THE WILD ONE

THE WILD ONE

NICK PETRIE

WHEELER PUBLISHING

A part of Gale, a Cengage Company

Copyright © 2020 by Nick Petrie.
A Peter Ash Novel.
Map by Jeffrey L. Ward.
Wheeler Publishing, a part of Gale, a Cengage Company.

LIBRARY OF CONGRESS CIP DATA ON FILE.
CATALOGUING IN PUBLICATION FOR THIS BOOK
IS AVAILABLE FROM THE LIBRARY OF CONGRESS

ISBN-13: 978-1-4328-7651-7 (hardcover alk. paper)

Published in 2020 by arrangement with. G. P. Putnam's Sons, an imprint of Penguin Publishing Group, a division of Penguin Random House, LLC

Printed in Mexico
Print Number: 02   Print Year: 2020

This book is for all those who have found themselves far afield without a map

Fall down seven times, stand up eight.

— Japanese proverb

He not busy being born is busy dying.

— Bob Dylan

A NOTE ON ICELANDIC
PRONUNCIATION

Icelandic is a challenging language. Here's a brief, unscientific guide to pronouncing some key names and places in the book. Emphasis is always on the first syllable, and the R is rolled.

To avoid confusion, I've kept accent marks but omitted special characters not used in the English language. Apologies to Icelandic speakers for this gross oversimplification of your mother tongue, not to mention my inevitable mistakes.

NAMES

Eiríkur — EYEE-reh-kur
Grímsson — GRIMS-son
Óskar — OH-scar
Eiríksson — EYEE-reeks-son
Hjálmar — HYOUL-mar
Bjarni — BYAR-nee

Freyja — FREY-yah
Axel — AHK-sel
Ingo — ING-go
Yrsa — IR-sah
Thorvaldur — TOR-val-ther

PLACES

Reykjavík — REYK-ya-vik
Seydisfjordur — SAY-this-fyur-ther
Egilsstadir — EY-eel-stah-thir
Mývatn — ME-vatn
Akureyri — AK-oo-rai-ree
Blönduós — BLUN-du-os
Skagaströnd — SKA-ga-strond
Vatnajökull — VAT-na-yo-kut

OTHER

Lögreglan — LOH-reh-glan
Mathöll — MA-thull
Bakarí — BAKK-er-ee

10

PETER ASH'S ICELAND

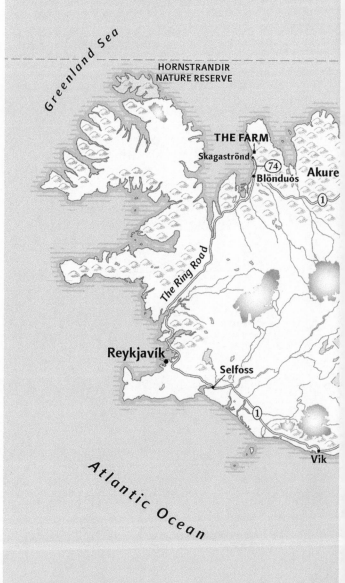

Greenland Sea

HORNSTRANDIR
NATURE RESERVE

THE FARM

Skagaströnd

74

Blönduós

Akure

1

The Ring Road

Reykjavík

Selfoss

1

Vik

Atlantic Ocean

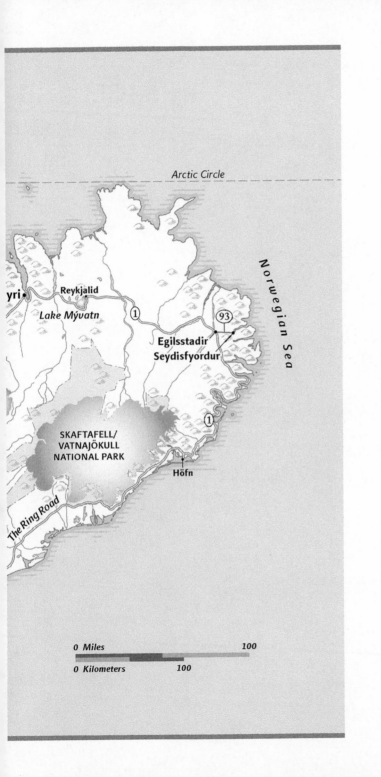

1

TWELVE MONTHS EARLIER

Óskar wakes them both by jumping into their bed, a warm and wiggly bundle of excitement. Erik groans, and Sarah buries her head under the covers. It's barely dawn, and the Air and Space Museum doesn't open until ten, but Óskar doesn't care. He wraps himself around his father's neck. "Happy Sunday," Óskar whispers loudly, seven years old and unable to contain himself. "Happy Family Day!"

Sunday is Family Day, when Óskar gets to choose an activity they will all do together. For more Sundays than Erik cares to think about, the Air and Space Museum, with a food truck lunch on the Mall, has been Óskar's choice. But Erik is still mixing batter for Family Day pancakes when Sarah's phone rings with a work emergency. She gives Erik an apologetic look and runs upstairs to put on work clothes.

15

Erik can't face yet another Sunday fighting the tourists for a glimpse of the moon lander without her. Instead, he drops to his knees on the dirty kitchen floor. "Óskar," he says, "I have an idea. What would you say to a Viking adventure in Rock Creek Park?" They have been reading Neil Gaiman's book on Norse mythology together, and the big park has plenty of wild sections and epic landscapes.

Óskar cheers and jumps around the house, climbing the furniture while Erik stuffs a backpack with sandwiches and extra clothes and a thermos full of hot chocolate, knowing that Óskar will happily wander all day if he's warm and fed. December weather in Washington, D.C., is nothing for a pair of real Vikings.

After a long and muddy day of exploration, they arrive back home at the last unrestored town house in Adams Morgan. Óskar sprawls on the floor amid a chaos of Lego and buttery crusts of toast, while Erik stands at the open refrigerator, waiting for Sarah to text him back.

It is unlike Sarah to ignore her phone. Erik reminds himself that his wife runs her own small cybersecurity company, and a client emergency could well be a very serious thing. She might not be home until midnight or later, and dinner won't wait with a hungry boy in the house.

Erik is the one who likes the predictable pleasures of domestic life. Sarah, on the other hand, thrives on emergencies. She still loves late nights dancing in clubs where the floors are sticky and the music is loud enough to lose yourself until daybreak. Erik is happy to be her designated driver because his pleasure comes from watching his brilliant, buttoned-down wife slam around the dance floor in ripped Levi's and an ancient biker jacket, alarming the bartenders. On the wildest nights, she pulls him into the back of their minivan, where she frees him from the confines of his pants, then wiggles her tight and sweaty jeans down to her ankles to get him inside her with delicious and slightly alarming efficiency.

His family, of course, loves Sarah's wild side.

Erik has chicken thighs braising and a green salad coming together when, to his surprise, Sarah bangs through the back door, her scuffed leather bag slung over one shoulder.

As usual, Sarah's crisp, professional look has come undone during the course of her workday. Her sandy hair falls free from its

17

ponytail, wisps hovering around her fore-head like stray thoughts. Her good wool coat is unbuttoned and the weight of her bag pulls her starched shirt askew and up the lush curve of her hips, making visible a crescent of pale skin at her waist.

Erik always finds this aspect of his wife profoundly sexy. His plan is to put Óskar to sleep as soon as possible, pour her a drink to vanquish the day, and then do his utmost to kiss his wife out of her clothing. The calendar says she's ovulating. Erik wants nothing more than another child.

Yet when he steps in to press his lips to hers, she holds him back with a hand on his chest. Her eyes remain dark and he knows she has not yet resolved her emergency.

"I need to show you something." She slips her bag off her shoulder. "Where's Óskar?"

"Busy." Erik tilts his head toward the tinkle of Lego and Óskar's voice mumbling numbers in the living room. "What's up?"

Sarah sets her laptop on the counter and types in her long and complicated password, automatically positioning her body to shield her keystrokes from prying eyes. Nothing personal, Erik knows, just long habit and sensitive client materials. She doesn't even use their home Wi-Fi, preferring a dedicated secure cell modem.

Then she steps sideways to make room for him at the counter, but keeps her torso angled to block the view from the door to the dining room. The door Óskar would come through. She hits a key and a paused video frame comes up on the screen.

It shows a dim room, two pale bodies entangled on a dark leather couch.

She presses Play. The bodies begin to move. There is nothing remotely sexy about it. Erik can tell immediately that something is profoundly wrong.

It takes him several moments, however, to realize exactly how wrong. The body on top is significantly larger than the body on the bottom. One is a grown man, his pants down to his knees. The other is just a girl. And she fights to get free.

Erik turns from the screen. "Sarah, what is this?"

"Wait." She checks over her shoulder for their son. "Keep watching."

"I'd rather not." Erik puts out a hand to block his view.

"Watch," she commands, and pulls his hand out of the way. The camera zooms in. The girl's face is a mask of pain and terror. She looks very young. The man's face is rapt, mesmerized by his own pleasure and power. He holds the girl down with a

19

practiced grip on the back of her neck.

Erik stabs out a finger and the video vanishes.

Sarah touches a key and the video returns. Her voice is calm. "Look at him, Erik. Do you recognize him?"

Erik blinks. He looks. He does recognize the man. He fumbles for the remote and turns on the small television in the corner of the kitchen. And there the man stands, as he does so often, on a futuristic set with his crisp haircut and a fresh shave and a microphone on his lapel, wearing a midnight suit and a blood-red tie.

The same man in the video with the girl. That same face. Mouth moving, always talking, charming his viewers. Right now his topic is regional stability and the protection of American interests overseas, but Erik doesn't hear a word. He can't stand it. He feels sick to his stomach. He unplugs the TV and looks at Sarah.

"Where on earth did this come from?"

2

PRESENT DAY

Peter Ash woke, gasping for breath, from a dream of gunfire. He could still feel the desert heat on his skin, and the memory of spent powder lingered in his nose.

Beside him, his elderly seatmate strained upward, one finger stabbing the call button overhead.

Peter blinked away the nightmare, wondering what he'd said or done in his sleep. He was a tall, bony man with shaggy black hair, a tired face, and the thoughtful eyes of a werewolf five minutes before the change. His green hiking pants were frayed at the seams, his Counterbalance Brewing T-shirt ghosted with old stains.

A beefy male flight attendant advanced up the aisle, broad face expressionless, hands open and ready. Watching him approach, Peter could tell the man had some physical training, and was probably tasked with controlling unruly passengers on this packed transatlantic flight.

Peter raised a hand and caught the other man's eye. "Sorry." It was hard to get the words out, his throat choked with the panic raised by the memories still burned into his brain. His T-shirt was damp with sweat and his mouth was dry as a dust storm. "Just a bad dream. Give me a minute, I'll be fine."

He bent to his bag stuffed under the seat and fumbled the flap as he dug for his pills. His seatmate had shrunk himself against the window, minimizing any contact. Passengers across the aisle were looking anywhere but at him.

"Sir." The flight attendant was almost on him. Peter's chest was tight, his lungs fighting for air. The cabin of the wide-body jet closed in hard. His fingers closed on the prescription bottle and he straightened up.

"I'm all right." He tried to believe it. "I just need my meds."

He fumbled the top off and shook four of the small pink circles into his hand. Then he found the last intact mini bottle of Reyka vodka in his seat pocket, twisted it open, and swallowed hard, pushing the pills down.

The dreams were new.

He'd come back from Iraq with claustrophobia bad enough to make living outside seem like a good idea. For more than a year, he'd slept alone under the stars or under a rain fly, high above the tree line of one mountain range or another, barely able to manage resupply in small-town grocery stores.

The post-traumatic stress came from kicking in doors in Fallujah, he figured. All those weeks of fighting house to house, room to room, clearing insurgents one doorway at a time.

Along with everything else he'd done.

He called it the white static, that feeling of electric overdrive that sparked up his brainstem, calculating firing angles, searching for exits. Nerves jangling like bare electrodes under the skin, his chest so tight he couldn't breathe, his fight-or-flight reflex gone into overdrive. When he first mustered out, he could only handle twenty minutes inside before the static turned into a full-blown panic attack.

In the time since then, he'd found a way forward. He'd made friends with the static, in a way, and a start at a new life. He'd found a veterans' group. He'd met a woman he didn't deserve, a woman named June Cassidy.

But he'd never had dreams, not like this.

Not until after Memphis.

Something had broken loose inside him there. Something he'd thought he had under control. Now it was roaming around in his head, knocking pictures off the walls, breaking the goddamn furniture.

In retrospect, this trip was a bad idea. He'd been in a hurry, had booked his tickets for same-day travel. Seats were limited and the schedule was brutal. He'd started in Portland, Oregon, changed planes and airlines in Minneapolis, then done it again in New York.

Long hours spent in the stale fluorescent clatter of airports, televisions blaring CNN and the Senate hearings at every turn.

More long hours with his oversized frame jammed into undersized seats, trapped in a cigar tube at thirty-five thousand feet.

His only exercise was pacing the aisles, his only sleep a few fitful naps. He'd hoped the Valium would help keep the white static at bay, but he'd been stuck inside for too long.

The static was losing patience.

The werewolf was coming.

He touched the little screen on the seatback. The plane icon was over Greenland now. Only ninety minutes to Reykjavík, Iceland, in late December. Where it snowed or rained for days at a time and the sun never truly rose, only brightening the sky for a few hours at midday.

He got up and went to the tiny restroom and splashed his face with water. He didn't look at himself in the mirror. He knew he wouldn't like what he saw there. On his way back to his seat, he plucked two more mini vodkas from the flight crew's service area and tossed them down in one go.

Maybe the dreams came from the Valium, fucking with him. It wasn't supposed to be a long-term solution. He'd read up on the side effects, and they weren't good. He sure as hell wasn't supposed to be chasing it with vodka, although the pills alone had stopped working months ago.

Maybe it was simply the price to be paid for getting back to some kind of meaningful work.

Or maybe he was just running away.

He told himself he'd quit the Valium once he got off the plane. He'd pick up his rental, find a place to park outside the city, and sleep it off, all of it. He had plenty of practice sleeping in a vehicle.

For now, he closed his eyes and drifted.

The airport's long, narrow halls were packed with people. Peter walked with the crowd to get his heavy pack and duffel, trying not to run, jumping out of his skin with the need to stand under the open sky and feel the wind on his face. Eight in the morning, and still dark outside. Daylight wouldn't come for hours.

At customs, the female agent behind the glass ran Peter's passport under the scanner. He heard a beep and her cool eyes flickered up at him. "Please wait a moment."

In less than a minute, two uniformed agents appeared as if from thin air, a man and a woman. The man collected Peter's passport from the scanner. "Sir, please come with us."

His English had just a trace of an accent. *Sir* became not quite *shir, us* became not quite *ush,* with a slight whistle to the sibilants. He was older than Peter, early fifties but slim in a crisp black uniform and fresh shave. His uniform had two tags, one in Icelandic on the right breast, LÖGREGLAN, and one on the left that read POLICE. There were no other markings of rank that Peter could see.

The woman was younger than Peter, but not by much. Her tag read CUSTOMS.

Peter took a deep breath and let it out. The white static crackled higher up his brainstem, vaporizing the haze of Valium

26

and vodka. His nerves twanged like a dropped piano and sweat gathered between his shoulder blades. He wanted nothing more than to get outside. "What's this about?"

The man saw Peter's rising tension and eased away from the woman, opening up the angles, giving himself room. He moved well enough, but he seemed unconcerned. There were a half-dozen other officers within view.

If he'd known what Peter was capable of, the things Peter had done, the things Peter was contemplating at that very moment, he would have been worried as hell.

The woman smiled with professional warmth. "Your name is Peter, right? I'm Sigrid. This is Hjálmar. Come with us for a moment, we'll explain everything. Would you like a coffee?"

Peter pulled in another long breath, then bent to pick up his duffel. He already wore the big pack slung over one shoulder. "Sure," he said. "Coffee would be good." Or a double bourbon, neat. Then another, washing down four more Valium.

He needed to get the fuck out of there.

They walked him through a door and down a hallway to a little kitchen alcove with a gleaming stainless-steel machine that could produce a dozen different coffee drinks with the push of a button. She made him an Americano. "Milk or sugar?" The mug was white ceramic, not paper, and warm in his hand. The coffee was better than he expected.

Past the alcove, a bright yellow door opened to a plain white room. It was furnished with a long laminate table and six plastic chairs. Inexpensive stuff, but elegant, lightweight, durable. Interrogation room sponsored by Ikea.

The man, Officer Hjálmar, held the door against the spring and the woman, Officer Sigrid, ushered Peter politely inside. Coffee in hand, he set his duffel on the table, then the pack. Officer Hjálmar followed and the door closed automatically behind.

It was all very civilized.

Peter thought about how hard it would be to kick his way through the wallboard. With his heavy leather hiking boots, not hard at all. His long leg muscles twitched. He wondered what might be on the other side.

Officer Sigrid gave him the smile again, as if he were a customer rather than a detainee. "Peter, please, have a seat. How is your coffee?" She was sturdy in her black uniform, comfortable in her skin. Everything she said and did was designed to put Peter at ease.

28

It didn't work.

Peter leaned against the wall. "Why am I here?"

"I'm told you had some trouble on the airplane," Officer Hjálmar said. "You were agitated. You shouted."

"I had a bad dream," Peter said. "I'm starting to think I'm still having it."

"You're sweating," Hjálmar said. "Are you nervous about something?"

"I have claustrophobia." Peter hated having to explain it, the weakness it implied. "I get panic attacks in small spaces. Like airplanes. And official rooms with no windows."

The man looked at Peter. "I'm sorry." Maybe some sympathy there, but he was still a cop. "Is that what the medication is for?"

Peter pushed back the shame that washed over him. At his inability to control himself, his inability to live a normal life. Eight years a Recon Marine, the tip of the spear, more deployments than he cared to remember. He was proud of his service, but it had changed him. He was still trying to figure out what he'd become, or was becoming. A work in progress, goddamn it.

But he had no use for sympathy.

"The medication is none of your fucking

business," he said calmly. "Again, why am I here?"

There was a knock on the yellow door. A female officer leaned in and said something in Icelandic. It was a beautiful language, sinuous and sibilant. That simple sentence sounded like poetry, Peter thought, even though he'd need two tongues to speak it.

Then she left and a new man stepped in.

He was plump, pink, and balding, one of those men who'd been middle-aged since he was seventeen. He wore a dark gray suit with a faint blue windowpane pattern that matched his pocket square and tie. He slung a long gray wool topcoat over a chair back and tucked both hands in his pockets. Not police or military, Peter thought. A civilian. And he'd always been a civilian. Peter could tell by the way he stood, the careless slouch of his shoulders. His soft, useless slick-soled shoes.

The static sparked at the base of Peter's brain, threatening to fill his head with lightning.

He pushed down the urge toward action, that familiar fight-or-flight instinct. It wouldn't help him, not now. Breathe in, breathe out.

The civilian nodded at the officers. "Please. Continue."

Sigrid spoke. "What is the purpose of your visit?"

Peter waved at the big pack filling a chair. "Hiking."

"In winter?" She turned on the smile. "You must be part Icelandic. You are signed up with a tour operator?"

"No. I'm renting a car."

Hjálmar shook his head. "This is not like" — he consulted Peter's passport — "your Wisconsin. Iceland can be quite dangerous, especially in winter."

"Don't underestimate Wisconsin." Peter smiled for the first time. "And I don't mind dangerous, either."

The civilian frowned. The two customs officers exchanged glances.

"Have you come here to die?" Hjálmar sounded concerned for the first time. "Suicide by glacier, or hypothermia? Because we don't want to put our rescue teams at risk, trying to save you."

"I don't want to die," Peter said. "I just want to get outside these walls, see some country. What's the problem?"

The civilian spoke a second time. "Let's see what's in his baggage, shall we?" He didn't sound Icelandic. He sounded American, maybe from the East Coast. Several generations of private schools and private

31

clubs and a long history of getting what he wanted distilled into a smug, nasal honk.

Peter said, "Who are you?"

The civilian looked amused. "That's not important," he said. "The luggage, please."

The customs officers glanced at each other again.

The man nodded once, just slightly, but he didn't like it.

The woman went to Peter's pack, popped the buckles, loosened the straps. She began to lay out his things on the table. Tent, poles, fly. Stove and pot. Sleeping bag and pad. All the other things he'd need to survive alone in open country. All of it excellent quality and well used. She laid out everything neatly. She left the folded silver emergency blanket and fifty-foot coil of Kevlar-core rope in the top compartment.

"The duffel as well."

The woman set her jaw but moved the bag to a chair and opened the zipper.

There was something odd here, Peter thought. These cops were annoyed. They didn't like taking this soft man's orders any more than Peter liked being in that room.

This wasn't about some panic attack on the plane.

Sigrid pulled out more hiking gear, along with town clothes and the carry-on he'd shoved inside at baggage claim, a simple day pack with his laptop and charger, a thin insulated jacket, a Ziploc bag of homemade granola bars, his travel documents, his pills, and a few books.

She held up the books. "You are a reader?" Peter nodded. Sigrid smiled. "Iceland is a nation of readers."

Inside his guidebook, she found a photo of a man holding a mop-headed boy in his arms like a happy sack of potatoes. The boy was seven, loose-limbed and cheerful with dirty knees. He looked away from the camera as if already planning for his next mud puddle. The man was thirty-three, with a bushy blond beard and a face as empty as a stone. His deep-set eyes seemed too blue to be real.

The civilian stepped forward and tapped the photo with his index finger. "Who's this?"

"A friend," Peter said. "Cute kid, isn't he?"

The civilian's frown deepened, his lips like squirming pink worms. He held out his hand. "Give me your phone."

"I don't think so. I'd like some answers."

The civilian was definitely unhappy now. "Here's an answer for you," he said. "You are not welcome in Iceland. Unfortunately for you, there are no available seats back to the States until late afternoon, the day after tomorrow." He took an envelope from his jacket pocket. "Here is your ticket. You will be on that plane. These officers will see to your safety and comfort until that time, and they will escort you to your seat."

With the flight, that meant three more days stuck inside. Peter felt the static crackle and rise, pushing at the boundaries of his control. But he wasn't going to lose his shit in front of this asshole. He ignored the ticket envelope. "On whose authority, exactly?"

"It's unofficial." The civilian gave Peter a tight smile. "But real nonetheless. You are persona non grata here. Go home."

Breathe in, breathe out. Peter looked at the customs cops. "He can do this?"

They glanced at each other a third time. If something passed between them, Peter didn't see it.

Officer Hjálmar said, "In fact that is a bit unclear. We will require written confirmation from your superior."

"Cut the shit," the civilian said. "You have verbal orders. Do as you're told."

It was the wrong response. Hjálmar's face betrayed no emotion. He simply shrugged. His voice was mild. "There are procedures for these things. Forms must be filled out."

Peter suppressed a smile. Insistence on standard procedure was the most elegant form of bureaucratic resistance. As a Marine lieutenant, Peter had used the tactic himself, although not as often as he'd stomped procedure into the dirt in pursuit of his mission and the safety of his men.

"We have no reason to detain him," Officer Sigrid said. "To our knowledge, Mr. Ash has committed no crime. You can see he's in discomfort. He says he's claustrophobic, having a panic attack."

"And you believe him?" Anger and frustration radiated off the pink civilian like an IED's afterglow. The envelope trembled, just slightly, in his manicured hand. Peter wasn't sure why the man was so worked up. He wasn't the one being kicked out of the country.

"We do things a bit differently in Iceland," said Officer Sigrid. "We have a great deal of respect for the rights of the individual and the rule of law. We do not detain people without proper cause."

"You should see his file," the pink civilian said. "You'd feel differently."

"But you have chosen not to share that information with us," Officer Hjálmar said.

"This request is unofficial. From one nation to another."

"It is *extremely* unofficial," Officer Hjál-mar said. "We will honor your request that he leave the country. But lacking written orders from our superiors, Mr. Ash will not be detained today." He took the envelope with the ticket. "We will collect his rental car and hotel information. If he does not report here, to our office, four hours before the flight, we will dispatch officers to collect him."

The civilian burned hotter. He took his phone from his pocket. "Give me five minutes."

Officer Sigrid turned to Peter. "Perhaps you should pack your things."

Into his phone, the civilian said, "Get me the head of the customs police. Yes, even better, the national police commissioner." He listened, his back to Peter and the officers. "Then get his goddamn cell phone and forward me there. Now."

Peter tucked his equipment back into place with the efficiency of long practice. Sigrid took out a notebook and pen. Her smile was still professional, but now it held true amusement. "Your contact information?"

Peter gave her his cell number. "I don't have a hotel room yet." Or plans to get one.

A phone rang. He turned to watch Officer

Hjálmar remove his phone from his belt and raise it to his ear. "*Já,* Hjálmar."

The civilian turned and stared, the phone lowered from his ear. "You're the national police commissioner?"

Hjálmar put his phone away. "Iceland is a small country. Your request is unusual. We take these matters quite seriously."

The pink civilian was turning red. "Do you know who is behind this request?"

"Unfortunately, no. Not officially." Hjálmar turned to Peter and held out his passport and the envelope with the plane ticket. "I will walk you out."

Hjálmar led Peter past the glass booths and into the airport's modest main hall. Through the glass walls of the atrium, Peter could see snow swirling bright under powerful lights. The white static crackled in response. Sometimes standing by a big window helped the claustrophobia, but Peter was well beyond that point.

It was after ten in the morning and the sky was barely beginning to brighten. Peter was exhausted and hungry and impatient. He wanted badly to walk outside. Hell, he wanted to run. But he held himself there, taking deep breaths. He knew they weren't quite done yet.

Hjálmar watched Peter carefully. "I hope I haven't made a mistake."

"You haven't." Peter stuck out his hand. "I'm Peter. What do I call you?"

"Hjálmar, please." They shook hands. "We are informal here."

"Who's the guy in the suit?"

"Someone connected to your embassy." The man adjusted his shoulders, as if working out some kink in his back. "There is some weight behind their request. Eventually my government will be forced to honor it. If you do not return when you are due, we will collect you. And we will not be gentle."

Peter nodded. "I'll try to behave myself. But I still don't get why I'm not in a holding cell."

A smile flickered across Hjálmar's face. "Icelanders are independent people," he said. "We do not like being told what to do."

"Huh." Peter watched the snow blowing sideways, drifts gathering in unlikely places. "Me neither."

"You were in the military." Not a question.

"I was a United States Marine," said Peter. "Still am, I guess. It's not something that leaves you."

Hjálmar nodded. "I was a ground observer

38

with Norway in the first Iraq war. I had to go, I couldn't help myself. All these years later, I still remember the burned-out Iraqi tanks, the smell of their dead drivers and gunners. Like roasted meat inside a cast-iron pot."

The static foamed and sparked. Peter needed to breathe open air. "Did you become a vegetarian?"

"No," Hjálmar said, "I became a policeman. So I am asking. What is in your file that would concern me?"

"You? Probably nothing."

"Then why don't they want you here?"

"Honestly? I have no idea." For the moment, it was the truth. "Are we done?"

"Yes. I'll see you in two days."

Peter smiled. "Not if I see you first."

Then he stepped forward and the double glass doors slid wide and he walked into the biting, sunless cold. The hard wind in his face and the icy snow falling down the back of his neck felt like some kind of gift.

3

Despite the weather, Peter wasn't ready to get back into a vehicle just yet. He fished his phone from his pocket and sent a text.

Landed in Reyk. Someone from the U.S. Embassy wants me sent home, won't say why. I'm due back on a plane in 48 hours. Any ideas?

With the time change, it was six a.m. in Maryland. He wasn't expecting a response. But his phone buzzed immediately.

My husband is well connected at State. I'll look into it. But please don't let anyone stop you.

Will do.

Peter walked his bags to the taxi stand and knocked on the window of a Renault station-wagon. "Iceland 4×4 Rentals? On, uh —"

"*Já*, I know it." The driver started the motor without looking at Peter. The rear cargo hatch floated up. "Thirty minutes." The taxi's front passenger side had a pair of tall rubber boots in the footwell and a hardback book on the seat, obviously not space for passengers.

Peter stowed his gear. The static didn't mind a windshield, but it didn't like the enclosure of a back seat. So Peter climbed in and stuck his face to the window, getting as close to the world as he could.

The blowing snow and limited visibility didn't slow the driver. He had his wipers on high and the pedal down. The landscape was flat and white and barren of trees and visible vegetation. The sky had begun to brighten slightly, as if dawn was coming, but was still some way off. There wasn't much traffic. After four crowded airports, three flying sardine cans, and one detention room, Iceland felt blissfully empty.

Peter had skimmed the guidebook on the plane, trying to figure out what to expect. The island nation was the size of Maine, but with a quarter of the population: only three hundred thirty thousand people. More than two hundred thousand of those lived in and around Reykjavík, the capital city, in the southwestern section of Iceland.

Reykjavík itself was fairly temperate, because the Gulf Stream's North Atlantic Current carried warm ocean water up from

41

the Caribbean to northern Europe. In winter, the book said, Reykjavík actually got as much rain as it did snow. Iceland also sat at the junction of two tectonic plates, which helped warm the island further, and created a surplus of geothermal energy, hot springs, and volcanoes.

The northern part of Iceland, on the other hand, could get snow year-round, and the high mountain interior was filled with glaciers. Big sections were accessible only a few months a year, if at all. And Iceland's weather was unpredictable. Powered by strong Arctic winds, major storms could develop anywhere in a matter of hours, no matter the season.

The driver made a right into a rambling, piecemeal industrial park. He hadn't spoken since Peter got in the car. They passed sheet-metal buildings set among storage lots filled with rusted fishing equipment and concrete building components and rows of tiny prefab cabins sitting on blocks, waiting for a crane to load them on a flatbed. Few lights shone. Other than the taxi, nothing moved. It felt like midnight, rather than almost midday.

The rental agency was in the oldest, shabbiest section, a dented steel shed with a variety of four-wheel-drive vehicles parked haphazardly around it. The taxi meter read fifteen thousand krónur, which was about a hundred and twenty dollars. Peter was glad it wasn't his money. He paid the driver, then dragged his gear out of the car. The driver pulled away. All told, he hadn't spoken more than a dozen words the entire trip.

The rental office was plain, stifling, and close, with only a single small window. A door opened to a big garage section where an air wrench shrieked. The static rose up and filled Peter's head. It took everything he had to stay at the counter.

The rental agent was a young guy in a blue-and-white Iceland World Cup stocking cap and an oversized quilted flannel shirt. He wiped grease from his hands with a rag as he talked Peter through the paperwork. The agency provided coverage for gravel damage, he said, but river crossings and wind damage were Peter's responsibility.

Peter raised his eyebrows. "Wind damage?"

"Yes. Always park facing into the weather, so the wind doesn't bend the doors back. That's an expensive repair." He handed Peter a single key on a ring with no identifying information. "Your vehicle is outside," he said. "The white Mitsubishi Pajero on the left. Please remember that it requires diesel fuel. The wrong fuel is a very expensive repair." He gestured toward the door. "Safe travels."

Reykjavík proper was crowded with traffic and pedestrians. A small cluster of glass-clad towers crowded the waterfront, and a cruise ship sat in the harbor. Clusters of construction cranes rose high, and modern new apartment buildings grew on the lower reaches of the old city. Packs of tourists in expensive new parkas wandered aimlessly through the snow, standing in curious clumps with their shopping bags. Iceland was booming.

Peter parked the Mitsubishi on a busy street in front of a bakery, used a credit card to feed the meter, crossed at the light, and walked uphill into the old city.

He'd spent a lot of time overseas, but most of that was in combat zones. He drank in the flavor of this peaceful, prosperous foreign city. The snowy streets were narrow and clogged with traffic. The buildings got smaller and older as he climbed the hill, breathing in the open air. Oddly, the proportions of some buildings were very much like the barns in northern Wisconsin, where Scandinavian immigrants had settled. Heavily customized 4x4 vehicles lined the side roads, Jeeps and Toyotas and strange European campers, many of them vintage, often parked halfway up on the skinny sidewalks. In this fashionable European city, they looked like improvised moon rovers.

The fatigue that always followed the receding static tugged at him like rocks in his pockets. The long trip with little sleep didn't help. At a tiny coffee shop on a cobblestone courtyard, he sat under a narrow overhang to sip his rapidly cooling espresso while the snow swirled around him. With the low heavy clouds and the snow, the sky hadn't gotten any brighter. He wondered if this was all the daylight he would get.

He rode the wave of caffeine through a maze of narrow side streets to a hand-lettered sign on the side of a building. SNORRI'S RAVE CAVE. Below the sign, stone steps led down below street level. Swirls of brightly colored paint covered the concrete walls of the stairwell. At the bottom, a dented steel door, electric green, glowed faintly in the subterranean shadow. Another sign screwed to the door gave the hours: 20:00–???

That was eight p.m., six hours away. He tried the knob, but it was locked. He rapped on the door with his knuckles. The dull

45

sound seemed to disappear into the falling snow. No answer. He took the rental key from his pocket and used the steel to sharpen his knock. Still no answer.

He found an outfitter's shop, where he bought a better sleeping bag, good to twenty below. His old gear was still sound, but Iceland seemed to call for an upgrade, and his choices would likely narrow significantly once he left Reykjavík.

Exercise always helped with the static, so he walked the city with his shopping bags, working his travel-stiff muscles on the hills. His stomach growled and he realized he hadn't eaten since the day before, so he stopped for a bowl of Thai noodles and chicken from a takeout window and ate standing in the street. Finally he walked down to the Mitsubishi and drove along the harbor road until he found a half-empty parking lot sheltered from the traffic noise by a wide earthen berm.

The espresso wore off as he drove, leaving him in a black pit of exhaustion. The drifting airplane unconsciousness of Valium and vodka wasn't the same as real sleep. It had been too long since he'd had a full night's rest without gunfire dreams.

The Pajero was a full-sized SUV with the boxy feel and diesel rattle of a truck. The rental company had removed the back seats and converted the vehicle into a kind of camper, with a slim plywood storage shelf, a hinged tabletop, and a little couch that unfolded into a bed. It was a small space, more like a two-man tent than anything else, but even with all his gear, there was enough room for Peter to stretch out comfortably. He cracked the windows for ventilation, then kicked off his boots and rolled into his new sleeping bag. The view was of the swirling snow and dimly lit sky. The wind howled in his ears like something wild.

He closed his eyes, hoping he was too tired to dream.

Knowing that it didn't matter. He would dream anyway.

4

The dream was always the same.

Peter stood in a dusty street, binoculars fixed on the face of a small brown man with sad eyes and a thick black mustache. The man sat behind the wheel of a faded blue Toyota Camry rolling toward a makeshift checkpoint at the edge of Sadr City, an impoverished Baghdad neighborhood at the heart of the insurgency.

The afternoon air was still and thick. It tasted of burned metal and raw, rotting meat.

Four of Peter's Marines stood sweating in full battle dress by a pair of Humvees parked in a V, blocking the road, waving at the Camry to stop. It was make-work duty, designed to keep Peter's Recon platoon occupied until their next real mission. The sad-eyed driver was coming too fast. This was a year into the insurgency, and the driver should have known to slow down.

More than that, Peter's Marines shouldn't even have been there.

When the driver was a hundred meters out, Big Jimmy Johnson stepped from behind the hood of his Humvee, M4 slung and hands held palms-out, knowing the riflemen and turret gunner behind him would have his back. Big Jimmy smiled his big peacemaking smile, a smile so wide and infectious that it made hardened insurgents smile back out of pure human recognition. Peter had thought more than once that, if every U.S. servicemember had Jimmy's smile, the insurgency would have been over before it started.

No matter that they shouldn't have been fighting that wrong war in the first place. The weapons of mass destruction didn't exist. All those people dead for nothing.

The sad-eyed driver got closer. He put a hand up. He said something, nobody knew what. His eyes got wide. But he didn't slow down.

Big Jimmy shouted. Raised his rifle. Made it clear in word and deed that the man should stop or there would be consequences. Bad things would happen. The driver got closer. A voice came through Peter's earpiece. "Lieutenant? Do we fire?"

The sad-eyed driver became more agitated. He took his other hand off the wheel and waved his arms. He wore a pale button-down shirt with short sleeves. His face was freshly shaven. He shouted. He didn't slow down.

Behind his own Humvee, Peter kept his binoculars on the man's face. A car bomb had hit an Army checkpoint the day before. Another had blown up a Sunni market that morning. The sad-eyed man still didn't stop. "He's too close," Peter said. "Okay to fire. Light that fucker up. Repeat, light him up."

The Marines fired their M4s. The windshield filled with impact stars, but the dusty Camry kept coming. When the turret gunner let loose with the fifty-cal, the deep thumping sound was almost physical in the thick, foul air. The Camry shook on its springs as it turned into Swiss cheese. Steam came from the punctured radiator. It wasn't until the tires were shreds and the engine died that the car finally lurched to a stop.

There was no bomb. It turned out that the Camry's brakes didn't work. Later, Peter discovered that the driver was a Sunni, facing death threats from his Shia neighbors. He was fleeing his home, scared out of his mind, reacting poorly, in a car that, once started, didn't want to stop.

His young wife and two small children

were huddled out of sight in the back seat. Probably so his neighbors would think he was just going to work, and not frag everyone in the car.

They had died anyway.

Peter had given the order and a family had died.

The driver hadn't even slowed down. It was a righteous call, by the book. Nobody had questioned it. Until the dreams started, after Memphis, Peter had barely remembered it.

How many calls like this had he made? How many more innocents had died in that dumb fucking war? How many children?

At the time, Peter hadn't wanted to learn their names. He didn't want to make it personal. He was doing his job. They all were.

It was personal, anyway.

When you take a human life, whether through action or inaction, how could it be otherwise?

The honest truth was that Peter hadn't hated the war when he was fighting it. He was often desperate or exhausted or scared shitless, but once he'd reconciled himself to the fact that he could die at any moment, his war had changed. It became a place to test himself, to improve his skills. He'd signed up to fight for his country, but that was before it all went bad. Then his mission became to protect his men. Get them home alive.

No, the *real* honest truth was that, more often than not, he'd fucking loved the war. Standing with his brother Marines, armed and armored before an assault, amped up and focused and ready to take the fight to the bad guys. Wordless patrols through the corn along the Tigris while the insects screamed. Night drops into the dry, bony mountains of Afghanistan, with Pakistan just over the next ridgeline. The beauty of pink tracers curving through the darkness as the remains of his platoon huddled behind a crumbling stone house, praying for the bombers to save their asses before the flankers eliminated their cover. High as a kite on terror and adrenaline.

He'd felt alive, then. Well and truly alive.

But that was then.

Civilian life wasn't the same. Not at all.

Of course, civilian life wasn't supposed to give you nightmares, either.

A VA doctor had prescribed him the Valium. The VA loved their drugs.

The Valium helped, until it didn't. It was a tranquilizer in the benzodiazepine family, and it was easy to build up a tolerance. It was also addictive.

Now, he woke sweating in the cold dark truck, wondering how many more faces would swim up out of the past to visit his dreams.

5

The snow was falling faster when Peter left
the Mitsubishi to walk the narrow, winding
streets of Reykjavík. The wind pulled on his
coat, but a warm yellow glow poured
through shop windows and restaurant door-
ways, illuminating the old city in reflected
light. Tourists in enormous parkas and
locals in wool sweaters headed out for
drinks and dinner. Peter's stomach growled
again. You burned more calories sleeping in
a cold car than in a warm bed.

The sign above the steps to Snorri's Rave
Cave was lit now, too. Black lights in the
cracked concrete stairwell made the painted
walls glow in luminescent swirls that grew
more vivid with each descending step. The
steel door at the bottom shone an unearthly
green. Peter tried the handle again. This
time, the door opened.

He found a low, darkened vestibule with
an unmanned coat check and an empty

doorman's podium. A red velvet rope hung from two metal stands, blocking the entryway to the club. Peter kept his coat, stepped over the rope and down another flight of stairs. The static foamed up his brainstem. He hoped he could find his guy quickly. Peter had never been a nightclub person. Now less than ever.

From the entrance, Peter had thought Snorri's Rave Cave would be small, but at the bottom of the steps he found a large, high-ceilinged space, several large rooms connected by wide, arched openings. The basements of multiple adjoining buildings had been dug deeper and merged. The original rough foundation stones were exposed, but they somehow stood atop crisp new concrete walls, the lines of the steel forms still visible. Standup tables ringed the room. Rope lights hung from the ceiling in wild, tangled loops.

The static sparked higher. It didn't like the windowless club, or the way the arched openings between the joined spaces limited his sight lines. He felt its pressure at the base of his skull, the muscles of his shoulders and back and neck tightening with the tension. He found himself checking the corners and scouting the exits, as if he'd find an insurgent with an AK hiding behind one of the long leather couches. He clenched his teeth against the static's rising insistence. He'd been getting better, goddamn it.

It was barely eight o'clock and the house lights were still bright. The dance floor was huge. Concrete mixed with broken glass, then polished to a fine sheen, glittered underfoot. At the far end, a DJ with a shaved head and a long, braided beard assembled his equipment on a raised platform. The heavy bass and insistent rhythms of electronic dance music poured from high speaker towers.

A wooden bar ran down one side of the room, where a pair of bartenders in crisp white tuxedo shirts chatted with early customers, and two barbacks methodically stocked the coolers. Peter put his elbow on the polished oak and caught a bartender's eye.

"I'm looking for Bjarni," he called over the music.

"There are many Bjarnis." The square-shouldered young bartender reminded Peter a bit of the well-fed farm boys he'd grown up with. Except for the fat gold ring in one ear, along with the stylized black tattoos peeking out from under the rolled-up sleeves of his tuxedo shirt, which made him look like a pirate dressed for the prom. He wore his straw-blond hair short on the sides and long on top, not a great look in Peter's opinion. Maybe it was a Viking thing. His square, clean-shaven face was polite and uninterested. "Which one?"

"Bjarni Bergsson. He works here, right?"

Peter only had a year-old photo of a face blond-bearded to the eyeballs and half-hidden in a long tangle of hair, with a prominent black metal nose ring. He'd looked on social media for others, but there were half a dozen of Bjarni Bergssons in Reykjavík. He wasn't sure if Bjarni still worked at the club, but if not, maybe his former coworkers might know where to find him.

"Why do you want this Bjarni?"

"It's personal. About his family."

The bartender swiped his hair out of his eyes with a practiced hand. "You are American?"

Peter nodded. "Is he here?"

The bartender glanced over his shoulder down the bar, then turned back to Peter. "He's late. But he should be here soon." He had the same soft, sibilant Icelandic accent. "If you are staying, cover charge is two thousand." About twenty dollars. "The club will fill soon. Beautiful women, great music.

Dancing."

Peter would rather be on June Cassidy's front porch, watching the stars and listening to the wind in the trees, but that was a wide ocean and a continent away. "Sure." He took four of the colorful Icelandic bills from his wallet and held them out. "Two thousand for the cover charge. Another six for you to point out Bjarni when he gets here." If the static let him stay that long.

The bartender nodded again, slipped the money into a pocket, and walked down the bar to the taps. A minute later, he came back with a pale, foaming pint. The inside of his right arm was covered with a large tattoo of a stylized Viking sword. A tattooed shield covered the other. "Our special Icelandic bitter," he said. "No charge. Our most popular beer."

"Thanks." Peter took a sip. It was definitely bitter, and strangely foamy, but also pretty good. Peter took a longer sip. He was hungry and thirsty. The beer would help with both, for a while. Drinking a single beer wasn't the same as draining a half-dozen airline bottles of vodka, was it?

There was a noise at the entrance as a dozen people clattered down the stairs. The women were dressed in sleek skirts and glittery tops that bared their arms and shoulders. The men wore tight jeans and shiny shirts and pointy-toed shoes. They were much younger than Peter, with sculptural hair. A doorman in a white tuxedo shirt and a black bow tie met them at the velvet rope to collect money and stamp their hands. The music got louder.

The house lights dimmed and the hanging ropes lit in a chaos of color. More people crowded in, talking and laughing. They were all better-looking than Peter, too. They probably didn't have so many scars. He guessed they weren't fighting static like white phosphorus in their heads, either.

Peter had never been a young adult, not really. He'd worked construction for his father and uncle all through high school. After that, he was a scholarship student at Northwestern, working his ass off during summers to make food and rent money for the year. Then he'd signed up for the Marines after the towers came down, and spent the next eight years in the fight.

No wonder he was having trouble figuring out what to do with himself now that it was over.

He drained his beer. The bartender brought him another, just as bitter and foamy. Peter looked at him with raised eyebrows. The bartender shook his head.

"No Bjarni." Peter could barely hear him over the sound system.

The music got louder still. Peter could feel the thump of the bass against his skin. The house lights faded to black and lasers flickered on, narrow beams strobing across the ceiling. Peter put his back to the polished wood of the bar and watched as the growing crowd began to edge onto the dance floor. He saw luminescent chemical glow sticks ignite one by one as people cracked the seals and shook them, blurring bright in their hands. The DJ called out and the music changed, speeding up.

Then, as if someone had flipped a switch, everyone began to dance.

Somewhere near the bottom of his second beer, Peter realized he was feeling better. The static was still there, but its pressure had receded without his noticing. The music was growing on him. His head was lighter than it should have been from a few pints of beer, although not in a bad way. He felt clear as a windowpane. He probably should get something to eat.

The club had gotten warm. Peter shed his coat and found an empty stool at a corner table. The other people at the table smiled at him, and Peter smiled back. Icelanders came in all shapes and sizes, but they were all beautiful. They wore luminous bracelets and necklaces in a dozen colors, made with the same bright chemicals as the glow sticks. He pointed at his coat, then the stool, and they nodded. He draped his coat over the seat like a hunter at a Wisconsin tavern. Blinking at the lights, he felt the beer in his bloodstream.

He was still too warm, so he peeled off his fleece and laid it over his coat. His bare arms tingled where it met the air. He couldn't take his eyes off the lasers flashing overhead. The music pulsed in his bones like a good infection. A young woman at the table locked eyes with him. She wore an electric green necklace doubled up as a headband. She stood and took his hand and led him onto the dance floor.

She was blond and pale and slender as a reed. In her early twenties, she was way too young for Peter, but she pulled him into the crowd like an electromagnet. He couldn't let go of her hand if he wanted to, and he didn't want to. She wore a crop top of some shiny metallic fabric that showed the taut muscles of her belly when she raised her arms. Her skirt was short and loose and filled like a bell when she spun on her toes. Her dark pupils filled her eyes. Peter had never been much of a dancer, but without conscious decision, he found himself on his toes, moving to the rhythm.

The press of people should have set the static raging and driven him out of there, but it didn't. The static rose, yes, but instead of feeding the urge toward fight or flight, it extended the boundaries of his senses. He felt connected to the crowd like he never had before. The static merged with the music and lifted him. His feet and hips and shoulders flowed like liquid. The dance floor was a temple to a God he'd never before imagined.

He was part of a group now, all swirling together in the pulse of the music. The women swung their hair, arms in the air, and the men spun on the toes of their smooth-soled shoes. Everyone wore the colorful glowing bracelets or necklaces or held swirling glow sticks, which trailed light behind them like tracers in the night. Peter felt warm and strong and graceful, his shirt damp with sweat from the movement and exaltation of the fast, driving rhythm.

He took off his T-shirt and threw it high over the raised arms of the multitude of dancers. He was just a single small molecule, but also part of the larger organism, the universe of love. His feet were slower than he wanted, so he took off his boots while he danced. The magnetic young woman, laughing, took them from his hands before he could throw them into the air. She went away and he slipped around the glittering floor in his hiking socks, his entire body floating high and humming with joy. He was connected to everyone, and they to him, by the grace and power and beauty of the music.

Eventually he was barefoot, naked but for his white featherweight long underwear slung low on his hips. Under the strobing LEDs and flickering lasers and luminescent jewelry, in the center of a circle of glittering young women, he danced like a wild man.

Oblivious to their hungry eyes, their fingertips trailing across his electric alabaster skin, he was a whirling kinetic sculpture of bliss, his corded arms and shoulders taut and gleaming with sweat like some beautiful ecstatic primitive finally released from his darkened cave into the bright world for the first time.

6

When the tuxedo-shirted bartender pushed his way into the circle of dancers, Peter didn't want to stop. It took him a while to come back to himself.

The young bartender was stronger than he looked. He took Peter's arm and pulled him close to shout into Peter's ear. "Bjarni."

"Oh," said Peter, remembering. "Where?"

"Outside. Having a cigarette."

"Okay." Feet still moving to the music, Peter held out a hand to the others, to his organism. "I'll be right back. Save me a place." He could barely hear his own voice.

The bartender towed him, dancing, through the crowd. "Where are your clothes?"

"I don't know. Somewhere. I don't want to wear them. Do I need them?"

"This is Iceland. December. You need clothes."

"I don't want to lose Bjarni."

The bartender leaned into Peter and stared into one eye. "You drank both beers."

"I was thirsty." Peter smiled. "I feel pretty good."

"I see that." The bartender shook his head at Peter in his sagging long underwear bottoms. "Come. Where are your clothes?"

Peter pointed to the distant corner where he'd met the young woman, at the chair with his coat and boots, but his shirt and pants and socks weren't there. Peter had thrown them into the crowd. The bartender said something in Icelandic, shaking his head. He pushed Peter's bare feet into his leather boots and pulled the coat around Peter's bare shoulders. He didn't tie the boots or zip the jacket, but Peter didn't mind. He was still too hot. His skin felt like an electric pink glow stick.

The bartender gestured toward a rear exit. "Go. Bjarni is there." Peter set off, still dancing, his loose boots sloppy on his feet.

They climbed endless stairs into a narrow dead-end alley. The night air was cool and refreshing. The wind had stopped for the moment, but the snow still fell in fat, heavy flakes. Perfect white mounds piled high on the lids of trash cans and the windowsills of the stone buildings that shrank the sky around them.

One of the barbacks leaned against the stone. He was short and wide in a rough wool sweater and jeans. Smoke trickled upward from a cigarette held between his thumb and forefinger. His hands were the size of soup bowls, and his face was thick with unmown beard. Peter said, "You don't look like Bjarni."

The barback said something to the bartender in Icelandic and pushed himself off the wall.

Peter turned to the bartender. "What did he say?"

"That's Dónaldur." The bartender finally smiled. "He said we will take you to the bakery."

The short barback flicked away his cigarette. "It means we are going to kick your ass."

Still feeling the love from the dance floor, Peter didn't quite understand. It must have showed on his face.

The young bartender rolled his thick shoulders. "I am Bjarni, you stupid American." Then he stepped close and swung a low, heavy fist toward Peter's stomach.

Peter danced sideways without conscious thought, the music still humming in his head. The punch didn't touch him. He

66

wasn't understanding. "You're Bjarni? Why didn't you tell me that from the start?"

Bjarni came at Peter again with a long, looping roundhouse to the chin. Still feeling the music, Peter did an elegant shuffle and watched the knuckles pass. He had all the time in the world to hit back, but he didn't want to hurt anyone. We're all just human beings, aren't we?

"Why are you upset?" Peter asked. "I just want to talk. I'm looking for your cousin Erik. I'm trying to help."

Dónaldur moved in from the side and tried to hit Peter in the kidney. Peter deflected with a forearm and pushed the shorter man stumbling back with a hand to the chest, having suppressed his own long-trained reflex to step into the opening and put the man away quickly with an elbow to the temple or a punch to the throat. He was still feeling good, part of the great human tribe. A lover, not a fighter.

"You know what happened to Erik." Bjarni's face was twisted with anger. "You people are responsible."

"I don't know what happened," Peter said. "I just want to help Erik do what's right. What's best for his son, Óskar."

Bjarni came at him in a rush, trying to bowl him over with his size.

These guys weren't very good at this. Peter stepped aside like a bullfighter, then swept away Bjarni's outstretched arm and spun the man into the stone wall of the building. But somehow Bjarni had caught hold of Peter's open jacket and yanked him off balance in his sloppy boots. While Peter adjusted, Dónaldur stepped inside and hit Peter with a short right to the ribs. Bjarni came off the wall in a hurry.

Peter tried to slip to the side, but had somehow stepped on his own untied bootlace so his foot couldn't move. He'd already committed his weight and felt his center of gravity shifting irrevocably toward the snowy street.

He tried to turn the fall into a roll, hoping to keep his rhythm, but the jumble of trash cans got in the way, and he couldn't find his feet in his too-loose boots. The music in his head went silent.

Then Bjarni kicked him in the stomach hard enough to knock him off his knees. Dónaldur stepped in and caught him in the hip. Stuck among the trash cans, Peter covered up as they took turns, grunting with each deliberate blow of their heavy-soled rubber boots. Not how a pro would have done it, Peter thought abstractly, but the two had more than enough enthusiasm to compensate.

A red blossom of pain in his thigh. "Go home."

A kick to the chest, caught on his arms. "For you there is nothing here."

A boot to the back. "Next time we throw you in a crevasse."

A steel toe to the meat of his ass. "You will be lost for a thousand years."

When they stood away, breathing hard, Peter wasn't having fun anymore. He'd lost his coat and his boots. He lay hurting, shirtless, and curled into himself on the snowy pavement, his thin long underwear soaked with melt.

The radiant human joy was gone. A bottomless growl grew somewhere deep inside him. Black sorrow and rage flooded in, darker than he'd ever known. The static exploded.

As a short pair of legs wound up for a field goal, Peter rolled and caught the kicking boot with both hands, then twisted Dónaldur off his feet to a hard landing by a recycling bin. He put a bony knee into the fallen man's thick chest and launched himself off the cobblestones, barefoot and nearly naked, steaming in the snow. He looked at Bjarni with blood in his eye. He roared like some raw creature newly uncaged.

Bjarni blinked, startled. He bent, scooped up a stone doorstop and came at Peter with it. Cold and aching, Peter was slower than he should have been, but he still stepped inside the blow. He caught the man's thick right wrist with one hand and locked his elbow with the other. They stood close, struggling. Bjarni's sword and shield tattoos dark against his pale skin. He smelled of stale cologne and alcohol and wet starched cotton.

When Peter broke the man's arm, it made a *snap* that he felt in his teeth.

Bjarni made a sound like a trapped rabbit.

Peter heard the dull scrape of thick bottle glass rising off rough pavement. Dónaldur among the recycling.

Peter released Bjarni and was half-turned toward the sound when he felt a bright starburst at the back of his head. His knees evaporated and he fell face-first into the snow.

Now a frenzy of wild boots from both sides. The Icelanders were hurt and angry and Peter's brains were scrambled. He used his arms to protect his neck and skull. There was no way this ended well. It didn't take much to kick a downed man to death. He had to get off the ground. He got his knees under him but a steel toe to the ribs knocked him sideways.

His reception was fading. He was getting cold.

The kicking stopped. They leaned in. Dónaldur's forehead wrinkled in concern. He favored one leg. Maybe Peter had twisted his knee. "Uh, Bjarni?"

Peter could only see from one eye. The other was swelling shut.

Bjarni didn't look happy. His arm hung at a strange angle. Peter had done some damage, at least. "This is Iceland. Outsiders do not mess with Icelanders. Do you hear me? Forget Erik. Forget Óskar. Go home. Do not come back."

"Hey, guys." Peter's voice was raspy. They leaned in farther. "Your beer sucks."

Bjarni went to kick him again, but Dónaldur put a hand on his good arm and said something in Icelandic.

Then they were gone. He heard the metallic slam of the club door. Feathery flakes of snow floated down from the city-lit sky. An empty vodka bottle lay by his head. He imagined a dent in his skull the shape of its base. "Goddamn Vikings."

Barely able to hear himself over the pounding of his head.

Made worse because of what was lost. That profound feeling of connection in the club. Alive and dancing in the presence of God.

The wind came up and raked across his bare chest. His long underwear bottoms were soaked through. His coat. Where was his coat? And his boots. Shit. It was embarrassing enough to get a beatdown by a farm boy in a tuxedo shirt. Even worse to die from it. He grunted and made it to his hands and knees, but no farther. Oh, he hurt. And he'd been having such a wonderful time.

Footsteps came softly in the snow-muffled night.

"Mary and Joseph." A voice rose and fell. He felt a hand warm on his bare shoulder. "Can yeh stand, laddie?" Then a quick laugh. "I see you're a bit worse for the drink. Some days a man needs to blow the cobwebs out. But I've got you now."

A musical accent. Irish. The hand found his underarm and pulled him up with surprising strength. "Be proper criminal behavior to leave a man in this weather with no clothes, innit?"

Much as it hurt to be on his knees, it hurt worse to be upright. Peter forced himself to stand erect, taking census of the damage.

Too early to know if there was anything permanent.

A pale, black-haired face peered at him. "Good Christ, that's quite the punch-up you've had. Got a name?"

Did he? "Peter." He hawked and spit blood.

"It speaks. I was gettin' worried. I'm Seamus Heaney, like the poet." Pronounced *Shay-mus*. Dark eyes under thick black eyebrows, the shadow of a black beard beneath pale skin. "Did you see who jumped yeh, lad? Shall we call a copper and make a complaint?"

Peter shook his head, then stopped. It hurt too much.

"Ah, we're peas in a pod, we are. I'm not so fond of the coppers myself. How about a doctor? Surely they have a hospital in this lovely city."

"No doctor," Peter said. "Sleep."

"You Americans, cowboys every one. Where's your hotel, lad?"

"No hotel. Car."

"You must be joking. It's gone midnight. And well below freezing." He peered at Peter's grim face. "Perhaps not. Well, let's get your clothes on before you catch your death." The Irishman helped Peter into his snowy coat, then peered around at the icy

73

cobbles and toppled trash cans. "Is there nothing else you were wearin', lad?"

"Clothes in the club." Peter struggled to get his bare, wet feet into his cold leather boots. It was harder than it should have been. He felt like he was running on three cylinders. Beat to shit, yes, but how had he gotten this drunk on just two beers? Unless there was something else in those bitter, foamy beers. Fucking Bjarni.

He scooped a fat handful of snow from a windowsill and put it to his swollen eye, then limped slowly down the alley. He'd been colder.

The Irishman called after him. "Lad?"

The nightclub stairwell was around the corner. People stood smoking and laughing on the pavement, shining and sleek in their club clothes, oblivious to the weather. One by one, they caught sight of him. Conversation stopped. They stared with wide eyes.

Peter looked down at himself, half-naked like some mountain troll crawling from his midnight cave. Swaying on his feet, one eye swelling shut, his shaggy, sweat-soaked hair beginning to freeze in the cold. The bottomless pit of his war memories yawned open before him. The white static climbed his spine.

Whatever they'd dosed him with, it had turned sour. He didn't feel like dancing anymore. He felt like beating a bartender to death.

He bent to tie his boots and almost fell. The Irishman caught him.

"Come on, lad. Where's your car?"

Peter shook his head. The shining people whispered to each other.

The Irishman put a strong arm around his shoulder and turned him. "We're leavin'." He spoke into Peter's ear. "Tomorrow's another day. Best we go before these eejits snap your photo and put you on social media. You want your mother to see you like this? Or worse yet, your wife?"

Peter tilted with the slope of the hill. Gravity pulled him down toward the bay, his mind blown wild with the winter wind.

By the time he found his car, most of the late-night tourists and party people had disappeared. The parking lot was nearly empty, and the still-falling snow had erased all footprints and tire tracks. The Mitsubishi loomed out of the darkness, snowclad like an old, rounded boulder.

The door was locked.

Peter reached for the key in his pants pocket, then remembered he'd lost his pants. That explained why his legs were so cold.

He patted his coat. No key. No wallet or phone, either. All in his pants. Shit. His brain definitely wasn't working right. He was going to twist Bjarni's head off his goddamn neck.

"Lad, you'll stay with me, all right?" The Irishman put a hand on his shoulder. "Just the one night. No grab-arse, don't worry. I can lend yeh some clothes. You'll be warm and dry."

Peter shrugged off the hand, then turned and slammed the back of his elbow into the Mitsubishi's slightly-open rear passenger window. Dull pain bloomed. The glass cracked. He hit it again and it spider-webbed. Once more and it buckled inward. "I'll be fine." He pushed his hand inside and unlocked the door. He cleared his throat. "Thanks. I owe you one."

He climbed inside while the Irishman watched. Beads of melt gathered on the man's raven-dark hair. His eyebrows furrowed. "You're sleeping in your hire car?"

"You don't know a goddamned thing about me." Maybe said with more force than he'd intended.

The Irishman shook his head, then turned and walked away. Peter climbed into the back and shook out his new sleeping bag to let the down loft. An odd diffused light filtered through the film of clinging snow. Wind pushed more snow through the broken window.

His whole body ached. His eye throbbed. Shivering, he knelt and dug into his duffel for dry tops and bottoms. He told himself it was like changing his clothes in a tent. He told himself he was in a mountain meadow, and tomorrow the sun would come out. Stomach tight with tension and growling with hunger, he crawled into his sleeping bag and waited for his heat to fill the down.

He didn't want to know what time it was. He didn't want to close his eyes. He could feel them waiting for him in the darkness, the Iraqi family he'd killed in the dusty Baghdad street. His punishment. Maybe welcome for all that. Maybe he didn't deserve to forget them, any of them.

His breath caught in his throat. What the hell had he been thinking? He was trapped in this godforsaken winter-bound land with no spring in sight, when his entire being screamed to be outside.

Fuck it. He found the pill bottle and shook two into his hand. Then two more.

He gulped them down dry.

For the pain.

7

TWELVE MONTHS EARLIER

They eat supper together like any other night, even if Sarah is unusually quiet and the food grows cold on their plates. Erik tries without success to wipe the video from his memory while Óskar tells his mother tall tales of their adventures in Rock Creek Park. Recitations of pi are not allowed at the dinner table.

After Óskar has cleared the plates, Erik and Sarah remain in the warm, flickering glow of the candles Erik lights at every evening meal. In the living room, Óskar sprawls on their big white couch, boneless as a squid and spellbound by a game on the family tablet. The tablet is a rare treat when there are Lego to play with and books to read. Óskar knows something is up but the game sucks him in anyway.

Quietly, Erik says, "Where did that video come from?"

Sarah gives Erik a tight shake of her head. Her lips are pale at the edges as she presses them together. The muscle below her right eye has begun to twitch. Sarah is trying to keep herself contained, but Erik is a dedicated student of her ways. He knows these signs.

"Sarah. Tell me what happened."

"The Prince's server got hacked last night. I spent the day up to my neck in it."

"The video came from the hacker?"

She shakes her head.

Of course, Erik thinks. The video came from the Prince.

Most of Sarah's clients are nonprofits, who get hacked nearly as often as for-profit corporations, although the crimes rarely make the news. The hacks are more often for ideological reasons than financial ones. The Women's Reproductive Health Coalition and the National Voting Rights Initiative have more enemies than Erik ever imagined.

Sarah does, however, have one corporate client. Her first real client, the client who helped get her one-woman firm off the ground. Although she would like nothing more than to free herself from him, the client won't let her go. He is too influential, too connected. A few quiet whispers in the right ears would ruin her business. Her career.

In private, when she talks about him, she refers to him as the Prince. A kind of shorthand.

The muscle in her cheek often twitches after she's seen him.

Even now, Erik notices, Sarah deliberately avoids using the man's true name. As if to speak it aloud would make this problem more real. Erik is eerily reminded of the old tales of summoning the midnight gods of the underworld, tales Erik is too intelligent, too rational, to take literally. Yet somehow he has adopted the same habit.

The Prince is the rare Washington power broker with no media presence, because he prefers to work in the darkness. He has no ideology or political affiliation, and is dedicated only to the cause of filling his pockets and broadening his reach. He has been investigated many times, but never indicted. He has somehow managed to avoid falling under the laws that regulate the lobbying industry. He's an attorney and a consultant, so his clients remain secret.

Sarah keeps a private catalog of his sins, gathering ammunition for the day when she might slip his grasp. But this sin is of an entirely different magnitude.

That video confirms every unpleasant suspicion Erik might have had about the Prince. And worse. He thinks about how the lens panned across the moving bodies, how it zoomed in on the faces. Somebody was behind the camera. The same person who set up the whole thing. Erik can only imagine its value, evidence of a public figure's crimes. The ways it might be used.

He says, "Did you catch the hacker, at least?"

She shakes her head. "Lost him in the Maldives." She means the hacker came in through a series of proxy servers, hiding his tracks with each step.

"Did the hacker find the video?"

"I don't think so," she says. "He didn't even get past my secondary firewall. The file was on a hidden drive I found when cleaning up the mess." She looks at Erik. "Although, if the video got out, that wouldn't be so bad, would it?"

"You're not considering —"

"I am."

"We need to think about this, Sarah."

"You think I'm not?" Her voice is low but fierce. The twitch in her cheek has reached her lower eyelid. She is furious. "That video should be in the hands of the police."

Through the door to the living room,

Óskar looks up from the tablet.

"It's more complicated than that," Erik says. "You have a nondisclosure agreement. You'll be exposed. Your business will be ruined. *We'll* be ruined. The lawsuit alone will kill us, even if we win."

"Are you kidding me?" Sarah can no longer contain herself. Her glare could spit a lamb and roast it. Her hair, fallen from its ponytail, rises on the electricity in the dry winter air. "That man goes on television every night and tells half of America what to think. What to believe. What's *moral.* That's reason enough. But to know that the Prince has it? And what he might do with it?"

Sarah's emotions are contagious. This is part of why Erik loves her, the deep currents of her passion. It is easy to get swept away. Nonetheless, he requires himself to keep his voice calm. He puts his hand in hers. "I'm saying, there's a lot at stake." He angles his head at the living room. "It's not just us."

She squeezes his hand. Her grip is astonishing. He watches her face. The twitching becomes more pronounced. When the upper eyelid begins to spasm, the likelihood grows that she will throw something. There are two sides to passion, after all.

"I'm with you," he says. "We want the same thing, okay? To do the *right* thing. Now we just talk about how to achieve it. Before we do anything rash, we need to talk with an attorney, someone who specializes in these things. Agreed?"

He glances at the living room. Óskar's eyes are glued to his parents.

The boy has been listening, of course. Óskar is only seven, but he misses nothing.

"Why don't you go for a walk," Erik tells Sarah. "While I put the tiny Viking in the bath, and to bed."

Óskar speaks up. "I don't want to take a bath."

Erik smiles at the boy. "Tomorrow is Monday, yes?"

"Yes," Óskar admits.

"Monday means school, yes?"

"Yes," Óskar says grudgingly. Despite the fact that he's skipped two grades because of his photographic memory, he still finds school boring beyond belief.

"Then tonight, a bath," Erik says. "And in bed, I will read you the story of Thor and the sea serpent."

Sarah squeezes Erik's hand again, but more gently. The tremor in her cheek has subsided. "A walk is a good idea," she says. "I'll do bedtime tomorrow."

But, of course, she won't.
Because by ten the next morning, she will be dead.

8

PRESENT DAY

For Peter, it began three days before, when Tom Wetzel had called, looking for a favor. Peter's first question was how Wetzel had found him.

Wetzel answered, "I won't ask your secrets, you don't ask mine."

Peter and Wetzel had been new lieutenants together in Afghanistan. Wetzel was capable enough, but hard for Peter to respect because he twisted himself into knots finding reasons to stay inside the wire. It wasn't enough to protect him, though, and he got sent to Germany with mortar fragments in his ass. An undiscovered knack for paperwork manifested during his recovery, and he ended up commanding a desk at Pendleton for the rest of his tour. Now he was some kind of corporate hotshot and he wouldn't tell Peter what the favor was, not until he'd signed a nondisclosure agreement.

It was sensitive, Wetzel said. Peter would have to travel internationally. There might be some heavy lifting, but nothing Peter couldn't handle. He'd be on the side of the angels. The money would be better than good.

Peter didn't care about the money.

When he'd left Memphis the summer before, returning with June Cassidy to her home in Washington State, he'd begun running the valley perimeter again, seven miles of steep, narrow trails with a forty-pound ruck on his back. The dreams had punished him every night. He'd added the waterfall climb, a thousand vertical feet of spray-slick granite, then another two miles through the high grassy meadow above. The rest of the day was spent weeding the big garden or repairing one of the valley's many old buildings. Working until his muscles ached and he stumbled with exhaustion.

It still wasn't enough to let him sleep without dreaming.

His subconscious kept reminding him of his many failures and bad decisions.

He knew, rationally, that the decisions were impossible. Made under pressure, in the heat of the fight, with lives other than his own at risk. He told himself this again and again. He couldn't make the right choice every time. Failure was inevitable.

But the back of his mind felt differently. The conflict between what he knew was right, and the wrong things he'd done. The things he'd had to do. To save himself, to save his people. He'd saved some. But so many others had died. Bystanders. Victims.

A married couple and their young children, in a car without brakes. Just trying to get someplace safe.

Collateral damage, my ass.

In December, he'd sat with June on the sleeping porch he'd built onto the back of her farmhouse. Since Memphis, when the static had gotten worse again, they didn't sleep together there, although they still did the other things they used to do. The unmade bed was a tangle of sheets.

Outside the floor-to-ceiling windows, it was clear and cold. The ground was almost frozen, and soon the snow would start to pile up. June wore a fleece vest and a wool hat and thermal leggings and two pairs of socks. Peter wore a threadbare T-shirt and faded mountain pants gone thin at the knees. He could see the high valley walls from every spot on the porch. He'd designed it that way. The walls had felt sheltering, once. They didn't feel that way anymore.

"Tell me you're not going to do it." June wouldn't look at him.

"I'm not going to do it."

"But you want to."

He felt the spring wound too tight inside him, the same old urge toward action. "I want a lot of things," he said. "World peace. The Packers in the Super Bowl. The perfect breakfast burrito. Will I get them? Maybe, maybe not."

"Peter, what the hell *are* you going to do?"

He didn't answer. It was a conversation they'd been having for too many months. June had been after Peter to find work outside the valley. "Start roofing houses," she'd said. "That'll let you stay outdoors. Or find a job with one of the local outfitters, take people on backcountry expeditions. Get back to a normal life. Make some new memories."

How to explain to her that none of those ideas felt much like living. Nothing could compare to the relentless, dread-filled thrill of a firefight. But the addictive, overwhelming dopamine rush of combat was inextricably tied to the suffocating guilt of surviving it, not to mention all the things he'd done to keep his men alive. And the fact that he'd failed at that basic task, many times over. It was an ugly feedback loop, and he was stuck in it.

"You're not talking to me," she said, "not like you used to, not about real things. That's what worries me the most. You're locking it down when you need to be letting it out. I'm afraid you're going to explode."

"That's why I went to Memphis," he said. "A kind of atonement. For the war."

"Atonement for what? Doing your goddamn job?"

"I know you're right," he said. "Intellectually, I know it. But it doesn't *feel* that way. I don't know that it ever will."

"That's why you need to move your life forward," she said. "Please. Just take the first few steps. Let me help."

He wished she was mad at him. Anger he could deal with. Hell, he was *good* at anger, especially lately. Instead she felt sorry for him. And there was nothing worse than pity.

He didn't tell her that he'd started thinking about going back. Despite the drawdown, there was plenty of overseas contract work for someone with Peter's experience. Executive protection, corporate mercenary stuff. He knew a lot of guys who had gone that route. Maybe he should stop fighting it. Maybe armed conflict was in his blood. Maybe it was all he had left.

He found himself standing on the cold plank floor without any recollection of getting to his feet, big hands twitching on bony wrists. He felt her eyes on him. As always, when June looked at him, he knew she was really seeing him. More clearly than anyone ever had. He wondered if that was a good thing.

Early that morning, she'd watched through the kitchen window as he packed his truck.

She reached out to him now. "Peter, please. Sit with me. Just a few minutes."

The long muscles in his legs ached with the need to move.

She got to her knees and crossed the bed toward him. "It's cold out here." She bunched his T-shirt in her fist and pulled him toward her. "Why don't you warm me up before you leave?"

He could feel the heat radiating from her skin. "Are you using sex to bend me to your will?"

"Maybe." She smiled and unzipped her fleece. Beneath it she wore a creamy button-up sweater that hugged her curves. "Think it'll work?"

"Only one way to find out." He leaned in and kissed the side of her neck. Worked his way slowly, gently, down to her collarbone.

She made a soft sound. She undid the top button on her sweater, then the next, and the next. He leaned in to kiss the freckles on her shoulders. She wore no perfume. Her own scent was more than enough, mysterious and intoxicating and utterly addictive.

Her voice was husky. "Are you going to visit Lewis?"

"No," he said. "Death Valley." Peter helped with the buttons. Beneath the sweater, she wore a simple cotton camisole. "Just for a few weeks. Maybe the desert will remind me of Iraq and knock something loose."

"Is that really a good idea? To spend all that time in your own head? You don't always have to go right at something, you know."

"I'll be stuck with myself anyway," he said. "You're leaving for Washington the day after tomorrow."

June was an investigative reporter, and she was working a side angle on the bombings in Venezuela and everything that had followed. Peter couldn't believe they were actually talking about a new war. Maybe that's why the static had gotten so bad.

June slid one strap of the camisole down her arm and Peter reminded himself to focus. When she dropped the other strap, her arm across her breasts was the only thing holding the fabric in place. She gave him a smile halfway between sweet and wicked.

"Let's recap," she said. "You're not meeting that corporate guy, Wetzel."

"Oh, no. Definitely not."

"Why don't you stop at Don's on the way." Don was a therapist in Springfield who'd given him some tools for working with the static. "Maybe he can help with the dreams."

Peter tugged at her arm and the camisole fell down. "Sure thing," he murmured. "You bet." He kissed his way along the freckles on the top of her chest.

"Mmm. You'd agree to pretty much anything right now, wouldn't you?"

In response, he cupped her bare breast in one wide, knuckly hand and ran his rough thumb across her nipple. Her breath caught and he felt a shudder pass through her body.

"You'll come back to me." It wasn't a question. "I need you to promise." She shivered and raised her arms as he tugged the camisole over her head. "This conversation isn't over, Marine."

Peter scooped her up into his lap. "Can it be over for a few minutes?"

She grabbed him by the ear, pulled him

close, and bit his lip. "Shit, Marine. This better take more than a few goddamn minutes."

He felt her smile against his. "Woman, will you please stop talking?"

"Never." She laughed her low, bubbling laugh. "How would you know what to do next?"

9

Peter never made it to Death Valley. He never even made it to Springfield.

He was on I-84 headed west from Hood River, low dry hills to his left, the Columbia River wide and shining on his right, when his phone rang again.

It was Tom Wetzel. Peter considered letting it go to voicemail. Instead he turned up the volume to hear Wetzel's voice over the rumble of the big V-8. Wetzel was so wound up, he didn't even say hello.

"There's a woman coming to see you. She's on a plane right now."

"Wetzel, I'm not doing it. I told you already."

"You'll have to tell her yourself. She lands in Portland in forty minutes."

"Wetzel. Whatever it is, I'm not doing it. I have other plans."

"Fine. Tell her that. After you listen to her story."

"Was this your idea?"

"Listen to her story, Peter. Then call me back."

"I thought you weren't giving me details without a nondisclosure."

"For now, I'll trust you. We'll talk after, okay? She'll meet wherever you like."

Peter sighed. "There's a place called Lardo in Portland, corner of Southeast Twelfth and Hawthorne."

"Corporate money and you pick a place called Lardo?"

"You called me, remember?"

Peter got off the freeway at Glisan, drove west through the rain past Voodoo Donuts on Sandy, then turned south on SE 11th toward Hawthorne. Portland was where the hipsters had moved when they got priced out of Brooklyn, San Francisco, and Seattle. He counted construction cranes between swipes of his wipers and wondered where the hipsters would go once they were priced out of Portland.

Hawthorne was an evolving neighborhood east of the Willamette River. Modest older houses and commercial buildings mixed with new mid-rise condos that looked the same as new mid-rise condos everywhere else. Soon, Peter figured, every town that used to be interesting would be homogenized by the relentless planet-wide flow of money. Somebody's version of progress, he supposed.

Lardo still looked like the Portland he remembered. A low-key, pork-oriented sandwich place set in a funky corner building across from a gas station and one of the few remaining food cart lots. Along with a dozen sandwiches, Lardo served local beer on tap and dirty fries made with jalapenos and parmesan and crispy chunks of pork belly. It also had wide windows that helped tamp down the static, even on a dark and wet winter afternoon where the clouded sun had already fallen past the horizon.

Passing the place in search of parking, Peter saw a black sedan at the curb, a thin plume of exhaust curling from the tailpipe. An angular man in a black suit stood on the sidewalk under a wide umbrella, watching Peter's truck as it drove by.

Peter left the Chevy around the corner and walked back in the rain.

On Lardo's covered patio, its empty tables and chairs padlocked together for the cold season, a woman waited. Slim and poised, she wore a long, tailored coat the color of midnight, unbuttoned to the weather. Beneath it he could see a single strand of pearls as big as marbles.

She stood with her back to the interior light. Rain hammered on the patio cover. He couldn't see her shadowed face. "Mr. Ash?"

Pending the nondisclosure agreement, Peter didn't know her name. He held out his hand. "Please, call me Peter."

She took it, and didn't let go. Her hand was thin, its bones feeling somehow loose under the skin. For all that, her grip was strong and tight, like that of a pond skater fallen through the ice. "I'm Catherine Price." She cleared her throat. "Thank you for meeting me."

He smiled. "Tom Wetzel is very persuasive." Her face was still hidden in the darkness. "Shall we go in?"

Catherine Price hesitated, gripping his hand in both of hers. A car came around the corner, sweeping the patio with its merciless headlights, and now he saw her ravaged face. Lines of grief carved deep as canyons, heavy bags under her eyes that carried everything her invisible makeup and elegant clothes tried to hide. She'd been a classic beauty once, until some unfathomable disaster had crash-landed into her life.

The disaster she'd come a long way to tell Peter about.

She didn't waste any time.

"Twelve months ago, my son-in-law murdered my daughter and abducted my grandson," she said. "They've never been found. The boy is now eight years old. His name is Óskar."

Behind her, the restaurant glowed with warmth and light. Couples sat across from each other, holding hands.

Three minutes before, Peter had wanted nothing more than a cold beer and a hot sandwich and to get back on the road. To reach the campground outside of Springfield before his sleepless night caught up to him. Now, though, he found himself missing June Cassidy more than he'd ever thought possible. He couldn't remember why he was headed for Death Valley. Her farmhouse on the dry side of the mountains was only a few hours away. He could get there before she'd gotten into her PJs. They could walk through the orchard together under the star-washed sky. They could lie in his hammock, wrapped in a down comforter, and keep each other warm.

Instead, he said to Catherine Price, "Let's talk in your car."

He owed her that much, at the very least.

10

The angular man with the black umbrella opened the back door for Catherine Price, eyeballing Peter as he walked around to the far side of the enormous sedan. Peter opened his own door. The man with the umbrella stayed outside in the rain.

Inside, it was warm and dark, lit only by the instrument panel and the streetlights outside. It smelled of damp wool and rich leather. The back seat was bigger than Peter's childhood bedroom. He felt the unruly static slowly begin to rise in the enclosed space. He wanted to find a reason to turn her down. "Tell me about it," he said.

Catherine Price seemed smaller in the car. She pulled her coat around herself more tightly. A black satchel handbag sat open beside her like a hole on the seat.

She stared across the seatback at something he couldn't imagine. Her profile in the dim amber light was the timeless profile of anyone caught by the meat grinder of war, the murderous vagaries of weather, or the vast cruelty of the sea.

"Do you have any children, Mr. Ash?"

"No."

"Once upon a time," she said, "I had two."

He saw it then, the bottomless ocean of grief only held back by her last reserves of self-control.

She took a breath like someone diving into the deep end of a pool. "William, my oldest, died four years ago," she said. "Black ice on the highway, his car went through a guardrail. His wife was with him. She died, too. She was pregnant." A vein pulsed in her forehead. "A year ago, I lost Sarah, my daughter, at the hands of her husband, Erik." She turned to look at Peter, her face sidelit, spooky. "But it's possible I haven't yet lost my grandson."

"Surely, the police," Peter said.

"The D.C. detectives tell me they believe my son-in-law took my daughter's life. They have physical evidence and no other suspects. He left the country almost immediately, taking my grandson. He bought two one-way tickets to Iceland. He grew up there, has family there. And the D.C. police have no jurisdiction."

"But the Icelandic police," he said. "Inter-pol —"

"They can't find him. It's possible his family is protecting him. They say he hasn't left the country. We asked a Norwegian private security firm to investigate, but their person spent weeks in Iceland and got nowhere. He filed his final report after he was injured badly enough to end up in the hospital. That was ten months ago."

"Something new happened," Peter said. "That's why you're here now."

She nodded. "Three days ago." She stopped, cleared her throat, started again. "Three days ago, Óskar's school bag turned up in Reykjavík Harbor. It was a Lego backpack. He begged for that bag for months. Sarah bought it for him before he started first grade. He even slept with it. When it washed up in the harbor, it still held his favorite book and his stuffed bear and his collection of little Lego people. He kept them in a plastic peanut-butter jar with a lid, along with his membership card for the Lego Club. His name was on the card. The air in that jar is the only reason the backpack remained afloat in that frozen ocean."

Her grief rose in her like a breaking wave. He watched her struggle for control. She went under for a moment. Then she reached out and grasped Peter's hand and somehow pulled herself back to the surface.

"The day I heard, I called the security firm we had hired before. They were sympathetic, but instead of seeing a sign of hope, they saw it as a confirmation of my grandson's death. His backpack appeared to have been in the water for quite some time. They felt Iceland was too empty, too wild, to find my Óskar. Or even to find his body. They suggested I simply accept what had happened, and try to move on." She caught herself again. "I spoke with a dozen more security companies. Large international firms. None of them would do the job. They said there was no hope." She shook her head, looking down at her hands. "I know it sounds ridiculous, but I believe that he's alive. I can feel it. I *know* it."

She looked up at Peter. "Will you help me?"

"I'm not sure I can," he said. "I don't know what Tom Wetzel told you, but this isn't what I do. Ma'am, I'm just a regular person."

"Tom tells me you were a Marine officer, among the best. He says he's seen what you can do."

Peter closed his eyes. More than anything,

he wanted not to do this. "I'm not quali-fied," he said. "I have no credentials, no authority. I'm not a policeman."

"I've tried all the policemen," she said. "I need somebody else. Someone who will care enough to keep trying. Someone who won't stop until he finds my Óskar."

She took a rectangular package from her purse. It was a brown cardboard document folder with accordion folds and a flap cover that fastened with a string. She unwound the string and reached inside. She didn't have to fish around to find the photograph. The heavy paper was soft at the corners and worn at the edges from where she'd held it many times before. It showed a serious, bearded man holding a smiling blond boy in his arms, a boy already looking for his next mud puddle.

"That's my Óskar," she said. "And the man who murdered my Sarah. Please bring little Óskar back to us."

Peter put his knuckle on the picture. "That's Erik?"

She nodded.

"I have to ask. Are you looking for re-venge? I won't kill him."

He didn't say that he didn't kill people. He'd killed more than he could count, some for good reasons. It was the rest that haunted him.

"Dear God, no," she said. "I just want to salvage something good from all this. I want you to find my Oskar, that's all. Find him, contact the police, and I'll do what's needed to bring him home."

She held out the folder. Her hand was shaking.

"My family has more money than we'll ever need. My late first husband had a knack for it. I'll give you whatever payment you want." She pushed the envelope toward him. "This is fifty thousand dollars to start, in cash, along with a credit card for expenses. The card has no limit. Anything you need, buy it. If you need more cash, just ask. The police report is in here, along with everything from the other investigators. Start with his family. His family is the key."

"Mrs. Price," Peter said. "I really don't —"

"Please." Her voice cracked in the quiet car. Her eyes were luminous. "Just look at the police report, that's all I ask. I'm fifty-nine years old. Both my children are dead and gone. I'll never have another. And that man has taken my only grandchild."

Peter watched as a tear slipped loose and slid down her ruined cheek. He wanted to brush it away, but he didn't. Her grief was hers to carry. It might have been the only thing keeping her together. The only thing she had left to hold.

He thought of that child's lonely backpack adrift in the bay. With only the air in a plastic jar of toys to keep it from sinking to the cold, rocky bottom.

"Mrs. Price, what's your grandson's favorite book? The one they found in his bag?" Peter kept his voice gentle. He made sure to speak of the boy in the present tense.

Her voice fluttered. "*Where the Wild Things Are.* By Maurice Sendak. Do you know it?"

Peter pulled in a deep breath, then let it out. He reached out and took the heavy folder from her hand.

"I do."

When Peter got out of the car, the angular man with the umbrella walked around to meet him in the street. He had long narrow limbs and a pale hatchet face pocked with acne scars. "Are you going to do what she's asking?"

The rain blew sideways and the gutters were ankle-deep in runoff. Peter tucked the folder under his coat. The static was happy to be outside.

"I don't know," he said. "Probably."

"Another guy tried. It didn't go well."

"She told me."

"You any good at this?"

Peter raised a shoulder. "Guess I'll find out."

The angular man leaned toward him almost imperceptibly. More a matter of attitude, a shift in weight, than a change in actual angle.

"I been with Mrs. Price almost ten years," he said. "Before that I was twenty years a D.C. Metro street cop. Narcotics, gang task force, you name it. I'm just saying. So you know who you're talking to."

"I figured you'd been something like that," Peter said. "That's why you're wearing a clip-on tie with that nice suit. You don't want a noose on your neck for somebody to hang you with."

The other man gave Peter a hard smile. "What I'm saying is, you better not just be taking her money."

"I'm not taking any money," Peter said. "Not yet. And if I do, it'll just be for expenses."

The angular man processed this information, gauging its truthfulness. "How come?"

"Somebody has to." Peter walked past the other man. He didn't mention the other reason. The simmer of static rising, thrilled at the prospect of being useful again. Another chance at atonement.

"Wait."

Peter stopped.

The angular man held out a card between two fingers. "I'm Novak. You get in trouble, call me."

Peter scratched his chin. "Does Mrs. Price always take you with her when she flies?"

Novak nodded. "Where she goes, I go."

"You stay at the house with her?"

"There's a guest apartment for security. But I'm full-time on Mrs. Price."

Peter nodded, took the card, then turned and walked toward the restaurant, feeling the weight of the heavy brown folder under his arm, sheltered for the moment against the hard-blown rain.

He hadn't even opened the folder and already he had questions.

Why did this guy, Erik, kill his wife?

Why did Catherine Price need a bodyguard?

And what the hell was he going to tell June?

11

Peter found a table in the rear where he could get his back against a wall, see all the exits, and had a good view out the wide windows to the street, to keep the static happy. Although the static would have been happier without the television replaying footage of the smoking tanker that had been bombed off the coast of Venezuela.

After the waiter took his order and brought back a Jubel Ale, Peter opened the folder and laid out the contents. Along with the worn photo of serious Erik and little Óskar, there were two thick sheaves of paper held together by purple binder clips and a fat yellow padded mailing envelope.

He upended the envelope over the table. Five banded stacks of crisp new hundreds spilled out, along with a matte-black credit card and a tiny thumb drive. He assumed the drive had the same information as the paperwork in digital form. The name on the credit card was Price Consulting.

At the next table, a young couple sat with their beers halfway to their mouths, staring at the neat stacks of money. Then their eyes turned to Peter in his knee-torn Carhartts and worn flannel shirt. They looked younger than Peter had ever remembered being. He smiled politely, reloaded the padded envelope, and tucked it back into the folder.

The first binder clip held police information about the murder of Sarah Price, at least a hundred pages. Skimming, Peter looked at the initial incident report from the first officer on the scene. The evidence inventory, which included a .44 caliber revolver with three spent shells and two intact rounds. Reports from the fingerprint and ballistics technicians. The coroner's report. Interview notes and transcriptions. Purchase records for the revolver and the plane tickets. A statement from someone at Homeland Security to the effect that their records showed that Eiríkur Grímsson and Óskar Eiríksson had left the United States on Icelandair. Paperwork about frozen bank accounts and credit cards.

Peter wondered what strings had been pulled to get the police to part with this information, and who had pulled them, whether official or otherwise. Money had a way of opening doors that were otherwise closed.

The last page was a printed copy of an email from a detective Philip Moore. He regretted to inform Mrs. Price that the investigation had reached the limits of the MPD's jurisdiction. The case had been referred to the Icelandic arm of Interpol. He'd included contact information at the end of the email, everything from Iceland's Interpol office to Moore's own cell.

After that came a thin 9×12 envelope holding four large glossy photographs. The first was a head-and-shoulders shot of a serious young woman in rectangular glasses, hair pulled back in a tight bun, wearing a starched blouse and jacket. Sarah Price, Peter assumed. The rest of the images showed a dead woman in a dark business suit, shot in the face, her body sprawled out on a pale sofa saturated with blood. They were images that no parent should have to see. Peter couldn't imagine why on earth Catherine Price had included those last photos, unless as some form of self-punishment.

There was nothing to tell why Eiríkur Grímsson had killed Sarah Price and taken their child.

Peter looked at the time. Three hours later in Washington, D.C. Peter picked up the phone, but got no answer. He left a message.

"Detective Moore, my name's Peter Ash. Catherine Price said I could call you. I'm trying to find her grandson, Óskar. I'm hoping you can help." Before Peter could get to the next section of papers, his phone rang.

"Phil Moore here. Who the hell is this?" A voice like a scrape.

"Thanks for calling back," Peter said. "Óskar Eiríksson's backpack washed up on the beach in Reykjavík. Mrs. Price asked me to go to Iceland and take another look. Do you remember the case?"

"Yeah, she called me about the backpack." A sigh came over the line, long and thin as an unraveling thread. "Listen, Catherine Price is a great lady. She's been through a lot, and I couldn't do shit for her. That's the only reason I'm calling you back. But this is my first night off in two weeks, so make it quick. Whaddaya need?"

"I'm looking at your paperwork on her daughter's murder. Did you ever figure out why Sarah Price was killed?"

"We never found anything like a motive. Maybe she was fucking her personal trainer. Maybe he was fucking the nanny. Maybe he was just looking for an excuse. Who the fuck knows?" The sound of ice rattling into a glass. "You must be private, right? You ever been a real cop?"

"Never," said Peter. "I'm not police. I'm just doing this as a favor." And because he couldn't sit still.

"Well, motive is overrated, buddy. Sometimes you never find out why. It's all about the evidence."

"And the evidence pointed to Erik Grímsson."

"Absolutely. With the best Metro PD experts and a clear chain of custody. These people, Catherine Price and her husband, they got plenty of money and they're connected all the way up, so we were more than careful. We found the gun at the scene, registered to Erik Grímsson, with his prints all over it. The ballistics match the rounds we dug out of the wall. His prints were on the shell casings. And he shot her three times in the face, which is a very personal way to kill somebody, by the way. My guess, he either felt real guilty about something, or real angry."

Peter asked the question directly. "You're convinced he killed her?"

"I'm sure of it." Peter could hear Moore breathing through his nose. "Okay, look, the case is a year old, and Grímsson's long gone. We'll probably never touch him.

Maybe if we're lucky, he'll fuck up somewhere and the locals will grab him. But I've been a cop a long time, and I'm telling you, he's guilty as hell. Plus, he ran where we couldn't follow. Why would he run if he didn't do it?"

Peter wasn't doubting, he just wanted to know more. "Why would he take the boy with him?"

"Maybe it was for protection, like a hostage. To get his in-laws to back off."

"Did he ever make that demand?"

"Not that I heard about, although his in-laws probably wouldn't have told me if he did. That kind of money, they make their own rules. Maybe they're putting money in an overseas account for the guy, because they don't want that kid to suffer any more than he already has. Not that I blame 'em. You know we think the kid was with him, right? When he did it?"

"Jesus."

"You said it, buddy. And this case is nothing compared to the shit I've seen. Teenagers shooting each other over a pair of shoes. Mothers throwing their babies off the fire escape because God told them to. Fathers killing their whole damn families because they were tired of paying child support. I'm telling you, people are animals. Five more years of this shit and I'm gonna retire and forget all about this life. Move to Key West and run a charter boat and screw all the tourist ladies who'll have me."

"Well," said Peter. "Thanks for your time."

"No problem, buddy. Now I'm gonna hang up and finish getting drunk, then watch basketball until I fall asleep on the couch. Don't ever become a cop."

Peter went back to Catherine Price's papers.

The second sheaf came from the Norwegian investigator, who had done a fair amount of work before he ended up in the hospital. He'd begun by making a list of members of Erik's extended family, including photos lifted from social media, which was apparently a major form of communication for Icelanders. Then he'd used public records to create a detailed profile of everyone he could find. The Norwegian had computer skills Peter lacked. The profiles were impressive. They included home and work addresses, any property and vehicles he could find, their occupations, and any criminal history.

The histories were interesting. Scanning the paperwork, Peter found a robust multigenerational tradition of physical assaults. The fights often involved alcohol, and seemed to be the men of the family confronting men they weren't related to, going all the way back to Erik's great-grandfather, Thorvaldur, who was ninety-six. Thorvaldur's last criminal complaint came at the age of ninety-two, when he'd assaulted another farmer with a hay fork. The punctured farmer was sixty years younger, and had ended up dropping the charges.

In fact, not many criminal complaints had led to arrests. Very few arrests went to trial. Maybe they were all wrongly accused, Peter thought. Or they had friends in high places. Or they were very good at intimidation.

The family would lead Peter to Óskar, Catherine Price had said.

Iceland was the Wyoming of Europe. Geographically isolated, economically challenged, a fierce, hard place for fierce, hard people. Family ties and endless struggle were what allowed people to survive, even thrive. They were proud of their Viking heritage. The tourist boom hadn't changed that, not yet.

Clearly, the family was a problem.

After the background work, probably all done from his desk, the Norwegian had gone into the field to interview the family members in person. He'd started with Erik's cousin, Bjarni Bergsson, because he was the only family member Erik was known to have made contact with after the murder, and he was based in Reykjavík.

Bjarni had been uncooperative.

He'd broken the Norwegian's nose.

A copy of the doctor's diagnosis was attached.

Next, the Norwegian had talked to Erik's mother, Greta. She was a vulcanologist at the Institute of Earth Sciences, and she lived in Selfoss, an agricultural community an hour's drive from Reykjavík. Bjarni had obviously put word on the family grapevine, because when the Norwegian arrived at her house, she slammed the door in his face. Unfortunately, it happened before the Norwegian managed to get his face entirely out of the way.

When the Norwegian sat in his car the next morning, waiting for her to leave for work so he could brace her again, a pair of unknown Icelanders stopped by and told him to leave. Their request resulted in minor damage to his rented Volvo. The repair estimate was attached.

It occurred to Peter that the Norwegian investigator, while great at digging up information on the internet, might not be suited to fieldwork. At least not with this family.

Erik's older brother, who owned a glacier excursion business, had bombarded the Norwegian with ice balls, then stomped the investigator's camera and phone into the hard-packed snow.

Another cousin ran a high-end guesthouse outside of Skaftafell. She'd set her sheep-dogs on him, then pulled rocks from her yard and pelted his car as he drove away. The medical paperwork noted twelve stitches in the Norwegian's calf and a rabies shot. Another auto repair estimate was attached.

Obviously, none of them admitted to knowing where Erik and Óskar had gone.

Between these pleasant home visits, the Norwegian had called Erik's relatives who were living abroad. Icelanders often left home to gain work experience overseas, especially after the financial disaster that followed the collapse of Iceland's banks. Erik had moved to Washington, D.C., Erik's father lived in London, his sister in Edinburgh, another brother in Toronto with his wife and kids. A half-dozen more aunts and uncles and cousins were spread all over Europe and Australia.

None of them had returned the Norwegian's calls.

The family grapevine had a long reach.

The Norwegian's last stop was Seydisfjordur, where two of Erik's uncles docked their fishing boat. But the boat was gone when he arrived, and after waiting for three days, it hadn't returned. Either they were fishing in the North Atlantic or their boat had sunk, because the Norwegian never found them. He never made it to the family farm, either.

12

The farm was more of a family compound, Peter realized. Catherine's documents included a Google Earth photo blown up to blueprint size and when he unfolded it, he saw green hills and fields that stretched from the mountains to the sea. The Norwegian had marked the farm boundaries in different colored pens. Like a grade-school geography report, Peter thought.

Outlined in red, the main farm stood at the base of a high, rocky promontory. Founded more than two hundred years ago, and owned now by Erik's grandmother, Yrsa Thorvaldsdóttir, it had grown to cover a wide, fertile plain, then jumped the main road and continued down to a broad, open bay with a gray beach. The scale was small enough that Peter could see braided streams, a wandering gravel driveway, and the long, straight lines of ditches draining the inundated meadows to make them usable for cultivation.

The photo must have been taken in summer, because the ditch bottoms were bright yellow with flowers. They were probably dandelions, one of the few flowering plants hardy enough to thrive in the Icelandic climate. Icelanders couldn't afford to consider them weeds.

Wrapping around the promontory on each side, two more farms spread out like raised wings, their borders drawn in black and blue. The farms were owned by Erik's grandmother's brothers, and although the fields stretched away from the headland, each farm's buildings all stood fairly close to one another. An easy walk, Peter figured, from one farm to the next. A few hundred meters at most. A close-knit family.

With the big barns making up an outer perimeter and the smaller farmhouses with their backs protected by the high promontory, all of them surrounded by a network of drainage ditches that must be wide and deep to be visible in the satellite photo, the entire compound reminded Peter of nothing more than a fortified medieval village.

Peter could picture that first tiny, turf-walled house, built more than two hundred years ago, when Iceland was still an unsettled wilderness in the middle of a mostly uncharted northern ocean.

The Norwegian had been on his way there when a jacked-up silver SUV came up behind him and ran him off the road. The Norwegian didn't recognize the make or model. The license plate had been smeared with mud.

When the rented Volvo rolled down the rocky slope, every air bag had inflated. Still, the resulting injuries had forced the doctors to put the Norwegian in an induced coma for five days.

In his final report, the investigator fired his clients and made note of his final invoice, which was not included in Peter's papers and must have been enormous.

The Norwegian had made an effort, Peter thought. And paid for it.

These Icelanders weren't fucking around.

How was it that Wetzel had thought this was something Peter could do?

Even more troubling, why did Peter want so badly to try?

Unfortunately, he already knew the answer to the second question.

Nobody had tried to kill him since Memphis. If he went to Iceland, someone might try to kill him again. In fact, it seemed likely.

Peter didn't want to admit that the simple prospect of dying made him feel more alive than he'd felt in months.

There was definitely something wrong with him.

It wasn't the first time he'd considered this.

The question was, did he need fixing?

June certainly thought so.

13

He finished his dinner and was going through the papers again when his phone rang. It was Tom Wetzel. "You met with Catherine Price," he said. "Tell me you're going."

Peter didn't remember Wetzel being this relentless. His battalion nickname had been Wetzel the Pretzel. Maybe corporate life had stiffened him up.

"I haven't decided yet. I'm still reading the file she gave me. Mrs. Price has legal custody of the boy?"

"Absolutely. I'll email the paperwork if you want to see it."

"I do," he said. "Tom, what happened with Sarah Price? Does anyone have any idea why Erik might have killed her?"

"I don't know. When you find him, you can ask."

"Were they fighting about something?"

"I don't know that, either. Look, I'm running point on this for Catherine, but I actually work for Jerry Brunelli, Catherine's husband. I'd only met Sarah a few times. We had a professional relationship. Can we get back on task, here?"

Peter looked at the name on the black credit card. "What kind of work does Price Consulting do?"

"We're a political consulting shop. Government is complicated. People hire us to help get stuff done."

"Like what? Pass legislation? Win contracts?"

"Whatever the clients need. Why are you asking?"

"I was wondering why Catherine Price has a bodyguard."

"In this town, perception is everything. A bodyguard is a D.C. Lamborghini, the ultimate symbol of importance. You have no idea how much money is floating around Washington."

This was classic Wetzel the Pretzel. "Tom."

Wetzel sighed. "My understanding is that Novak's more of a driver. He pulls the car around, holds the umbrella, picks up the dry cleaning."

"You ever meet Novak? I don't see him running errands. He seems pretty focused on taking care of Catherine."

"He's a former cop, Peter. He's got a mission mind-set, just like you and me."

"Has there ever been a threat?"

"We're a small shop, but we do a serious business. We pull the levers, you know? But some levers don't like to get pulled."

"You didn't answer my question."

"This isn't Iraq, Peter. People play for keeps in this town, but a big move is a grand jury subpoena, not a gun in your face. Anyway, if everyone liked us, we wouldn't be doing our job, right? It's just the cost of doing business."

"And that's nothing to do with Sarah's murder. Or Erik."

"Absolutely not. I'll send you the nondisclosure now. You can see why we need you, right?"

"No," Peter said. "I don't. I was an infantry officer, not a cop."

"That boy doesn't need a cop. The Norwegian investigator already did that work. That boy needs someone strong and resourceful enough to face that family and find a way to get him back home. If you know someone better who can be there tomorrow, let me know."

Peter could think of any number of people. He was the wrong man by every measure. Never mind that he wasn't anyone's idea of an investigator. Any good he'd done in the world had largely come from dumb luck, a stubborn streak, and a fierce desire to be useful.

To make some kind of atonement for the things he'd done in war, and afterward.

He looked at the crisp stacks of paper held firm by Catherine Price's neat purple binder clips, their orderly edges a vain attempt at containing the chronicle of violence and pain within.

The padded envelope lay open, carrying its useless freight of money and hope.

The finger-worn photo of stone-faced Erik and little Óskar stood propped against his half-empty beer glass.

None of his reasons mattered, Peter knew.

He was going anyway. Even if he had to pack himself onto an airplane to do it.

He said, "Do you know anything else that isn't in the report?"

"Did you see the video?"

"No." Peter fished through Catherine Price's envelope. "On the thumb drive?"

"That's it. You should take a look. You'll get a sense of Erik. Maybe provide some motivation."

14

Peter packed up and walked back through the rain to his truck, where he fired up his laptop, found the video file on the thumb drive, and hit Play.

The screen showed Óskar on his mother's hip, arms around her neck. His face was dreamy, half-buried in her hair, his lips moving as he talked to himself. Peter could see the straps of a backpack over his shoulders, sky blue with the yellow Lego logo.

"Such a lover boy." Catherine's voice. She must have been holding the camera.

"Ugh. He's a *heavy* boy." A smile quirked the corner of Sarah's mouth. She looked different now than she did in the photo Peter had been given, not so serious. Her thick-framed rectangular glasses perched atop her head, her sandy hair down and blowing in the wind. Then she glanced at the screen, realized she was on camera, and wrinkled up her face. "Mom, please."

"What? It's a beautiful day." The camera closed in on Sarah and Óskar's faces. In that simple act of observation, Catherine's unconditional love was evident in every moment.

With the camera closer, Óskar's voice was loud enough to be understood. He wasn't talking to himself, he was reciting numbers. "Three point one four one five nine two six five three five eight nine . . ." The digits kept coming, spilling out of him.

Sarah raised one arm and pointed. "Hey, Óskar, look at the trees. Aren't they pretty?"

The boy blinked and turned to look. "Wow," he said. "Wow, wow, wow!"

He released his mother's neck, slid from her arms, and hit the ground running, dumping the backpack to the grass as he ran toward the trees.

The camera tracked him across a lumpy green field backed by a row of trees wearing fall colors. A park. The screen bounced as Sarah and Catherine hustled to catch up.

The boy sprinted from tree to tree, skinny arms and legs pumping. "What kind is this tree? How about this one? And this one!" After all his time in war zones, Peter had almost forgotten what it was like to watch a child run without fear. How could the boy be so small, but still so wild and free? It made Peter want to run alongside, seeing the world the way he did. All that joy and excitement and energy.

Óskar stopped at a flame-orange maple with broad, spreading limbs and wrapped his arms around the trunk in a hug. No, not a hug, he was climbing up the tree like a monkey.

The camera jolted, forgotten but still taking video. "Is that a good idea? What if he falls? What if he hits his head?" Worry clear in Catherine's voice.

"Hey, kiddo?" Sarah sounded calm, a good mother. She held his backpack in her arms like a baby. "Be careful, please. Not too high."

"He's fine." A man stepped under the tree, looking up into the branches. Erik, his face almost invisible under a thick blond beard. His voice was deep. "How's the view up there?"

"I can see forever!" Óskar's voice was high and excited. "Which way is our house?"

Then a soft *crack* and a panicked yelp. A thrashing of branches, the slow ticking fall of leaves knocked loose.

Sarah's hands clenched into fists, but her voice stayed steady. "Óskar? Are you okay?"

"A branch broke. I sorta slipped?" A quiet but rising panic. "Now I'm stuck. I can't get down."

"You're doing fine," Erik called. "You're a Viking, remember? So be strong, hold tight with your hands, and find a place for your feet."

"Sarah," Catherine said, "he's seven."

"He'll figure it out," Erik said, staring upward. He looked exactly like his photo. "When I was his age I was climbing mountains, chasing lost sheep."

More thrashing of branches. "Mama?"

Sarah's voice was low. "This isn't Iceland, Erik. Parenting isn't a spectator sport."

"He's more capable than you think." Erik kept his eyes trained on the branches. "How else will he learn?"

"I'm his *mother.*" Sarah dropped the boy's backpack and reached for the lowest branch. "Jesus, Erik. Sometimes kids need help."

She wore a cardigan and high-waisted jeans and ballet flats. She did not appear particularly athletic. Yet she pulled herself up onto the first branch, then the next. "I'm coming, Óskar. Hold tight, okay?"

Limb by limb, she climbed until she vanished into the flame-colored leaves.

Erik remained on the ground, his expression hidden under the heavy beard.

Then the video ended.

Peter wasn't a father, and he wasn't sure

what to make of their argument. He'd grown up without a lot of oversight, and he'd definitely fallen out of his share of trees. Right now, though, he couldn't stop seeing Erik's face.

The depth of feeling in his eyes was startling. The eyes of a man who would do anything.

Peter uploaded the data stick from his laptop to the cloud, then used Catherine Price's credit card to make reservations for the first flight to Reykjavík, leaving that evening.

He spent the next few hours on his laptop, learning everything he could about Iceland's culture, geography, and winter weather.

In the end, he didn't tell June anything. He didn't even call her.

He told himself that she already thought he'd be off the grid in Death Valley. She had her own work to do. She wasn't expecting to hear from him for two weeks.

He just got on the plane and left.

15

When Peter woke in the back of the Mitsubishi, the storm had softened and a giant plow was roaring down the road beside the parking lot. The Reykjavík curbs were piled high with thick, wet snow. Everything inside the 4×4 was damp from the weather that had blown through the broken window.

Peter's head throbbed painfully in time to his heartbeat. His right eye had swollen completely shut, rendering him blind on one side. Blood clotted his hair where Dónaldur had clocked him with the vodka bottle. His back and ribs and legs ached where each boot had hit its mark. Even his elbow was sore from breaking the Mitsubishi's window the night before.

Losing his pants, with his phone and wallet and key, was obviously a setback, too.

On the plus side, his skull seemed to be intact, and he still had all his teeth. The truck's clock said it was after noon, which meant he'd slept something like twelve hours. The midwinter sun was hovering somewhere near the southern horizon, brightening the clouds.

He gulped ibuprofen from his first-aid kit, then unwrapped alcohol wipes to clean his swollen eye and the split skin on the back of his head. He was probably too late to actually sterilize the wounds, but the sting of the alcohol got him focused. The hardest part of getting dressed in the car was putting on his socks.

In his still-damp coat and boots, he walked up the hill into the old city, feeling his stiff body begin to loosen up. He wondered why Bjarni and Dónaldur hadn't simply killed him and tossed him in a dumpster. The family had already run the Norwegian off the road.

Maybe Bjarni was softhearted. Maybe the family didn't want to risk any more attention. Maybe it was just harder to hide a body in the city.

It didn't matter. Peter still had a job to do.

He stopped at a newer apartment building with a covered entrance where he could stand out of the snow and keep his good eye on the stairway to Snorri's Rave Cave. It wasn't due to open for hours, but Bjarni would have to come to work eventually.

He thought about the night before, dancing in the club. That purity of feeling, as if he were linked by some gossamer thread of humanity with every person there.

He wasn't sure he'd ever felt like that before.

Certainly not since his last deployment.

What did it say about him, that the only time he felt connected to something larger than himself was in a running firefight with his platoon or high as a kite on some club drug slipped into his beer. Or alone and off-trail on the side of a mountain, miles from so-called civilization.

The snow came softly down. He was hungry and cold and long overdue for coffee. His head throbbed. His swollen eye tightened. The day got darker. But the white static was strangely silent.

He found that he missed it.

He didn't want to begin to think about what that meant.

Peter had let his guard down, in the club.

It wouldn't happen again.

He would be as ruthless as these Vikings obviously were.

The snow had mostly stopped and shopkeepers were shoveling their sidewalks when

Bjarni came around the corner in a dirty red coat and familiar rubber boots, a day pack slung over one shoulder. The white static finally woke, sparking high. Fight or flight. Peter had a definite preference.

As Bjarni passed the apartment entrance, Peter stepped out behind him, grabbed his hood, and slung him around to slam him face-first into the building. The day pack fell to the ground.

Bjarni said something guttural in Icelandic, then pushed off the wall with one hand. When he spun to meet Peter, his eyes widened in recognition. One sleeve was empty, his right arm slung under his coat. Even with just one good eye, Peter had no trouble thumping Bjarni in the temple with his sore elbow.

Bjarni's eyes fluttered and his knees buckled. Peter caught him under the armpit and held him up. "Viking my ass."

A gaggle of tourists in immaculate new outerwear walked past, staring. Peter hung Bjarni's good arm around his shoulder and clamped his hand around the man's wrist to hold him, just two local drunks trying to keep it together. Bjarni stomped at Peter's instep, but Peter shifted and the heavy heel slipped off the outside of Peter's boot. Bjarni tried to pull his hand away at the

135

same moment, not the worst idea, but Peter just tightened his grip and leaned in.

"Stop fighting or I'll hurt you."

Bjarni kept thrashing, so Peter popped him on the broken arm. He wore a fiberglass cast inside the sling — lucky Bjarni had gone to the doctor — but Peter's hands were hard, and the break was fresh. Bjarni froze in place, face rigid, paralyzed by the pain. The tourists kept walking, shaking their heads. Icelanders.

"Where's your wallet?"

"You are crazy."

"Yes. Where's your fucking wallet?"

Bjarni shook his head. "Back pocket."

"I'm going to take it now. If you try anything, I'll break your other arm. Got me?" Peter watched the muscles flex in Bjarni's face.

"*Já.*" Yes.

Peter released Bjarni's shoulder and fished out the man's wallet. It was a thin, black leather envelope with his national ID and a bank card with a few high-denomination krónur folded between. The ID didn't have an address. Peter put the wallet in his own pocket.

"Give that back."

"Maybe later. What's in the bag?"

"My shoes, for work. A book."

"Any weapons?"

An arrogant tilt of the chin. "This is Iceland, not America."

Peter raised an eyebrow. "I forgot, you just use your boots here."

Bjarni opened his mouth, then closed it again.

Peter patted Bjarni's coat pockets and fished through the bag. He found keys and mittens and a pair of black shoes and Ken Bruen's *The Guards*. At least the guy had good taste in books. He put a knuckly hand on Bjarni's bad arm. "Where are my things from the club? My phone and wallet and key. My goddamn pants."

He watched Bjarni weigh his options. To help him along the path to truth, Peter drummed heavy fingers on the cast. Bjarni's eyes tipped down. "At my home."

"Then that's where we're going. Do we walk or drive?"

"I cannot be late for work." Bjarni said.

"Look at my face." Peter pointed at his swollen eye, his cheek gone black and blue. "You think I feel bad for you?" He scooped up Bjarni's bag. "Now, do we walk or drive? Or should I break something else?"

Bjarni had a banged-up little Skoda hatchback parked just down the hill.

16

They drove along the Saebraut, snow piled waist-high and lumpy beside the road. People walked the seawall on the left, with the dark bay beyond like a hole in the night. Peter had Bjarni's bag at his feet. He wondered where they'd pulled little Óskar's backpack out of the water.

Bjarni turned right on Snorrabraut, which cut back up the hill and through town. The Skoda was a stick shift, and he had trouble driving with one hand, which suited Peter just fine. It would make Bjarni less likely to try fighting in the car, although Peter knew he'd try something eventually. The square-shouldered Icelander with the sword and shield tattoos didn't have the submissive slump of a man who'd given up. When it came, Peter would be ready. Even if he only had one good eye.

Snorrabraut was a major thoroughfare, four lanes packed with small cars and big trucks and enormous yellow-orange buses. The buildings were mostly concrete, three or four stories tall, built right up against the sidewalk and each other. Snowflakes melted on the windshield, shining in the approaching headlights.

They crossed over a highway and came to a long stretch of parkland on the right, with low trees and shrubs half-buried in white. Icelanders had long ago cut down almost all of their native trees for building materials and fuel. New plantings grew very slowly in the subarctic climate.

Peter already had the city map in his head, so he knew where they were, but he didn't know where they were going, and he didn't speak the language. Bjarni could be taking him anywhere. A Viking longhouse packed with cannibals seemed as likely as anything.

"Give me your phone."

Bjarni looked at him, astonished and offended. "No."

People were so attached to their phones. "Really?" Peter rapped his knuckles on the other man's cast.

"Aaah, shit, fuck you. Okay. I must pull over."

Bjarni found a spot to stop. Peter kept a grip on the other man's seat belt, in case he tried to slip the buckle and run, but Bjarni

139

just fished his huge smartphone from his inner coat pocket and handed it over.

Peter woke the phone and saw a photo of three men in a snowfield, wearing winter climbing gear, their arms around each other's shoulders. Two enormous men with cropped hair and graying beards flanked a younger man, clean-shaven and handsome, with empty eyes and a wool hat pushed back on his head. Erik Grímsson was the man in the middle. Maybe the two others were his uncles, the fishermen? Bjarni would have taken the picture.

Peter held up the phone. "What's your security code?"

Bjarni made a face, but stuck his thumb on the button and the phone's main screen came up.

The phone's language was set to Icelandic or Norwegian or something, but Peter recognized the app icons. Global capitalism at work. He found the map function. "What street do you live on?"

Smirking, Bjarni rattled off an impossibly long word or words Peter couldn't begin to decipher, let alone spell. Peter shook his head, opened the glove box, and unearthed the car's paperwork. It had Bjarni's name and what looked like an address. Or, at least, there was a number and a word that began and ended with the same sounds, sort of. He held up the paper. "This?"

Bjarni made a sour face and nodded once.

Peter told him, "Keep driving."

Bjarni ground his teeth and put the car in gear.

While Peter tweaked the phone's settings and put the address into the mapping app, Bjarni got them back onto the road, past a long, narrow inlet, and into a tree-filled neighborhood on a small peninsula sticking out into the sea. The map app identified it as Karsnes. The houses were mostly painted concrete with a modern look. Peter liked the clean Icelandic architecture.

Bjarni stopped at a modest single-story home with wide windows and a low-pitched roof, hiding behind a screen of trees. Tire tracks showed in the snowy cobblestone driveway, which had been shoveled just enough to get the car out.

Bjarni didn't move from his seat. The muscles clenched in his jaw. "What do you want from me?"

Peter wanted him inside the house, where he couldn't make a scene. "I told you," he said. "My phone, my wallet, my car key, my pants." He gave Bjarni a toothy smile. "And your cousin, Erik."

Bjarni just looked at him. He was trying

for empty eyes, but couldn't quite manage it.

Peter took the keys from the ignition, unlatched his seat belt, and opened his door. He still hurt all over. "Come on, I can't wait to see your place. What's for dinner?"

Bjarni muttered what sounded like a potent Icelandic curse, and followed Peter to the house.

At the narrow entrance, Peter handed Bjarni the keys and hung back while the big man unlocked the house. Peter didn't know what might be waiting inside, so he bumped Bjarni off-balance and slipped past to turn on the lights.

He saw an open-plan living area decorated in Icelandic Bachelor Pad, with cross-country skis leaning in one corner and snowshoes piled in another. The wide front windows might be nice when the sun was out, but in the midwinter darkness, they just reflected the pale lamplight back like mirrors. The static didn't like any of it.

Bjarni came in behind him, and Peter pointed at the low couch. "Sit."

Broken arm or not, square-shouldered Bjarni looked bigger indoors. He glared while Peter poked around. Coats and trekking packs in a closet by the door. Four plastic crates in the corner held climbing gear, crampons and harness and rope. A simple kitchen was separated by a counter and stools. The furnishings were inexpensive and utilitarian, but well-made, even elegant in their Scandinavian simplicity.

"Do you have any guns in the house?"

"No, no." Bjarni made a face. "Too expensive. It takes several years for a license. You must take classes, learn safety. And what would I shoot, a sheep?"

As if people only used guns to kill animals, Peter thought.

He locked eyes with Bjarni. "Don't move," he said. "I'm going to look around."

Down a short hallway, he found a bathroom and two bedrooms. The big bedroom was Bjarni's: an unmade bed and dirty laundry. The small bedroom was storage for fishing equipment and car parts. The bathroom was tiled in gray, floor to ceiling, with a glass shower stall and a central floor drain. One kind of shampoo. A single toothbrush at the white sink. Nothing that a kid might use. No sign that Erik and Óskar had ever been in the house.

He heard a noise and pulled a fluffy white bath towel from a heated bar.

He peeked into the hallway and saw

Bjarni, grim-faced and coming fast. He'd shed his coat and sling. The heavy white fiberglass cast ran rigid and right-angled from his wrist to his armpit. With his free hand, he swung a short-handled folding shovel, blade-first, directly at Peter's head.

The static made its rapid calculations. Even sore and half-blind, Peter's advantages were speed and mobility. Fighting the big Icelander in a corner of the tiny bathroom wasn't the best choice. The narrow hallway would keep Peter at the point of the shovel, but he'd have more freedom to move.

He ducked out of the bathroom and backpedaled down the hall. With a left-handed grip on one end of the towel, he snapped the other end at the Icelander's face. Bjarni slammed on the brakes and raised his broken arm to brush the heavy fabric away. The shovel tip carved a crisp curve from the wallboard.

The Icelander recovered quickly and swung the tool back and around, the dark sword tattoo on his forearm flashing as he pivoted his wrist like a samurai to keep the shovel in motion. It looked like the same black NATO-approved entrenching tool Peter had been issued as a Marine, with the same short folding D-handle and strong, sharpened blade.

As a weapon, it was far less effective without two working arms, but neither would matter if the steel bit bone. Trying to get past the sharp end would be asking for a new nickname, like Lefty or Eight-Fingered Pete. A direct hit would split his skull like an uncooked potato.

Either Bjarni had some weapons training or he'd seen a lot of kung fu movies.

Regardless, he came on.

The whirling blade drove Peter shuffling backward down the hall to the bedroom door, which stood open behind him. Still in reverse, he pulled the other end of the towel into his right hand and backed into the bedroom. The furnishings were spare, just a low mattress against one wall and a doorless armoire in the corner. Peter only had one good eye, but now he had space that Bjarni, still in the hall, did not.

He retreated until Bjarni was in the doorway, the shovel restricted in its movement but at the height of its orbit and beginning its descent. He raised the towel taut between both hands and caught the heavy blade on the thick fabric, then brought his hands together, threw a loop of strong cotton around the handle of the stalled shovel, and pulled.

Taken by surprise, Bjarni didn't have time

to correct. Stuck in the doorway with his free hand limited by the immobile cast, he instinctively tried to keep the shovel. It was the right idea, but Peter had two working arms. He yanked Bjarni forward onto his toes, then took two quick steps inside and brought his bony knee up hard into the other man's groin.

Bjarni folded at the waist with a noise like a lonely kitten. Peter caught the man's big square head in the crook of his right arm and hit him three times in the stomach with his left fist. Bjarni dropped the shovel, knees buckling. Rather than hold him up, Peter pushed him away. Bjarni fell backward and curled into himself.

Peter scooped up the shovel, then took a long step and booted the fetal Icelander hard in the meat of his ass.

The adrenaline blasted through Peter's veins like a power surge.

Alive, alive, he was most definitely alive.

Breathing hard, he said, "Tell me we're not done so I can kick you into next week. Please. Are we done, fuckhead?"

Bjarni's eyes were wide and panicked, his good hand clutching his crotch, his mouth gulping air like a beached fish.

"Shit," Peter said. "You'll be all right. Come on, give me your hand."

Shaking his head, he helped the Icelander to his feet and down the hall to the couch.

17

While Bjarni sank into the cushions and tried to create a safe space for his aching balls, Peter examined the folding shovel. The blade's black finish had worn away at the business end, leaving the curved tip shining and polished by use. One edge was serrated, for chopping roots, branches, and, if you ran out of ammunition, the enemy. Peter had one just like it in the back of his pickup.

An excellent tool for backcountry camping and the zombie apocalypse. And maybe for a fucked-up Marine on the loose in Iceland.

"Let's start with something easy," Peter said. "Where's my stuff from last night?"

Still short of breath, the Icelander nodded at a wall unit on the far side of the room, bookshelves over cabinets.

The storage crates from the corner had been spilled onto the floor, where Bjarni had evidently dug for the shovel. Kicking aside a climbing harness and ice axe, Peter found his phone and wallet and car key atop a stack of well-thumbed Yrsa Sigurdardóttir paperbacks. His cash and the black credit card were still in the wallet. His pants, belt, and fleece were folded neatly on a lower shelf.

Peter transferred his things to his pockets, put his clothes by the front door, then turned back to Bjarni. He twirled the shovel in his hand, the weight comfortable and familiar. "Next question. What did you put in my beer last night?"

The Icelander shook his head. His voice was a croak. "I don't know what you're talking about."

Peter tested the shovel blade with his thumb. Recently sharpened. There would be a metal file around somewhere. He made a mental note to look for it. Then he kicked away the coffee table and swung the little shovel again, the blade coming closer to Bjarni's face with each orbit. The Icelander's eyes got wider. "Bjarni. What did you dose me with?"

Bjarni's breath came back. "*Já,* okay, shit. I gave you some Molly."

"I don't know what that is."

"MDMA? Vitamin E?"

Peter shook his head.

"Ecstasy," Bjarni said. "A party drug. Synthetic, very good quality. Medical grade. It made you feel good, I think?" He tried to smile, but it came out as a grimace.

Ecstasy was the classic club drug. It was supposed to lower your inhibitions and increase your feeling of social connection. And Peter *had* felt pretty fucking good. One with the universe and dancing like a freak until Bjarni and Dónaldur had kicked the shit out of him in that alley. Now the only thing that kept him from jumping out of his skin from the static was the rush of the fight still washing through him. Adrenaline had always been Peter's drug of choice.

He poked at Bjarni's chest with the sharp tip of the shovel. Bjarni stiffened on the couch. "Did somebody give you the drugs? Tell you what to do?"

Peter was thinking about the embassy man who'd wanted Peter to go home so badly he'd gotten him kicked out of the country.

Bjarni raised his palm and gently redirected the blade. "Why would anyone do that? Who is there to tell me? I sell Molly at the club." He gestured at the house. "You think I afford this place as a bartender?"

"Then why dose my beer with that shit?"

"You asked about my cousin." Bjarni

glared at him. "The last time someone asked about Eiríkur, two men broke my jaw and sent me to hospital. I had nothing but beer, *skyr,* and smoothies for two months."

Two men? That incident wasn't in any of the reports Peter had seen. "Where's the rest of your dope?"

Bjarni opened his mouth, then closed it again with a sigh. "In the freezer, under the cod cheeks."

Peter took a backward step toward the open kitchen. "If you move off that couch I'll break your head. You got me?"

Bjarni raised his hands. "*Já, já,* I got you."

With one eye on the Icelander, Peter put the E-tool on the kitchen counter, then dug under plastic bags of frozen vegetables and vacuum-packed chunks of fish parts until he found a yellow DHL mailer filled with thumb-sized clear plastic Ziplocs. Inside each was a small pile of pale powder.

He put the mailer on the counter and opened the fridge. A lonely block of cheese, a moldering cabbage, a half package of hard salami, and a few cans of beer. Also three cardboard cartons of milk, which seemed like a lot.

The first carton was almost empty. The next was unopened. The third, tucked way in the back, was stuffed with money.

151

He carried the mailer and the milk carton back to the living room with a jumbo bag of frozen peas and a smile. He tossed the peas to Bjarni. "Put those between your legs, it'll help with the swelling."

Bjarni arranged the peas carefully in his crotch, then looked sourly at the milk carton and the yellow mailer. "Tell me what you want."

"I want your cousin Erik. Tell me where he is and I'm gone. I'll even leave your dope."

Bjarni shook his head. "Why do you continue to ask about Eiríkur? He is dead."

"Wait. What?"

"He is dead. Your people killed him. Last winter."

Peter watched the Icelander's face, but couldn't read him. "My people?"

"Who else came looking for him? The men who broke my jaw. Your people."

Peter hadn't seen anything about that in the Norwegian's report, either. Something wasn't adding up.

"Do the police know about Erik?"

"Please. My family, we do not talk to police. Besides, they would take him away for medical examination. Eiríkur is family. We buried him on the home farm."

Easy enough to claim, Peter thought, and

152

a convenient explanation of why Erik couldn't be found. Also unprovable without digging up the body. Maybe Erik was still alive.

"Why would they kill him?"

"Why ask me? I do not know. Ask your people."

When Peter had met Catherine Price, her emotions had been bare as bedrock scraped clean by a bulldozer. She hadn't cared about Erik. She wouldn't have sent a team of killers. She'd sent Peter to save the boy.

"How about Óskar? His mother and father dying must have been pretty traumatic. Is he okay?"

Bjarni glowered at him. "Óskar is also dead. What kind of men kill a child? What kind of man are you?" Bjarni leaned back into the couch and folded his good arm across his broken one. "Some things are sacred. I say nothing more."

Bjarni's stone face was pretty good. Peter still didn't know whether to believe him. If Erik and Óskar were dead, why was someone trying to get Peter sent home? Unless there was another reason Peter didn't yet know.

Changing tactics, he pointed at the DHL mailer with its cargo of little powder-filled bags. "How many doses in there?"

Bjarni blinked. "About two hundred."

"How much for one?"

Bjarni just shook his head.

"Come on, I had fun at the club. How much?"

"Forty euros each. Five thousand five hundred krónur." Then, despite his aches and the bag of frozen peas in his crotch, the big man brightened. "How many do you want? I will give you a good price."

Peter wasn't buying, although he admired Bjarni's commitment to salesmanship. "How many did you give me last night?"

Bjarni looked away. "Four doses. Two in each beer."

"Seems like a lot for one person."

Bjarni shrugged. "You looked as though you needed it."

Peter wasn't going to have that conversation.

"So you've got about eight thousand euros in product." Peter picked up the milk carton and spilled the contents across the coffee table. Euros and krónur and dollars in neat, rubber-banded folds. "That's gotta be another ten thousand euros, at least. Maybe fifteen."

The look on Bjarni's face told Peter he was underestimating.

"That's a lot of money," Peter said. "Tell

me where Óskar is and I leave now. Your money and dope stays here."

"I told you, Óskar is dead." Bjarni set his feet and leaned forward, shifting his weight. "Money is just money. Family is everything."

"So you said." Peter stepped into the kitchen and took the folding shovel off the counter. When he came back, Bjarni was still struggling off the low couch. It was always harder to get vertical after a beatdown. Bjarni looked at the ice axe in the scattered pile of winter climbing gear.

Peter shook his head, the shovel resting on his shoulder. "Stay down, stupid. You're going to get hurt."

Bjarni made it to his feet and moved forward, scooping up the ice axe with his free hand. The sword tattoo danced on his forearm, and he held his heavy cast before him like a shield. He'd been kneed in the balls and pounded in the stomach and kicked in the ass, not to mention getting his arm broken, but he was still on the attack.

Stubbornly protecting his family.

Peter almost liked the guy.

Bjarni brandished the axe. It was longer than the shovel but far lighter, so it would be quick and responsive. The serrated steel pick, designed for punching ice, gleamed in

155

the lamplight. A good weapon, and a bloody one, if it made contact.

Peter sighed. Bjarni came at him, axe raised.

Peter snapped the shovel around at the end of one long arm and smacked the Icelander in the side of the head with the back of the blade. But gently, more or less.

Bjarni's eyes rolled back and he did a few knee-wobble dance steps. Peter stripped the axe from his hand and caught the cast at the crook of the elbow, then eased the other man back to the couch.

"You're okay." Peter was fairly sure it was true. He went back to the kitchen and returned with two tall cans of Viking Beer. He popped the tops and held one out. "Are all you Icelanders like this?"

Bjarni grabbed the beer like a lifeline. He drained it without appearing to swallow, then looked at Peter with one bleary eye. "Like what?"

Peter sighed again. "Hard heads."

"Hells *já.*" Even beaten down, balls aching, unable to stand, Bjarni jutted his chin at Peter. "It doesn't matter what you do to me. Family is everything. I give you nothing."

Peter closed his eyes for a moment.

He didn't know whether Bjarni was telling the truth, or just telling a story to protect his family. Either way, Peter wasn't going to get anything more out of him.

Fucking Vikings.

18

TWELVE MONTHS EARLIER

After a bath and a story, Óskar snores in his
bed. Erik and Sarah sit again in the dining
room, a cheap phone on the table between
them. It's nearly midnight.

Erik hoped Sarah would calm down during her walk. Instead she found a little
market on 14th Street NW that sold disposable phones, bought one with cash to keep
the phone invisible, then used the mobile
browser to research attorneys. She used the
same phone to leave a message with the
answering service of Ginger Mulanax, a
firebrand California whistle-blower specialist.

Sarah is, after all, a cybersecurity expert.

Mulanax calls back an hour later. She is
on speaker now, her voice warm and strong,
explaining how the federal whistle-blower
statute works.

"People become whistle-blowers for many

reasons," she says. "Patriotism is one. So is pride in your work. Sometimes embarrassment or shame. But in essence, you would be informing on your employer, often revealing proprietary information, so there's a huge amount of personal risk involved. Official whistle-blowers have to go on the record and cooperate with prosecutors, secretly record business conversations, obtain company documents. It's this cooperation that protects a whistle-blower from being sued by his or her employer."

Erik looks at Sarah. He wants to make sure she understands the weight of this. It is like going into business with the government. So much is outside your control. The muscle in her cheek is twitching again.

Behind Ginger Mulanax's voice, they hear the low murmur of voices. The attorney is calling from a dinner party. She doesn't even know their names. She keeps talking.

"It's important to note, however, that resolving a case can take years. It can be incredibly stressful for you and your family. Your role will almost certainly be known to the company well before the case is resolved. You'll be fired. You'll likely be named in a countersuit. All your relationships at work will be ruined. And it may be very difficult to find another job in your field."

"That does not sound promising," Erik says. "We have a young son."

"You need to know what you're getting into," Mulanax says. "It's not for everyone. But the federal government wants to encourage people to come forward, so the statute sweetens the pot a little. Whistle-blowers have the right to anywhere from fifteen to thirty percent of any fines levied and monies recovered by the government. That can be millions of dollars, or tens of millions. For some people, that money is enough to offset the difficulties. But there's no guarantee you'll get a nickel. You're going to want to think about this, long and hard, before you decide."

"What if we don't care about the money," Sarah says. "Is there a way to lessen the risk and speed up the timetable?"

"You just want the people caught?"

"I want him punished," Sarah says.

Not *them,* but *him.*

If Erik had any doubts before, he has none now.

It's personal for her.

Of course it is.

"I'm an attorney," Mulanax says, "so I can't advise you on a path outside the law. But many jurisdictions have a pipeline for anonymous tips. Any tipster would need to

160

assemble enough documentation to compel the prosecutors to begin their own investigation, and do it in a way that protects the tipster and keeps their role a secret. It's harder to do than most people think. If the company is big enough, they'll have information controls in place. Once they know they're in trouble, they'll come looking. Without invoking the whistle-blower statute, a tipster won't be protected from legal reprisals."

They talk for a few more minutes, and Ginger Mulanax returns to her dinner party. Sarah powers off the phone and removes the SIM card. Her face is flushed red. Erik's heart sinks.

"We already have the documentation," she says. "We have the whole hidden drive. We can release everything and pretend the hackers did it."

"What do you mean, you have the hidden drive? I thought you just had that single video."

"There's more than one video," she says.

"What? How many more?"

She isn't listening. "I already made a back door into the server. And we don't need to find a prosecutor, either. We just copy the drive to an offshore server and send a link to reputable journalists, somebody at the

Post or the *Times*. That or publish the video online somewhere, along with the drive address and the password. The internet will do the rest."

Erik cannot believe what he's hearing. "You were planning this all along," he says. "From the moment you realized what that video was."

She puts her hand on his arm. It is hot to the touch. "We can do this," she says. "Don't you want to see him punished?"

"It's not that simple," he says. "What if something happens to us? What about Óskar?"

But Sarah isn't listening. She's already reaching for her laptop.

The whole night, Erik thinks, neither of them have even dared to speak the man's name.

Now they are trying to bring down his whole dark empire.

19

Peter left Bjarni on the couch with the frozen peas in his crotch, a shrink-wrapped halibut steak against the side of his head, and false assurances that he'd leave Bjarni's car keys and phone at Snorri's Rave Cave. He took the money from the milk carton, along with the E-tool and the ice axe, but he left the tiny envelopes of medical-grade MDMA.

Most of them, anyway.

The storm had eased but the temperature had dropped. The wet snow had frozen into a hard crust. He wanted to check his phone, but drove the little Skoda a mile before pulling over to the side of a busy road, in case Bjarni came after him again. With a pointy stick, maybe. The goddamn Viking probably had a harpoon in his garage.

Peter had two texts and four voicemails.

The first text was from Catherine Price,

163

in response to his text about the embassy man after leaving the airport. *My husband is talking to his contacts at the State Department and trying to solve your problem with the embassy. He will call you when he has something.*

The second text was from June. *Drive safe. Call if you need phone sex.* Then a smiley face.

She still thought he was driving to Death Valley after a visit with Don, his shrink.

Peter closed his good eye and felt the little car rock in the wake of the tractor-trailers flying by.

He was not a good person.

It occurred to him, not for the first time, that he didn't deserve her.

The voicemails were all from a single number, which the caller ID listed as Hjálmar, followed by the Icelandic word *Lögreglan.*

Police.

In the first voicemail left the afternoon before, when Peter was sleeping off his jet lag in the Mitsubishi, Commissioner Hjálmar had invited Peter to dinner at his home. "I promise, I will not serve fermented shark or dried fish or any of that crap, just a hearty Icelandic meal of lamb with brown sauce, mashed potatoes, and cabbage salad."

In the second voicemail, left at eight o'clock the night before, when Peter was walking down the steps to Snorri's Rave Cave, Hjálmar had invited Peter to an after-dinner drink. "I suppose you are not checking your phone," he said. "But in case you get this, I invite you to a drink at Ölstofan. It is a civilized place. They have excellent Icelandic beer and spirits. I stay up quite late. Please call anytime."

Peter wasn't used to the cops being quite so polite. Or having the national police commissioner leave personal messages on his phone.

The third call came at midnight, when Peter was high on Ecstasy and getting the shit kicked out of him in a snow-covered alley. The commissioner's tone was much more businesslike. "I call to remind you that you must notify me or my assistant of your hotel and your rental car. You must also report to the airport within thirty-two hours for your flight back to the United States."

The fourth call came just a few hours ago, while Peter was waiting for Bjarni by the apartment entrance. The commissioner's voice was again cordial, even cheerful. "*Halló,* it is your friend Hjálmar. You will not escape without Icelandic hospitality. I invite you again, dinner tonight. I will text you the restaurant to make it easy to find."

The commissioner's persistence about dinner was not a good sign.

The restaurant was in the heart of the old city.

Peter drove the long way around.

He parked Bjarni's Skoda in a snowdrift behind an ancient Volvo camper, then walked through the white streets toward the rented Mitsubishi. He'd left it in the narrow lot between a row of mixed-use buildings and a high berm that sheltered the cars from the cold ocean wind.

The temperature had dropped even further, and the weather came horizontally off the bay, tearing fine snow particles off the berm and streaming them into the night. The party people weren't out in this section of town, just a few local pedestrians hurrying for home. If the cops were watching, there was no way Peter could sneak up on the Mitsubishi without being noticed.

So he played the part of the winter tourist and climbed the berm to look at the white-capped water and the glittering concert hall across the sea road, his good eye watering in the wind. Then he turned to admire the city and look for watchers. The exhaust plumes from a running engine might not be so visible in the gale, so he looked for clean windshields with a body behind the wheel. It was well below freezing, and felt much colder. Peter figured even an Icelandic cop would want heat during a long wait.

He saw several wind-scoured windshields but no people, so he walked down Saebraut, cut through a gas station dug into the berm, then walked back along the row of apartments. No exhaust plumes from this vantage, either, and nobody shivering in a cold car. Maybe Commissioner Hjálmar hadn't found Peter yet. Either that or the Icelandic cops were hiding under the snow.

He picked up his things from the Skoda and walked to the Mitsubishi. Nobody looked twice at the tall, battered man with clothes rolled under his arm, an ice axe in one hand and a folding shovel in the other.

He kept Bjarni's keys and phone. He wasn't going to give the big Icelander another chance at him. Also, when Bjarni had unlocked the phone with his thumb, Peter had taken the opportunity to change the passcode and the language. He could use an extra phone. At the very least, it might take longer for Bjarni to alert the rest of the family.

Peter needed all the help he could get.

■ ■ ■ ■

He parked outside Grandi Mathöll, an industrial building on the working water-front that had been converted into a large, well-lit space with counter-service food stalls on three sides and a wall of windows on the fourth. One burger place even had a compact kitchen built into the shell of a Chevy Step Van. Long family-style tables and benches took up the center of the hall with a view through the tall windows. The wind blew the snow sideways, but Peter could still see glimpses of the illuminated city across the harbor, and a pair of ships hauled for repairs onto the rocky beach.

Televisions high on the walls showed ongoing coverage of the Venezuela thing. That lacquered American commentator was really pushing the idea of a new war. Although, he wasn't the one who'd have to go fight, was he?

The static didn't like the televisions or the enclosure, especially with only one good eye, but if he concentrated on the view, it helped. So did the fact that the exits were clearly visible and the place was half-empty at that time of night. And he needed to work on being inside, and he needed to eat. He was acutely conscious of his swollen face, but nobody looked at him twice. Either folks were very polite or brawling was a national pastime.

He ordered a giant grilled sandwich from one stall, lamb chops and roasted new potatoes from a second, and a Viking Beer from the bar. Iceland didn't appear to be big on green vegetables. The food came on wooden trays covered with brown butcher paper. Peter sat alone by the window, angled toward the harbor, and fell on his supper like a wolf.

As Peter saw it, he had two challenges. The first was to talk with Erik's family without getting beaten to death or killed in a car wreck. The second was to deal with the Icelandic police. The embassy man's demand required that Hjálmar put Peter on a plane back to the States in less than twenty-four hours. Peter needed more time than that.

He wondered again who had the pull to get him thrown out of Iceland. He was still waiting for Catherine's husband to hear back from his contacts at the State Department. Peter wasn't going to wait. He needed to move faster than the speed of government.

He thought, too, about his conversation

with Bjarni. He didn't know whether he believed that Erik and Óskar were dead. If they were, he still owed Catherine a confirmation of that fact, so she could put aside her hope and truly mourn. If they were still alive, he'd find them. Either way, his task was much the same.

Although Óskar's survival was no guarantee that the boy would actually be loved or even cared for. When Peter was growing up in northern Wisconsin, his own family had taken in many runaway kids, children abused or scarred or locked out of their own homes by parents who had claimed to love them. Who'd nearly loved them to death. Peter had seen too much of that damage to wholly believe any family's claims of love and devotion, no matter what Bjarni had said. The Icelandic family's police file was too thick. If Óskar were alive, Peter had to believe that he would be better off with his grandmother in Washington, D.C.

Then there was the question of Sarah Price. As Detective Moore had noted, shooting someone in the face was a very personal way to kill. Most murders, even premeditated murders, had simple, personal motives. Jealousy or greed. Anger or fear. Yet nobody seemed to know why she was killed.

There had to be a reason. It would be nice if Peter could figure out what it was.

This was no longer a simple search for a missing child. If it ever had been that.

He could only imagine what June would say about this.

Which was why he wasn't going to tell her about any of it. She had her own work to occupy her. She wasn't expecting to hear from him. There was no cell service in Death Valley's wild empty spaces. Peter had two weeks before she'd start to worry. He'd be back well before that time was up.

He told himself that a child's life was at stake. That it was better to beg forgiveness than ask permission. That he'd give June the whole story when it was done.

As if, by this single lie of omission, he weren't opening some vast, possibly unspannable chasm between them.

20

His supper in ruins, Peter opened his day pack, set Bjarni's phone on the table beside his own, then reached into the pack's laptop sleeve. He'd only used that space to keep Catherine Price's folder from crumpling during the long trip to Iceland, but the deep padded sleeve had turned out to be a half-decent hiding place for documents, as long as the police didn't want to actually find anything.

He leaned the photo of Óskar and Erik up against his empty beer glass, then paged through the Norwegian investigator's report. The Norwegian had been on his way to the family farm when he'd been run off the road. It had happened right after he'd tried to find Erik's uncles on their fishing boat.

The Norwegian was a much better re-searcher than Peter would ever be, but he seemed more comfortable on the internet than in a hostile environment. Peter wasn't about to get chased off by Vikings with snowballs. He'd knock on some doors, introduce himself, and see what happened.

Not that it was an actual plan, of course. But Peter had used similar tactics in the remote corners of Afghanistan, where the locals had been fighting invaders since before Alexander the Great. They knew the territory better than Peter's platoon ever would, and were experts at ambush tactics. They'd disable a convoy with IEDs, appear out of nowhere to kill or injure as many Marines as they could, then melt back into the landscape like ghosts.

Peter's solution to that particular problem was to take part of his platoon into a known ambush zone on purpose, ready for the fight with his backup on speed dial. When the bad guys made their move, Peter's spotter would call in the artillery or air support while the rest of the platoon would ride in to pour on the hurt.

Of course, Peter didn't have air support in Iceland, or any other kind of backup. His friend Lewis, who was usually happy to lend a hand, was spending two weeks in California with his wife, Dinah, and their two boys. So it wasn't really the same plan.

Peter was on his own, headed downrange,

looking for trouble.

It was disturbing how comforting that felt.

"There you are." Peter turned his head to see Hjálmar standing in what had been Peter's blind spot. "I see that you ate your supper without me."

He wore a short black jacket, blue jeans, and snow boots. Civilian clothes. No bulge at his belt, no sag in his coat pocket. The police didn't carry guns in Iceland, Peter reminded himself. Although Hjálmar could have a radio in his back pocket. He certainly had a phone somewhere.

"I was too hungry to wait." Peter felt the heat radiating from his eye. The back of his head throbbed. "I was just about to call you."

"Of course." Hjálmar's eyes moved from Peter's face to the pair of cell phones to the papers spread out on the table. He seemed to be alone, which was a good sign. "Outlanders require proper permissions to work in Iceland. Perhaps you did not know this."

"It's more of a hobby," Peter said. "I'm reading up on Icelandic history. Tracing genealogy."

Hjálmar didn't believe a word of it. "And the bruises on your face? Is that a hobby also?"

Peter put on a sheepish look. "A girl asked me to dance. A couple of guys decided they didn't like me. Maybe I had too much to drink? Some guys just like to fight, I guess."

The commissioner glanced at Peter's corded arms and his wide, knuckly hands. "And you? Do you like it?"

The bruising on Peter's forearm would look defensive. Peter's hands would back up this story, too. They weren't red or swollen because he generally tried not to hit people with his fists. Elbows and forearms were much more effective.

"I don't like losing," Peter said. "How'd you find me tonight?"

Hjálmar tried to hold back a smile but was not entirely successful. "It is my work."

"You found the agency where I rented the car," Peter said. "I assume my rental has a GPS, in case I get lost or have an accident, but those are usually pretty cheap. They only ping every few hours. So why didn't I see you watching?"

The Icelander had the grace not to gloat. "I left my personal car in the parking lot with a cellular-linked camera on the dashboard. I had a coffee watching live video on my laptop."

Hjálmar was better than Peter had expected. Plus he got points for style. Peter began to gather his papers. "Please, sit. Can I buy you a beer? This Viking Beer is good stuff."

"Unfortunately, I cannot. I am on duty."

The gusting wind pushed against the glass like a giant's hand. Peter felt the pressure change inside the building. "Wow."

Hjálmar shook his head. "The coming storm will be worse. A big one."

Peter raised his eyebrows. "This isn't a big one?"

"Not really," Hjálmar said. "Our weather people compare the coming storm to our last large storm, five years ago. It lasted three days. In East Iceland, we measured winds at two hundred sixty kilometers per hour."

"That's too bad," Peter said. "I was hoping to get out of town for a few hours."

"I do not recommend you attempt to leave Reykjavík. With this storm, it is possible to die from exposure or avalanche. And I must mention, your flight to America leaves in" — he checked his watch — "twenty hours."

"You know, I had almost forgotten." Peter tucked his things into his pack. "I could really use a few more days."

"I am sorry. That is not possible."

Peter nodded. "How many officers do you have waiting outside?"

"None," Hjálmar said. "We are civilized human beings, are we not? So we take the civilized path. I offer you my guest bedroom for the night. It was my son's room, he lives now in Berlin. Tomorrow, after coffee and a fine Icelandic breakfast, I drive you to the airport."

"Let me guess." Peter smiled. "The storm has you short on manpower."

Hjálmar sighed. "The wind blew off the highway three tour buses. The drivers did not correctly judge the weather."

Peter stood from the table and shrugged into his coat. "I hope nobody was hurt."

"Do you know," Hjálmar said, "I am now police for more than thirty years. What I have learned is this. It is easy to see only the worst parts of people. It is easy to lose trust, to grow hard as a stone. That is one way. Another way is different. You see people for who they are. You are prepared for them to be bad. But you hope to see them do something good. You are often disappointed, but not always. And you continue to hope."

"And you're the second way?"

"No," Hjálmar said. "I am the third way. I am hard as a stone. But still I hope. Will you disappoint me?"

Peter shouldered his pack and walked around the long table toward the other man.

Peter was three inches taller, two decades younger, and outweighed the commissioner by at least twenty pounds.

Hjálmar stood almost formally, feet apart, hands clasped behind his back. "I have no baton or pepper spray," he said. "If you leave now, I will not attempt to stop you. But the civilized path will no longer be possible. Only the barbarian's path. I do not think you will like the barbarian's path. Although perhaps you are familiar with it."

"You checked up on me."

"I run also Iceland's Interpol office." Hjálmar was slightly apologetic. "We have a good relationship with your FBI. They confirmed that you are not a suspect in a crime. The request to send you home did not come from them. They would tell me nothing else."

"I live a simple life." Peter stood six feet from the older man. "There's nothing else to know."

"So why, I wonder, does someone at your embassy want for you to leave Iceland?"

"If you tell me his name, I might be able to get an answer to that."

"The name on his credentials was David Staple. When I called him at the embassy today to follow up, I was told they had nobody there by that name. When I spoke directly with the ambassador, she told me that she could not comment on State Department personnel."

"Huh." Peter considered the options. "So, the order to kick me out of Iceland. Where did that come from? The embassy, or Staple?"

"The ambassador would not comment on that, either, although she was very diplomatic about it. Either way, someone does not like you."

"Can't be. Everyone likes me. Even you." In truth, Peter could come up with a long list of people he'd pissed off. "You have David Staple's number in your phone from when he called you at the airport. You could call him back, set a meeting, ask him directly. Clear this whole thing up."

"I do not work for you," Hjálmar said kindly. "I am deporting you. Remember?"

"Right," Peter said. "I forgot."

"You understand that Staple himself does not matter. A request from your State Department, even an informal request, carries a great deal of weight."

"What if I told you I came to Iceland to find a child. The American son of an Icelandic man who apparently killed his American wife, then fled to Iceland with his young son."

"Ah." Hjálmar nodded. "You are looking for Óskar Eiríksson. The boy's backpack came ashore in the last storm. I know you are not law enforcement or you would have contacted me directly. You work for Mrs. Price, like the Norwegian before you."

"You know about this case?"

"Of course," Hjálmar said. "We are a small country. We do not have so many international fugitives that I cannot give them my full attention. Also, I spoke with Mrs. Price several days ago."

"You spoke with her personally?"

"Of course. It is her grandson's backpack. Her daughter who is dead. Who else would I ask to do this thing, my assistant?"

"Do you think the boy and his father are still in Iceland?"

"We continue to search but have not yet found him. We have spoken with Erik's family members and friends many times. They invite us in for coffee and pastries. Most Icelanders are quite polite and well behaved. We also watch his finances, but he has not attempted to access his American or Icelandic bank accounts. He has not used a debit or credit card. He has not applied for legal employment or government support. He cannot rent an apartment without using his identity card. We believe someone shelters

180

him, most likely a relative."

"What can you tell me about his family?"

"We have what I think of as new Iceland and old Iceland," Hjálmar said. "The new Iceland is tourism, technology, and work overseas. If you've seen Catherine's investigator's report, you know that some of the family has relocated abroad permanently, others work overseas for part of the year. For example, Erik's mother, a vulcanologist, has been in Indonesia since May, studying the recent eruptions there. Erik's brother owns an excursion business at Vatnajökull, and his cousin owns a guesthouse near Skaftafell, but they are also partners in a nightclub in Barcelona, so they spend much time there. In fact, they are there now. And Erik and Óskar are not."

"How do you know?"

Hjálmar smiled. "The new Iceland branch of the family has become friendly with my officer stationed in Vik, who is their neighbor. He takes their dogs when they leave town. They have given him keys to their homes. Each time he visits, he finds no evidence of man or boy."

So much for the snowball throwers and camera stompers. "What about the old Iceland part of the family?"

Hjálmar shook his head. "Very different,"

he said. "And a very old family, from the time of settlement in the north. Prosperous in the old way, with fish and sheep and hay. Rich in land, not krónur, and a long history of lawless, violent behavior."

"The Norwegian found their criminal records. It looks like small-time stuff."

"We know much that is not official. Iceland's history is filled with centuries of brutal poverty and famine. To survive, northerners had to be strong and hard. We believe two brothers who own a small fishing business are actually smugglers, using Iceland's location between Europe and America. We suspect them in several murders, although officially the victims are merely missing because we have not found the bodies."

That wasn't so small-time. "But the family wouldn't have the money or connections to influence David Staple."

"I do not believe so. And it is not their way. They are more, ah, direct. But that is not the question I ask." Hjálmar scratched his chin. "Who knew you were on your way to Iceland to find Óskar?"

Peter was a little embarrassed that he hadn't thought of it himself. When the backpack was found, Hjálmar had called Catherine Price. Had Hjálmar called someone else? Had Catherine?

He changed the subject. "What if I told you Erik and Óskar were dead. Murdered, their killers never found."

Hjálmar looked at him without expression. "I would ask for the source of this information."

"His cousin Bjarni."

"Ah." Hjálmar permitted himself a modest smile. "This is a better explanation for your bruises. Do you believe Bjarni Bergsson?"

"I don't know. Maybe it doesn't matter. I'll keep looking, and learn the truth either way."

Hjálmar regarded Peter for a moment. "Bjarni is just a pup. The smugglers, Eiríkur's uncles, are quite dangerous. If you find Óskar, what will you do? You are one man."

"I have your cell number," Peter said. "I guess I'll call you."

"If that is the case, perhaps we should have a coffee." Hjálmar extended a hand at the table. "Surely you have other questions?"

Peter smiled. He wasn't going to sit. The commissioner was stalling for time. But Peter had one last question. "If you had to guess, where do you think he might be?"

Hjálmar frowned. "I do not wish to guess. However, the farm in Nordhurland Vestra is a possibility. It is a large holding. He would have work and shelter and family. But we have been there many times, looking for Eiríkur and the boy, and have not found either one. There is risk for the family, too, because if they are harboring a fugitive, there would be a penalty. It is possible they would lose the farm. For these reasons, I think Seydisfjordur, to the east, is more likely. Eiríkur's uncles own a fishing boat and a small processing facility there, and we are told that Eiríkur is close with them." He shrugged. "When the boat leaves the pier, we cannot follow. They may have already taken Eiríkur and Óskar to Europe."

Outside, the sound of the wind rose and fell. Peter was running out of time. He adjusted the pack on his shoulders. "It's been nice talking with you," he said. "But I've got to go."

"Please," Hjálmar said. "I ask you again, come with me. As my guest."

"I can't." Peter took a backward step toward the door. "I'm sorry, Hjálmar. You've been very civilized."

Hjálmar put out his hand, palm up. "Perhaps you would care to surrender your passport, as a gesture of good faith?"

"No," Peter said. "I wouldn't." He turned away.

"This is an island," Hjálmar called after him. "You are now in the computer system. Every person, on every airplane and every ship, departs Iceland only with the permission of the customs police. Unless you are a very strong swimmer, you will not leave."

When Peter walked outside, he heard sirens on the wind, coming closer.

The pack thumped on his back as he ran for the car.

21

He drove the Mitsubishi too fast, the big engine wound up, fat tires slipping on the snowy pavement even in four-wheel drive. There was only one road in and out of the harborfront. He was certain that Hjálmar had already told the dispatcher what Peter was driving, including the plate number.

He made it past the Saga Museum and through the roundabout without meeting a police car, although he saw their blue and white lights flashing off the high pale fronts of the buildings to his left. At the next roundabout, he swung left back into the old city. Time to get rid of the big 4x4.

He drove with the heater up high and the windows down in an effort to keep the static from overwhelming him. It didn't help. He was getting outflanked on every turn. This whole thing was getting away from him. He was no closer to finding Óskar. If he ended up in a holding cell, he'd have succeeded only in making negative progress.

He steered through the tight maze of streets, small apartment buildings, and commercial blocks built right up against the narrow buckled sidewalks. He passed groups dressed for the clubs, talking and laughing despite the snow and cold and wind. Almost eleven and they were just getting started.

Bjarni's dented little Skoda sat at a snowy curb, right where Peter had left it.

It was a narrow, one-way road with parking only on the left and no legal spots. Peter bumped the Mitsubishi up the opposite curb. The walk was so skinny that the truck was tight to the wall of the building yet half in the road. He shouldered his heavy pack and duffel, his day pack hanging from one hand. He still had Bjarni's keys.

A dirty mountain bike leaned against the Skoda's back end. A square-shouldered man in a red coat pulled open the driver's door and folded himself awkwardly into the small seat.

Peter didn't have time for this shit. He dropped his gear and grabbed the man's arm to pull him from the car. Through the coat, he felt the hardness of the cast. Bjarni turned, mouth open to speak, until he saw Peter's face and froze in place. Seeing something there that Peter didn't want to think about.

Peter said, "You rode your bike here? With all this wind, on these icy streets? With a broken arm?"

"Taxis are expensive." Bjarni was indignant. "And I did not want a parking ticket." He jutted his chin at Peter. "You said you would leave my things at Snorri's, but you did not. I am glad I brought my extra keys."

Peter held out his hand. "Give them here." He could not believe this fucking Viking.

Bjarni shrank back and turned away, trying to protect his cast. "No."

Peter couldn't bring himself to hit anyone else that night. He grabbed Bjarni's ear and pulled. "Keys. Now."

"Ow, okay." Reluctantly, Bjarni held out the keys. "Where is my phone?"

"Get out."

Peter heard sirens again. The big Mitsubishi would grab the eye, parked with two wheels on the walkway on the wrong side of the road. Time to go.

Bjarni pulled away and rubbed his ear. "Why do you want my car? You have one already."

"You can have it." Peter held out the 4x4 keys. "Think of it as an upgrade. Take it."

Bjarni scowled. "It is a tourist rental. Impossible to park, and not yours to give. I want my own car. I *like* this car."

Peter didn't have time to debate the merits of the shit-brown Skoda. The sirens were getting louder. He needed to keep moving if he wanted to stay outside. If he wanted to stay in Iceland. If he wanted to find Óskar.

But if he left square-shouldered Bjarni behind, he was likely to tell the police what Peter was driving. Hjálmar could add car theft to Peter's growing list of offenses.

"Fine, you can give me a lift. But I'm driving." He pushed Bjarni's thick shoulder, shoving him across the transmission hump.

Peter threw his gear into the back, then popped the hatch and jammed the mountain bike into the cargo bay for good measure. The tire hung over the bumper and the hatch wouldn't close. It didn't matter. He climbed into the driver's seat and got the hell out of there.

He found his way to the Saebraut, the shortest path out of town. He used his turn signals and kept to the speed limit. The cold winter wind swirled through the open rear hatch. Snow began to collect on the dashboard. Peter could barely feel his fingers. He might as well have been riding on the roof.

Bjarni looked concerned. "Where are we going?"

189

Peter saw a bus station coming up at the end of a monolithic strip mall. "Right here." He turned left at the light and pulled into the parking area.

"Buses will not run in this weather," Bjarni said. "Already three are off the road. It was on the news."

"I'll spend the night in the station, where it's warm." Peter opened his door. "You've only got one good arm. Let me help get your bike inside the car. It's too cold to drive with that hatch open."

"Thank you, but I have it." Bjarni climbed out and walked around to the back. He pulled a lever and the rear seatback flopped forward, making more room. He shoved the bike inside one-handed. "See? All is good." He closed the hatch with a *thud*.

Peter hadn't left his seat. He popped the clutch, hit the gas, and the little car jumped forward, the movement slamming his door shut.

In the rearview, he saw Bjarni standing flat-footed on the asphalt with his mouth open, coat blown wide by the wind, watching him go.

Peter really wished he didn't feel sorry for the guy.

He drove until he saw an ocean of cars and

trucks surrounding a big white building, part tow operation, part auto shop, part junkyard. The shit-brown Skoda would look right at home. He parked out of sight from the street and sorted through his gear, trying to ditch the duffel and fit the essentials into his heavy pack. He wanted his hands free. How much crap did one man need?

Then he dropped the keys on the floor, hauled the bike out of the Skoda's cargo bay, shouldered into the sixty-pound ruck, and pedaled away.

In the time it took him to ride two kilometers, the wind knocked him over four times.

He left the bike behind the glass-fronted Land Rover dealership and found a secluded spot in the lee of a slope under a copse of evergreens, where he used Bjarni's folding shovel to dig himself a shelter in the frozen snow. The exertion warmed him. The dealership opened in nine hours.

He lay in his sleeping bag, rolled into his ground cloth like a burrito, wide awake in the middle of the night. His head throbbed.

Maybe he was becoming nocturnal. Like a vampire or some other predator. It was better than sleeping, he thought. Better than the dreams.

He dug into his pack for his headlamp and the photo of Óskar in his father's arms.

Erik's bearded face with its indecipherable expression. Óskar ready to escape at any minute. But it wasn't enough to remind Peter of what he was doing there, dug into the snow while the wind tried to blow him into the North Atlantic.

He took out his dying phone and pulled up the video Catherine Price had given him. Óskar reeling off random numbers in his mother's arms. Óskar dropping his Lego backpack to run across the grass and climb the flame-orange maple. Óskar stuck in the tree. His father calling, "You are a Viking. Be strong." His mother climbing up to save him, then vanishing into the leaves.

It was different now, wondering if Erik and Óskar were dead. But still Peter watched again and again. Trying to lock Óskar into his memory, so he'd know the boy's face, his voice, the way he ran and walked and moved his hands.

By the third time through, Peter thought to wonder about Óskar's numbers in the beginning of the video. By the fifth time through, Peter was pretty sure Óskar was reciting the first twenty-seven digits of pi.

He looked at the time. Four hours earlier on the East Coast. His phone battery was almost drained. He called Catherine Price. She picked up on the second ring.

"Have you found Óskar?" Her voice was filled with hope.

"Not yet," Peter said. "The national police are pretty enthusiastic about putting me on a plane home. Although I did get a name on the embassy guy, David Staple. Has your husband made any progress with the State Department?"

Her voice dropped from the weight of her disappointment. "He's still waiting to hear from his contacts there," she said. "I'll text him the name, maybe that will help."

He didn't want to tell her that Óskar might be dead. She already carried that fear. Instead, he asked about Óskar's numbers.

She said, "Óskar has a photographic memory, just like his grandfather — like his genetic grandfather, my first husband, I mean. And he's in love with pi. Do you know pi?"

"I do." Pi was the mathematical constant that described the ratio of a circle's circumference to its diameter. As far as mathematicians had determined, pi went on forever without repeating or demonstrating a pattern, making it both an irrational number and a transcendent number. In the seventh grade, in a pimply, ill-conceived attempt to impress a girl, Peter had memorized the first hundred digits. He'd since lost all but the first six, 3.14159, until Óskar's voice brought them back.

"Well, Óskar knows the first four thousand digits. He'll begin to recite them at the slightest provocation, and he'll continue until you ask him to stop. He's quite a brilliant boy. When you bring him home —" Her voice roughened and he knew she was pushing down tears. She cleared her throat. "He'll be at a good school where he can develop his gifts. Instead of climbing rocks and trees where he might crack his head open every day."

Peter pictured her ravaged face, the lines carved deep with grief. He was afraid he was only adding to it. "After the Norwegian investigator, did you send anyone else to look for Óskar?"

"I tried," she said, "believe me. But nobody else would take my money. They didn't speak the language. They told me Iceland was too remote, too empty. They said I was better off with the police."

Those were good reasons, Peter thought. Yet here he was. And Erik and Óskar were still missing.

"When they found Óskar's backpack, who else did you talk to, before me?"

"I talked with my husband, because of his connections. He told me to talk to Tom Wetzel. And Tom sent me to you. Why do you ask?"

"I don't know," he said. "I'm just trying to figure out who the players are."

"Peter, I need you to call me." He could hear the strain in her voice. "Every day. I need to hear what you're doing, what progress you're making. Can you promise me that?"

"Catherine, I can't," he said gently. "I'll be traveling cross-country soon, and the weather is going to get bad. I don't know what kind of connection I'll have."

"Do what you can," she said. "Promise me that? You'll do what you can?"

"Yes," he said. "I will."

Then his phone went silent. The battery had died.

He found his headlamp and pulled out the photo of Óskar again. The father's bearded face. The boy in his arms, so full of life.

In the pale false light of the LED, Peter held up the photo by thin, worn corners.

He lay there amid the howling darkness and looked at the photo for a long, long time.

22

The slouching salesman clearly didn't believe Peter could afford to buy a Land Rover, even a used one.

Peter didn't blame the man. His eye was still swollen shut and the cut on the back of his head felt puffy and raw. The dreams were more vivid than ever, so he was bleary from lack of sleep, and he hadn't showered since he'd left Portland three days and four airports ago. In that time, he'd danced like a dervish, had two major panic attacks, lost one fight and won another. Standing by the floor-to-ceiling dealership windows, he could smell himself through the open neck of his coat.

But when Peter held out Catherine Price's black credit card, the salesman flashed a broad, surprised smile, stood up straight, and carried the card reverently to the manager's office, where they stood in hushed consultation. The transformative power of money. The manager made a phone call, then came out and shook Peter's hand.

He ended up with a seventeen-year-old blue Defender 110. With serious four-wheel drive and seating for nine, the utility vehicles were legendary for their toughness and durability, and widely used in Africa, Asia, and the Middle East. Peter's Defender had fabric seats and minimal dashboard controls, definitely not a luxury model. But it had a powerful engine and oversized tires with good rubber remaining, and the previous owner had tricked it out like an English redneck with a winch on the front bumper, a snorkel tube for crossing rivers, and a cargo basket on the roof carrying four spare gas cans and a disturbingly substantial snow shovel.

It wasn't Peter's green 1968 Chevrolet pickup, but it had a certain style.

The salesman looked confused when Peter didn't want the dirty truck washed, but was happy to sell him a pair of sand ladders and a bumper jack for crossing roadless areas. Then Peter pulled into an empty service bay, where he borrowed a wrench from a tall mechanic in black overalls and a commemorative World Cup sweater.

The mechanic scratched his beard as he

watched Peter remove the second- and third-row seats to make a sleeping bay in the back. He didn't mention Peter's swollen eye, or his pained grunts as he contorted his aching body to get to the seat bolts.

When Peter returned the wrench, he noticed the mechanic's safety-yellow work coat hanging from a hook on the side of his toolbox. The coat was worn and dirty but Swedish-made and designed for Nordic weather. Even better, he'd seen dozens of men wearing similar gear, all over Reykjavík. "Nice coat."

"*Já.*" The mechanic shrugged. "It is warm."

"How much do these cost? If you don't mind my asking."

"Too much," the mechanic said. "But they last. The best."

"May I see?" The mechanic nodded. Peter picked it up and pulled it over his fleece. It fit him well enough. The mechanic clearly didn't like Peter wearing the coat. Peter took it off.

"Can I buy this one? I'll pay you the same as a new one."

The mechanic looked at Peter with the frugal man's suspicion of an offer too good to be true. "It is not new."

"I know," Peter said. "I need to drive

198

north, but I don't think my coat is good for working in this weather." He took out a fat wad of Bjarni's krónur. "What do you think? Maybe with enough extra to buy some beer for your friends?"

The mechanic still didn't answer. Deeply skeptical. A female mechanic, working on a Volkswagen in the next bay, had straightened up to see what the conversation was about.

"Why don't you try my coat?" Peter had laid his own across the hood of the Defender. It was a gift from June, so he didn't look like a mountain bum when they went to town. "Not so durable, but warm."

The mechanic scratched his beard again, then looked at the female mechanic, who shrugged. He stepped forward cautiously, as if Peter was playing a trick on him, then pulled Peter's coat over his overalls. He looked at the female mechanic again. She raised her eyebrows, maybe seeing her coworker in a new light, then gave a grudging nod.

"It looks good on you," Peter said. "Keep it." He held out the wad of krónur. "And the money."

"You are certain?"

Peter nodded. "Please."

The mechanic shook his head at the

extravagance of outlanders. "Okay."

He took the bills and they shook on the deal. The mechanic had a grip like a hydraulic press. Peter put on his new work coat and climbed into the Defender. The mechanic came over and put his hand on the door frame.

"I do not want to give advice," he said. "But this weather is bad, even for Iceland. There is a storm coming. It will get worse. You should not go. Maybe instead go to the doctor?"

Peter smiled. "Thanks for the coat." Then he threw the truck into reverse, backed out of the service bay, and headed out into the snow.

In his Swedish safety yellow and the fat-tired Defender crusted with dirt, Peter had officially gone native.

It was oddly bright out, probably because the previous night's heavy wind had wiped the clouds from the sky. The Defender's heater was still working hard. There was no built-in thermometer for the exterior temperature, but the previous owner had epoxied one to the side mirror. In Celsius, it read twenty below zero, which was about zero Fahrenheit. Not bad, if you grew up in Wisconsin.

Of course, it was only noon. Things would get a lot colder when the sun went down.

Driving out of the city center, he plugged Bjarni's phone into the cigarette lighter to charge. The cold was hard on battery life. His own phone's battery was so dead that the phone wouldn't even turn on.

He parked in front of a supersized strip mall in a busy commercial area, then went surfing on Bjarni's reviving phone. He found a nearby hostel with an open room and made a reservation on the hostel's website with Catherine Price's black credit card. He didn't like using the card, because it could leave a trail for Hjálmar to follow, but unless Peter wanted to get naked in the parking lot and give himself a snow bath, he really needed to take a shower. With soap. Otherwise they'd lock him up as a hazard to public health.

He couldn't check into the hostel until four, but that was fine.

He had a few other things to do first.

First, he went to Bónus, a big grocery store with a lot of boxed and canned and frozen foods. The food selection made sense on an island where most food arrived in shipping containers. They had fruits and vegetables, but apples were five dollars apiece. He paid cash for several weeks' worth of food he could eat without cooking, like bread and butter and cheese and cured sausage.

He also bought a roll of tinfoil, although he wouldn't be cooking with it.

At a gas station that doubled as a kind of convenience store, he filled his tank and his spare gas cans, and picked up a handful of preloaded gas cards, because he couldn't use cash at the unattended pumps outside the big cities. He also bought a new local smartphone with a front-loaded data plan, and a handmade wool hat with goofy earflaps that partially covered the sides of his face. He'd seen a lot of locals wearing them.

In his hat and safety-yellow coat and six-day beard, nobody gave him a second look.

Peter Ash, master of disguise.

23

The United States Embassy was a modest, older three-story concrete office block with no redeeming architectural features, set in a snug neighborhood among small apartment buildings and single-family homes on Reykjavík's central hill.

Peter parked a quarter block from the embassy and continued up the one-way street on foot to get a look. The sun had gone down and the streetlights had come on. The building's blank face was bright with security lighting.

Iceland was a small, low-risk posting, which explained why the building was set right on the street, with no gated compound, no barbed wire or guard tower. Still, a row of rectangular concrete planters stood waist-high along the front of the building, projecting into the street and narrowing the road to a single lane. The planters might have looked decorative, but with hidden steel reinforcement sunk deep underground, Peter knew they could stop a heavy truck or absorb the blast of a car bomb.

The other security measures would never be mistaken for decoration. The windows were protected with thick metal grates, an array of obvious cameras watched the street, and a pair of armed men were stationed by the door. Their large mustaches and longer hair told Peter they were not Marines. Embassy guards, especially in Europe, tended to be groomed within an inch of their lives. Peter was glad. He didn't want to embarrass a fellow Marine. Private security was a different matter.

He had a map of the area in his head, but on the ground, the streets were a jumble of curves, angled intersections, and one-way residential lanes. The exception was a busy thoroughfare paralleling the embassy to the west, with a historic church and the National Gallery on one side and a small lake on the other. From there, it was a direct half-kilometer to the highway.

The snow had been cleared, although some ice remained on the uneven sidewalks. He circled the block on foot, then climbed back into the Defender. He could see the embassy entrance from the driver's seat. The truck's previous owner had rigged the cigarette lighter to work even when the engine wasn't running, so Peter unplugged Bjarni's phone from the charger and plugged in his own.

When it collected enough juice to wake up, the screen flashed with text messages and missed calls. Catherine Price wanting a progress report. June asking about his appointment with the shrink in Springfield.

Feeling like a bad person, Peter ignored the messages and tore off a generous rectangle of tinfoil, folded it in half, then in half again, and laid it on the passenger seat.

Then he called Hjálmar's cell phone.

"*Halló,* my friend Peter Ash. Your time is perfect. I have not yet had lunch. May I invite you?"

Peter heard a soft commotion in the background. "Thank you, Hjálmar. Lunch sounds great. First, I was hoping you'd give me the cell number for David Staple. I have some questions."

A pause. "Why would I do this for you? It would only make trouble for me."

"You don't like him, either. He's using you. Icelanders are independent people, remember?"

The commotion in the background continued. Peter heard whispers. He smiled. It was good to know the Icelandic cops were human.

"Okay," Hjálmar said. "I will text you David Staple's information. After you finish with him, you call me back. We will have lunch, then I will take you to the airport."

"Sounds great, thanks."

Peter didn't know how hard it would be for Hjálmar to track his phone. But Peter's refusal to go with Hjálmar the night before would have made picking him up a priority. If the police had the capability, they would use it.

He figured the only reason they hadn't found him yet was the fact that he'd drained his phone battery. But they'd had the overnight hours to get themselves ready. Wasn't Europe supposed to be the home of the nanny state? They probably knew what he'd had for lunch. Which was exactly nothing, because despite buying four bags of groceries, he'd forgotten to eat.

Hjálmar's text arrived. Peter made the call.

"Who the hell is this?" Definitely Staple. Peter could practically see his outraged pink face.

"Hi, it's Peter Ash. We met at the airport a few days ago?"

"You? Son, you better be there now, or on your way. Your flight leaves in, what, four hours? Otherwise you've got Interpol on your case. You'll go home in handcuffs."

"About that," Peter said. "My rental car got towed. Any chance you can give me a lift?"

"Jesus Christ. You're pathetic."

"I thought you wanted me to go home," Peter said. "You can walk me to airport security yourself. They make a good cup of coffee."

Staple sighed loudly. "Where are you now?"

"Do you know that big modern church on top of the hill, where all the tourists take their pictures? It's not far from the embassy. That's where you are, right?"

The embassy was a wild guess. Staple could have been at the Hilton, or lunch, or anywhere else. It didn't really matter. Staple would want to be at the church when the police grabbed Peter, just to make sure it happened. He hadn't gone to all that trouble getting Peter kicked out of Iceland just to drop the ball now. Mostly Peter didn't want Staple to hide out where Peter couldn't get at him.

"Yeah, but I'm in the middle of something," Staple said. "Give me an hour. Meet me at the statue out front of the church."

It was a ten-minute walk. The hour would

give the police time to get set up.

"Great," Peter said. "Thanks so much for your help."

Then he called Hjálmar back. "All set. Where do you want to meet for lunch?"

Hjálmar seemed to be in a chatty mood. "What kind of food would you like to eat? We have traditional Icelandic, of course. Thai food is always good. Let's see, there is Gló, which has very good vegetarian . . ."

Clearly Hjálmar would talk until Peter's phone gave them his location. Peter laid the phone atop the quadrupled rectangle of tinfoil while Hjálmar yammered on: ". . . sushi, steak, fish, a new pizza restaurant called Flatey . . ."

Hjálmar kept talking as Peter folded the foil around the phone. When he crimped the final edges tight, the sound abruptly cut off as the improvised Faraday cage blocked the signal and killed the connection. Next thing, Peter'd be making himself a tinfoil hat. Crazy, maybe, but even the paranoid have enemies.

Peter had two working assumptions. Staple would tell Hjálmar they were meeting at the church. And Hjálmar hadn't gotten a fix on Peter's location.

If Staple wasn't actually at the embassy, Peter would know soon enough. If not, he'd find the man at the church. Wait out the police and take him then.

He wondered again exactly who Staple was.

Peter was sure that Hjálmar, as the national police commissioner and the local head of Interpol, made it his business to know the main players in the staff of every embassy, especially the American embassy. Hell, Hjálmar was probably on the invitation list to every embassy party. Staple acted like a big wheel, but Hjálmar didn't know him.

Which meant that Staple was new on the country team, or he wasn't actually on the embassy staff. Which led to another question. If Staple was such a big wheel, why did he end up at a small, obscure posting like Iceland?

Maybe he'd screwed up, Peter thought. Got sent away for his sins, whatever they might be.

But that still didn't account for the ambassador's refusal to acknowledge to Hjálmar that Staple worked at the embassy. Or to officially confirm the request to refuse Peter's entry.

What if Staple was some kind of spook? From one of the intelligence agencies. That would account for his attitude, his credentials, and the unofficial nature of the request.

But Staple didn't seem like a spook. He just seemed like an asshole, and not a particularly capable one. In fact, Staple's attitude had annoyed Hjálmar so much that he'd turned Peter loose on Reykjavík for two days.

The embassy's front door opened and Staple appeared. He carried a paper cup of coffee, but nothing else. He wore the same slick-soled dress shoes, his long topcoat, a scarf, but no gloves or hat. Which meant he'd been in a warm vehicle. Even Staple wasn't self-important enough to walk in this weather without better clothes.

If Staple was in the upper echelon at State or the CIA, he might have a driver, but nothing idled at the curb. Staple just walked through the gap between the planters and turned up the sidewalk toward Peter and the row of angle-parked cars.

Peter tugged down his new hat with the earflaps and put Bjarni's phone up to further hide his face. Even though the Defender's windows were rolled up, he did his best Swedish Chef imitation, just to be saying something that sounded vaguely Scandinavian. Peter had always liked the Muppets.

As Staple passed, Peter watched his eyes

210

flick across the dirty Land Rover, the worn safety-yellow coat, the semi-goofy hat and six-day beard. But Staple didn't seem to see anything alarming, because he didn't break stride, just pulled a fat key from his pocket.

A black Renault flashed its lights at the far end of the row.

Definitely no driver. Which was good. Peter didn't want to have to hurt some new hire stuck driving visitors.

He left the Land Rover and hustled after Staple. His boots found the few patches of bare pavement on the icy sidewalk. He carried a hiking pole in one hand, the other hand held to his ear as if he were still on the phone.

"Já, já." He spoke loudly. *"Nei. Reykjavík. Já. Björk. Takk fyrir. Oh, já."* That was pretty much all of Peter's Icelandic. It was a notoriously difficult language to learn, maybe because its closest relative was Old Norse. Still, if Peter gave a shit what Staple thought, he'd have been embarrassed.

Staple didn't seem to notice at all, just took a big slug of coffee. He held the cup in his right hand, which meant it was likely his dominant side. Peter closed in from behind, watching where the other man stepped.

When his right foot landed on a reasonably smooth patch of ice, and his weight was fully on it, Peter stuck the spike of the hiking pole into the leather back of the man's expensive, slick-soled dress shoe and pushed.

Staple's right foot slid forward on the ice and flew into the air, followed immediately by the left. His arms pinwheeled. His hips followed his legs. Staple was, for a moment, fully airborne.

He landed first on his left hip, then his elbow and shoulder, neck bent to protect his head. He lay there unblinking, trying to process what had happened. Peter tucked the hiking pole under his arm, woke Bjarni's phone, and took a few photos of the man's face. "Work with me, baby. Looking good."

The shock of the fall faded, replaced with confusion and pain. Staple's winning personality reemerged as he raised himself onto his good elbow. "What the fucking fuck? Who the fuck are you?"

It was almost enough to make a Marine give up swearing. Peter put away the phone and pulled off the earflapped hat. "Hello, David."

Recognition dawned. "You?"

"Yep." Peter reached down and yanked open Staple's topcoat, the buttons popping like stray rounds. He dropped a heavy knee onto the man's soft chest.

Staple grunted and twisted on the ground but he couldn't dislodge Peter. "You are in deep shit. We are going to destroy your life. You'll be living in a cardboard box by the time we're done with you."

Interesting that the guy didn't threaten him with federal prison or foreign rendition. Peter smiled pleasantly. " 'We'? Who's this 'we,' exactly?"

Staple snapped his mouth shut and pushed at Peter without effect. Not a physical guy.

Peter slapped him hard across the face. The blow shocked Staple into stillness. He wasn't used to getting hit, so probably not trained as a spook. Peter tore open the man's suit jacket and searched the pockets. He found a big smartphone, a passport wallet, a State Department ID, and the envelope with Peter's plane ticket. He flipped through the documents. The passport and other ID all gave his name as David Staple.

Peter tucked everything into the depths of the safety-yellow coat. He showed Staple his teeth. "Why do you want me out of Iceland? Who's running you?"

Staple only pressed his lips tighter. Peter slapped him again. He didn't have a lot of time.

Staple tried to get his hands up to protect

his face. He was shaking. Anger, adrenaline. And fear, too. But of Peter, or someone else?

Peter knocked Staple's hands away and hit him backhanded. Staple's mouth began to bleed. "I could kill you right now," Peter said. "Give me a goddamn name."

Staple's shakes got worse. Definitely fear. His voice was hoarse. "He will squash you like an insect."

"Hey." A voice behind him. "Hey!" The embassy guards stood on the sidewalk, not half a block away. They hadn't seen what happened, but were responding to the shouting. Still bent over the man, Peter took up his hiking pole and cracked Staple on the temple with the butt of the handle. Staple's eyes fluttered like a geisha's. Peter pressed the man's pink thumb into the phone's button, but it was the wrong kind of phone for that.

"*Já,* I see him," Peter called over his shoulder to the guards, trying to sound like a local with poor English. "He falls on the ice. He does not wear boots."

One man stayed by the embassy's fortified planters, the other walked toward Peter. "What happened?" He had his coat open and his hand on the butt of his sidearm. Mustache or not, these guys were plenty serious.

214

Peter was tempted by the idea of a rare pistol in Iceland, but he didn't want the situation to escalate. He pulled the earflap hat down low on his head. "Tourist." He shook his head at the guard, disgusted. "You help." He rose and turned back to his truck, grinding Staple's phone into the sidewalk as he did.

He backed out of the parking spot, but instead of driving forward past the embassy, he continued to reverse until he hit an intersection. The way he'd seen locals drive, it wasn't out of character. It was also the simplest way to avoid the embassy cameras.

Peter had just bought the Defender.

He didn't want it to become a siren magnet just yet.

Reykjavík was getting smaller by the minute.

24

Peter parked outside the Litla Guesthouse, hoping that the hostel manager hadn't charged his credit card yet. Peter was gambling his need for a shower against the possibility that Hjálmar had called Catherine, gotten the card number, and found Peter's reservation.

He circled the block and looked for police cars and wondered how he'd gotten exactly nothing from a soft target like Staple.

Well, not nothing, exactly. He'd learned that Staple was more afraid of the man who'd sent him than he was of Peter kneeling on his chest and hitting him on the face. Either Staple was a harder man than Peter had thought, or the man pulling his strings was pretty scary.

Still, Peter was no closer to figuring out what the hell was going on. Definitely no closer to finding Erik and Óskar. He'd have to leave town for that.

The Litla Guesthouse was set in an odd little building on a busy corner across from a bus stop and a butcher shop. According to the website, it was a European-style hostel for budget-minded travelers, which meant that the bedrooms were private, but the bathrooms were shared, along with a common kitchen and dining area. It was the first place Peter had found where he could get a room on a few hours' notice. The manager had already emailed him his room number.

The main door opened onto a tiny, unheated landing with a narrow stair leading up. The overhead light was out, and the rough-plastered walls reminded him of the concrete construction in Iraq. The static reacted immediately, sparking up his brainstem. He began to sweat in the cold.

Shit, he was getting soft.

The only way out, he told himself, is through.

The bathrooms were at the top of the stairs. He locked the door, stripped off his clothes, and let the scalding torrent pound his shoulders. The Litla Guesthouse clearly didn't believe in low-flow fixtures.

The static rose up. Hello, old friend. Breathe in, breathe out. If he closed his good eye, he could pretend he was standing under the waterfall in June's little pocket valley.

June was always after him to take better care of himself. Regular meals, regular sleep. Here it was, almost suppertime, and he still hadn't had breakfast. Hell, he hadn't even had coffee. He told himself the shower was a good start.

Standing there, he wondered what it meant that he didn't want to tell June where he was and what was he was doing. But he knew already.

He hadn't called her because he didn't want to lie to her. Because that would be crossing a line. An important one.

Peter lived a life outside the boundaries of society. He worked no regular job. He didn't even have a valid driver's license. He lived on the dwindling remains of his combat pay, unwilling to touch the windfall he and Lewis had taken from a Milwaukee profiteer.

Lewis insisted half the money was Peter's, but it felt tainted by what they'd done to get it, no matter their intentions. Peter didn't even want to take Catherine's money.

He wanted his motives to be pure.

But he knew they weren't.

Hadn't he enjoyed beating Bjarni down? The crack of his arm, breaking?

That righteous anger had blazed up like he was some kind of avenging angel.

He'd felt it in Memphis, too, that glorious rage. It had gotten away from him. No, he told himself. Be honest. He'd released it, like a beast from its cage.

He was afraid, lately, that he could no longer remember the man he'd been before the war. He'd left that man behind in some ancient valley in Afghanistan, or some mud-walled city in Iraq, without even a backward glance. It had been necessary, he knew. To protect his people. To survive. He wasn't wishing he'd died back there. But who had he become?

A man who lived only by the rules he made for himself. A man who honored those rules with everything he had. Because without them, he was truly an outlaw. Capable of anything.

A barbarian, like Hjálmar had said.

Lying to June would be breaking the rules.

He thought again of leaving her. Because he would surely hurt her eventually. If not Peter, then the predators he sometimes hunted.

Under the burning flood, mind like a tornado, Peter scrubbed until his skin was raw.

Until he heard a pounding on the bath-

219

room door, then a muffled voice. "Dude. How long are you gonna be in there?"

Peter cleared his throat. "Use the other bathroom."

"The toilet's clogged. Dude, I ate some of that fermented shark meat. I really need to get in there."

Peter turned off the water. "Three minutes."

He was glad the mirror was steamed over and he couldn't see himself more clearly.

The bathroom opened onto a central hallway, bedrooms on three sides like spokes on a wheel, the common room and kitchen on the fourth. Peter came out in clean pants, a fresh thermal top slung over his shoulder, trying to dry his hair with a backpacker's towel without reopening the cut on his scalp.

A skinny guy with a patchy beard and an unnaturally pale face pushed past without looking at him. The bathroom door slammed.

A man with a swimmer's build in an Ohio State sweatshirt stood in the kitchen doorway, laughing. "I coulda told him not to eat that stuff."

A woman in form-fitting fleece came to the doorway with a plastic spatula in one hand. Silver bracelets jangling, she rested her other hand on the man's arm. But she was staring at Peter, shirtless and sweating from the steam and the static, eye still swollen shut, bruises turning green on his ribs and chest and shoulders. "Wow," she said. "What happened to you?"

At the table behind her sat a man with midnight hair and the dark shadow of a beard on his pale face. "The lad was jumped," he said. "Behind a nightclub." The Irish accent was clear. "Do yeh remember me?"

The man who'd picked Peter off the ground and gotten him to his car. "I do. Seamus Heaney, right?"

A smile creased the Irishman's face. " 'Tis, indeed, just like the poet. And you're Peter. Come in, let's have a look at yeh."

The guy and girl faded back into the kitchen and Peter stepped forward into the Irishman's searching gaze. "I'm afraid I was rude to you that night," Peter said. "I owe you thanks and an apology."

"Nah." Seamus waved it away. "I'm sure I'll do you far worse before we're done. Because tonight, you're buyin' the whiskey. We'll do it proper and you can tell me how you came to be in that snowy place."

Peter thought of young Óskar, living with the knowledge that his mother was dead.

His grandmother was waiting. "I'd like that," Peter said, "but I have to go. I've got to get to the Eastfjords and I'm trying to beat the storm."

"D'y'know," the Irishman said, "I'm about done with Reykjavík myself. Would you care for company on the Ring Road? I've got a good vehicle. Be safer in this weather if we made a convoy."

Ohio State looked at the girl with the bracelets. "Actually, we were thinking of leaving ourselves. What good is coming all the way to Iceland if we never leave Reykjavík?"

Peter wasn't going to endanger anyone else. Plus he didn't want to have to explain himself. "Sorry, I've got to meet somebody. I'm already packed."

The Irishman nodded. "See you down the road, then." But he wasn't done. "Listen, boyo, we don't know each other well enough for me to be giving you advice, but I'll give it anyway." He tipped a knuckle at Peter's swollen eye. "Yeh might want to get some antibiotics on that. Don't want to get yourself an infection, right?"

The first flakes of snow hit Peter's windshield as he pulled onto the highway out of town.

222

25

TWELVE MONTHS EARLIER

It's after three in the morning when Erik spoons coffee into the filter, turns on the machine, and waits for the familiar gurgle.

Their third pot since midnight, and Erik's mouth tastes like he's been chewing one of Óskar's stinky socks.

Sarah sits at the dining room table with her laptop, her fingers flying across the keyboard like a concert pianist's. She is finalizing the configuration of a mirror server at a cloud farm in Iceland. They both know that the physical location of the hardware is irrelevant, yet even Erik is comforted by the connection, however tenuous, to his family.

The mirror server will be a secret, remote, real-time copy of the Prince's server, including the hidden drive, with all the data intact. The mirror server will also track all changes across the original system, and keep a copy of all files. Even hidden, deleted files.

The mirror server will be invisible, Sarah swears.

Erik is still unsure whether they're doing the right thing.

He slides Sarah's second laptop toward him. It, too, is invisible, untraceable, layered with multiple security protocols. The drive icon stares at him from the screen. He clicks it.

A row of folders appears. They are named GOVERNMENT, INDUSTRY, OPERATIONS, and PROJECT.

When Erik moved to Washington, he was appalled that the area had no decent local football team — in fact, they didn't even call it football. So Erik decided to follow the most prominent D.C. sport. With the passion of a convert, he's been hooked on the drama of American politics ever since.

So when Erik opens the GOVERNMENT folder and finds a long row of video files, he recognizes most of the names.

The files are in chronological order. He clicks on the newest.

It's a wide-angle video of a doughy man standing in a hotel room. Gingerly, he picks up a leather overnight bag and upends it over the bed. Bundles of banknotes tumble out. He looks in the direction of the lens, annoyed. "What do I look like, a city councilman? You want your issue to come up before my committee, I need to see six figures. And put it in a numbered account like a professional." He shakes his head and pushes past the camera. "We're done here."

The man is a prominent member of the House of Representatives. He is a senior member of the Committee on Armed Services.

Erik goes back to the INDUSTRY folder and looks at the files. He knows these names, too. Defense contractors, tech companies, financial firms. Again, the files are in chronological order. The newest file shares a name with an international oil company. Erik clicks on the file.

Two men in crisp summer suits and cowboy hats sit at a long wooden conference table. The view is from the tabletop, so Erik thinks the camera must be in a pen or coffee cup or something. Whoever is pointing it does a pretty good job of capturing faces. One man is midforties and thick through the neck and chest. The other is at least seventy, lean, and leathery.

The younger man says, "You're our damn consultant. Why can't you move the needle on this?"

A cool baritone answers. Erik recognizes the voice, one of the Prince's underlings. "We've taken steps, as we've discussed, but despite the efforts of our influencers, Congress as a whole remains understandably reluctant to get involved. We need more voices. We won't see organic support until public opinion changes."

The men in cowboy hats glance at each other. The older man raises his eyebrows. The younger one speaks. "What'll it take to do that?"

"Anything that will provide fodder for public hearings," says the underling. "Actionable intelligence on WMDs would do the trick. Risk to American lives, threats or damage to American holdings. Some kind of major provocation."

"The refineries have already been nationalized," says the younger man in the cowboy hat. "How about the embassy? Or a tanker? Bombs seem to get the public's attention."

"I'm a consultant." The underling's baritone cools further. "Explosives are outside my area."

"I sincerely doubt that," the older man says. "Not if the price is right."

"You want me to find someone to bomb the American Embassy in a hostile foreign country?"

"I would never suggest such a thing." The older man has a slow drawl. "I surely wouldn't want anyone to get hurt. Especially Americans." He gives a thin, dry smile. "Not too many, anyway."

"I'm sorry," the baritone says, "but I need you to be more clear."

The older man looks at the younger man. The younger man aims a thick finger at the camera. "You know what we want. Do what you did last time. Start a goddamn war."

The video ends with the finger pointed directly at Erik.

He navigates back to the OPERATIONS folder. He clicks on the most recent file.

The video starts. Another motel room, as seen from a fish-eye lens somewhere high in a corner. Four men stand around the bed. "It'll be the easiest thing in the world," says a small man with his back to the camera. Erik spent a year at Oxford, and he knows an Irishman when he hears one.

A man with a shaved head and a heavy beard speaks. "Easy enough for the man staying on dry land." Also Irish, Erik thinks. "Where do we get the goods?"

"If hard men like yourselves can't find high explosives somewhere between Miami and Maracaibo, I've got the wrong lads for the job." The small man lifts an athletic bag and drops it on the bed. "Operating expenses and a plan of the vessel. The first half of your fee will be wired tonight. We may require a second operation involving an RPG attack on a building in the city, for an additional fee. There's no shortage of money to be made here. Are we agreed?"

"Aye," says the man with the heavy beard.

The other two men nod. "Aye," they say.

Erik returns to the main drive and goes to the PROJECTS folder and finds the newest file.

He clicks. A man sits on a steel chair, which itself stands on a broad sheet of black plastic. More plastic hangs from the walls behind him, held up by silver strips of tape.

The man wears a rumpled pinstriped suit. His wrists are tied to the arms of the chair with cloth strips, and his hair is plastered to his scalp. His eyes are swollen and red, as if sick with the flu or a bad hangover. Erik wonders if the man was drugged.

He stares balefully at the camera. "What the fuck do you think you're doing? I'm a United States senator. Do you know the kind of shitstorm that's coming down on you right now?"

For all his bluster, Erik can tell the man is shaken. He doesn't know where he is or how he's found himself in this position.

Offscreen, a voice speaks. It is mechanical, metallic, some kind of electronic voice modulator. It reminds Erik of a man in Blönduós who had throat cancer and needed a device to speak. "You were offered an opportunity. You did not accept. It appears you are a rare man of principle."

The senator blinks several times. "Maybe I was too inflexible. We are all adults here. Tell me what you want."

A wide-backed man steps into view. He wears a black tracksuit zipped to the neck, black leather gloves, and a black full-face mask with a white stylized skull printed on it. Almost no skin is exposed. Still, there is something about him that Erik finds familiar. The man is big compared to the senator, but his movements are tight and controlled.

The white skull glances toward the camera.

The mechanical voice speaks. "Begin."

"Wait, no." The senator's eyes flick from the camera to the white skull and back again. He is hyperventilating. "Your offer was more than fair. Tell me again about the, ah, the opportunity. Please."

A mechanical chuckle. "Unfortunately, the opportunity is no longer available. Now you are an example to others." The voice sharpens. "Begin."

The man in the skull mask steps behind the chair, picks up a thick roll of silver tape, and runs a strip around the senator's head, covering his mouth. He is quick and efficient. The senator doesn't even know what's happening until it's done. He screams through his nose and thrashes in his chair but he's held helpless.

Erik puts his finger to the pause button but he does not allow himself to press it. He needs to know how bad this is. He needs to know why he is risking everything.

The man in the skull mask returns to the front of the chair, bends his knees slightly, and adjusts his shoulders. Then, his hands a blur, he hits the senator in the stomach, the groin, and the face.

The senator rocks back from the force of the blows, then curls in on himself. The skin of his cheek is split. Blood streams down his face. Snot bubbles form at his nostrils.

The white skull observes for a moment, a craftsman inspecting his work, then strikes again, this time more deliberately and with exacting precision. Then again. And again. The microphone picks up the exhalations of his effort, the flat smack of leather on skin, a faint animal whine.

When the white skull stops again, the senator's face is no longer recognizable. He slumps in the chair. His breath sucks at the tape around his mouth.

The white skull looks back at the camera.

"Good enough," says the mechanical voice. "End it."

Erik does not want to watch this, but he is frozen. He cannot help himself. The video plays on.

The white skull cocks a fist. The senator's eyes widen and he thrashes against his bonds. The chair legs rattle on the floor. The skull pauses for a brief moment, perhaps waiting for something. Perhaps saying a prayer, although that seems unlikely. Then the fist flashes down too quickly for Erik's eye to follow.

It strikes the senator in the center of the throat.

The white skull steps back and lowers his hands. The senator's thrashing increases. He is choking to death. The sound is horrible.

Erik forces himself to watch until the bound man is still.

Then he scrolls back to the beginning. He uses a screen tool to capture a picture of the man's face from the first moments of the video.

He puts the image into the secure search engine.

There are thousands of hits. The man was the junior senator from Michigan. He was a former Naval officer and federal prosecutor known for his moral opposition to war. He was found beaten to death behind a bar outside Detroit.

Erik remembers following the story, which was in the headlines for weeks. The FBI's inability to find the killer is considered a major failure of law enforcement. Michigan's governor appointed the senator's wife to fill out the remainder of his term. She has announced that she will run for his seat in the next election. Her fundraising is already at record levels.

Unlike her husband, Michigan's newest senator is running on a platform of a robust national defense.

Closing the laptop, Erik feels a hole in his stomach that has nothing to do with the amount of coffee he has drunk. "This is bad," he says.

Sarah doesn't look at him. "I know." Her hands keep moving on the keys.

"Have you seen any of these videos? They're killing people."

She doesn't stop working. "I know."

"Sarah." He puts a hand on her keyboard to still her fingers. She finally looks at him. He can't read her expression. He says, "What about us? I'm scared."

"Me, too." She moves his hand away. "I'm almost done."

26

PRESENT DAY

Peter drove alone across a white, treeless plain punctuated by dark rocks. Distant hills gave the landscape a jagged edge. The wind gusted unexpectedly, a drunken giant shoving the Defender from its lane. The snow was up to his wheel hubs. The sun was a distant memory.

Highway One was called the Ring Road because it circumnavigated the island. If he drove far enough around its fourteen hundred kilometer length, he'd end up back where he started. Peter didn't know if he should find that fact comforting or distressing. He figured that depended on where he was standing at the time.

The Ring Road bore little resemblance to a modern American highway. For most of its length, Highway One was just two lumpy, narrow lanes with only periodic yellow plastic markers poking up through the snow to indicate where the ragged asphalt ended and the untouched landscape began.

The only other traffic was the occasional tandem tractor-trailer running fast toward the safety of Reykjavík. The big Mercedes and Scania rigs were almost exactly as wide as their lane, and they didn't move over or slow down for anything or anybody. When they passed, the heavy Land Rover shuddered like a toy, blinded in their wake for three or four heart-stopping passes of the wipers. Peter kept both hands on the wheel.

The coming storm had both complicated and simplified his plans.

Before he left Reykjavík, he'd pulled up Iceland's weather website — www.weather.is — on Bjarni's phone, trying to decide which direction to drive. The website was a public resource, created and maintained by the government because Iceland's weather was so extreme and variable that it was often hazardous.

Hjálmar had told Peter that the most likely places to find Erik and Óskar were the farm and the fishing boat. The farm was on a peninsula jutting out into the Greenland Sea, about three hundred kilometers north of Reykjavík, but the weather website showed the north road closed by snow in five places. Peter didn't want to get stuck.

Seydisfjordur, where the fishing boat docked, was seven hundred kilometers to the east, and the road was still clear, even if the weather map showed the rising storm as a giant white spiral, howling in from that direction.

Hjálmar had no reason to think Peter was dumb enough to run into the teeth of an arctic hurricane. He'd figure Peter was hunkered down in Reykjavík. He certainly wouldn't mobilize much-needed officers during a storm emergency with no good cause. Or so Peter hoped.

Bjarni, on the other hand, was dumb enough to come after him. In that shit-brown Skoda. With one good arm.

Peter also liked the fishing boat as his first stop because the Norwegian had been run off the road after visiting there. He didn't want to admit to another reason. There were only two fisherman uncles. He could handle two fishermen, couldn't he? He wasn't so sure about a half-dozen farmers descended from the same Viking stock that had settled Iceland eleven hundred years before, and spent the next ten centuries repelling Spanish pirates and Anglo-Saxon slavers.

Besides, if Peter didn't find Erik and Óskar in Seydisfjordur, he could keep driving the Ring Road and approach the farm from the opposite direction.

It was six at night when he left Reykjavík. He hoped to get to the fishing dock by six the next morning.

Three and a half hours and 180 kilometers later, he stopped outside the town of Vik, his last guaranteed chance for gas until Höfn, almost 300 kilometers away. The roads weren't recently plowed, but the fat-tired Defender was making reasonable time. Peter didn't understand what all the weather fuss was about.

Vik was a handsome little seaside town, with a classic steepled white church on a hill framed by the angular mountain behind it, although both disappeared in a whiteout as he watched. The N1 gas station was minimal, just a pair of twenty-four-hour pumps on a broad, unplowed slab with no cover, standing beside a shuttered white concrete building that had seen better days. The building's roof sported a giant Coca-Cola sign that rattled and shook with each gust of wind. The map showed the ocean less than a quarter mile off the road, but it remained unseen and unheard in the night.

Peter remembered the recommendation of the truck rental clerk and parked at the pump with the windshield facing into the gale. Even with the vehicle standing still, the sound of the wind against the skin of the truck was a low, eerie song played on a strange instrument. As he got out of the Defender, the wind tore the door from his grasp and slammed it shut. His open coat blew off his shoulders and flapped on his arms. The flying snow felt like birdshot on his exposed face and hands. He hoped there was an open bathroom somewhere. He didn't like the idea of taking a leak in this breeze.

While the thirsty Defender guzzled, he fired up his new Icelandic phone to check the roads. The route north to the farm was still closed, and the route east to the uncles' fishing dock in Seydisfjordur was still open. The time stamps were only thirty minutes old. The map showed dozens of the little yellow icons for storm conditions and blowing snow, but so far, the weather wasn't too bad by northern Wisconsin standards.

Then he checked the forecast and saw that the giant white storm spiral had slowed offshore. It hadn't even made landfall yet. Maybe Peter wasn't giving Icelandic weather enough credit. But it just made him more determined to keep driving before the weather truly turned to shit.

When the Defender had drunk an entire

gas card, he climbed back in the truck and found the Norwegian investigator's number in Catherine Price's papers. The time was an hour later in Oslo. He wondered if the Norwegian was the type to keep his phone on after work.

"*Halló,* Kristjan Holm."

"Hello, Mr. Holm. My name is Peter Ash. Can we speak English?"

"It's very late. What do you want?" Holm's voice was thin and reedy, his accent faintly British, his irritation clear.

"I'm sorry to bother you. I'm working for Catherine Price. Looking for her grandson, Óskar, in Iceland. Do you have a minute to talk?"

Kristjan Holm didn't say anything for a moment. Peter heard a mechanical clatter in the background, as if he'd ridden an old bicycle over a bump. That seemed unlikely given the time of year and the fact that Holm was probably looking at the same storm from the other side of the Norwegian Sea.

"Mr. Holm, do you remember the case?"

"Yes." Peter heard the flare of a match and a sharp intake of breath. Holm had just lit a cigarette. "How far have you gotten?"

"Not very," Peter said. "I found Erik's cousin Bjarni." Peter didn't want to mention getting dosed with MDMA and then beat up. It was embarrassing enough to have lived through it. "I'm on my way to Seydis-fjordur to talk with Erik's uncles."

The Norwegian took an impossibly long draw on his cigarette. Peter could hear the crackle of the burning paper. Another draw like that and Holm would be down to the filter. Maybe he smoked the filter, too. "How many people do you have?"

"Just me," Peter said.

Holm gave a short chopping laugh without a shred of humor in it. "Did you not read my report? Are you this unintelligent? Or perhaps you simply have a fetish. You like pain."

"Bjarni told me Erik and Óskar were dead."

Silence for a moment. Maybe he was blowing smoke rings. Then, "Do you believe him?"

"The police have been looking for a year. It might explain why they can't find them. What do you think?"

"If you are asking if they are good police-men, I would say yes. If you are asking if they are corrupt, I would say no. Iceland has little history of that. You have met Hjál-mar, yes? The other police I have met are like him. Very professional."

"Hjálmar thinks the best places to look are the fishing boat and the farm."

"There are more places to hide than the police might consider, or have the people to search. If you look, you will see many abandoned farm buildings still holding back most of the weather. Or one could build a turf house, the way Icelanders did during the settlement time, and for centuries after. However, both the farm and the fishing boat offer work and the protection of family. I think the farm less likely because if Erik and Óskar are found, there is a legal risk to the family. But as I said, there are other possibilities. The police don't have the manpower to search every broken-down farmhouse or caravan."

"Neither do I," Peter said. "So if Erik and Óskar are alive, the farm and the fishing boat are my best bets. But if they're dead, who'd have killed them?" Peter heard the mechanical clatter again. If it wasn't a bicycle, what was it?

Holm said, "Normally I would think the family. But every member of Erik's family defended him to me, denied that he was involved with his wife's death. So maybe it wasn't the family."

"Or maybe you didn't talk to the right person."

"Correct. Maybe it was Erik's uncles. He brought the police to their doorstep. Hjálmar believes they are smugglers, by the way. Maybe that's why they came after me, too."

"Or maybe it wasn't the family," Peter said. He told the Norwegian about David Staple from the State Department, trying to keep Peter out of the country, and Bjarni's claims about two men looking for Erik. "Maybe it was someone else. That would change things."

"Yes. It would mean that Erik didn't kill Sarah."

"I talked to Phil Moore, the Washington, D.C., detective," Peter said. "He's convinced Erik killed her. Although he couldn't give me any kind of motive for the murder."

"Detective Moore only thinks about his retirement," Holm said. "You have to find Erik. Maybe he's dead, maybe he's alive. But if you find Erik, you'll find the boy."

"Do you think they're still alive?"

"I hope so," Holm said. "Besides, if they are dead, why would someone want you out of Iceland? Unless there is something still to discover."

"Good point." It was helpful, talking to the Norwegian about this. Better than just bouncing ideas around in his own head. Peter missed Lewis. "Listen, why don't you join me here? You must want to hit back, after they ran you off the road like that."

Holm cleared his throat. "You have no idea what these people are like."

"I'm learning," Peter said. "But you've already met them. I could use the help. How long would it take you to get here?"

"Most of my work is on the computer," Holm said. "Background checks, security interviews. I work for big companies, like Equinor and Orkla. Before Catherine Price, I didn't leave my desk very often. After what happened in Iceland, I'm not leaving my desk again."

"The pay is good," Peter said. "Double your normal fee."

"I can't."

"Okay, triple your fee. Quadruple it, if you want." The thought of an actual trained investigator with knowledge of the family was appealing. He should have called Holm before he even got on the plane. "Don't you want to get back at these guys? Or have you forgotten about the boy?"

"I haven't forgotten anything." Holm's thin voice was flat. Peter heard the mechanical sound again. "The auto crash damaged my spinal cord. I'm paralyzed."

That explained the sound. Holm's wheelchair. "I'm so sorry. That must be difficult."

He heard another match flare. "I should feel lucky. I can still use my arms. I can empty my own shit bag. That's what my wife said when she left. Anyway, I can't help you."

Peter thought again about Holm's written report and how much information he'd found on the Icelanders. Peter was definitely not a computer person. And he couldn't very well ask June for help with research.

"I have another idea," he said. "Would it be okay if I sent you something? You won't have to go anywhere, just some computer work. Charge me whatever you like."

Holm sucked in another lungful of smoke. "Do what you wish, but you won't hear from me. I'm done with that family."

Then he hung up.

Peter had already sent himself the picture he'd taken with Bjarni's phone, the facial close-up of Staple lying on the sidewalk outside the embassy. Now he took pictures of Staple's passport and U.S. driver's license and the now-expired plane ticket home. He texted all of them to the Norwegian investigator, with a note.

This is the man from the U.S. State Department who convinced the customs police to remove me from Iceland. What can you tell me about him?

244

Then he sent one last text. *If you don't want to help with this, I understand. I'm sorry for what happened to you. I'll make them pay.*

27

The long-haul trucks had vanished and Peter had the highway entirely to himself. The road clung to the contours of the landscape, steep winding river valleys alternating with long stone fingers that reached far into the sea. Rock walls on the left, a precipitous drop on the right, a riot of angry ocean far below.

In the occasional flat spots, he saw houses and barns abandoned to the weather. The Norwegian was right, he thought. The police could spend years searching these old buildings and never find Erik and Óskar.

Every hour or so, he turned the Defender into the wind, stopped in the middle of the road, and stepped out, engine running, to stretch his legs and gather a handful of clean, cold snow to put on his eye. He wasn't sure, but he thought the swelling had started to go down. His face felt less tight, and he was getting a glimmer of light on that side.

He left the main highway at Egilsstadir, turned east, and arrived at the harbor village of Seydisfjordur just after eight in the morning. The sky was still dark, but the snow shone with ambient light. His mouth tasted like a goat's armpit and his body ached from the tension of driving through the gusting wind and snow. Still, the roads had remained passable. The worst of the storm had not yet arrived.

Seydisfjordur sat at the innermost point of the fjord, where an empty parking lot waited at the ferry terminal for the weekly boat to Denmark and the Faroe Islands. The streets followed the contours of the water, and the houses were painted in bright, cheerful colors. The sheer stone walls of the valley rose like ramparts around the village and channelled the wind into a steady southeast gale.

Peter found the uncles' address at the edge of the village, between a fish processing facility and the fuel storage depot with its squat tanks like snow-frosted cupcakes. A boxy red building crouched midway between the road and the shore, the corrugated metal siding loose and humming in the wind. Behind the unlit building, parallel to the shore and partly hidden from view, a fishing boat lay against a plain concrete pier. The boat was festooned with lights and the pier was edged with yellow paint. Safety first.

Peter drove the Defender down a narrow gravel access road to a grubby oceanfront storage yard beside the pier, and parked in partial concealment between two faded shipping containers, but where he could still get a good look at the boat.

She was bigger than Peter had expected. Maybe twenty meters long, she had a high, ocean-going bow, followed by a pair of tall crane masts for hauling nets and offloading fish, then the long working deck with the cargo hold beneath, and a rounded two-story superstructure at the stern. On the overhang shielding the curved windows of the wheelhouse, someone had hung a varnished wood plank with *Freyja* painted in bold blue letters.

The *Freyja* was definitely not a new vessel. Her graceful curves spoke of an earlier era, when the vast, capricious power of the ocean was something to be negotiated with, rather than overcome by sheer mechanical might. Cascading streaks of rust on her hull made it hard to see the vessel's true colors beneath. The wind rocked the *Freyja* up against the ancient tractor tires used as dock bumpers, so at least she was still afloat.

A slender gangplank with rope rails angled down from the high gunwale to the pier, where a heavy four-door flatbed truck with disintegrating door panels waited beside a newer black Dacia station wagon with an elevated suspension. Neither vehicle's engine was running, but the snow had been scraped from their windows the night before.

The vehicles and their license plates matched what the Norwegian had found registered to Eiríkur's uncles, Ingo and Axel Magnusson.

Peter sat and watched the *Freyja* while his brain cried out for coffee. He ate some bread and cheese and tried not to think about a hot breakfast. The back of his head still throbbed where the vodka bottle had hit him. He touched it with his fingers. Did the skin around the cut seem warm, even a little puffy? He tried not to think about that, either. Instead, he thought about where Erik and Óskar might be.

If the boy had truly witnessed his mother's death, he would be traumatized. Bjarni had told Peter that family was everything. If that was true, they'd want what was best for the boy. Which would probably mean getting back to some kind of regular life. The comfort of family, and the familiar routine of school. It was another argument, as if Peter needed one, for bringing Óskar back to Catherine.

The red building certainly didn't look like any kind of home. The wind would blow right through that rattling siding. The boat must have crew cabins and some kind of heat, but it looked ready to sink at any moment. Either way, this fishing pier was no place for a traumatized child.

Maybe that was the problem with Peter and June.

Maybe that's what she was trying to tell him.

Why she was trying to get him to change.

His life was no place for a child, either.

With the engine off, the Defender was cold, and the sky remained impossibly dark. He shivered and thought about getting himself to the desert after all, someplace warm and dry where the sun kept shining. Maybe June would come with him, if she could get away from her work. They could hike the canyons during the day and make a campfire feast at night. Dance naked and make love under the stars. Although June had a limited tolerance for sleeping outside. He wondered again if they could actually make a life together. If they were just too different. If he was ruined for all that.

He took out his Icelandic phone and brought up the video of Óskar running in the park. Climbing the tree. His mother climbing after him, vanishing into the leaves. Peter had been up for almost twenty-four hours. He didn't have time to sleep. He didn't want to dream. He glanced again at the clock. It was 8:47 in the morning.

In a few minutes he'd dig out his camp stove and make some coffee in the back.

He closed his eyes, just for a moment.

He stood in a hot dusty street with a radio in his hand, watching the old sedan roll toward his checkpoint, a small, sad-eyed man behind the wheel. The car came closer and closer. Big Jimmy stepped out from behind the Humvee with his M4 and a friendly smile, patting the air with his palm to indicate that the driver should slow. The sad-eyed man made frantic gestures. The car kept coming. Light it up, Peter said. The squad emptied their magazines. When Peter walked to the ruined car, he saw the woman and two children huddled in the back seat, covered in blood, an entire family dead because their brakes didn't work. They stared at him through open eyes.

He jerked awake.

It was still dark. He glanced at the clock. It was only 8:49.

He still held his phone in his lap. It buzzed again and he realized it had woken him.

The number began with +47, the country code for Norway.

28

Staple is a staff attorney for the American State Department. Not at the embassy in Reykjavík, but in Washington. So he does not work for the ambassador."

No hello, no good morning. "You've been up all night."

The Norwegian's voice was flat. "I no longer sleep well."

"Me neither," Peter said. "How did you find out about Staple?"

"I have access to six databases of current American government employees. It's public information. I know Staple's salary. I thought it would be higher."

"So maybe it's not the ambassador trying to kick me out of Iceland."

The scrape of a match, the start of a fresh cigarette. Breakfast of champions. "Staple should not be able to do so, either. He is a low-level functionary."

"He didn't act like one," Peter said. "He

acted like somebody important."

"Perhaps that is an old habit. I found his employment history. When he was twenty-eight, he was an attorney in your White House. After that he was a partner in a multinational law firm. Then he worked for a United States senator. Then back to the law firm."

"And now he's a low-level lawyer at the State Department?" This wasn't the typical D.C. revolving door, where a career alternated between power and wealth, adding to both along the way. Something had happened to Staple. "What about the plane ticket?"

"I found payment for a ticket on Icelandair, Reykjavík to Washington, D.C., on his personal credit card account, along with a second round-trip ticket, which must be his own. Purchased at the last minute, so they were quite expensive."

"If he paid for the tickets himself, he definitely wasn't on State Department business."

"Yes. I will keep looking for other affiliations."

"Thank you." Peter looked out the window at the red shed and the two parked vehicles and the rusting boat tied to the pier. He wasn't sure how to ask his next question. "Listen, I was thinking about the people that drove you off the road. Did the police ever find them?"

"No. And I couldn't help. I didn't see the driver's face. I couldn't even be certain of the car's manufacturer, only the type and the color. They could only search for a large silver SUV. Nobody in Eiríkur's family owned such a car. The police were certain it would be damaged. They went to the local repair shops where that kind of damage might be repaired. They spoke with tow drivers. They reviewed insurance claims. Eventually they reviewed every silver or gray SUV registered in Iceland. All such cars were accounted for. They found nothing. As if it didn't exist."

"You didn't imagine the car, right?"

A deep inhalation of tar and nicotine, the crackle of burning paper. "Icelanders love their automobiles, and they have many amateur mechanics. It would be possible to get the SUV repaired without reporting the accident. Or it could have been blue, painted silver the year before, and the car registry never updated. Or it could be entirely unregistered and now sits inside a barn, waiting for the police to stop looking."

Peter scratched at his growing beard. "Do

you think the police have stopped looking?"

"I don't know. Perhaps not. Iceland is mostly a peaceful place. The police take their work seriously."

"They're not the only ones," Peter said. "I thought you were done with this."

"I told you, I no longer sleep well." The *clink* of a mug on a countertop, the faint rattle of the wheelchair. "Also, I need the money. But let me ask you a question. When I took the job, I did not know how dangerous Erik's family was. But you do. You are alone in a wild and empty place. You risk your life for this boy. Why?"

"Somebody should," Peter said. "And I like to be useful."

He didn't mention the dead he saw in his dreams.

On the boat, two men stepped through a door in the lower superstructure.

"I have to go," Peter said. "I'll call you in a few hours."

29

On the *Freyja,* the men walked to the waist-high rail and down the gangplank, which sagged beneath their weight. They wore dirty orange coats unzipped and flapping in the growing wind. No gloves or hats, the white stubs of cigarettes poking from their bunched fists. Faces hidden beneath unruly gray beards.

The men in the photo on Bjarni's phone, standing with Eiríkur on a snowy slope somewhere. Ingo and Axel Magnusson. Erik's uncles. Neither one looked much like him.

They looked like NFL linemen. Only bigger.

Like trolls or some other oversized creatures out of myth or history. From the Norwegian's file, Peter knew the uncles were on the far side of middle age, but they were no less powerful for that. Thick-shouldered and barrel-chested, these were men who had done hard physical labor for decades, who thought of getting drenched and frozen and hurt as a normal part of the workday.

Peter had known men just like Ingo and Axel. He'd served with them, had worked beside them. He was one of them, in a way. But he was a lot smaller than these two.

Just watching them, Peter found himself shrinking into his seat, as if trying to make himself invisible. It was an atavistic reaction — ancient, gene-deep instincts hijacking his rational mind. A monkey hiding in a tree as apex predators prowled below.

Ingo and Axel were going to be a problem.

He had never minded facing a big man before. It was a matter of skill, leverage, and desire, and Peter had all those in spades. But there were two of them. They were enormous. And Peter had just one good eye. Why make it harder than it needed to be? An elephant gun, that was the thing. Maybe a squad of Marines.

The enormous uncles somehow managed to shoehorn themselves into the little black Dacia wagon, which settled deep on its springs. Peter watched as it lurched around the corner of the red warehouse and strained up the hill to the road.

Hjálmar had thought the uncles were living on the boat. Aside from the red building, the Norwegian investigator had found no other apartment or house in their name. They definitely had another vehicle, somewhere, or they used to. The silver SUV that had forced the Norwegian off the road and into a wheelchair. Maybe they had another apartment in town, too, someplace more suitable for a child.

Only one way to find out.

When the little station wagon turned onto the road into town, Peter cranked up the Defender and followed.

Maybe he'd find an elephant gun on the way.

Ingo and Axel drove a half mile and parked in front of the Bistró Skaftfell, a three-story building with a restaurant on the first floor and an art gallery upstairs. The snow began to fall in earnest as Peter left the Defender behind a brightly painted rental camper and walked back, his coat unzipped, his hat jammed in his pocket, freezing in the wind. Any self-respecting Icelandic bistro would have coffee, right?

To keep him awake on the long drive from Reykjavík, Peter had put an app on his new phone to teach him basic Icelandic. He was up to a few dozen words, including "farm" and "boat." So he knew that Lokad, the sign on the bistro door, meant the place was closed.

But he could see customers through the low front windows, and a young man in a white apron moved behind the counter, so Peter stuck his head inside. The ceiling was low. The static flared, and not just because of the space. Ingo and Axel sat at a long table by the window with six other men in similar work clothes. None were Erik. Jesus, the uncles were huge even in that small space. Coffee cups and plates with pastries were spread out in front of the group, a feast of fat, carbohydrates, and caffeine. On the back wall, a television showed the ever-present footage of the crisis in Venezuela. This time the footage was of the giant rust-colored U.S. Embassy in Caracas, damaged in an RPG attack.

"Opid?" Peter asked. Open? In an effort to avoid notice, he was still trying to pass for an Icelander. His safety-yellow coat and uncombed hair and scruffy beard did most of the heavy lifting.

"Já, já." The young man waved him in. He wasn't Erik, either.

If Ingo and Axel noticed Peter, they didn't seem to care. They were talking with the others.

Peter stepped to the counter. *"Góden dag.*

Kaffi?" He was nearing the limit of his vocabulary, but the man in the apron had the usual Icelandic reserve. If he took note of Peter's sudden sweating from the static, he was polite enough not to mention it. He just nodded at the trio of different sized cups and raised his eyebrows.

Peter raised one palm above the other to indicate the largest size, then raised two fingers. *"Bakarí"?*

The counterman pointed around the corner, where a glass-fronted case held a dozen varieties of sugary deliciousness. Suddenly, Peter was starving. He loaded a paper bag, glanced at the menu, figured the total in his head, rounded up, and handed over a few bills from Bjarni's wad of krónur. *"Takk fyrir."* Thanks.

The counterman nodded. *"Takk takk."*

At the long table, Uncle Ingo and Uncle Axel were deep in conversation. They had taken off their coats and leaned back in groaning wooden chairs. Peter collected his coffee and walked out into the worsening weather.

He hadn't found an apartment, but with the uncles at breakfast, he had a new plan. He didn't know how much time he had, but he meant to make the most of it.

30

He left the Defender on the far side of the road, nose-out in an unplowed parking lot, and dug a flashlight out of his pack. He considered grabbing Bjarni's folding shovel, because it was the only thing he had that would serve as any kind of weapon, but decided against it. He jogged to the red metal building with its small raised loading dock. A steel I-beam for a rolling chain hoist poked through the wall like an afterthought. Beside the dock, open steel steps led to a rusty door.

He climbed the steps and tried the knob.

The door was unlocked.

When it closed behind him, the interior was cold and completely dark. The static rose. Peter felt his chest begin to tighten. With his flashlight and one good eye, he found a wall switch and flipped it.

Fluorescent flicker lit a single large space. Beside him stood a cluster of gray forklift bins loaded with thick coils of rope and aluminum net floats the size of beach balls. An open mending frame filled one corner with a faded blue net spread across it, torn holes arranged at a comfortable working height. Repairs were in process, the bright new strands as thick as a pencil. The whole place smelled of fish and the sea.

He found no bunkroom or small apartment carved out of the frozen space. He didn't even find a heat source.

Ignoring the screaming static, he followed his flashlight down a sagging interior stair. The lower floor would be at ground level, with more loading doors for easy access to the boat. The fish smell was much stronger. The siding rattled in the wind.

He turned on the lights and saw a long wooden trough with wood rakes for pulling fish down to scarred cleaning tables. A fish-cleaning line, antique but clearly still in use. Rows of gray plastic tubs were stacked along the back wall beside a counter with a hand-cranked knife-sharpening wheel. Definitely old-school.

Aside from the lights, the only real signs of modernity were a commercial icemaker for cooling the fish and radiant electric heaters mounted on the ceiling. The heaters were cold to the touch.

No sign of living quarters, not even a cot and sleeping bag. No Erik, no Óskar.

The clock was ticking. He cracked the dockside door and peered out. The four-door flatbed was still there, but no Dacia wagon. No other human visible on or near the *Freyja*. Just snow, falling harder still.

Trying to look like he belonged, he walked to the gangplank and climbed aboard.

The *Freyja*'s working deck was stacked with more empty gray bins. Vicious-looking fish gaffs lay clipped in easy reach below the side rails, varnished handles gleaming in the floodlights. The wind was bitter. The pilot-house windows were bright. Peter undogged a round-cornered hatch and listened at the opening. He heard nothing. He took a deep breath to calm the static, then stepped over the bulkhead and inside.

He stood inside the ship's galley and common area. Built-in benches flanked a dining table, the wood finish and upholstery reminding Peter of a suburban breakfast nook from the 1970s. The tiny open galley had a marine stove on gimbals and high shelves with rails to keep the cups and plates from flying off in heavy weather. Lockers held cans and boxes of easy-to-prepare food. Despite the substantial supply of Reyka vodka, everything was clean and in good repair. The sink held no dishes. The steel stove was polished to a high shine.

Tick tock. Peter ducked down a ladder, static flaring, to a small landing with two doors, one to each side. He opened the left door and saw a wide bunk built into the curved side of the hull, with storage for personal things below and a narrower bunk above, hinged up and out of the way, with no mattress. The wall opposite held a built-in desk and storage locker, with unhealthy plants lashed into open shelves beside Icelandic-language books. There was just enough space for a grown man to change his clothes, if he was careful about it. The porthole was the size of a dinner plate.

The cabin to the right was the same, only messier. Both cabins had pictures taped to the bulkheads, tropical beaches and swimsuit models and family snapshots. Very homey. The only things missing were a half-knit sweater and a ship's cat.

Peter opened lockers and held up clothes. Everything was sized for giants, both cabins. The uncles, who obviously lived on the boat. Their boots were size seventeen triple-wide. No kids' books or clothes, no Lego. No Erik or Óskar. No sign of anyone living aboard except the uncles.

The static climbed Peter's spine. He couldn't hear anything outside the boat. He imagined the uncles climbing out of their clown car, then tried not to think about it. Down a half ladder, he found the engine room, all heavy metal and color-coded paint, but not a spot of rust. Cabinets full of mechanical tools, a workbench with a pump rebuild in process, lockers loaded with spare parts. No pallet on the floor, no sleeping bag.

Tick tock. One last possibility. Moving quickly, he climbed back up the ladders, past the cabins and the galley, to the pilot-house. He found a spoked ship's wheel and a sagging leather captain's chair flanked by banks of elderly marine electronics. A chart table with rolled maps in a rack and a built-in bench that wasn't long enough to sleep on.

The brass and chrome gleamed. The broad, curving windows looking out over the harbor were clean.

Outside, the black Dacia station wagon rolled down the gravel drive and onto the pier.

31

Peter didn't like how easily big Uncle Ingo and Uncle Axel unpacked themselves from the small car. They were quicker and more limber than anyone their size had a right to be.

He dropped to his knees and peered under the chart table and pilot's controls. If this were his boat, he'd have a shotgun stashed somewhere he could get at it quickly. Nothing. Did nobody in this country use gunpowder? He opened drawers looking for a handgun and found nothing but an orange-handled fishing knife in an orange rubber sheath. He shoved it into his back pocket. Not much good, but better than nothing. Get moving. If they caught him inside this tin can, he might never see daylight again.

He clattered down the ladder and pushed open the hatch just in time to see the uncles step from the gangway to the deck, fresh cigarettes in their fists. They stared at him.

Peter felt like a seal at a polar bear convention.

Up close, the uncles looked very much alike. Their round, wind-worn faces were creased by years of squinting into wind and sun and snow. They had the noses of street brawlers, crooked with previous breaks. Their beards were yellowed at the lip from the smoke of ten thousand cigarettes. Their hands were huge, scarred and thick from years of cleaning fish and mending nets. Their stomachs would have the hard kind of fat.

The slightly smaller uncle said something in Icelandic. His face remained expressionless, but his tone of voice was clear enough. What the fuck are you doing on my boat?

Peter felt the adrenaline rise up in his blood, but he just held his hands up, palms out, like it was all a big mistake. "Sorry, I don't speak Icelandic. English?"

"*Já,* I have some English," said the same uncle. He had a voice like an idling bulldozer. Being slightly smaller than his brother made him only the size of a prize bull. He wore a gray hand-knit sweater under his coat and a gold pirate hoop in his left ear. "You are the American. You broke Bjarni's arm."

"Bjarni started that fight," Peter said. "I

268

could have done much worse. You are Ingo and Axel?"

In Icelandic, the one with the gold hoop said something to the other, who nodded silently. Peter thought he caught the Icelandic word for "farm."

"I am Ingo." The talker jerked his head at his silent brother. "He is Axel. What do you want?"

Peter wanted this to end without a fight. "I'm looking for Óskar Eiríksson. I just want to know if the boy is all right. I'd like to see him, to talk with him. Then I'll go."

The uncles looked at each other, then back at Peter. Neither man spoke. Their massive hands flexed restlessly.

"Bjarni told me Erik and Óskar are dead," Peter said. "Is that true?"

Ingo regarded his cigarette, then dropped it to the deck and stepped on it. Axel rolled his shoulders like a boxer between rounds.

Peter said, "If something happened to Erik or Óskar, it had nothing to do with me or anyone I know. Has anyone else talked with you?"

Ingo's lips twitched in the tiniest of smiles. His eyes crinkled up at the corners. It made him look like Óskar, just a little.

"So many questions, Mr. American. But I have a question for you." The smile grew wider. "Can you swim?"

Behind him, Axel gave a rhythmic grunt. Peter realized the bigger brother was laughing.

No, this was no place for a child.

Axel stepped left to block the gangplank, still holding his cigarette. Ingo stepped right and slipped a two-foot fish gaff from its clips under the rail. The sharp steel tip shone bright under the floodlights. With Peter's vision limited to just one eye, he kept his head on a swivel. Two on one was always hard, but these two would be harder.

The fjord was chunky with ice. If they threw him in the water, it would kill him. Even as big as they were, even with their nicotine lungs, they could walk faster than Peter could swim with his clothes on. They'd certainly be able to beat him to any place he might scramble out, and keep him swimming until the hypothermia got him. He'd be lucky to last fifteen minutes. Even if he somehow managed to reach dry land, he'd be soaking wet on the east coast of Iceland in December with a storm coming on strong. Unable to do more than shiver and wait for the uncles to arrive and throw him back in, a fish too small to keep.

The uncles stepped forward and he backed

away, keeping his distance. Letting them close was a bad idea. If they got their hands on him, he was done.

His open coat flapped in the wind. The superstructure loomed behind him. There was a narrow gangway on either side that would get him to the rounded stern, but that would just give them a smaller space to contain him. He still had the orange-handled fishing knife in his back pocket, but he'd have to get inside their reach to use it, and he'd have to kill them both quickly. Step inside and sever an artery. If they didn't smash him down first.

For men of their size, the uncles were impossibly fast. Even as Peter reached for the knife, Ingo stepped into Peter's blind spot and caught the windblown open front of the safety-yellow coat. Peter spun backward and counterclockwise to slip his grip, but when he finished the spin, Axel was already there to meet him. Peter raised his arm and slammed his elbow into the side of the big man's head, but Axel didn't even seem to notice. He just caught Peter's lower sleeve in one thick fist and held him.

Peter didn't wait for the other fist. His back now to both brothers, Peter raised his open arms in a gesture of surrender. But before they could improve their grasp, he dropped to his knees and slid his arms from the slick sleeves of the coat. Then he angled right, took three fast steps, planted a firm hand on the cold steel rail, and vaulted over the top and into thin air.

32

It was a long drop, eight feet or more. Off-balance, Peter landed hard and awkward on the snowy dock, but managed to push his momentum into an ugly forward roll. He wouldn't win any points for style, and his clothes got soaked in the slop. Still, he hadn't hit his head or sprained his ankle, so he called it a win and popped to his feet.

On the *Freyja,* the big Icelanders stared at him over the rail. They were too big to jump. Instead, they boiled toward the gangplank, shouting as they came.

Even with space to maneuver on the dock, this wasn't a fight Peter wanted. It was almost certainly not a fight he could win, not without a real weapon, not if he wanted to walk away in any kind of useful condition. Part of him wanted the fight, wanted it badly. The cleansing sweat and adrenaline and pain. But it wouldn't help him find Óskar. Especially not if he lost.

There was a time-honored tactic for moments like this.

Peter turned and ran.

The black Dacia and the four-door flatbed were parked at odd angles on the dock, nose-in toward the gangplank. The Dacia was closer, and the driver's side would give him some cover. Running, he put his hand to his back pocket and found the orange-handled sheath knife from the *Freyja*'s pilothouse. Feet still moving him forward, he pulled the blade and cut into the soft sidewall of the Dacia's front tire. He was rewarded with a quick blast of air as the tire went flat. Without slowing, he did the same at the back wheel. Nobody carries two spares.

The snow swirled, flakes flying faster still. He heard the uncles bellowing over the sound of the wind. They were behind him somewhere, probably on the dock by now.

Staying low, he ran around the rear of the Dacia and peeked. No uncles. How could you hide that much beef on the hoof? They weren't the kind to hide, anyway. Probably circling behind to keep him from leaving. He had to get away from the water. They could throw him off the pier just as easily as they could throw him off the boat. They'd just step on his head and that would be the end of it. But getting distance from the water wouldn't help if they could run him down on the road.

He ducked across the gap to the flatbed and jabbed the knife into a truck tire. The blade wouldn't go through the sidewall. It was a heavy-duty tire, and the thick rubber was hard with age. Head still on a swivel, he stopped to lean on the handle. It wasn't going in.

Axel ran past the front of the truck, saw Peter, but skidded on the too-slick snow, which gave Peter a few extra seconds. The valve stem was metal so cutting it wasn't an option. The knife was plenty sharp. Pushing harder, he wiggled the blade back and forth and finally heard a hiss. The tire wasn't flat yet, but it would be.

Axel finally managed to change direction, but he was staring at the knife in Peter's hand and holding back. Ingo appeared over the top of the Dacia and called out in Icelandic, making a plan. He still held the fish gaff in his fist, a two-foot wooden club with an eight-inch hook. Peter reversed away and around the back of the flatbed. The dock was still empty on that side. He jammed the knife into the next tire at the rounded curve of the inner sidewall, got it in far enough to stick, then carefully stepped down on the blunt end of the grip. The blade sunk to the hilt and the tire began to hiss.

Ingo came around the rear of the truck and Axel came around the front. The gaff hung negligently from Ingo's hand, like any other familiar tool. Peter tried to pull out the knife but it was stuck.

The storm was loud in his ears and the snowfall had accelerated again. Without the good yellow coat, Peter's fleece was heavy with moisture. Ingo and Axel came closer. Peter stepped on the flat of the knife handle, hoping to free it. The hiss turned to a soft *pop* and the tire sank, but the blade snapped at the hilt.

When they saw the blade break, Ingo and Axel ran at him, one from each side, tilting forward in their rush. Peter dropped flat to the slippery snow and the fishermen's thick torsos crashed together like a high-speed meat collision. He felt an impossibly powerful blow to his outer thigh, but before they could grab hold of some part of him, he pushed off the dead tire with his legs and squirted out onto the dock.

Then he was off, thigh aching but legs sprinting strong across the pier and onto the uphill drive, where his hiking boots dug deep and found gravel to grip. When he

276

made the top of the rise, he glanced over his shoulder without stopping. Ingo and Axel were coming hard, the gaff still in Ingo's fist, but Peter was a runner and the uncles were smokers and he was thirty meters ahead.

He ran across the road and up the low hill to the Defender, keys already in his hand. Thankfully they'd been in his pants, with his wallet and phone, and not his coat.

The Defender started without a hiccup. He threw it in gear and bounced down the snow-slick slope, slewing sideways onto the road just as the uncles made it, breathing hard, to the top of the drive. Ingo threw the gaff overhand and it hit the passenger side with a thump. Peter considered running them down with the Defender but figured it would be like hitting a pair of moose and he didn't want to hurt the truck. Instead he raised the single-finger salute and put the hammer down.

He had a moment of panic as the four tires spun down to pavement. Then rubber grabbed the road and he shot forward into the worsening weather.

Man, he was going to miss that damn coat.

33

Peter fled up the high-walled river valley. Plows for the previous storm had made high white banks flanking the road, and the wind dropped heavy new snow into the space between, narrowing the two-lane to a single track. There were no other tire marks. The Defender slewed sideways on the curves, and wouldn't go faster than eighty kilometers per hour. It had also developed a new and unpleasant rattle.

When he reached the top of the valley, he stopped the truck and walked around to the passenger side, where the rattle came from. He found the gaff's hook caught in the door hinge, the bright spring steel still vibrating with the weight of the hardwood handle. He worked it free and threw it into the truck, then looked behind him, his swollen eye throbbing in the cold. The sun had come up behind the clouds, and Peter could finally see farther than the limits of his own headlights.

Another vehicle was halfway up, a white plume in its wake. It was too far to see the kind of car, and he didn't want to take the time to dig out his binoculars, but it could have been a silver SUV. Maybe the same one they'd used to force the Norwegian off the road the year before. Maybe hidden in a barn for a year, waiting until it was needed again.

Peter wasn't going to wait around to get a closer look. He couldn't ambush them with the snow revealing every track. Without any weapon more serious than the fish gaff or Bjarni's folding shovel, direct confrontation was out of the question. For now, he could only outrun them. Down the road, he'd find a place to hit them.

He thought about what Ingo had said to Axel, on the boat, and the little bit of Icelandic Peter thought he'd understood. The word "farm." With little else to go on, Peter decided that single word meant that Óskar was at the farm. He had four hundred kilometers to figure out the rest of it.

He pushed the Defender hard back toward Egilsstadir, watching in his rearview as the other vehicle faded ghostlike into the snowy distance. In town, he estimated his lead at fifteen minutes, then burned three of those minutes when he stopped to top off his tank. The next section of the Ring Road was the least populated and most desolate. While the pump ticked off the liters, he took the tinfoil off his American cell and waited for it to find the network. He didn't know how much longer he'd have service.

His phone showed six texts. The first five were all from Commissioner Hjálmar, with time stamps going back sixteen hours. The tone was polite but increasingly insistent.

Mr. Ash was accused of assaulting an American citizen and government employee, which was a serious offense. He should contact Hjálmar immediately to tell his side of the story.

Mr. Ash would be late for his flight to America — he should contact Hjálmar immediately for a ride to the airport.

Mr. Ash had missed his flight. Hjálmar was happy to help him solve this problem and he should contact Hjálmar immediately.

Mr. Ash was out in the largest storm in twenty years. Conditions were dangerous and Hjálmar was concerned for his well-being. He should contact Hjálmar immediately.

Mr. Ash had not responded to any messages. Hjálmar was concerned he was in danger. Mr. Ash should contact Hjálmar immediately.

The man was relentless.

In fact, Peter was counting on it.

He texted back, *Sorry I missed our lunch but your country is too beautiful to leave. I'll buy you dinner when I get back to Reykjavík.* He didn't mention that he was going the long way around.

With that message, he hoped the commissioner's tech people would learn his nearest cell tower and get Peter's rough location. He didn't want Hjálmar entirely in the dark. He was going to need the police to get Óskar free from Erik's family.

Peter glanced at the road. Traffic was almost nonexistent in the deepening snow. Still no sign of the silver SUV.

He opened the last text, from an unknown number. *This is Jerry Brunelli. You're looking for my grandson, Óskar. We need to talk. I'll meet you at the Hotel Borg in Reykjavík at four p.m. local time tomorrow.*

Catherine Price's husband was coming to Iceland?

Peter replied, *On the other side of the country, can't get back. Please call.*

Brunelli responded immediately. *Too sensitive for phone. The restaurant at the Hotel Kea in Akureyri, seven p.m. tomorrow.*

Not negotiable. On my way to Helsinki.

Brunelli was flexing his muscles. Peter had no idea why, but it didn't matter. He hoped the man had found something. Akureyri was the second-largest city in Iceland, about three hundred kilometers away, and Peter had to pass through town on the way to the farm.

He'd planned to stop anyway. He needed to pick up a good coat, along with a few other things. He texted back, *OK. See you then.*

He wondered about Brunelli's motives. What had he found that he needed to talk about in person? Or had Hjálmar asked him to set the meeting? Was Brunelli even coming to Iceland?

It occurred to Peter that he didn't know enough about Jerry Brunelli.

34

Back on the Ring Road and headed north through deepening snow, Peter called the Norwegian, who sounded almost cheerful.

"*Halló.* I have made no progress. Only breakfast."

"Norwegian pancakes?" A staple of Peter's Wisconsin childhood, served with powdered sugar and homemade jam. He was hungry.

"French breakfast. Coffee and a cigarette."

"You're a gourmet. I have another request. Would you take a quick look into Jerry Brunelli, Catherine Price's husband?"

A short, rasping laugh. "A quick look is all that is possible. I tried last year, when my legs still worked. I found very little."

"He runs a political consulting business, there must be some public information, disclosure requirements, that kind of thing. He worked with Catherine's first husband, right?"

"Perhaps you know more than I do. His

online presence is minimal. No social media. The company's public website is very small, just contact information and a few paragraphs of text. Not even a photo. To be honest, I just wanted to make sure he could pay my bill, so I looked mostly at his financials, which are substantial. Why do you want to know?"

"Catherine said he had connections. He's coming to Iceland and wants to meet in person. It makes me wonder what his connections are." Although now Peter was wondering why a political consultant would want a low profile. Wasn't visibility one of the metrics of success in politics?

"I'll look deeper," Holm said.

After Peter turned off the phone, he rewrapped it in foil, then checked the rearview mirror again. He hadn't seen another car since he'd left town.

The silver SUV could still be back there, the driver biding his time. Peter wouldn't be hard to follow from a distance, either, with his tire tracks the only man-made marks on this snow-covered highway. It didn't take a genius to figure out where he was headed, and there was only one way to get there.

Maybe they had a favorite place for running people off a cliff. Maybe they just planned to catch him on the Ring Road, a hundred kilometers from nowhere. Maybe their SUV had a harpoon gun mounted to the roof. They'd shoot him through the rear hatch of the Defender, then reel him in and cut him up for shark bait.

He was more worried about Ingo and Axel than he was about the weather. So far, Peter wasn't terribly impressed by what Icelanders considered to be a big storm. Sure, they had some pretty good wind, but Peter had grown up on the shore of Lake Superior, where winter came early and hit hard, roaring down from Alaska and across the Great Plains.

His dad had put the plow on the pickup every October, and when Peter turned fourteen, it became his job to drive from neighbor to neighbor after a storm, clearing driveways and making sure nobody was stuck or snowbound. As an adult, while backpacking in the Rockies at high elevations, he'd been buried by fast-moving systems at least a dozen times. So Peter had seen his share of heavy weather.

An hour into his drive, the storm started to measure up to Wisconsin levels. The wind got stronger and the snow fell faster. He passed a barn with a cellular antenna bolted to the gable, but his phone had no signal, either due to the humidity or the cloud cover or some kind of equipment damage.

Visibility dropped. He slowed to fifty kilometers per hour, then forty. At thirty, he began to see what an Icelandic blizzard was all about.

The snow no longer fell, but came in dense windblown clouds that made it hard to see more than a few dozen meters in front of him. Sometimes he couldn't see the nose of the truck from the driver's seat. The phone was useless. He stopped frequently to clear the crust from his windows and wipers and headlights. He checked his back trail for the uncles, but the open country behind him had disappeared into swirling white.

Where the highway dipped down or ran in the lee of a long escarpment, the snow drifted high and only the tips of the yellow road markers showed the path ahead. Where the road ran across open sections, it was often scraped clean by the gale, so he could follow the dark river of asphalt laid out before him. In those sections, the wind was strong enough to shove the truck sideways, and slick black ice was often indistinguishable from pavement. More than once he found himself turning a slow pirouette on the road.

Still, the Defender was capable as hell. Peter had plenty of gas. There were no headlights behind him. He was slow, but the uncles, if they were still behind him, were slower. He drove on.

Staring out the windshield, trying to see the road through the swirling snow, his mind wandered. He thought about the video of Óskar climbing the tree, and his mother vanishing into the leaves after him.

He tried not to think about June, and failed.

The truth was, he was beginning to wonder if she was right.

He'd lost faith in the Afghan and Iraq wars early on, when it became clear that they were fighting the wrong wars for the wrong reasons, without any real thought of the consequences. He'd gone to Memphis, and now Iceland, as a kind of atonement for his part in those conflicts. A way to give meaning to the things he'd done.

It had to be for something, didn't it?

But maybe it was also a kind of punishment. Maybe part of Peter was afraid that, if he could put the war behind him so easily, if he allowed himself some kind of real life, it meant the war really *had* been for nothing, or *less* than nothing.

Maybe he wanted to prove he deserved to

be alive when so many others had died.

He really should have gone to talk with Don in Springfield.

The back of his head was killing him. He needed coffee. He needed sleep. Sleep without dreams of the past.

June had said it before, and the more he thought of it, the more he thought she was right. He wasn't going to stop dreaming of the past if he couldn't imagine a dream of the future.

But he wasn't sure he knew how to do that.

35

After three hours' driving, the storm had become unlike anything Peter had ever experienced. He found himself skirting the edge of a broad plateau that vanished into a pale void. The wind blew hard enough to rattle the wipers and the defroster was losing the battle with the ice.

He came to a turnoff leading to a small picnic area, marked by a small blue sign with an icon of a picnic table and pine tree. This wasn't exactly picnic weather, and no trees had grown on this barren plain for hundreds of years, if ever, but some earlier snowplow had cleared the drifts so the turnoff was passable. Peter needed to put some food in his belly, maybe close his eyes for a few hours, and he didn't want to stop in the middle of the highway in a whiteout storm. If the plow driver had managed to turn around and get back to the road, Peter figured he could do the same.

As it turned out, snow wasn't a problem. The pavement was polished bare by the endless wind. The surface gleamed in the last remnants of sun, with nothing between the pavement edge and the slope down to the wild, empty land beyond. On a nicer day, it actually would have been a great place for a picnic, and maybe a hike. The dashboard clock read 13:27.

The parking lot sloped gently downhill and away from the access road. Mindful that he needed an exit plan, Peter pulled around in a slow circle and parked at the highest, flattest spot with a straight path back to the highway. The wind came from basically the same direction, so he didn't need to worry about his door getting bent back on its hinges. He left the engine running. Before getting out, he made sure every door was unlocked. It would be pretty stupid to get stuck outside his truck in this weather.

When he tried to open the door, the force of the storm pushed back like something alive. Adjusting, he pulled his hat down, shifted his center of gravity, put his shoulder to the metal, and stepped outside. The footing was slick and the wind gusted high. It blew the door shut and pushed him flat-footed toward the rear of the truck, his feet sliding across an invisible ice patch. He caught himself with a hand on the roof rack and looked down. The parking lot was not covered with asphalt, but with smooth black ice.

This was not a good place to stop. He pulled himself forward again, wrestled the driver's door open, and hopped inside, pulling his legs out of the way before the windblown door cut them off at the knees.

That small shift of weight, along with a new blast of wind, was enough to start the truck moving. Sliding backward, an inch at a time, down the modest slope and away from the highway.

At first, the whole thing seemed to happen in slow motion.

The Defender's big tires were an asset in snow, where their treads could grind and grab, but the size of the tires seemed to have the opposite effect on this slick ice. The weight of the vehicle created a thin layer of melt, which acted as a lubricant under the rubber. The tires weren't metal-studded. The truck was dead weight on four rubber ice skates.

The hardest part, apparently, had been starting the slide. Once that inertia was overcome, the high-sided vehicle acted like a sail. With a slow, stately grace, the wind turned the truck broadside to the gale. The truck began to pick up speed.

Peter watched through the passenger-side window as the Defender approached the downhill edge of the parking lot. It was an eerie sensation, to be sitting behind the wheel but moving sideways. Soon, he thought, the tires would hit snow or exposed gravel and the truck would lurch to a stop.

The Defender slid faster still. As it got closer to the edge, Peter leaned into the passenger seat and peered out and down. From that position, the surface looked like the top of frozen rapids. The dark ice extended seamlessly onto the rough shoulder without losing any slickness. Beyond that was an equally smooth transition to the steeper slope that dropped twenty meters down to the empty open snowfield below.

Doing nothing wasn't going to stop this slide. He put the truck into gear and eased off the clutch, giving almost no power to the wheels. Nothing changed. The shoulder got closer. He goosed it gently, but knew immediately that it was the wrong thing to do. The friction of the turning wheels increased the layer of melt between the ice and the rubber, which only added to the slickness.

The wind rose to a prolonged howl.

Outside the window, the world turned white.

The truck slid ass-first down the long embankment and into the deep, drifting snow.

36

TWELVE MONTHS EARLIER

The eastern horizon gleams crimson through the living room windows. Soon, the clock radio upstairs will begin to play WAMU, but neither Erik nor Sarah have been to bed.

While Sarah sits at the dining table and reverses course through the Prince's system, erasing the evidence of her work as she goes, Erik roams the house until Óskar's footsteps thump overhead. He thunders down the stairs in his Batman pajamas and announces that he is starving. "Like, to death, Dad."

Erik leaves Sarah at her laptop and goes about the business of making breakfast. His little family may be standing at the edge of a cliff, getting ready to jump, but Erik finds a temporary calm in the simplicity of feeding a hungry boy. Óskar definitely has a Viking's appetite.

Sarah's fingers dance across the keyboard.

Across from her, Óskar drains his glass of milk, then licks the wreckage of eggs and sausage directly from his plate.

"Óskar," she says.

He looks up at her, caught in the act. "Mom. It's the best tool for the job."

She smiles too brightly. "I know, honey. Hey, can you do something for me? I need you to take a picture of these." She walks around to slide the laptop in front of him.

Erik comes from the kitchen to look over her shoulder. Her screen shows the URL for the hidden drive on the mirror server, a web address almost two lines long and unintelligible to a human being.

"Click," Óskar says. "Got it."

Sarah opens a new window. This one shows a sixteen-by-sixteen grid of random three-digit numbers. The server's access code.

"Wait," Erik says. "Is this a good idea?" To involve Óskar, he means.

"You wanted security," Sarah says. "If we keep no electronic or physical copy of the passcode, it prevents any kind of side-channel attack. Without it, 256-bit encryption is essentially unbreakable. The mirror server data will remain intact even if they physically destroy their own server."

"It's okay, Dad." Óskar glances at the grid

of numbers, then turns to look at his parents, one by one. "This is a secret, right?"

Erik feels the breath go out of him right then.

"Yes, honey," Sarah says. "It's a big secret."

"Then I'll put it with pi," Óskar says. "I already had four thousand." He turns back to the screen. "Click. Now I have more."

While the pit in Erik's stomach turns into a black hole, he fills two travel mugs with coffee, then loads Óskar's lunch in his Lego backpack while Óskar gets dressed and brushes his teeth. Sarah fusses with her laptop for a few more minutes, erasing the night's work from her own equipment, then changes into a fresh work outfit.

At the door, she says, "It won't look right if I don't show up."

"Call me afterward," Erik says. "I want to know you're okay."

Sarah nods and heads for her car.

In two hours, someone will shoot her three times in the head.

37

PRESENT DAY

The Defender landed almost softly, with its nose pointed uphill. The wheels turned slowly on the slick slope, and the boxy rear end was jammed firmly in the high drifted snow. Peter would have preferred a harder landing. At least he'd be on solid ground.

He put the truck in neutral and climbed out his door and up to the roof rack, where he unstrapped the burly snow shovel and jumped off the back and into the bottomless drift. Up to his waist in the snow by the rear bumper, the big truck looming over him, he began to dig. Without the protection of the safety-yellow coat, he wore only a thick fleece top that was anything but waterproof.

His plan was to get down to the frozen gravel, where he could plant the foot of his rescue jack on something solid. With the back bumper braced, he could excavate the

297

rear wheels and get his sand ladders wedged underneath to bridge the soft snow. Because the truck sat on a slope, it would want to slide backward, so he'd almost certainly have to jack it up a few times. It would be a long night, but with a solid platform under the tires, he could coax the truck out of the drift and onto flat ground, where he'd work his way across the lumpy, barren snowscape until he found a place to get back on the raised road.

It would be a lot easier if he could use the winch, he thought. But there was nowhere to attach the hook. No trees, no rocks big enough to stay put. No other truck to use as an anchor.

The thought of another vehicle made him automatically glance up to the road. He didn't want to see one. He doubted that the men inside would be there to help. Thankfully, the road was dark and empty. He shook his head at the idea that being alone in this situation, with the snow eating his car and the wind stealing his heat, was the better option.

Well, hell. He'd dug his share of Humvees out of the sand using these same tools and techniques. He could do this.

Then the engine coughed.

Peter knew he still had plenty of gas. The

angle of incline wouldn't be a problem, not for a Land Rover. What would make the engine run rough? Then he realized that the backward slide had probably packed the truck's tailpipe with snow. If the engine couldn't expel the exhaust and bring in new combustion air, it would die. Without that big diesel power plant, things would get a lot colder. He attacked with the shovel, trying to get down below the bumper.

The blade was too wide for this thick, dense drift. He tried to take small bites, but it was taking too long. He should have bought a regular mason's spade instead of trusting this fat scoop. The engine's cough got worse. Trying to take a bigger bite, he felt the telltale crack through his gloves as he overleveraged the fiberglass handle. Fuck. No amount of duct tape would make it strong again. He snapped the handle against his knee, dropped into the hole with the naked blade in both hands, and kept working.

It was a calculated risk. If the truck settled abruptly, he could get pinned, and the cold would kill him. But if the engine died and he couldn't restart it, he'd almost certainly be dead anyway. At least hypothermia was a peaceful way to go. He dug harder.

He finally found the tailpipe just under

the left bumper. Totally clogged. The engine was gasping now, unable to bring in combustion air, smothering on its own trapped exhaust. He banged the pipe with the bent shovel blade, hoping the hot metal of the tailpipe had partially melted the plug and the snow would slide out. The snow didn't move. He needed some kind of ice pick.

He grabbed the shovel handle and worked the sharp end into the pipe, trying to clear as much as he could. The handle was too thick, and only packed the snow in tighter. Now the engine began to truly choke. It needed an emergency tracheotomy. He leaped out of the hole, pulled open the truck's rear door, and fumbled inside for a telescoping hiking pole and pulled it apart. The sections were hollow. He jammed the largest section into the packed pipe and pulled it out, filled with snow. He got a gasp of exhaust through the small open core. The engine didn't die.

He whacked the pole section against the truck, knocking it clean, then jabbed it into the tailpipe in a new place, expanding the airway. The engine still wasn't happy, but it was catching again. He made two more holes before he'd gotten enough free space that the rest of the snow would slide out. The Defender let out a noxious cloud, then settled into its regular cheerful rumble.

Peter knelt in the snow, wiped out by the effort. He hadn't even truly started digging himself free. His face was freezing and the rest of him was soaked in sweat and snowmelt. He really missed the mechanic's yellow jacket. He needed to get into better clothes. When he got to Akureyri, he'd gear up again.

Clearly, he hadn't been paying Iceland the proper respect.

It wasn't just Bjarni and the enormous uncles that Peter had to worry about.

Turned out, Iceland was trying to kill him, too.

He climbed into the Defender to grab the E-tool he'd taken from Bjarni. When he climbed back out, he found that the storm had somehow found a new gear. The snow came faster. The wind blew harder. Its wild, unearthly cry was unlike anything Peter had ever heard. A screaming choir of demon sopranos who couldn't carry a tune.

He jumped back in the hole and began to dig again, working to clear the drift from under the car and behind it. The roaring snow stung his eyes and face, and the white-out hid everything outside the reach of his hands. He quickly realized that, while the folding shovel was tough enough to take any punishment Peter could dish out, he wasn't making much progress. The blade was barely larger than Peter's cupped hands, and fresh snow blew into the hole almost as fast as he could take it out. He couldn't get ahead of this storm, not for long. He was going to have to stop for food and sleep. His swollen eye ached in the cold. His head pounded. The vodka bottle's divot felt hot.

Breathing hard, he leaned against the drift and watched the hole he'd made fill again.

He had enough food and gas to stay fed and warm for a few days. Eventually the plow driver would pass through again and either stop to help or call one of Iceland's famous volunteer rescue crews.

Unless the uncles showed up first.

He jammed the broken shovel blade into the snow to act as a windbreak for the exhaust, packed the rest of his tools in the truck, then climbed the icy slope to the driver's seat, where he turned the heat up as high as it would go. He stripped off his wet things and hung them over the passenger seat to dry. Shivering in the cold, he pulled on fresh long underwear and laid out his sleeping bag in the tilted back. He wouldn't be comfortable, but he'd survive. The storm couldn't last forever.

The wind was so loud it was like standing inside a cymbal's crash. He'd never sleep in all that noise. The only thing he could see outside was swirling snow. He might as well be locked in a small, white room. The only thing missing was the padded walls. The static rose, sending sparks up his brainstem as it complained about the enclosure.

"What," he said aloud. "You'd rather be outside in that miserable weather?"

As if in response, the static crackled higher, jabbing electric tendrils into his brain. Despite the cold, Peter began to sweat again.

"I thought you were supposed to be watching my back," he said. "Now you're just trying to get me killed."

Great, he thought. He was talking to himself.

If he couldn't get the truck dug out of there, it was going to be a long few days. Just him and his broken brain and the white static screaming like a banshee.

He was pouring sweat but couldn't stop shivering. He dug for warm socks and discovered the handful of little packets he'd taken from Bjarni, the same shit Bjarni had dumped into Peter's beer.

Why had Peter taken the packets? He was a beer and bourbon guy. He didn't even smoke pot. But he'd liked that MDMA. He understood why it was called Ecstasy. He'd felt connected to every other person in that place.

It had also damped down the static in the club.

He sure wouldn't mind feeling like that again. Even if there was nobody here.

It would be dumb as hell to take one of those packets now, right? Stuck in the snow in the middle of nowhere? He wasn't that desperate. He wasn't.

He told himself this while the inside of the truck got smaller and smaller. First a psych ward, then a detention cell, then a coffin. The glass had fogged from his panic sweat and wet clothes. He cracked a window to vent the moisture but felt the temperature plummet and rolled it back up. The static rose higher. He reached for the door handle and had to invent reasons not to pull it. As if the killing weather wasn't enough.

The static's electric roar grew louder than the wind.

Fuck it. The club drug wasn't Peter's only option.

He riffled through his groceries and found the small bottle of Reyka vodka he'd bought. He cracked the seal and washed down four Valium from his dwindling stash.

Only four pills left.

He needed sleep without dreams.

Just a few hours of peace, that's all he wanted.

38

He dreamed anyway.

The dusty street in Baghdad, so real he could smell his own rank sweat and the acrid stink of spent gunpowder, could feel the road grit under his bootsoles. The dead stared back at him. His heart racketed in his chest.

He woke shivering in the early morning, aware of some change in his environment. It took him a moment to realize that, aside from the bass rumble of the engine, the world outside was silent and echoing in his ears.

The wind had died. His clothes had dried. The windows had unfogged and he could see outside again.

The sun was nowhere in sight, but the night was strangely bright. The snow glowed as if lit from beneath. The clouds had washed away and a billion glittering stars shone in the sky. On the other side of the windshield, a shimmering green curtain stretched across the northern horizon.

He pulled on clothes and boots, checked the gas gauge, and climbed out into the still, frozen night.

The air was crystalline, as if there were no atmosphere. The milky spray of stars and the electric waves of the northern lights felt close enough to touch. Low, dark mountains wrapped the rim of the plain, making a jagged line against the sky like torn edges of the world. As if this small, high place had somehow ripped away from everything solid to rise into the sky and float unknown and aching through the universe, utterly empty but for Peter.

It was profoundly cold, and getting colder by the minute. His stomach trembled, and his limbs shivered uncontrollably. His nostrils froze shut with each inhalation of breath. His eyeballs hurt, leaking tears that turned to ice on his lashes. Every bit of exposed skin felt scraped raw.

He had to get the fuck out of this place.

Back in the tilted truck, his skin burned as the cells thawed. Needing calories to burn for heat, he stuffed himself with bread and cheese and chocolate while he ransacked the car for the warmest clothes he could find. No coat worth a damn, but yesterday's fleece had dried. He layered up like a polar explorer. When he pulled on his hat, he felt a wet spot on the back of his head.

He touched it with his fingers. The wounded skin was spongy and weeping, definitely infected. He needed antibiotics. No wonder his head hurt.

Fucking Vikings.

They'd probably stopped to wait out the storm, too. With the change in weather, they'd get back on the road. They'd keep coming. Peter didn't blame them. It's what he would do, too.

He climbed back outside, filled his gas tank from the jerry cans on the roof, and began to dig.

He made it down to solid ground to set the jack and stabilize the truck, then started excavating the rear tires. He laid the sand ladders behind them and reversed the truck six feet to the edges of the ladders while the front tires sunk into the snow. Then he jacked up the rear bumper and moved the ladders and did it again. And again. Six feet at a time. Hoping with each iteration that the wide tires would finally float the truck over the snow and he could drive himself free. But the Defender was heavy, built for a beating. It sank every time.

He'd managed to move the truck forty-two feet, maybe a hundred more to go, when he heard the sound of a diesel engine on the road at his back.

He climbed up the drift to look, hoping for the snowplow.

Instead he saw a pale SUV, slowing to a stop on the highway. Was it silver? It looked just like the Mitsubishi he'd rented and abandoned in Reykjavík. It came from the southeast, just like Peter.

This was as good a place as any, he thought. Out in the open, the odds were better than on the pier with the killing ocean right there. Peter's arms were tired, but he was fed and warm and dressed for action. He took the fish gaff from the back of the Defender, glad of its weight in his hand, and waited.

The door opened on the SUV. A figure got out and looked at Peter over the roof of the car. Either he was very large, or he was standing on the running board.

Then the figure gave a big wave and stepped down to the road. He still looked large, but it might have been the puffy white coat he wore, with the deep, fur-trimmed hood that hid his face. Avoiding the skating rink pretending to be a parking lot, the figure walked nimbly down the embankment and across the rocky white plain. As he came closer, he threw back the hood.

It was Seamus, the Irishman, his black hair and unshaven face dark against the clean, bright snow, his breath steaming like a dragon's. He nodded at the fish gaff in Peter's hand. "Are ye catching any?"

Peter stepped forward to shake his hand. "Not a goddamn thing."

The Irishman was good in the snow. He drove his pale rental SUV another quarter mile down the highway until he found a place where the land rose and the embankment was slightly less steep. He angled down the crusted verge, slowly but in total control, as if driving to the store on a fine spring day. On the wind-scraped plain below, where the snow was only a few inches deep, he navigated the scattered rocks and uneven ground to the deep drift where the Defender sat idling.

After that, it was a simple matter to hook the Mitsubishi's winch cable to a tow hook bolted to the Land Rover's bumper. Peter laid the sand ladders ahead of his tires and put the gearbox in low. With the winch helping, it didn't take long to haul Peter's truck out of the drift. Peter followed the big Mitsubishi on the same wandering track back to the highway.

They made it up the embankment without trouble and stopped on the road. Seamus stepped out into the killing cold. Peter did the same, looking over his shoulder at the highway stretching back across the rim of the plain. He'd lost sixteen hours to that snowdrift. The wind had scoured the pavement clean.

Despite the temperature, Seamus stood with his puffy white coat unzipped, showing the black wool sweater and jeans beneath. He took a silver flask from his hip pocket, took a sip, then held it out. "Care for a drop?"

It was barely eight in the morning. Peter shook his head. "Where'd you learn to drive like that? You don't get this kind of snow in Ireland."

The Irishman took another sip. "I've been all over, lad. You pick up a few things along the way."

Peter was tempted to pull out his stove and make coffee, but he didn't want to linger. "That storm's not done with us. Let's keep moving."

"Agreed." Seamus climbed back into the pale SUV and roared off.

Closing the distance, Peter saw the Mitsubishi's license plates.

They were from Great Britain, not Iceland.

Which meant the Irishman's milk-white SUV wasn't a rental after all.

39

The sun rose low in the light blue sky as they dropped down from the high plateau. Ahead and behind, the cliffs stood caked in wind-sculpted white as if frosted by the world's largest spatula. Seamus drove more slowly than Peter would have liked, but the road was unplowed since the day before and Peter didn't mind keeping the Mitsubishi where he could see it. By early afternoon they'd passed through Reykjahlid, a tiny town still mostly buried in snow, and curved north around Mývatn Lake, shining like a tarnished silver plate.

The Mitsubishi looked strange through Peter's windshield, and he couldn't figure out why. For some reason, it reminded him of a three-legged dog the platoon had briefly adopted at a combat outpost along the Pakistani border. The dog had run with its hips slightly out of line with its shoulders, as if whatever event had taken its back leg had also somehow bent the entire animal at a slight angle only detectable at speed.

The sun was long gone by the time they saw Akureyri, Iceland's second-largest city, climbing the hills across the dark fjord. After three days in the wilderness, the bright-windowed buildings and the cruise ship strung with Christmas lights seemed like something out of a dream. Or maybe it was Peter. He had the Defender's heat turned off, but he was still sweating. It was mid-afternoon but it felt like midnight.

At the end of a long causeway where the river drained into the sea, they came to an N1 station with a few cars filling up before the storm returned. Peter tapped his horn and flashed his lights. Seamus turned off the road and stopped at an open pump. Peter looped around to the far side of the island. Diesel gurgled through the hoses, its fumes sweet in the thin, cold air.

Peter looked across the pumps at the Mitsubishi. He still couldn't figure out what was strange about it. It looked normal enough from the side. Seamus had his door open, head down, collecting food wrappers and crushed coffee cups for the trash. Peter walked around for a better view.

The Mitsubishi wasn't a camper conversion like Peter had rented, just a regular

SUV with three rows of seats. He glanced down at the front passenger tire. It was worn unevenly, the tread almost gone on the outer edge. Which meant the front end was badly out of alignment. Which in turn might be why the vehicle looked somehow off, the front end rolling slightly out of line from the back. Like a three-legged dog.

He ran his bare hand along the passenger side fender. Instead of a smooth clean curve, he felt the telltale ripples of a hurried repair. If he knocked on it, he knew he'd hear the dull thud of two-part epoxy rather than the metallic *clang* of sheet metal.

Peter looked closer at the milk-white paint. It wasn't opaque, but translucent. A cheap spray job, not a factory finish. Along the inside of the open door, he could see the original color. Silver.

On the driver's side, Seamus straightened up with his hands full and saw Peter standing there. "I believe we're due a meal, lad. I'm thinking whiskey and red meat." He was slim and pale inside his open coat.

"Sounds perfect." Peter walked toward him. "I have to run a few errands and meet a guy at seven. How about eight o'clock?"

"Another meeting?" The Irishman looked at him. "I'm starting to believe you're not truly on holiday."

"What makes you say that?"

"The beating you took, a real tourist would have gone to the clinic," Seamus said. "Might even have gone home. Instead you braved a hurricane to make your meeting in Seydisfjordur, and again to get here. Also, you've changed cars. But I can't tell if you're the fox or the hound."

"I'm a little confused myself." Peter took out his Icelandic phone and thumbed open the camera app. "Listen, you really saved my ass, digging me out of the snow back there. How about a selfie?" He went to sling an arm around the Irishman, thumb already on the button.

"Lord, no." Seamus knocked the phone down and almost out of Peter's grasp. The Irishman had extremely fast hands. "I'm old-fashioned. Graven images and all that. No offense."

"None taken." Peter turned off the camera and tucked his phone away. "For the record, I wasn't trying to steal your soul."

The Irishman's smile was bright but his eyes were dark. "I've no soul left to steal, boyo. I was ten years a copper, a black bastard from Belfast. I've seen things a man can't unsee." He brandished his silver flask. "Explains why I'm so fond of the drink."

It also explained the Irishman's friendly

questions, and the way he stood, boots shoulder-width apart, right foot slightly ahead of the left. A policeman's readiness for what might come.

But it didn't explain the Mitsubishi.

Peter heard the whine of an airplane engine coming from the north. The single runway of the local airport was directly behind them. He glanced up as a small turboprop chased its landing lights down through the clouds. Then Peter caught movement in the corner of his eye and turned to the road.

Two cars appeared under the lights of the causeway, headed into Akureyri.

A black Dacia Duster, followed by a shit-brown Skoda.

The Defender was on the far side of the pump and partially hidden from view. Peter stood in the open. The bright causeway was maybe twenty meters away.

The uncles filled the Dacia like walruses in a fishbowl, but they kept their eyes pointed forward. Bjarni wore his red jacket and drove with his window down. He glanced at the N1 parking area but didn't seem to notice Peter. He didn't even touch his brakes. He just followed Ingo and Axel toward town.

The man had driven a stick-shift hatchback a thousand kilometers through an arctic hurricane with one broken arm. These Vikings were something else.

Seamus noticed Peter watching the cars. "What's that about?"

"The people I'm meeting," Peter said. "They're early."

40

He made a plan to meet Seamus for dinner, then set off toward town, hoping like hell he didn't see anyone he knew, not until he was ready. The streets were full of cars, a busy shopping day before Christmas. Peter realized he didn't even know what day it was.

He turned off the sea road into a long municipal parking lot, where he passed an unoccupied police Volvo. He angled into the next row of spots and there they were, the black Dacia Duster and the shit-brown Skoda, side by side. Also empty. No Bjarni, no Ingo, no Axel. No cops.

They were all in town, on foot.

He drove out of the lot and past the Hotel Kea, where he was supposed to meet Jerry Brunelli at seven, then up a long curving hill to a tall gray modernist church overlooking the city. He left the Defender on the far side of the church's parking lot, snug between a jacked-up Blue Bird minibus and a rusty Ford F350 with a camper on the back.

He wasn't hiding, he told himself. He was being strategic.

If Hjálmar had in fact convinced Brunelli to arrange the meeting, Peter didn't want the police to find the Defender. He'd need it for a few more days, at least. He was still waiting for Kristjan Holm's report on the man. He checked his Icelandic phone for a message, but there was nothing.

But he had another question for the investigator. He found the stealth video he'd shot while attempting to set up the selfie with Seamus. Most of it was useless, but somewhere between sky and pavement, he'd somehow managed a quick, clear capture of the man's face.

He isolated the image and sent it to the Norwegian along with the Mitsubishi's license plate number. *Who is this guy? Says his name is Seamus Heaney. Irish? Police?* Hoping Holm could work some investigator database magic.

Then he pulled a fleece hat down low, grabbed his day pack, and walked to the edge of the church parking lot, where a wide pedestrian stair dropped down the hill.

At the bottom of the steps, the beige bulk of the Hotel Kea stood across from a street that had been narrowed to one lane as a kind of pedestrian mall. He slipped through the strolling crowd of locals and tourists, his good eye peeled for Bjarni and the uncles.

That would be a good name for a band, he thought absurdly. *Tonight at Snorri's Rave Cave, please welcome Iceland's favorites, Bjarni and the Uncles!* He blinked and felt a wave of dizziness. He was not at his best. The wind blew ragged and strangely warm. A thin, cold rain began to fall.

Head on a swivel, he went shopping. First, he bought a new orange-handled fishing knife at a tourist shop because he felt naked without some kind of weapon. Then he went to a 66°North store, Iceland's answer to The North Face and Patagonia, where he found a waterproof coat and winter bibs that had been designed, according to the serious young salesman, for the Iceland Rescue teams. With his good eye on the door, Peter asked if they came in white. He was hoping to blend into a snowy landscape.

The salesman stared at Peter like he was mentally challenged. "The clothing is designed to be visible." He spoke slowly, to make sure Peter understood. "This is Iceland. If things go badly on your expedition, you may need to be rescued."

Peter settled for black. He could always

pretend to be a rock.

As he paid, he asked the salesman where he might find a pair of snowshoes. The man suggested several sporting goods stores, but said it would probably take a week or more, as they'd have to come from overseas. He was happy to recommend several tour companies that could take Peter into the mountains. The big storm was circling back around, he said. Peter would be much safer on a tour.

Peter looked up at a pair of vintage steam-bent snowshoes hung on the wall as decoration. The wood frames, rawhide webbing, and leather bindings looked in decent shape, and they were sized to float a man with a full pack. He pointed and tried to look rich and stupid. "How much for those?"

The salesman closed his eyes and sighed.

It took four phone calls and a great deal of Catherine Price's cash, but Peter left the store wearing his new black coat with the winter bibs in a shopping bag and the big snowshoes tucked under his arm.

Watching for familiar faces and safely camouflaged among the tourists in his spotless, high-end outerwear, he realized he still had an hour to kill before his meeting with Brunelli. He walked until he found a *bakari* with a row of damp tables under an awning. Inside, waiting to order, he glanced at the television, expecting to see more talking heads, or maybe footage of the burning American tanker or the RPG attack against the embassy in Caracas.

Instead he saw Commissioner Hjálmar being interviewed in front of a shiny building.

The date was noted in the bottom corner of the screen, indicating the footage was from the day before. The day after Peter had left Reykjavík. The sound was off, which didn't matter because Peter only had two dozen words of Icelandic.

The video changed to uniformed police on a city street. Beyond them, a glimpse of what could only be a body covered with a plastic sheet. The snow was dark red around it.

The screen changed again, this time to a photograph of a man's face, probably from a passport. A passport Peter had taken from the man and stashed in the glove box of the Defender.

On the crawl, Staple's name.

Next came Peter's own passport photo. His own name on the crawl.

Peter didn't need to speak Icelandic to know the news.

Staple was dead and the police thought Peter had killed him.

41

He looked around. People were talking and eating. Nobody was watching the television.

In Peter's passport photo, he was clean-shaven and impossibly young. Now his face looked like a punching bag, and his un-shaven scruff was dark and rough.

He got back in line and ordered two large cappuccinos, trying not to look like a murderer. The young woman at the counter smiled and took his money. When his coffees came, he carried them outside to the chairs under the awning and sat with his back to the shop window and his hood pulled low and his good eye on the street. Hiding in plain sight.

He took out his phone and found an English-language Icelandic news site. Staple's murder popped up as the lead story. The website ran Staple's photo right beside Peter's. It was a huge deal, the nation's first murder in three years, and particularly gruesome. The police believed Staple, an American tourist, was killed with a knife, stabbed from behind. He was found stuffed under his car almost twenty-four hours after Peter had mugged him outside the embassy.

Someone had asked Staple — had almost certainly paid him — to keep Peter out of Iceland. Why kill him now?

To shut him up, Peter assumed. Unless the mugging outside the embassy had changed something, although Peter couldn't figure out what. Maybe they'd killed him to throw suspicion on Peter, to give the police a more urgent reason to find Peter and put him out of commission.

If that was the plan, it was certainly working.

It didn't matter why Staple was murdered, or that Peter hadn't done it. What mattered was that Hjálmar was no longer merely annoyed that Peter had walked away from the arrest at the food hall. He wouldn't be distracted by the storm. He would be actively working to locate and arrest Peter. That was a problem.

Most of all, it mattered who'd taken the man's life. Because Staple's assassin had been bird-dogging Peter's tracks this whole damn time.

He stood abruptly, looking up and down

the street. He had to walk. He had to keep moving. Then he knew.

It was the Irishman, of course.

But who the hell was behind the Irishman?

He called Holm and got no answer. Shit.

The rain turned to sleet.

He crossed the street to a narrow pedestrian path that angled up the hillside. The snow-shoes were awkward under his arm. He climbed to a winding road that ended above the hilltop church where he'd left the Defender. His binoculars showed no police cars, no black Dacia or shit-brown Skoda, no watchers in the rain, so he walked down to the parking lot. The Blue Bird minibus was gone but the rusty pickup with the camper on the back was still there.

He unlocked his truck and nobody stopped him. He offloaded everything but the orange-handled knife and his binoculars, then started down the long diagonal steps toward the blocky concrete hotel where he was due to meet Brunelli. On the other side of the central railing, a bearded man and a boy climbed the stairs, hand in hand.

Peter couldn't see their faces. They were below him, the man in a hip-length brown leather jacket, the boy in a bright blue parka. Their wool hats were beaded with water. Engrossed in a quiet conversation, they climbed without haste.

A dozen steps below, the man raised his eyes to Peter and nodded a polite greeting. The boy stared at Peter's swollen eye and leaned into his father. The man didn't look anything like Erik and the boy was too young to be Óskar. But how badly Peter wanted them both to be here, alive and well and together.

The sleet stung his battered face. Peter raised his hand to wipe his eyes and found that he still held the binoculars. He had work to do.

He scanned down the stairs, which ended at the corner of the hotel. He had no view around the corner to the entrance. He wondered if Brunelli had caught the news and called the police. It was bad tactics to make an appointment and keep it, but it was even worse to keep it without recon.

Through the lenses, he saw a small, faint cloud appear briefly against the line of the hotel wall. It vanished, then came again. A plume of breath in the cold air. Someone was standing on the far side of that corner, waiting.

Peter hopped the side rail and slipped laterally across the slick hillside, trying to get a glimpse around the corner of the hotel.

He was a black shape on white snow and he hoped the shadows were deep enough to hide his passing. He stopped behind a sparse evergreen tree, still not far enough to get an angle on the corner, but now he had a good view across the street. At the mouth of an alley, a man leaned against a red Jeep and watched the hotel entrance. Something familiar about him, that athletic slouch. Peter raised the binoculars again.

He'd seen the man before, in the hallway of the Litla Guesthouse in Reykjavík.

The grad student with the swimmer's build in the Ohio State sweatshirt.

Peter scanned farther, looking for stillness in the thinning sea of pedestrians, and found Ohio State's friend, the young woman with the spatula and the silver bangles on her wrist. She wore a dark parka and stood at the back of the raised hotel patio, sheltered from the wind with views down both sides of the intersection.

Peter dropped to the snow and slid farther across the hillside until he came to a concrete retaining wall that rose a half meter above the snow and, on the other side, dropped four meters to the sidewalk below.

Sheltered in the retaining wall's slim shadow, he could finally see around the corner of the hotel. A third figure stood out of the light, a very large man almost invisible in a watch cap and a gray utility jacket. Peter had never seen him before.

The sleet came down hard, dampening the sound from the street. The snow was cold and wet against his legs and butt. Ohio State and Spatula Woman weren't Hjálmar's people. They'd been with Seamus at the Litla, so Peter assumed they were with Seamus. But who the hell was Seamus with?

Peter dug out his phone and called Holm again.

The phone rang and rang. The downside of modern communication, Peter thought, was that everyone knew who was calling before they answered.

When the Norwegian finally came on the line, he was more abrupt than usual. "Tell me you didn't kill David Staple."

Of course Holm had seen the news. Staple's death and Peter's picture would be all over his feed.

Peter kept his voice quiet. "I didn't kill David Staple." It was a good sentence to practice. If Hjálmar caught him, he'd need to be convincing.

"I shouldn't be talking to you." Holm's voice rose. "Interpol could charge me for assisting in a crime. I should hang up right now."

"So hang up," Peter said. "But first let me tell you about this SUV I found."

Holm didn't say anything, but he didn't hang up, either. Even the wheelchair was silent.

"It's a big white Mitsubishi," Peter said. "Recently painted. Used to be silver or gray. It's had some repair work done on the front end, like it was in some kind of collision."

The cheap cell gave off the eerie silence of a digital connection. Peter missed the faint carrier hum of the old rotary phone in his parents' kitchen. It was a comfort, reminding him that someone was still listening on the other end of the line. Just the thought made Peter feel like some kind of antique unsuited to the modern world. He was too young to feel so goddamn old.

Then the Norwegian lit a cigarette, and the crackle of the slow burn came over the line. "Okay," Holm finally said. The wheelchair rattled softly across some threshold. "That's the plate number you sent earlier?"

"Yes. And the photo of the man driving it."

Fingers clacked across keys. "The plate is for a Mitsubishi Pajero. The color is given as silver. Registered in the United Kingdom to a man named Seamus Heaney. Like the poet." More keystrokes. "A citizen of Ireland? He is not Icelandic?"

"He says he's Irish. He sounds Irish to me."

"You talked with him?"

"He dug me out of a snowdrift this morning."

"Why would he do that?"

"Good question. I'll ask him."

"What?"

"We're supposed to meet later. For dinner. He says he was a cop in Belfast. Maybe you could find out a little more about him?"

Holm took another long drag on the cigarette. "*Já*. I will." He exhaled. "Thank you, Peter."

"My pleasure. Did you have time to look into Brunelli?"

"Ha." The laugh like a bark. "First let me tell you about David Staple. Remember how he started at the White House, worked his way up to a nice law partnership, but somehow ended up as a low-level attorney at the State Department? I found out why. I didn't think it was important until just now. Staple resigned from his partnership when the *Washington Post* revealed that he was a person of interest in an FBI investigation into money laundering. For something called the True IRA."

"Oh, shit," Peter said.

The original Irish Republican Army was a separatist group responsible for many decades of political bombings and assassinations throughout Ireland and England, until the 1998 Good Friday Agreement made an uneasy but growing peace. But the most violent element of the IRA had formed a splinter group called the True IRA, which was less political and more criminal, pursuing everything from gun running to bank robberies to murder for hire, all over the world.

"Oh, *já*," Holm said. "David Staple never went to trial, of course. Lawyers never go to jail. But I wanted to learn about his early career. Do you know who Staple worked with at the White House? Someone whose career turned out very differently?"

Suddenly it fell into place.

Peter thought about the boy, reciting pi to four thousand places. What other things did he carry in his head?

On the steep and slippery slope, the wind rose cold from the north. The sleet turned into snow.

42

Monday traffic is worse than usual. Erik gets Óskar to school on time but is stuck on the Beltway, still miles from his office outside of Rockville. When Sarah calls, it's automatically sent to the car's speakers.

"My key card didn't work," she says. "Tom Wetzel was there but he wouldn't let me in."

"Did he give you a reason?"

"He said they're releasing me from my contract. They found a new cyber provider. A better fit, he said." Her voice is hollow over the sound system.

"Did Jerry say anything yesterday?"

"Yeah," she says. "He thanked me for coming in on a Sunday."

The only thing that changed overnight was the fact that Sarah copied Brunelli's secret hard drive to a server in Iceland. Erik understands immediately. Somehow, they

334

learned what she'd done.

Erik can't get those videos out of his head.

He is less than a mile from the Rockledge exit, where he can get off the Beltway and reverse course, but in this traffic, it might take him ten minutes to reach the ramp. Erik, ever the prudent driver, is stuck in the middle lane. He puts on his turn signal to get over, but the neighboring car won't let him in.

He says, "Where are you now?"

"In the car. On my way home."

"I have an idea. Let's go somewhere for a few days. Just drive south."

"You know, I had the same thought. I already picked up Óskar at school. I'm going to grab a few things from the house."

"Let me do that. You keep driving. I'll meet you at that pancake house in Virginia Beach."

"I just pulled up. It'll take five minutes."

"Please." Erik is trying very hard to pretend not to be scared to death. "Let me. You keep going." He can't stop thinking about the man in the skull mask, pulling on his leather gloves.

"Erik, I've got this." He hears the slam of a car door, then another. "Óskar honey, we're going on a little trip. Mommy's going to pack a quick bag. Should we take your

Lego guys?"

Signal on, Erik looks over his shoulder again, but the guy in the next lane won't let him in. Erik turns the wheel anyway. He hears a horn, but he doesn't stop, just cuts through to the breakdown lane, where he accelerates toward the exit. "Sarah, don't hang up. Keep me on the phone, okay?"

She gives a short laugh, the one that tells Erik she's nervous. "I love it when you're a worrywart."

Erik hears her keys jangle as she unlocks the house. The slap of the storm door behind her. Their son quietly reciting his numbers.

He makes it across the overpass and back to the Beltway, weaving through traffic like those aggressive drivers he has always hated. He's almost to Connecticut Avenue when he hears Sarah's footsteps going up the squeaky old stairs. She says, "Óskar, I need you to pay attention, okay? Put your Lego guys and your book in your backpack, please."

"Mama, can I bring Bear-Bear?"

"Great idea, honey." Óskar's feet thump away. "Now, where did I put my swimsuit?"

Erik doesn't want to distract her, but there's more than one reason he wanted to go to the house himself. "Sarah, you know my fire safe in the closet?"

"Yes." Her voice is muffled. She's put the phone down. He hears the clatter of hangers.

"I need you to get something out of it."

"I've already got the emergency cash and our passports from the drawer." She's annoyed. She thinks he's mansplaining their escape.

"Open the safe." Erik tells her the combination. "Look under the insurance folder. There's a gun."

"What?" Sarah doesn't like guns.

When Erik first moved to the district, one of his new coworkers told him how easy it was to buy a firearm in Delaware. He bought the revolver years ago, but somehow never found the right time to tell Sarah. His work group goes to the range at lunch, once a month. Erik's become a pretty good shot.

"I'll explain later. Just take it."

"I am *not* comfortable —"

Behind his eyes, Erik sees the man with the skull mask. "Take the damn gun, Sarah."

"Jesus Christ," she mutters. "Okay. Fine. Is this thing loaded?"

"Yes." He knows he shouldn't, but it makes him feel better anyway. He keeps the gun locked away, after all.

"Erik." She is pissed. "Is it safe?"

"Yes. You have to cock the hammer before you can shoot. That's really hard to do by accident."

"We are not finished with this topic." She sighs. "Is there anything else you want me to pack?"

"Just go." He is trying not to shout.

"Okay, okay." She calls, "Óskar, come on. Time for our adventure." Erik hears their feet hurry down the squeaky stairs. "I don't want to stay in Virginia Beach, though. How about —"

A loud triple rap interrupts her. A knock at the front door.

Erik's heart stops in his chest.

She says, "Erik, is that you?" Her voice sounds like it's right in his ear.

"No, I'm still in Chevy Chase. Don't go to the door. Go out the back. I'll pick you up at the Philz on Adams Mill."

"Shit. There's a man in the backyard. How the hell did he get in the backyard?" She's breathing a little hard now, moving fast.

The triple rap at the door again, louder.

"Óskar, buddy, get behind the couch." Her voice is low and steady. "Now. Like you're hiding in your fort, okay? Good boy. Don't say a word. You stay there and stay quiet until I tell you it's okay. Here, take this. Daddy's on the phone but you can't talk to him."

"Mama?"

Another triple rap, this time even harder.

Sarah's voice drops again. "This is stranger danger, honey." Stranger danger is what Óskar's school calls their active shooter drill. "You stay down and stay quiet. You are hiding from everyone, got it? Say, 'Yes, ma'am,' and then be very, very quiet."

"Yes, ma'am." Óskar's voice is a whisper, but Erik can hear him clearly now because the phone is in Óskar's hand.

The front door slams open. Sarah gives an involuntary *yip.*

Erik swerves into traffic at the Western Avenue traffic circle, cutting off a line of cars. Everybody honks and Erik jumps in his seat, realizing the sound will be heard from the phone in Óskar's hand. He hits Mute on the dashboard and flies past Military Road toward Nebraska, where he runs a red light.

"What the hell do you think you're doing?" Sarah is armored in outrage. "Get out of my house, all of you."

"Oh, Sarah." Jerry Brunelli's smooth baritone. Unworried, unhurried. "Silly, stupid Sarah. You stuck your fingers into things that are not your business. And after all I've done for you, too."

"I don't know what you're talking about, Jerry. I'm glad you fired me, though. Because I don't want to work for a piece of shit like you, anyway."

"Now, now, let's not say things we might regret." Erik can hear the smile in Brunelli's velvet voice. The Prince of Darkness. "Fitz, take her bag."

"You can't —" Erik hears a rustle, then a muffled slap. "Give me that back."

"The thing is, Sarah, you're not my only cybersecurity contractor. We have a keylogger on the system. We have a record of every keystroke. We know where you've been. What I don't know is what you've done with my files." A rustling sound as Brunelli fishes through her bag. "Laptop password, please."

"Go to hell."

"Fitz."

Another slap, this time a sharp *crack*. Erik thinks of the man in the skull mask, the precision of his blows, and knows why he seemed familiar. It's Fitzsimmons, Brunelli's silent bodyguard.

Erik needs to go faster. He swerves into oncoming traffic and brushes against a pickup truck, clips off his side mirror. He squeezes the wheel too tightly. His hands are screaming.

"There's no coming back from this, Jerry.

That's assault."

"Oh, Sarah." Brunelli chuckles, deep and rich, and lets it build into a laugh. Then his voice turns cold. "Where's young Óskar?"

"Don't you touch him, you disgusting —"

Another slap.

"Maybe I'll pick up Óskar from school, bring him home early. I know the headmaster. I'm on their board of directors. Can't you see that I do what I want, Sarah? Exactly what I want. I always have, and I always will."

The rustle of clothing, a grunt, a squeak. Sarah fighting to get free. Erik stays in the oncoming lane, weaving through traffic, but he's too slow. There are too many cars.

"I know you made copies of my files. But I don't know where they are. Tell me now and we're done. You and your son walk away." Brunelli's voice hardens into a hammer. "Now, Sarah."

Erik can practically see her face. Flushed red, furious, her hair flying free. Dear God, he loves her, he will do anything for her and Óskar both, he will give anything. He swerves around a city bus, narrowly misses a beer truck, the squeal of his tires gone silent as his ears strain to hear everything coming through the speaker. Please, Óskar, don't say anything. Don't do anything. Just hide behind the couch and breathe. Keep breathing.

"All right," she says. "Let go of me. Let *go,* you prick. I made a copy in the cloud. I'll show you."

Erik imagines Fitzsimmons releasing her. Sarah straightening her jacket, pushing her hair out of her face.

More footsteps. "I better do it." A third voice. Tom Wetzel, Brunelli's deputy. "You never know what she might do with a few keystrokes on that laptop. What's your password, Sarah?"

"Give me my bag," she says. "There's a flash drive in the bottom. You need that software to navigate to the server."

"No," Erik says, loud inside his car. "No, Sarah, no." He rides the horn and runs the light at Tilden.

Her bag is always a mess. Nobody can find anything in there, nobody but Sarah. And Erik knows there is no flash drive. Sarah didn't trust them. They're not secure.

"Give her the bag," Brunelli says.

Erik can see her taking the strap and reaching inside. He won't get there in time. He hears a familiar *snick* as she pulls the hammer back. Sarah always did have strong hands.

Everyone talks at once.

"Gun." Fitzsimmons.

"Don't — shit —" Wetzel.

"Stop." Brunelli.

BANG.

For a moment, silence.

Then Brunelli's voice, cold as ice. "God-damn it, what a mess. You *idiots.* Tom, how hard can it be to take a gun away from a girl?"

Wetzel's baritone is quiet. "She was stronger than she looked."

"Maybe you're just a pussy," Brunelli says. "Now we'll never find our files." He exhales loudly, recalculating. "Okay. Tom, finish it. Make it look good. Fitz, you call our friend with Metro, let him know what's coming. Maybe he can be in the neighborhood."

Softly over the speaker, Erik hears a faint keening sound.

Óskar, still hiding with the phone behind the couch. Trying not to cry.

Erik careens forward, desperate, out of his mind, too fast, too far away.

"Two more in the face," Fitzsimmons says. "Makes it personal."

Wetzel clears his throat. "In the face?"

"Do it or I'll do you." Fitzsimmons's voice is hard.

BANG. BANG.

343

The padded *thump* of the gun hitting the carpet.

Brunelli sighs. "You really fucked this up, Tom. Better get started on fixing it."

"What about the gun?"

"You're wearing gloves, Tom. Leave it. But take the laptop."

Fitzsimmons says, "Hello, Phil? There's been an incident. Time to earn your retirement supplement. No, no siren. You were driving by and heard shots. The front door was standing open. You think the husband did it. Here's the address."

The voices fade.

Oh, Sarah.

Erik passes the National Zoo. He is eight blocks away, now seven, now six.

Óskar's keening gets louder and louder, until it blocks out every other sound.

At the curb, Erik abandons the car and sprints up the front steps.

"Óskar?" He runs through the front door, his voice rising. "I'm here, Óskar, I'm here."

He stops short in the living room. Sarah lies across the couch. Her face is gone. Blood everywhere. His head spins.

He clutches his skull with both hands as if he could crush it. He wants to go to her. He wants to kiss her, but there is nothing

344

left to kiss. He wants to fall to his knees. He wants to die himself, but he can't. For the boy's sake, he must live.

"Óskar? Óskar, where are you?" The boy has gone silent. Erik bends at the side table and sees his son's small huddled form behind the couch. "Come out, Ós. I've got you. Come out."

The boy crawls toward him. His face is pale and still. There are no tears, not yet.

"Don't look, Ós. Close your eyes." He lifts Óskar into his arms, presses the boy's face into his shoulder. "Keep them closed. I've got you. Hold me tight."

Óskar clings with arms and legs. Erik scoops up Sarah's two bags and Óskar's backpack and hauls them out the door. Carrying everything. Even when he throws the bags in the car, he knows he will carry it all until the end of his days.

"Okay, buddy. Into your booster seat." But Óskar won't let go. Erik has no time, he has to get out of there before Brunelli's policeman comes. He climbs into the driver's seat with Óskar's arms still locked around his neck. He puts the car in gear. "Time to go on an adventure. Time to be real Vikings. Ready?"

Óskar keens softly. Erik holds him tight. Everything he loves is broken beyond repair.

He can only think of Iceland, the last place he has left. It might still be a home for Óskar.

In Iceland, he will know what to do.

43

PRESENT DAY

Lying hidden on the cold, snowy hillside above the hotel, watching Ohio State and Spatula Woman through the binoculars, Peter asked the Norwegian, "How did you dig up info on Brunelli? I thought he kept a low profile."

"His online presence is minimal now, but the deep web has many hidden artifacts, if you know how to look. I found the ghost site for his first company. The biographical information there was enough to get me started."

"And?"

"Do you know the Defense Intelligence Agency?"

"Yes." The DIA was the Defense Department's intelligence arm.

"Brunelli was a civilian employee there, one of Donald Rumsfeld's deputies in charge of planning and analysis. He was on a White House task force after 9/11. I found David Staple on that same task force."

"I'm curious, what was the focus of Brunelli and Staple's working group?"

"The search for Saddam Hussein's weapons of mass destruction."

WMDs were the main justification for the 2003 invasion of Iraq. The invasion that took funding and troops away from Afghanistan. The invasion that destabilized Iraq and led to its civil war and the violent end to countless lives, some of whom were Peter's friends.

Not to mention the wreckage of a blue Toyota with broken brakes on a dusty street in Baghdad. The death of a family of four. For no reason at all.

Weapons of mass destruction that were never, in fact, found.

"So Brunelli's a real fucking prince," Peter said. "But he's Catherine's husband. Why would he want to keep me from looking for Erik and Óskar?"

"You will have to ask him," said Holm.

"Oh, I fucking will," Peter said. "When did Brunelli leave the DIA?"

"In 2005, he started a lobbying operation with Catherine Price's husband Ken, who was at the CIA at the time."

"Cashing in their chips while we were still

winning the war," Peter said. "But that's not what he's doing now, right?"

"It's difficult to know what he's doing now, exactly," Holm said. "In the past, he was registered both as an agent of foreign governments and as a lobbyist, as your law requires. His clients included African dictators who later received an American arms package, and corporations hoping to evade prosecution for bad behavior. He even represented Sinn Féin, the political arm of the IRA. Today, however, his name is no longer listed on those registries. He appears to act purely as a consultant."

"Why would he do that?"

"All his work is now secret. He can do anything he wishes without government oversight."

After Peter got off the phone, he climbed the hill to the church parking lot, then retraced his steps along the winding upper streets and down the steep pedestrian path to the main shopping street, where he walked toward the Kea Hotel. As he passed Ohio State and Spatula Woman, they detached from their stations to drift along in his wake. They definitely weren't grad students. If he wasn't actively looking for them, he'd never have known they were on his trail.

Whatever they were, they gave Peter plenty of room, enough for the lurker in the watch cap and gray utility jacket to slip into the gap. Peter figured him for the primary assaulter. As he walked into the hotel, the static crackled like a power surge.

44

Tom Wetzel stood at the window of the crowded hotel bar. He was tempted to look at the talking heads on the television — with all the talk of war, they had some five-star testifying about military preparedness in a closed session — but kept his eyes focused on the street, waiting for Ash. Somehow, the man had gotten much farther than Wetzel had expected.

He'd stayed in contact with a few carefully selected Marines over the years. He hadn't seen Ash in person since that deployment in Iraq, but they knew some of the same people and Wetzel made a point to keep in touch. A regular background check helped fill in the details.

Ash was a classic example of the kind of man who thrived in combat but failed at life afterward. He'd been a recon platoon commander for eight years, one of the most demanding jobs on the planet, but showed no evidence of employment since he'd mustered out. He didn't own a home, in fact appeared to have no permanent address. His parents' address was listed on his driver's license, but it had expired years ago. His credit report showed no debt, but no income, either. Taken together, it painted a picture of sporadic day labor, post-traumatic stress, and likely drug addiction.

In other words, like so many veterans, Peter Ash had fallen off the edge of the world.

A sad, sad story.

Of course, these same facts explained why Wetzel had kept track of the man, and why Wetzel had chosen him for this particular job. His history of violence and high probability of failure.

Because even Jerry Brunelli, with all his powers of persuasion and coercion, couldn't talk Catherine Price out of sending somebody to Iceland when her grandkid's backpack had washed ashore. There was too much at stake, especially now, to leave it to chance. So Wetzel had dipped into his list of losers, men on the margins, and found the right man for this job.

A man without a home.

A man who wouldn't be missed.

That was the original plan, anyway. Wetzel had a new plan now, one that made him look like a genius. Ash would be blamed for all kinds of things.

Because people would accept the obvious explanation. That Peter Ash, a broken man, had gone off like a bomb and innocent people had died.

Such a tragedy.

As Wetzel watched, a tall, gaunt figure appeared out of the snow and angled toward the hotel entrance. He wore a hooded black coat, but his head was bent and the hood was up and Wetzel couldn't make the ID until the figure straightened and turned to look through the bar window.

When he saw Ash's pale, grim face under the tangled beard, despite his own certainty of the rightness of his path, Wetzel felt the fear tighten like a noose.

The fear had been with him as long as he could remember. Fear of his father's anger, fear of a bad grade. Fear of not getting into college, fear of flunking out. At bottom was the constant, grinding, and relentless fear of falling through the cracks, like his own parents did. Wetzel was nine when the mine that fed their town shut down. With five kids and only minimum-wage jobs left, his parents had blown through their savings, lost their house, and landed in a third-hand single-wide with a leaky roof on borrowed land, every day disguising desperation as hope.

Wetzel had thought college and ROTC would be a way out of all of that. Becoming a Marine Corps officer would take away that ungrounded feeling, that fear of falling.

And it worked, at least for a while. He was a motivated student midshipman, and graduated with honors. At The Basic School, he was an exemplary leader of men. He passed every test they gave him.

Until Iraq, when the tests gave way to the ugly realities of war and Wetzel saw things clearly, maybe for the first time. He could die here for real. Or worse, be grievously wounded and permanently disabled, turned into a complete waste of space, and for what? For men he'd just met, men he barely knew? Men who'd barely made it through high school, who had no future in the world. Not like Wetzel's future, which he now saw was so very bright, if he could just survive this deployment.

War didn't make Wetzel fearless. Instead, it made him ruthless.

He sent other men to fight outside the wire, using every reason he could muster to minimize his own risk. He told himself he was more valuable as an officer than a casualty, and that he was building up his squad leaders, but he knew neither came close to the truth. The real truth was that preserving his skin was more important than men he was assigned at random, far more important than his country, which saw Wetzel only as cannon fodder. Securing his future was more important than anything else. Nobody else mattered. He had to save himself at all costs.

He blamed what happened next on Ash, who'd been a new lieutenant in Alpha Company. While Wetzel made the rational and intelligent choice to step back, avoiding a bullet, Ash stepped forward to take it on the chest plate. The enlisted men loved him for it.

Ash wasn't one to point fingers or blow his own horn, but he didn't need to. Wetzel's captain had watched Ash's platoon and the way his men responded and drawn his own conclusions. It made Wetzel's rational caution look like weakness. His captain told Wetzel to get his ass outside the wire with his men.

In the end, to save himself, Wetzel had to be ruthless enough to step in front of a mortar shell.

The resulting wound got him sent back to Pendleton with a Purple Heart and metal under his skin that he'd carry for the rest of his days.

No, Wetzel didn't mind what would happen to Ash now.

He didn't mind at all.

One of Tom Wetzel's many talents was the ability to carry a grudge.

Wetzel watched as Ash pushed back his hood, walked into the crowded bar, and surveyed the room. Beside the Euro-tourists with their well-bred cheekbones and flashy gear, the damaged Marine stood out like a winter wolf at a thoroughbred dog show. Wetzel was glad to see Fitzsimmons approaching through the snow, a dozen strides back but reaching for the door handle.

"Hello, Tom." Ash put out his hand to shake. "Where's Brunelli?"

Ash's grip was strong, but Wetzel was pleased to see that he looked like shit, one eye bruised and swollen, face pale and glazed with sweat. Seamus had told Wetzel how bad things were, but his description hadn't conveyed the reality, which was much better than expected.

Wetzel smiled. "Sorry, I'm here by myself. Jerry's still in Reykjavík, stuck in a meeting."

Ash still held Wetzel's hand. His grip was

getting tighter. Ash stepped closer and Wetzel could smell the man's unwashed funk along with something else, an odor that reminded him of goat meat left too long under the hot Iraqi sun.

Wetzel tried to pull his hand back but Ash wouldn't let go. His grin was too wide and showed too many teeth.

Wetzel's fear had him now. He wanted to look for Fitzsimmons but didn't. Instead he reminded himself that he was a principal in a major international consulting firm with a current net worth of 6.6 million dollars, an achievement reached only by being ruthless on his own behalf. His car was a Lexus, his watch was a Rolex, and his condo had a view of the Potomac. He was winning, and he was going to keep on winning, no matter what.

Sometimes he told himself that in the middle of the night, when he couldn't sleep.

Ash said, "What's so important we had to meet in person?"

"I'm just checking in," Wetzel said. "Making sure you have what you need to finish the job."

"What job is that?"

"The job you signed up for," Wetzel said, faking patience. "Find the boy and deliver him to the police. So Catherine can take

357

him home."

"What's the boy got, Tom? Something in his head, that's my guess. Something worth a lot to somebody. Óskar's got a photographic memory, but I'm sure you know that."

How had Ash come up with that? Wetzel didn't know, and it didn't matter. "Dude, what the hell are you talking about?" He put on a sympathetic look and kept his focus on Ash as the door opened and Fitzsimmons slipped through. "Are you all right?"

Ash's bony grip only got stronger. His eyes had a strange light. "You were never a great Marine, but I didn't think you'd turn into a total piece of shit," he said. "What the hell happened to you?"

Wetzel ignored the pain and put his free hand on Ash's shoulder to help lock him in place.

"Nothing happened to me, dude. Working for Jerry is no different from being a Marine, except the pay is much, much better. I'm still a patriot, still doing the dirty work that nobody else wants to do. And right now, the job is to find Catherine's grandson."

Wetzel was not, in fact, a patriot, but he saw things more clearly than ever. Working for Brunelli actually *was* like being a Marine, in that the entire Iraq war had been for the benefit of the politicians and the defense contractors. The job then, as now, was to advance the agenda of the powerful, to be their strong arm. Patriotism was bullshit. Altruism of any kind was bullshit. There was only yourself and what you could take.

Fitzsimmons slipped easily through the crowd. Despite his bulk, nobody looked at him. They knew what he was and made space without conscious thought. Wetzel felt a flare of pain in his hand as Ash squeezed tighter. Behind him, the door opened again and the husband–wife team came in like hunting dogs who'd spotted their quarry. They split up to flank Ash on both sides. Soon they'd enter his line of sight, but by then it wouldn't matter. In ten seconds, Wetzel would win again.

Ash's nostrils flared as he sucked in air. His pupils were dilated, and sweat gleamed on his forehead. His grip was strong but his eyes flickered like a failing circuit. It was a little disappointing to see him in this condition, Wetzel thought. He'd wanted payback, but this was almost a mercy killing.

Fitz loomed closer, the syringe small and low in his fist, the uncapped needle gleaming. Ketamine was fast. The flankers were four steps away. Wetzel smiled wider.

Then Ash moved, and Wetzel understood the depths of his miscalculation.

He'd thought that Ash was crippled and broken, his postwar failures a result of permanent and significant damage.

Now he understood that Ash wasn't disabled at all, just different. Rewired, repurposed. Remade into something new.

45

Peter let the static build and watched Wetzel's eyes. When they flickered over Peter's shoulder, Peter slipped left and yanked Wetzel forward hard, propelling him through the now empty space where Peter had just been. As Wetzel passed, Peter spun and shoved him in the center of the back, crashing him into the arms of the lurker in the watch cap, who held something delicate in his outstretched fist, thumb raised like a suicide bomber with a dead man's switch.

Peter saw a slim needle and a clear plastic plunger. Still in motion, he grabbed the lurker's thick wrist below the gray sleeve and used his momentum to force wrist and fist sideways, punching the needle into the meat of Wetzel's hip.

The reflexive clench of the lurker's fist pushed the plunger down. Peter released the wrist and the tight fist jerked back in

361

response, breaking the needle under Wetzel's skin.

Peter had no idea what kind of shit had just gotten pumped into Wetzel, and he didn't care. He hoped it was no pleasure cruise. Wetzel had been ready to shoot that same shit into Peter.

Wetzel clearly knew what had happened, because he froze in place as if waiting to see how bad it would be. The lurker in the watch cap was jammed up behind him, reaching for Peter around Wetzel's torso. He had bright nailhead eyes in a face like a gravedigger's shovel, the kind of face that made farm animals flinch and good citizens hurry across the street.

Peter wanted to smash that face, but Wetzel was in the way. The static crackled a warning and Peter turned to see Ohio State coming fast. Peter sidestepped right and threw out a hard arm to catch the man's neck in the crook of his elbow in a classic clothesline that left Ohio State's boots climbing the air and his shoulders dropping to the floor.

Two down. Peter spun again and saw Spatula Woman closing with a dreamy half smile on her face and her thumb unfolding an ugly knife. In his half-second's hesitation over hitting a woman, she had the brutal blade open and her weight over her toes, looking far too comfortable for Peter's liking. Behind her, Wetzel's knees were mid-buckle and the lurker in the watch cap had a hand in his armpit to shove him aside.

Adrenaline burned hot and the static filled his head. The world moved in slow motion, but Peter knew this was not the time. There were too many people. Some tourist would get hurt. It was time to go.

Wetzel tumbled into a waiter, who tipped his tray of drinks. In the crash of glass, the crowd erupted into chaos. Spatula Woman's dreamy smile sharpened as she advanced.

Peter slipped behind the careening waiter and fled around the bar and through the dining room, where he shouldered open a swinging door with one last look at the lurker in the watch cap, nailhead eyes shining as he bulldozed through the packed people.

The door flapped shut and Peter was in a long, narrow kitchen with a half-dozen white-coated cooks intent on their work and oblivious to the racket from the dining room. As he juked through the living obstacle course, a few heads turned to look at the tall intruder, but nobody said a word.

On the far end, he found stairs down into darkness, a walk-in cooler, and a steel door with a crash bar. Peter slammed through the door and found himself standing at the bottom of the steps to the church parking lot.

He jogged upward, looking over his shoulder. When he saw the man in the watch cap bang through, followed by Spatula Woman and a wobbly Ohio State towing Wetzel by the collar, he picked up speed.

He made sure they got a good look at the Defender before he popped the clutch and roared away. But he never took it out of second gear on the hill road, and before he got to the main highway, he detoured into the big municipal parking lot.

The black Dacia and Bjarni's Skoda were gone, along with the police car. The pale Mitsubishi was there, though, the cabin dark but diesel exhaust floating from the tailpipe. At the far end of the lot, Peter finally turned onto the Ring Road, but kept his speed under the municipal limit of thirty kilometers per hour and one eye on his mirror.

After a minute, the Mitsubishi pulled out behind him.

Two minutes later, another pair of headlights bounced into view. The lurker and the grad students in the red Jeep, Peter hoped.

He'd done all he could to let them catch up.

He passed the sign for the city limits and accelerated. The road ahead was dark and empty and mostly clear, despite the heavy snow falling. There would be a plow truck up ahead somewhere, rumbling through the night.

He wanted to find a spot to take them before he caught up to the plow. He needed speed and decent traction and a tight, blind curve.

46

The road ran straight through kilometers of silent winter farms and homesteads. The headlights stayed steady in his mirror, a half kilometer behind him.

As the world turned white and empty, the static softened and the adrenaline began to fade. With the absence of that gasoline in his veins, he felt the crash coming like a black avalanche. His head throbbed and his bad eye itched. He was sweating under the coat. He unzipped it and peeled it off his shoulders with shaking hands.

Despite Spatula Woman's ugly knife, he didn't think they'd meant to kill him in the hotel bar. If they'd wanted him dead, they'd have tried to take him on the patio outside. Fewer witnesses, and more room to use a weapon. No, the syringe had a purpose.

Maybe it was meant to control him, make him seem drunk or passed out. They could haul him out of the bar, laughing the whole time, and kill him later.

After they'd found Óskar. Because Óskar must be alive. Otherwise why go to all this trouble to stop Peter?

Suddenly Peter remembered the black credit card. Catherine had given it to him, but the card had Brunelli's company name on it. Brunelli had tracked every purchase Peter had made. His ticket to Iceland, the Defender he drove, even the Litla Guesthouse, where Seamus had found him again.

Shit. Peter fished it out of his wallet, cracked the window, and pushed the black card out into the darkness.

Wetzel the Pretzel had been playing him from the very beginning.

Now the headlights crept up behind him. He thought of how the Mitsubishi had run the Norwegian's Volvo off the highway from behind, and stepped on the gas.

The road came to a long hook around a broad rocky headland. He pulled ahead of his pursuers, but found no driveway or other wide place that would allow him to turn and face them head-on. So he pressed forward, using his forearm to wipe the sweat from his eyes. His head began to throb again.

The headlights came up behind him

again, following closer this time. He was running at 130 kilometers per hour, too fast for the narrow road and the falling snow, his wipers flapping frantically. He understood now that he might not get to choose the ground. He might have to fight them as they came, four on one.

He wished Lewis was with him, or Manny Martinez, or Big Jimmy, or any of the other men he'd known, his wartime brothers. He'd been an idiot to do this alone. He'd been an idiot for many reasons. He still didn't know anything about what had happened to Sarah Price, or why.

In his rearview, the headlights came still closer. Ahead, the road curved sharply to the left. Fuck it, he thought, there's more than one way to do this. He downshifted hard to shed speed without flashing his brake lights. Behind him, the headlights bounced and lurched as the other drivers braked too hard and too late. They'd either slam into his rear bumper or steer away and fly off the curve. He was trusting the Defender to stay on the pavement.

As he felt his tires begin to slip, he saw a car off the road on the right, a snow-covered sedan with a lightbar and police markings. But the windshield was clear. Was that a shadow in the driver's seat?

He upshifted and found traction to power through the curve. The dark police car didn't move. In his rearview, both pairs of headlights had vanished. Either his pursuers had lost the road, or they'd killed their lights so he couldn't see them coming.

The police car vanished behind him. He looked over his shoulder but the night remained black in his wake.

When he faced front again, he saw three big vehicles blocking the road a half kilometer ahead, showing faint amber on their fenders.

Then, as if on cue, three bright sets of headlights came to life and three lightbars flashed red and blue in the cold winter night.

A sedan, a station wagon, and a big SUV were parked in an aggressive wedge, blocking the narrow road. The land fell away on both sides so Peter couldn't simply drive around them. Snow blew in white ropes across the bare asphalt as the wind scraped the raised road clean.

The heavy Defender was more than a match for the smaller Volvo wagon and sedan. He could hit the gas and crash through their weak spot, but they'd only come after him harder. He thought about turning around to run back the way he came, but the lighter, nimbler vehicles would have no trouble keeping up. Either way, they'd know his vehicle and have his plate number. They'd call for reinforcements and chase until he ran out of gas.

Peter knew how this worked. He'd done his share of chasing.

As he slowed, four figures got out of the vehicles, bulky in their cold-weather gear. The reflective tape on their sleeves and pant legs shone in Peter's headlights. They adjusted their equipment belts and Peter was glad not to see the familiar shapes of holsters and pistol grips. This meant he probably wasn't facing the Víkingasveitin, the armed Icelandic SWAT team known as the Viking Squad, called out for major incidents. These four were likely just local police, well trained and capable, but equipped only with batons and pepper spray.

They waved their arms, as if he somehow might not have noticed them in the road, then held out their palms for him to stop.

The static began to crackle again. Peter checked his rearview. The headlights were gone, but he knew Brunelli's people were still back there. He thought of Óskar, running across the grass. Maybe carrying something in his head, something worth killing for.

Peter wanted to crash through and keep driving. He wanted to find Óskar and keep him safe.

But he didn't have a choice.

It was possible he might still talk his way out of this.

47

One of the officers detached himself from the group and walked toward Peter. With the swirl of snow and headlights in his eyes, Peter couldn't make out the man's face, only that he wore a fur-lined hat with a six-pointed star on the front and earflaps snapped under his chin. Taking care to stay well to the side of the heavy Land Rover, the officer made a throat-cutting motion with the blade of his hand, indicating that Peter should kill his engine.

Peter did as directed, but left his headlights on and his keys in the ignition. He stuffed his phones into the top pouch of his day pack.

Next, the officer held his hand out, palm up, and gestured to the side, a polite invitation for Peter to leave his vehicle. It wouldn't be an invitation for long. Peter opened his door and stepped out. The wind slammed it shut behind him, and almost blew him off his feet. He hadn't put his coat on, thinking he might need an excuse to get back to the truck. Now he zipped up the neck of his fleece.

The officer beckoned Peter forward with a curl of his gloved fingers. Peter walked toward him. He still couldn't make out the man's face.

The officer plucked a radio off his chest and held it to his mouth. He spoke briefly, refastened the radio, then moved forward with the other officers in his wake.

As he stepped into the glow of Peter's headlights, Peter saw his face clearly. It was Hjálmar.

Peter had underestimated him again.

The three officers began to close the gap behind Hjálmar. Peter saw batons and pepper spray on their belts. No pistols yet.

Peter's head was killing him. He should have put on his coat.

Hjálmar raised his voice over the wind. "Your eye is not looking well, Peter. Have you seen a doctor?"

Peter called back, "You know I didn't kill David Staple."

Hjálmar's smile was gentle. "You did knock him to the ground, however, not long after we last spoke. You took his wallet and passport."

"True," Peter admitted. "But if I planned to kill him, would I have asked you to help me find him?"

"Perhaps you became angry," Hjálmar said. "He fought back and you lost control. It was an accident. Crimes of passion are quite common in Iceland."

"I sent you a text not long after Staple was killed. The cell tower records will show that I was in Seydisfjordur."

"We will check those records," Hjálmar said. "I am sure you are correct. Although I must mention that you would not be the first person to lend your phone to a friend. Also, I am curious. How do you know when Staple died?"

Peter didn't like how this was going. The static crackled high. Despite the cold and the wind, beads of sweat ran down his temples. He kept talking.

"I think Staple was killed by an Irish national named Seamus Heaney. He drives a Mitsubishi Pajero with front-end damage. Its original color was silver. He ran Kristjan Holm off the road." Peter hooked a thumb over his shoulder. "He was right behind me on that last curve. He's after Óskar."

Hjálmar didn't say anything. Peter pressed on.

374

"The FBI investigated David Staple for laundering money for the IRA. Before that, he worked with Jerry Brunelli, Catherine's husband. Brunelli works with all kinds of bad guys. Erik didn't kill Sarah Price, someone else did, maybe Brunelli or one of his people. You need to call the FBI."

"An excellent idea," Hjálmar said. "I will call your FBI." The three bulky cops flowed around him, closing in. "Come with me, we will sit in my office and talk to them together."

Peter held up a warning hand. His head pounded. He was running on fumes. "Goddamn it, Hjálmar, you know why I'm here. To save Óskar."

"Yes, I know." Hjálmar's face was calm and kind. "But who will save you, Peter? You want to do the right thing. Let me help. We will make this easy. We will find out what happened. Nobody wants to hurt you."

Peter remembered that he had several Valium left. They'd go a long way toward easing the pressure in his head, along with a long swallow of vodka. Although he knew they wouldn't help, not really. They'd just put off the problem until later.

The officers edged closer. Peter's neck and shoulders were clenched tight. His head felt ready to explode. They would put him in a car. They would put him in a cell.

He thought of Óskar again, running through the grass. His purity and innocence.

His mother's face as she climbed up to save him.

What the boy had seen since that moment. What he'd been through.

No, Peter could not rest. Not yet.

He shook his head. "I can't, Hjálmar. I just can't."

"I'm sorry, Peter. You must."

Hjálmar raised a hand and the night grew suddenly brighter. A vehicle had come up behind the Defender, unseen and unheard in the snow and the wind, and only now had turned on its headlights. Peter threw a quick glance over his shoulder, fighting the blind spot of his swollen eye, and saw the snowy police sedan from the curve, the spotter now blocking his escape.

He whipped abruptly back to face Hjálmar and a wave of dizziness hit him. Pain spiked through his head and the world faded to gray. It only lasted a few seconds, but when he could focus again, the two biggest officers were already on him.

With strong hands, they'd moved him off balance, face-first against the side of his truck. "Sir, you are under arrest. Do not resist." One man held Peter's bent left wrist

376

behind his back in a compliance hold, preparing him for the cuffs. The other man stood to Peter's right, reaching for his free hand. The third man stood back, ready to jump in.

The static flared high, like an electric arc.

The burly officers leaned in, using their body weight and the pain of his bent wrist as leverage. Police were usually very good at the basics of physical control, and these two weren't rookies.

But they'd never tried this with a man like Peter, and they'd made a mistake. They should have put him on the ground. It was easier to control someone on the ground.

He felt the hands on him shift. As the man on his left reached for his cuffs, the pressure on Peter's wrist decreased slightly. Adrenaline burned like rocket fuel. Now was the time.

He knew the men behind him intimately, how they stood, their centers of gravity. He felt the flaw in the control grip. Both were right-handed. They wore their batons in front-draw holsters just ahead of their left hips. All Peter needed was a baton and one good eye and he could crack their skulls like eggs. The static soared, lightning in a thunderhead, just waiting for release.

Hjálmar must have seen it. "I can help

you," he called. "If you let me. Please."

Peter struggled to contain himself. He could break free, he knew, but he had no friends here. No contacts beyond Hjálmar himself. He didn't speak the language. He'd be a wanted man in a foreign land in midwinter on an inhospitable island in the middle of the North Atlantic.

He needed to learn why Sarah Price had died.

He needed to save Óskar.

He needed Hjálmar's help.

These cops were just doing their jobs. He didn't want to hurt them. He wasn't an animal. Take a breath. Hang on to your shit, brother.

The static raged. The wind roared. Peter took a breath, then another. The officers adjusted their holds. He allowed them to capture his free hand behind his back, and the moment was gone.

He felt cold steel on his skin and heard the *click* of the pawl as the cuffs closed, first on one wrist, then the other.

Three steps away, Hjálmar took his hand off his holstered baton and called out in Icelandic. The burly officers took Peter by the biceps and pulled him away from his truck. The third officer retrieved Peter's coat and day pack from the Defender. The spotter got out of his snowy sedan.

"Hjálmar," Peter called. "We need to talk."

The wind rose higher still. It smelled like a frozen sea. The commissioner shook his head. His face was hard, all kindness gone. His voice carried over the sound of the storm. "We are done here."

Then he turned and walked away.

The two burly officers grabbed him tighter and muscled Peter toward the roadblock vehicles.

48

The cold steel cuffs bit into Peter's wrists as the officers ushered him down the snow-swept road. With every step away from the Defender, the static crackled higher, stronger. He'd never felt it like this, not while he was outside.

Before, the static had always come when he went into an enclosed space. It climbed his spine and filled his head with noise. If he got stuck indoors for too long, the static would spread farther, into his entire body. Eventually it would drown out everything, including Peter.

It would howl and rage, the way it threatened to now.

Because he was in handcuffs. And Hjálmar wasn't talking to him.

Peter had made a mistake. He'd hoped to have enough to convince the man, but he didn't.

Peter wasn't Hjálmar's friend. He was a

murder suspect.

As the cops moved him toward the sedan, Peter looked inside. Like any American police cruiser, the white Volvo had a steel grate between the back seat and the front, making a man-cage.

After the car, they'd move him to a holding cell.

His chest was tight. He had to work to breathe. Despite the cold, sweat soaked his clothes.

Before the dreams had ruined his sleep, when his main problem was his claustrophobia, a therapist had suggested he get used to the static. To notice and become comfortable with it, to treat it like an old friend. In the years before the dreams, Peter'd had a fair amount of practice at it.

Walking now across the windblown pavement, he forced himself to take deep breaths, to keep the oxygen flowing. He closed his eyes and pictured a place where he'd been happy, at the top of the thousand-foot waterfall overlooking the pocket valley where June lived. He stood there in his mind, with the green meadow behind him and the summer valley spread out below and hawks soaring on warm thermals.

Breathe in. Breathe out. Hello, old friend. We can make this work, right?

He had no choice. He would do this.

His muscles were taut as bridge cables. Another breath, then another. Eyes closed, trying to feel the warmth on his face as the police moved him along. Not better, but not worse, either.

Until he stumbled on a chunk of frozen snow and they caught him hard, lifting his arms behind him at a painful angle. He growled and felt the thunder in his bones.

Not their fault, he told himself, not their fault. But the handcuffs ratcheted tighter.

Behind him, Hjálmar spoke, his words torn to fragments by the wind.

The two burly police pushed him chest-first against the police Volvo and kicked out his feet, which banged his swollen face against the hard metal roof. He watched from the corner of his good eye as the third man patted him down and emptied his pockets. He put Peter's wallet, keys, and the orange knife into a clear plastic bag and handed it to Hjálmar with Peter's passport. The spotter came up with Peter's coat and day pack from the Defender.

Hjálmar tucked the passport into his breast pocket and the plastic bag into the top pocket of Peter's pack. The wind whipped at Peter's face. Thunder rumbled. Breathe in, breathe out. One of the burly officers opened the car door, then put a rough tactical glove on the back of Peter's head, directly on the tender skin split by Dónaldur's bottle.

The infected wound tore open. The cop bent him down and put him in the back seat. It took everything Peter had not to fight.

The door closed beside him with a solid *thump.*

Breathe in, breathe out. His hands were cuffed behind him. The doors wouldn't open from the inside. The steel grate was bolted to the seatback, the roof, and the side pillars. The officers stood outside and talked. Inside, the static raged.

He had windows on four sides, but he couldn't see past the storm. The wind moaned its dismay. Where would he be next? A cinder-block cell with a steel door, a steel bunk, a single flickering light in a cage on the ceiling. The chemical stink of industrial cleaner. Shit.

He tried to take a breath but his lungs wouldn't expand. His chest was wrapped in steel bands that tightened by the second. His skull pounded, his face throbbed with blood. He was so tired of being broken.

Outside, the police kept talking like they had all the time in the world. Peter put his hot face against the cool window. How long would he would be in that cell? Days, at least. Maybe weeks, until they decided what to do with him. If there was a trial, it would be months. He'd never walk toward the horizon again. He was going to die inside. He might die right here.

His mouth tasted like a thousand pennies. The adrenaline spiked and his vision narrowed. His heart hammered but he couldn't catch his breath. The static crackled and sparked high, then higher still, until something gave way.

The static burst out until it filled his mind. Lost to himself, his thoughts disappeared into forks of lightning that set the world ablaze. All he knew was an interior scream and the desperate need to be free.

He kicked heedlessly at the metal mesh of his cage. His wrists strained behind his back. Cut by the cuffs, he began to bleed. The mesh clattered and flexed but did not give way. Like a wolf in a trap, he knew that he didn't have the muscle or leverage to break it. His instincts gave orders. He turned sideways in the seat, hyperextended his long arms, and forced his tearing wrists down around the narrow curve of his ass. He pulled his knees to his chin and pushed the cuffs past his ankles and around his toes.

Hands now in front, he set his upper back to the steel cage and kicked at the rear windshield.

His heels hit hard. Years with the heavy pack had made him strong. He heard shouting. A fragment of stone from the Reykjavík alley was stuck in the lugs of his boot, and it hit with a *crack.* The laminated glass starred, then bowed outward.

The shouting got louder. Wind came at him from the side. He kicked the windshield from its frame. Salt air swirled and hands grabbed at him. Unthinking, he scrambled toward the hole and the hands lost their grip. His legs tensed and flexed and launched him headfirst through the opening and across the trunk to roll onto the cold hard pavement.

He gathered his feet beneath him.

The burly police ran at him in a rush.

The werewolf bared its teeth and sprang forward to meet them.

49

The two closest men came with hands open and ready. Wearing tactical gloves and equipment belts, they were trained to contain large, belligerent drunks and put them in handcuffs. The cuffs were supposed to neutralize the threat. They'd never seen a wild man kick his way out of a patrol car before.

He wore the cuffs in front now, but he still wore them. He was just one man, and they were four. They hadn't laid him facedown in the road before, and that was a mistake, but they would do it now. Two of them against a single man in handcuffs, they figured it would be easy.

They hadn't figured right.

To be fair, nobody would have.

The first cop closed and grabbed Peter's wrist to lock the joint and turn him. It was the first step toward putting him down.

But Peter's wrists were slick with blood and the blast of white static surged through him like a high-voltage current. His training kicked in as he slipped the grip but accelerated the spin. He bent his arms at shoulder height, came around at speed, and slammed the back of his left elbow into the cop's temple, swinging from his toes.

Still in cuffs, he couldn't give it everything, but he gave it a lot.

The cop flew sideways and pinwheeled to the asphalt, eyes rolled back in his head.

Peter reached down and plucked the man's baton from the sheath on his belt.

As he straightened to confront his next opponent, high on battle rage and adrenaline, he flicked his wrist down and out to snap the telescopic baton to its full length, three sections of spring steel and a heavy striking tip.

Peter had carried a baton on patrols in Iraq as an effective nonlethal weapon, and he liked it. The checkered grip felt good in his hand, and there was a disturbing, primitive satisfaction in hitting something, or someone, with a stick. The static screamed its approval.

The other burly cop was already coming fast on Peter's blind side and Peter turned to meet him. If the man registered what had happened to his partner, it didn't show in his face. He should have pulled back and slowed things down. He should have tried for another compliance hold. Maybe it was too late to reconsider, maybe he didn't care. He adjusted left in a late attempt to sidestep the baton, then dropped his shoulder and drove his fist toward Peter's gut with the full weight of his body behind it.

It wasn't a tactical move, but the strike of a brute-force brawler planning to power Peter to the ground. Under normal circumstances, it would have done the job. Peter would drop and the cop would kneel on Peter's back until someone showed up with leg irons or a Taser or a syringe full of large-animal tranquilizer.

That wasn't how it went.

Instead, Peter slid left to slip the body slam, the baton raised in a two-handed parry to push aside the punch, then whipped the baton around and down into the other man's extended right forearm. He'd aimed for the nerve cluster but heard the *crack* of bone, even over the scuffle of boots and the roar of the wind.

The man's eyes flared with the pain and he pulled his arm back automatically. But he didn't stop coming. He set his feet and lashed out with his open left hand to strike

Peter's neck and jaw and push him back.

Peter pivoted on his rear foot and moved his head to the left. The other man's hand found only air. Peter dropped his hips, snapped the baton down, and smashed the heavy steel tip into the other man's leading knee. It gave way under the blow and his momentum carried him down. He landed on his side, broken arm held protectively against his chest, bearded face grim, scrabbling at his equipment belt with his free hand.

Peter kicked him in the joint of his left shoulder. It knocked him flat with the shoulder locked up and his face white. In serious hurt and down to a single useful limb, the man scrabbled backward like a crab with missing legs, desperate to get out of the fight.

Peter filled his lungs with salty North Atlantic wind, feeling that delicious, terrible joy that only came in the full fury of a fight, that made him want to howl at the moon.

The two officers with Hjálmar had held back by the larger SUV, not wanting to get in the way. Now they glanced at each other, expressionless, and reached for their own weapons.

Peter had to get out of these goddamn handcuffs. The man he'd hit in the temple was just now raising his head off the ground, still hearing chimes. Peter saw a key ring on his belt, with the distinctive shape he needed. He dropped a knee to the man's chest, but before his blood-slick fingers could disconnect the ring, the other two officers snapped out their batons. The metal-on-metal *clack* was as distinctive a sound as a shotgun racking a round.

The chrome baton tips gleamed in the headlights as the pair of officers approached.

Peter abandoned the keys and backpedaled to give himself room.

These two were a little older, with gray in their beards, but no less large or capable. They'd been crisp and professional before, confident in their skills, maybe thinking their boss was overreacting. But the wild man before them was no late-night drunk. He'd taken down two brother officers in six seconds flat.

So they came in slow and with serious intent, feet firm, shoulders loose, hips angled for stability. Bright baton tips up and ready between their neck and shoulder, free hands raised to deflect or grapple. Two on one.

Peter held his baton in the same ready position. He saw the officers taking inventory of his limitations. Still stuck in the cuffs, he didn't have a free hand, which was a serious disadvantage in a stick fight. The cuffs also limited his swing and the roll of his wrists. One eye was still swollen shut.

Long past caring, Peter showed them his canines in a wolfish smile.

50

The baton was a force multiplier, its heavy tip moving far faster than any hand, and with more devastating force. The butt of the handle, held in the fist, could also wreak havoc at close quarters, pounding the ribs or neck or face. Any blow that truly connected would be consequential. A strike to the head could kill.

But a stick fight between trained men was more than a fight with sticks. It was a technical duel using the baton as both weapon and shield, to attack and parry and attack again, faster than the eye could follow. The secondary hand was equally important. The flesh too fragile to block a heavy baton blow, the open hand was used instead to deflect or redirect the other man's baton hand in mid-swing, creating an opening for a counterstrike or an immobilizing joint lock.

The cops spoke to each other in Icelandic,

then split their position, one circling to Peter's right to get behind him. With Peter's limited vision, this only improved their odds. These guys knew what they were doing.

Before the two graybeards could get comfortable, Peter feinted at the man in front of him, who moved his free hand forward to deflect Peter's wrist and swung his baton sideways to parry the blow. But neither arrived. Instead, Peter pivoted to the second man and snapped the heavy steel tip along the length of the blocking baton and into the fragile bones of the cop's hand.

He winced and his weapon fell to the pavement, but he made no sound as he stepped forward and jammed his free forearm inside Peter's guard and up through the space between Peter's cuffed wrists. Then he bent his elbow and cranked his arm back from the shoulder, using the cuff chain to capture Peter's hands.

It was a good move, perfectly executed, accepting the pain to immobilize Peter for his partner. There was something beautiful about it. Peter hadn't seen it coming.

But he didn't fight the trap. Instead he used his own body weight to swing the big man around like a square dancer, directly into the path of his partner's accelerating baton. The first man's thick shoulders were hunched with effort, and the heavy blow landed on his bunched muscles instead of shattering his collarbone.

Still, the pain was enough to make him reflexively relax his arm. Peter slid free and released his attacker to slam ass-first into his partner. Both stumbled, reeling, but somehow kept their feet. Peter scooped up the dropped baton in his right hand, holding it backward along the length of his forearm. Now he had a shield.

The two cops found their balance and began to circle again. One man had a baton, the other nothing but a hurt hand, but he was still in the game. The first two cops stayed well back and nursed their hurts. Hjálmar, looking over his shoulder, walked toward the farthest vehicle in the roadblock.

Peter needed these capable men out of commission. He needed his pack and his keys. He didn't want to give them time to regroup. Better they were off balance and reactive.

So he attacked both men at once.

He swung fast and hard, striking at hands, wrists, forearms, and knees, driving them back but not landing anything. They were playing defense, taking his measure, giving him room, controlling the play.

The handcuffs were the problem. With his wrists locked together, he was slower and his reach was limited. The cop with the baton was slipping or blocking everything Peter threw at him. And Peter didn't have that crucial free secondary hand to create space to strike.

Peter would get tired before they did. Hell, he was tired already. He'd make a mistake. He had to force some kind of change. He had to get out of there.

For the two graybearded cops, holding back was definitely the right tactical move. But they didn't like it, Peter could tell. He'd taken down two of their own, and their blood was up. Peter understood, he'd feel the same way. But he wasn't going to get anywhere unless they made a move. So he let his baton tip fall out of position, just a little. The kind of thing a tired man might do. An opening.

The big cop with the baton saw it and stepped in, swinging hard, trying to beat Peter down with brute force. Peter held up his right forearm with its weak, improvised shield. The other man's baton slammed down like a hammer blow. Peter managed to keep hold of his shield, but his wrist ached with the power of the strike. He was lucky his forearm wasn't broken.

But he hadn't managed to counterattack, and now the officer with the baton was truly after Peter, using his superior mobility to press his advantage. At the same time, the officer with the broken hand circled around on Peter's weak side, a distraction he couldn't afford to ignore. Peter circled and sidestepped, blocked two more heavy blows and counterattacked, but still wasn't making real contact.

His baton shield was bending under the onslaught. His right arm ached. Time was not his friend. In his next attack, he swung just a little too wide, opening up his torso, willing the cop with the baton to see it and make a move.

When the man committed to his swing, planning to end the fight by breaking Peter's ribs, Peter brought his shielded elbow sharply back to slip the blow, then continued the pivot to kick the other man on the hip, knocking him off balance.

The man wobbled. Peter brought his baton down and knocked him on the side of the knee. The cop made a face, shifted his weight, then swung for Peter's head, but Peter cranked his baton around and smashed the other man's forearm hard enough to break bone. The baton flew away and he went down hard.

The last cop standing had no baton and one good hand. He fumbled for his pepper spray, not that it would work in this wind. Peter smacked his gloved hand with the steel striking tip, then thumped the man's forward shinbone, a sensitive spot. When the cop stumbled back, Peter whipped the baton around and rapped the man's opposite ankle.

He yelped and fell on his ass. Peter kicked him in the chest to knock him flat, and again in the ribs to roll him onto his face. He knelt on the man's thrashing thighs and tore the keys off his belt ring, then got to his feet.

When the cuffs fell clattering to the asphalt, the four injured men scrambled away however they could, big veteran officers with fear clear on their bearded faces. Peter stood erect on the snowy road in the wind and cold and dark, breathing hard, feeling loose and wild and free. The crackle of static like something alive inside him.

Something he knew might just eat him from the inside out.

The adrenaline would only last so long. Soon would come the shakes and the crash. Black depression, shame, and regret.

They were officers of the law, sworn to their duty. They'd done nothing but try to keep the peace.

And Peter had hurt them. Cracked their joints, broken their bones. Smashed them down like cheap toys.

At least he hadn't killed anyone.

Not today, anyway.

He stalked toward Hjálmar, his back against the SUV, rear hatch wide open. Peter's pack held his new coat down on the road, but the sleeves flapped in the whipping wind. Peter could see Hjálmar's pain and anger over his fallen men.

"I'm sorry," Peter said. But he was still riding the static. His eyes gleamed like he could see in the dark.

"You will be." Hjálmar held something along the back of his leg, maybe a baton, hoping Peter wouldn't notice. Overmatched but still ready to step up. Peter liked that.

Hjálmar had surely called for reinforcements, although the roadblock was many kilometers from any town large enough to have resident police. The four battered cops were hunched together on the side of the road. Peter stood between them and their vehicles, facing Hjálmar.

"Step away." Peter had to raise his voice over the sound of the gale. "I just want my gear and I'll be gone." His pack held his keys and phones and wallet. He'd need the coat in the days to come. It might be the only thing that kept him alive.

"What do you think happens now?" Hjálmar said. "Where do you hope to go?" Peter knew it was a tactic, stalling for time, allowing the four beaten officers to regroup. But it was also a legitimate question. Peter didn't have an answer.

Instead, he raised his baton and advanced. "Step back or I move you back."

Hjálmar moved his hand out from behind his leg. It held a flat black pistol, pointed down at his side. "Get on your knees. Please."

Peter stepped closer. "I thought Icelandic police didn't carry guns."

"Some have them in the car." Hjálmar raised the pistol two-handed, the muzzle now pointed at the road near Peter's feet. "On your knees. Hands behind your head. Now."

Peter was eight feet away, then six. "You spend a lot of time with that weapon, Hjálmar? You know what it will do to a man at close range? You want to see that every time you close your eyes?"

Behind him, Peter felt the injured officers gathering themselves.

The barrel rose to center on Peter's chest,

Hjálmar's face pale in the dark night. Peter was four feet away, now two. The muzzle described a small circle in the air. Hjálmar was shaking.

"Pull the trigger or put it down. Walk away and we're done. Nobody else gets hurt."

Peter closed the gap. Arms down, hands bloody from his torn wrists, he stood with the muzzle tight against his chest. "Harder than it looks, isn't it?"

Hjálmar's shaking got worse. His finger was inside the trigger guard, but there was no pressure on the trigger. Peter abruptly swept the pistol from the older man's hand and away.

Backing toward the rear of the SUV, Hjálmar seemed relieved.

Peter glanced after the pistol, now buried in the snow somewhere beyond the edge of the road. He'd meant to keep hold of it, but his hands were clumsy in the cold. He'd never find it before they came for him.

Instead he stuck one arm into his snowy coat, then the other, while the still-rising wind tried to tear it free. With fumbling fingers, he fished his keys from the top pocket of the pack, and his orange-handled knife. The blade was very sharp. It sliced effortlessly through the sidewalls of the police tires, over and over. They wouldn't come after him without a tow truck.

As he walked past the open back of Hjálmar's SUV, he saw a small bag, faded blue with shoulder straps. Óskar's Lego bookbag. The boy would want his things. He shoved the bag under his arm and turned to go.

Then he remembered what Hjálmar had put in his breast pocket. He put out his hand. "Give me my passport."

The commissioner had recovered his dignity. "I will not." Now they had to shout to be heard over the wind. "You will be in an Icelandic prison for the next ten years, or twenty. I guarantee it. Unless you face extradition for crimes committed else-where."

"I could have killed your men."

"I will mention your restraint at your trial." Hjálmar gestured at his downed offi-cers. "How many men will go to hospital because of you? Will walk with a cane?"

"I'll add that to my long list of regrets," Peter said, and meant it. "My passport. Now."

Hjálmar reached inside his jacket and withdrew the small blue book. He gripped it firmly between his thumb and the knuckle of his index finger. Even though he held it down by his waist, the storm wind made the thick paper rattle.

Peter stepped closer, hand out and open.

Looking Peter in the eye, Hjálmar threw the passport straight up, as hard as he could.

The wind caught the little booklet. The cover opened and the pages fluttered like wings. The passport lifted high, rising into the night sky until it was lost in darkness.

Peter growled.

Hjálmar raised his chin. "We are a nation of laws. We will find you. You will be punished."

"I don't doubt it," Peter said. "When you find me, I'll have Óskar." He looked the older man hard in the face. "Make sure you get him to a safe place. Do you understand me?"

Hjálmar stared back without an answer.

Peter climbed into the Defender and used the heavy bumper to push through the roadblock, then roared northeast toward the gap in the mountains.

51

He left the main highway just before Blönduós, headed north on a narrow road between jagged mountains and the raging sea.
The storm was fully on him now, the snow
coming fast and hard.

He gripped the wheel firmly to stop his
hands from shaking. The adrenaline had
burned itself out and left him an empty
husk. He'd seen no police since the roadblock, nor any other pursuers, although he
knew they were behind him somewhere,
gathering.

In the aftermath of the fight, the wave of
dizziness had returned twice. Peter didn't
know the cause, but it didn't matter. He'd
been tired before, and sick, too. He was
strong. He'd be fine. He had work to do.

Past the turnoff for Skagaströnd, the road
changed from lumpy asphalt to washboard
gravel. The few farms in the flatter places
became even more distant. The midnight

land felt vast and wild. The plow hadn't passed by for twelve hours or more, yet he saw only two other sets of tire tracks in the snow. He did not find this reassuring.

As the road climbed a hill, the gravel turned to potholes and the truck rocked with the full force of the blizzard roaring across the Greenland Sea. He stopped on the high ground and stood on the running board with his binoculars raised, although he could still only see clearly from one eye.

The fallen snow brightened the land below, and the ambient light reflected off the bottoms of the clouds so that the cold, windswept plain lay before him, dark yet gleaming. The road ran through a wide network of hayfields lined out by drainage trenches, their geometry from that distance looking like the remnant of an ancient alien civilization laid out still visible on the earth.

To the east, above the fields, a steep promontory rose up five hundred meters, a stone wave waiting to break. In a semicircle around its base stood three clusters of buildings. The family farm, more than two hundred years old.

The family wouldn't be happy to see him.

But he wasn't going there just yet. When the tire tracks turned into the unmarked driveway, Peter kept driving. The blizzard would cover signs of his passage soon enough.

After twelve curving kilometers, he came to the place he was looking for, a derelict barn not far off the road. The structure's concrete walls were mostly intact, but the windows and doors were empty sockets, the wood rotted away long ago. It was the broken line of the collapsed roof that had caught his eye on the Norwegian's big satellite map. He'd needed a place to hide the Land Rover from the road, and he didn't want to worry about visitors.

The only sign of a turnoff was a high spot in the ditch. He eased across and found himself following deep frozen wheel ruts under the snow, an old tractor or cart path that led him around the side of the structure. The Defender's heavy-lugged tires churned through the knee-high drifts.

Behind the building, he saw an opening where the barn door had once stood, but realized there was something blocking the way. He pulled the Defender tight alongside the structure, hoping it was enough to get the truck out of sight from the road. He'd have to backtrack and check.

The storm roared and the snow swirled madly around the corners of the structure.

He had a moment of dizziness and had to wait for his vision to clear. He was sweating again, and very thirsty. When he opened his door, the wind took it from his grasp and bent it back on its hinges with a rending croak. "Oh, hell."

He got out and tried to push the door back in place, but it no longer fit into the opening. He looked closer and saw that the steel was bent and the hinges torn. The door wouldn't latch without major surgery.

He found a length of rope, sat in the driver's seat, and held the door closed as he tied its handle tight to the steering wheel. The repair would make it hard to turn a corner. He figured he'd better just keep moving forward.

He peered through the passenger window at the shadowed shape inside the barn. It was a big round-cornered box, half-hidden in dark drifts.

No, it was the back of an old camper.

He thought again about what the Norwegian had said about places to hide.

Suddenly Peter had a bad feeling.

With a flashlight in his hand, he climbed out of the Defender and walked into the dark barn.

The camper was a boxy cream-colored Winnebago Minnie Winnie with the distinctive orange W on the side, built on a Dodge van cab and chassis. From the late seventies, Peter guessed, and not treated kindly since. The aluminum shell was dented, the corner trim patched with peeling caulk.

There was no sign of life. The windows were frosted over. Peter looked up. Flakes fell through the barn's broken rafters but the roof was still mostly intact over the vehicle. A searching aircraft would never see it. A good place to hide.

The Winnebago's side door was dented, the lock broken. When he pulled it open, he caught the faint scent of cold iron. His bad feeling got worse.

Shining the light up through the open doorway, he saw a large, dark stain, thick on the threadbare carpet.

Shit, shit, shit.

Peter knew old blood when he saw it.

52

In the parking lot across the street from the Reykjavík bus station, Erik stands with his bags at his feet and Óskar heavy in his arms.

The day after his mother's murder, Óskar hasn't really stopped crying, even in his sleep. When awake, his arms and legs are wrapped around his father like a desperate octopus. He buries his face into the hollow of Erik's neck and whispers warm, damp numbers into the darkness.

When Bjarni rolls up in the ancient caravan, Erik's heart sinks. The old camper looks far worse than he expected. But he must remain positive for Óskar, so he bounces the boy in his arms. "Isn't this great, Óskar? We're having a real Icelandic adventure now."

Óskar lifts his head to regard the ragged beast. He pinches his mouth sideways as if cauliflower has landed on the dinner table, and Erik knows Óskar is not fooled.

Things are very bad, and this crap caravan is no improvement.

On Erik's way to Dulles International the day before, his phone began to ring. The caller ID said Thomas Wetzel. When it went to voicemail, Wetzel called again. Then again, and again, and again.

Past Dupont Circle, Erik saw an open parking spot and pulled over to turn off his ringing phone. Then he realized he needed the phone to buy plane tickets. He was right in front of Philz Coffee on Connecticut, so he turned off cell service and borrowed Wi-Fi from Philz. The only available seats were first class, but he bought them anyway. He wasn't going to be able to use that credit card much longer.

Everything he'd heard over Sarah's phone was burned on his brain, especially this: Brunelli had a D.C. police detective on his payroll. Erik couldn't go to the authorities. Having seen the videos on Brunelli's server, Erik had no illusions about the man's reach. If the police put Erik in jail, even overnight, he wouldn't see morning.

He couldn't even think about what might happen to Óskar.

With the tickets handled, he turned cell

service back on to call his cousin, who listened to Erik's impossible story in silence. Then said, "I'm so sorry. How can I help?" It was Bjarni who suggested the caravan, already for sale by a friend of a friend. He'd buy it that afternoon, and "forget" to register it in his own name.

When the call ended, Erik's phone immediately began to ring again. Soon it wouldn't be Wetzel calling, he thought. It would be the police, tracking the signal. He needed to get rid of it.

His phone was filled with pictures of Sarah, all he had left of her.

They were backed up in the cloud, but he was pretty sure they could track that, too.

As he pulled into traffic, he held the ringing phone out the window and let it slip through his fingers. The car behind him crushed it into a thousand tiny pieces.

Now Bjarni climbs down from the caravan. "It's not pretty, but the tires are good and the transmission was rebuilt last year. She'll take you where you need to go."

"It's wonderful, Cousin. Thank you so much." Erik takes out his envelope of emergency cash. "How much do I owe you?"

Bjarni waves away the money. "You're

family. Also it was a bargain, because the bathroom doesn't work. But I filled the gas tank and bought the things you asked for." Groceries, winter coats and boots, a good map. "But better not to call again, not for a while."

Erik understands. With the police on his trail, he is a danger to everyone he touches. But after Bjarni hugs them and walks away, Erik feels the desolation wash over him like the tide. They are alone. Sarah is dead. He wishes he, too, could cry for her loss, but he can't, not yet. They aren't safe. He can feel it.

Still, with the caravan rumbling beneath him and Óskar strapped into his passenger seat clutching his backpack, Erik feels something like hope for the first time since this all began.

The familiar sound of his own language in his ears, the cold wind of home.

The weather is good and the road north is clear of snow. He considered going east to his uncles, and he may yet ask for their help to get him to England, but Erik is tired of exile, tired of the life that drew him abroad. Without Sarah, he can imagine nothing better than raising Óskar in a crowd of cousins, mowing hay and shearing sheep for the rest of his days.

But he can't go to the farm, not yet. Not until he's sure the police have given up on finding him. His family will help him deal with Brunelli when the time comes. Sarah's death won't be for nothing. Óskar still carries the encryption code in his head.

For the last two hours of driving, he worries that the abandoned barn has collapsed in the dozen years since he's been there. But while more of the roof has fallen, he manages to nose the caravan inside and out of sight without having to do more than clear away a few rafters. Now he worries about the forecast. Erik needs fresh snow to cover his trail. Because Brunelli will use every bit of his influence to find them. The police will come looking. And after them, Fitzsimmons.

What can Erik do against them? How can he protect his son?

With Óskar in his arms again, he walks out into the darkness and looks up. The sky is filled with stars. The empty landscape shines crisp and clear in the cold night air. The waves boom against the shore a kilometer away.

"Óskar, do you see that big hill, with that flat spot on top?" He points away from the road, where the narrow plain rises into a rocky saddle. It is not a hill. It is a small mountain.

Óskar raises his head from his father's shoulder to look, then nods.

"On the other side, down below, is *amma* Yrsa's farm, where I was born. We were there two summers ago. You remember?"

Óskar gives his dad a look. Of course he remembers. Óskar remembers everything.

Back inside the little caravan with its brown cupboards and orange cushions, Erik seats Óskar at the table and spreads out Bjarni's map, its scale small enough to show buildings as dots. Erik puts his finger on the dot for the barn. "We are here. This is the hill. These are called topographic lines, their little numbers show the hill getting taller. Do you understand the map?"

Óskar nods.

Erik puts his finger on the saddle. "Here is the flat spot we looked at. Here is the way across. And here is the way down to *amma* Yrsa's farm. Can you take a picture to keep it in your head?"

Óskar nods again.

"Okay," Erik says. "If anyone comes, you run up this hill quick as you can, okay? Like a real Viking, all grown up. But here is the hard part. Are you ready?"

He locks eyes with his son. He does not

413

want to say this, but he must.

"You do not wait for me, Óskar. Okay? You do not stop, you do not rest, you do not look back. You *run*. When you get to the flat spot, you *keep* running, across the top and down to *amma* Yrsa's farm." He retraces the route with his finger. "They will take care of you until I get there. Do you understand me?"

His seven-year-old son stares at him without blinking. He refuses to answer.

"Ós, this is very important." Erik clears his throat. He can barely get the words out. "If anyone comes, you must do this. You must run without me. Say yes, that you understand. That you will do as I say."

Óskar's eyes fill and he launches himself from the couch into his father's arms.

With bottomless sorrow, Erik knows that his son understands perfectly.

The snow falls while they sleep and they wake to a softer world. After a breakfast of *skyr* and bread, Erik challenges Óskar to a Viking race up the hill. The rules are simple. Run flat-out, no stopping, no looking back, and hot chocolate is the prize. Óskar doesn't stop and he doesn't look back. Erik lets him win, but just barely. At the top, he points the way across the saddle toward grandma

Yrsa's house.

Ten days pass in the little camper. They eat *skyr* and bread for breakfast, cheese and bread and carrots for lunch, fish cakes and potatoes and cabbage for dinner. They play every card game Erik knows. They remember Sarah and cry. Erik tells stories of heroes and witches and pirates and monsters, the stories he learned as a child, but now he gives every story a happy ending. If Óskar is skeptical, he does not complain.

Each morning and each afternoon, they race up the hill. Like Vikings, Erik says.

Óskar doesn't stop. He doesn't look back. And with each trip, he gets a little faster.

Aside from themselves and the derelict barn, they see no other signs of human life. Just the snow, the mountains, and the sea. The caravan's electric heater works well, but Erik uses it sparingly. To charge the batteries and warm themselves, they only run the engine for a half hour during meals, but soon the caravan will need more gasoline. Soon they will need more food. The snow keeps falling, getting deeper. Erik is worried again, this time about getting the boxy old camper back to the road.

But he needn't have worried.

On the eleventh morning, while they eat breakfast and talk about superheroes, while the engine runs and the battery charges, a gray plume of exhaust rises through the barn's broken roof. On the dark road, a silver SUV approaches. Its headlights illuminate the faint, swirling cloud.

The SUV stops.

Two men get out.

Their doors close with a double *thump.*

They walk toward the barn.

53

Erik has been hiding blind for more than a week, and his ears have learned to sift through the variable noise of the wind for other sounds. The clatter of rockfall down the cliff face, the croak of timbers settling under the snow.

The caravan's diesel rumble blocks out these other sounds, but not this new double *thump,* which Erik recognizes instinctively. He scrambles into the driver's compartment to kill the engine, but he's too late. He hears the crunch of boots in the snow, then a voice.

"What a lovely spot for a hideaway."

The boots crunch closer. Erik drops to the floor and gathers Óskar into his arms. At the caravan door, a sharp knock.

The voice again, louder now. It sounds Irish.

"Begging your pardon for the intrusion, but I'm an investor from Ireland hoping to purchase land. Would you have a moment to chat?"

Erik says nothing, just puts a finger to his lips. Óskar buries his face in Erik's neck.

Again, the voice. "I know you're inside. I saw your exhaust from the road, and heard the engine running just now. I wonder, is your barn for sale? With a bit of work, it would make a lovely vacation home."

Erik's heart beats so loudly he is sure they can hear it. His mind races but gets nowhere. What should he do? How can he fight back?

The man knocks again and keeps talking. "I'm sorry to bother you, truly I am. I can tell you're a man prefers his own company, living way out here. But perhaps just a quick chat? If you're not the owner of the property, we're willing to offer a finder's fee if you can steer us toward him. Say a thousand euros? I have the money with me."

The Irish lilt is charming, but Erik doesn't believe a word. Who comes looking for vacation property in northern Iceland in late December? But he sounds so damned *reasonable.*

Erik tries to think of a way to see the man without being seen. He detaches himself from Óskar, then creeps away from the door to peek out the window over the sink. The glass is nearly opaque with wear, but a man stands directly outside, grinning right up at him, a dark shadow of beard in a pale face.

Behind the man stands silent, looming Fitzsimmons, looking like a statue in the cold.

Erik jumps backward into the darkness as if pulled by a string, but of course he is too late. They have seen his face.

The camper's thin door rattles and creaks as they test the lock. The metal is not strong.

The Irishman says, "You had a good idea, hiding here. I've done the same thing myself, finding an empty place to wait out the coppers. I was a copper, too, once upon a time, so I know how they think. Or how they don't think. Most coppers are so comfortable, they don't really understand a desperate man. But I do."

The door creaks again, then bangs in its frame under the force of a fist. Óskar attaches himself to his father. Erik says, "What do you want?"

"As you know, there was an unfortunate accident. A misunderstanding. In addition, your wife took some video files that don't belong to her. The police believe you killed her, but we know this is untrue. If we get our files, and proof that no further copies exist, you will be exonerated and walk away

419

a free man."

More crunching of boots in the snow. It's the sound of a large dog breaking the bones of a small animal. Erik imagines Fitzsimmons prowling around the caravan, looking for another way inside.

Then he realizes they haven't seen Óskar. They don't know he's there.

"Sarah saw some strange footage, that's all," Erik says. "She just got scared. She didn't take any files."

"I'm afraid you're misinformed, lad. Your Sarah was in a hurry, perhaps, and not as careful as she might have been. She didn't actually reformat her laptop. Our own expert went through that machine with a microscope. We know she downloaded the files. We know she uploaded them to another server before deleting them on her machine. We only want those files, and the server's data record as proof that there are no copies. That's all."

Erik doesn't answer. They are lying, of course. They want much more than they're saying. Erik knows too much. He wonders when they will understand that they can just break a window and reach inside. But of course, he realizes, they already know that.

"We even have the URL of the server," the Irishman continues. "But not the encryption key for access. That's quite a large number, is my understanding."

"I never saw that." Erik knows he needs a better answer to save Óskar, but he can't come up with anything.

On the other side of the door, the Irishman talks on. "A 256-bit protocol, our expert calls it. Says the software generates the key at random, then scrambles the numbers beyond retrieval. Quite clever, that. The software's instructions are to print a paper copy before it's scrambled."

"That's what she did," Erik says. "She printed a copy. But I don't know where she put it."

"Now, lad, I know that's not exactly true. See, our expert has your printer also. According to its datalog, the last pages printed were a chocolate cupcake recipe, five weeks past. So that encryption key was quite a mystery."

Erik holds his breath.

"Until I was informed," says the Irishman, "that your Óskar is quite good with numbers. Has a perfect memory, I'm told. And he's gone away with his dad. You bought him a plane ticket. You went through customs."

Erik cannot speak. Óskar's grip tightens. He makes the high keening sound of profound distress.

The door crashes again, louder this time. They're hitting it with something, a stone or a fallen timber. The metal is weak, it won't stand up, not for long.

"Come on, be a good lad. Open up. Give us what we want. We're your only chance at livin'."

For Sarah, the content of the videos, and how they might be used to start a war, was her primary motivation. But Erik doesn't even think of that now. All he can think of is Óskar.

What they might do to get those numbers out of his head.

What they will surely do once they have what they want.

Erik doesn't have a weapon. Why didn't he think to get a weapon?

Because he's not a fighter. He's just a programmer.

But he's also a father, and he will protect his boy. If all he can manage is to buy a little time, he will do that.

He scrabbles through the kitchen drawers. In one, he finds their only knife, a short blade he's used for peeling potatoes. In another, he finds an aluminum frying pan. These are not real weapons, but they will have to do.

Another crash against the door, harder this time. Can Erik kill a man? He doesn't know. To save his son, he will try.

He looks at Óskar. "Get your coat and go to the back." A curtain closes off the sleeping alcove, where a wide rear window looks out at the mountains. "When you hear me shout, you climb out the window and run. Just like we practiced. You run and you don't stop. You don't look back. You run all the way to *amma* Yrsa's house. I'll be right behind you, I promise."

Óskar's eyes are huge.

"I love you, son. Now go."

Blinking back tears, Óskar slips on his coat and picks up his Lego backpack. He climbs on the convertible couch and unlatches the sliding glass. Erik reaches back and tugs the curtain across the opening.

There is another crash and the caravan door buckles at the lock. Then it peels open and cold air floods in.

The small man bounds up the short steps with a grin on his face and Fitzsimmons right behind him. Erik raises his little paring knife in one hand and the frying pan in the other.

The pale man also has a knife.

His hand moves faster than anything Erik has ever seen.

He cries out in pain. The last thing he sees is the pale man turning to Fitzsimmons. "The kid is running. Go get him."

Erik is not alive to see the two men run up the mountain after Óskar. Trailing only by the length of a football pitch, they crash through the snow in their low boots. Their coats are good, but their thin socks and city pants are soon wet, then turn to ice. The wind cuts right through. Their chests heave with effort and their skin burns with the cold. They're not gaining on the boy, but they're not falling back, either.

The men are reassured to see that the boy is also not dressed for this weather. He wears pajama bottoms and no hat, yet carries a small bookbag on his back. But he is light enough to run on top of the crusted snow, and he must know their intentions, because he runs full-out.

He does not stop to rest.

He does not look back.

As if he knows exactly the manner of red death on his heels.

The boy is a Viking, after all.

The snow falls harder. The clouds drop lower. The men's legs tremble and ache. Ahead of them, the boy fades to a ghostly shape. Then he disappears entirely.

The smaller man stops, hands on his knees, breathing hard, and looks over his shoulder. The clouds are so thick that he can no longer see the barn. His own footprints are disappearing.

He says, "I don't believe I care to die in this godforsaken place."

The taller man stops to consider and catch his breath. The weather is only getting worse. "Think he'll come down?"

"Come down to us or freeze to death up there, he's dead regardless. There's no shelter for kilometers in any direction."

Their mission is to recover the encryption key, or, failing that, to vanish the man and boy. The second option seems most likely now.

"We wait below," says the taller man. "Give it twelve hours. He won't last twelve hours."

"Agreed," says the smaller man. "Let's get the fuck out of here."

They make their way downslope, following their own fast-fading tracks. They move the silver Mitsubishi behind the barn, then return to the caravan and step over the cooling corpse.

They make hot chocolate on the little stove. Their wet clothes steam by the heater.

They take turns watching out the rear

window.
The boy never returns.
Mission accomplished.

54

"Sir, we're still on mission." Wetzel held the phone to his ear as he slumped in the back of the Jeep. He didn't feel well at all. Fitz's ketamine injection had kicked in, and Wetzel could tell that the size of the dose was going to be a problem.

"You said that last time." Brunelli's voice was razor-sharp. "Mistakes have consequences. Tell me why this isn't yet another fuckup."

Wetzel felt a flutter of fear but kept his voice calm. "Yes, we missed him at the bar, but to be fair, he appears to have slipped a police roadblock, too. We know where he's headed. The new plan still holds."

"You said that last time, too."

They had been reactive from the start, Wetzel had to admit. First, Sarah Price's accidental discovery of the video records, and her resulting moral outrage that forced

427

Wetzel's hand. Then Erik's unexpected instinct for survival.

When Seamus and Fitzsimmons reported that Erik and the kid were dead, Wetzel thought he'd contained the problem. True, he hadn't been able to track down Sarah's hidden server, but with the kid dead, the data would be locked behind an unbreakable firewall. Eventually, when no further payment appeared, the hosting company would shut down the server, reformat the drives, and all that evidence would vanish.

But then the backpack showed up in Reykjavík Harbor, and Catherine Price had driven them nuts with her renewed conviction that the kid might still be alive. At her insistence, Brunelli had instructed Wetzel to put a plan in motion. He'd connected Catherine with Ash, then put David Staple on a plane to Iceland to flash his State Department creds at the locals. It seemed easy enough to get Ash sent back to the States, where Fitz would cut him into pieces and bury him in a shallow grave.

When the customs police had refused to cooperate, Brunelli had dug into the details again. Under his relentless grilling, Seamus and Fitz had admitted that they hadn't actually seen the kid die, had only assumed he was dead because they'd lost him in a blizzard. Wearing his backpack. Maybe, Seamus had offered, the backpack had washed down to the ocean with the kid's dead body?

Brunelli, who didn't like sloppy work or loose ends, had gone ballistic. If Fitz and Seamus hadn't been so useful, and so necessary at that stage of the operation, Wetzel was fairly certain Brunelli would have told him to kill them both. As it was, Wetzel was sure that order would come before too long. Brunelli didn't like witnesses, either.

The secondary plan, then, was for Seamus to follow Ash until he found the kid or determined that the kid was actually dead. Wetzel had even put Seamus on the same plane as Staple, figuring that even if Staple did his job, Seamus could put the repaired Mitsubishi back on the ferry to England, eliminating that old liability. Wetzel still hadn't thought that Ash would be a problem. When Seamus had reported finding Ash in an alley, drunk and beaten half to death, Wetzel had worried whether Ash would be any use at all.

Ash had surprised everyone by confronting Staple at the embassy. In retrospect, it was a sign of how difficult Ash would be to control, but at the time, Wetzel had just considered Staple a poor tool that had outlived its usefulness. When he told Seamus to eliminate the arrogant prick, Seamus had performed perfectly. The next day, Staple was a news item, Ash was a wanted man, and Wetzel had a new narrative.

It would have been easier if they could have taken him at the bar, moved him to the farm, and kept him sedated until they got what they needed from the family. Then they'd sink him in the bathtub and slit his wrists. The evidence would show that Peter Ash, decorated but damaged combat veteran, had overmedicated himself, murdered an entire Icelandic family, then taken his own life in a fit of remorse.

Even with Ash still under his own power, Wetzel knew the plan would work.

"Sir, the mission is sound," he told Brunelli. "Ash is running on fumes. We'll take him at the farm and improvise the rest. I'll call you when it's done."

The police wouldn't look too closely if they had a good story. The police never did.

55

As Peter climbed into the little Winnebago, the static flared and the walls closed in.

He aimed his pocket flash around the space. He found a single dark, crusted island on the carpet and an arterial archipelago on the window glass, but no second stain. A year after the murder, the unmistakable smell of death was faint but clear.

He felt a wave of dizziness and flashed back to that hot, dusty street. He stood beside Big Jimmy Johnson and stared into a blue Toyota Camry, where a family of four lay destroyed at his orders. The father behind the wheel, the mother with her children on the floor in the back. Blood and gobbets of flesh everywhere. Already the flies had begun to gather.

Then the children blinked their eyes.

They stirred from their rest and pushed aside their mother's arms.

He knew they were dead. He could see

their ruined bodies. But now they reached for him.

He crashed out of the camper and fell to his knees in the snow, trying to catch his breath.

Finally, with shaking hands, he strapped the bentwood snowshoes to his boots, then hoisted his pack and started walking. He was nowhere near a hundred percent.

Headed upslope with the ruined barn and the dark ocean at his back, he put the waking nightmare from his mind and concentrated on what he'd seen in the old Winnebago. That single stain on the floor.

Bjarni was telling the truth. Erik was dead.

But maybe not the boy, not yet.

Not if Peter could help it.

As he climbed, the dizziness returned twice. He felt a sharp pain in his head and the world faded to gray. He wasn't sure, but the spells seemed to be getting longer. He told himself they were power naps. Behind him, the storm was already erasing his tracks.

He skirted a rock ledge and arrived at a broad saddle where the land rose on two sides. He consulted his folded map, found a route forward, and walked on.

The world faded twice more as he worked his way toward the high promontory he'd seen when he first drove into the valley. Each time he emerged from the blankness, he found himself someplace he didn't quite recognize, walking ahead of marks in the snow that he didn't remember making.

He didn't understand why a simple infection would make him feel so funky. Maybe he'd caught the Icelandic flu. It didn't matter. He'd get over it. He kept moving.

Finally he arrived at the great knobby scarp that leaned out over the hayfields and farm buildings five hundred meters below. The arctic hurricane hurled itself across the dark abyss of the sea. Snow arrived horizontally, and the wind rattled the sleeves of his fancy new coat. Sweating, he checked the thermometer on his zipper pull. Thirty below. Measured in Celsius, but still impressive.

In the hard white crust of the outermost tip of the crag, he used Bjarni's folding shovel to dig himself a sheltered observation post. Behind him, huge dark fins of basalt poked up through the drifts, as if sharks the size of submarines circled just below. He counted back and realized he'd only slept maybe five hours total in the last three days.

Through his binoculars, the farm jumped into focus. In the ambient glow, it looked like something out of a picture book. Bright strands of Christmas lights hung along the eaves of the main house. Circular hay bales stood in long snowmounded rows. Drainage trenches divided the fields into neat rectangles. A half-dozen cars and trucks wore fluffy white hats, including Bjarni's Skoda and the uncles' Dacia.

Waiting, he munched frozen trail mix. He tried to make coffee but his Jetboil refused to ignite. His sweat cooled and he pulled his tent from his pack, thinking to shelter further from the storm. A gust plucked it from his hand and wrapped it around a high outcrop, where the wind played it like a tireless, talentless teenager with a new drum set.

Finally, as daylight seeped through the falling snow, a line of police cars appeared on the Skagaströnd road and streamed up the long driveway to the farm. Hjálmar had gotten new tires and mustered reinforcements. Officers leaped from their cars and ran to the house and barns. This would probably take a while.

Then the real world faded again and he found himself on that hot, dusty street, his tactical vest heavy on his shoulders. Big Jimmy was at his back. The faded blue Toyota was full of broken glass and ruined flesh. The dead children blinked up at him, then climbed out of their mother's bloody arms. They opened the car doors and stepped into the street, their mother on their heels, all of them reaching for him.

Peter should have been hot, but instead he was cold. His fingers were numb, and the tip of his nose burned. He opened his eyes and it was dark again. Hours had passed. His body shivered uncontrollably. The infected wound on his head was leaking down the back of his neck.

He raised the binoculars and glassed the farm. The police cars were gone.

Good, he thought. He couldn't stay in the open any longer.

He clambered to his feet, fumbled into the snowshoes, and hoisted his pack. Then began the descent into the ring of farm buildings arranged like a fortification against the outside world.

If the police were gone, Brunelli's people would be coming. Peter had to get there first.

Other than that, he was out of options.

His plan was simple.

Knock on the door.

Start talking.

Hope for mercy.

56

Half-blinded by the storm but cushioned by drifted snow, Peter followed the course of a fast-falling stream. As he walked, the world came and went, again and again. Sweating and shivering at the same time, he realized his fever had spiked. It was possible that he'd overestimated the healing power of exercise.

The land flattened and the stream widened as it wandered toward the sea. He turned toward the farm buildings, walking the bank of a laser-straight drainage trench with steep-angled sides, maybe five feet wide and five feet deep.

From above, he'd seen the cars parked at the largest farmhouse, so he walked in that direction. Lights shone from the eaves, and a wall of windows glowed with warmth and heat. He was looking for a place to cross the trench when the world vanished midstride.

It came back slowly. He lay face-first in a cold crust of white, snowshoes tangled behind him, his backpack weighing him down like a thousand years of history. The drainage ditch had turned the corner of the meadow, but he'd kept walking in a trance and fallen to the bottom. His limbs felt weak and his head hammered like a roofing crew on meth. Judging by the snow accumulated on his coat, he'd been gone for a long while. Racked by fever tremors, it occurred to him that, if he passed out again, he might never wake up.

He heard a low noise and looked up.

At the rim of the trench, a dog peered down at him and growled.

This was a sheep farm. Of course there was a damn dog.

It was black, brown, and white, shaggy with its winter coat. One eye was dark, the other light. It had no collar. An Australian Shepherd, maybe forty pounds but looking bigger with all that fur. It watched Peter with its ears up, alert, as if hoping Peter would do something interesting.

"What are you looking at?" Peter's entire body ached. The snow swirled dizzyingly. It might not have been the snow.

The dog came to its feet and bounced down to the trench bottom without apparent effort. A meter away, it dropped its shoulders slightly, intent and growling again.

"Give me a break." Peter swiped at the animal, but it evaded him easily. Not that he wanted to hurt the animal. Or could, in his current state.

The dog slipped in behind him and nipped at Peter's ankle.

"Hey." Peter jerked the leg back. The dog went for the other ankle. "Shit."

Peter shed his pack and lurched upright. He had limited options in the bottom of this trench. The snowshoes were not helping. One had already come loose, the strap broken. The dog waited patiently as Peter bent and freed himself with frozen fingers. It was possible that the dog was laughing at him.

When he finally stepped out of the straps, it came in again and nipped at his calf. "Jesus, okay." Turning, Peter scrambled up the steep side of the trench and into the farmyard. The dog came after him, alternating growls and feints at Peter's heels.

The Aussie was a sheepdog, bred to herd livestock.

Now it was herding Peter.

The lit-up main house stood fifty meters away, past the parked vehicles. A simple structure with a wide-gabled roof and concrete walls, big enough for a large family. Peter headed that direction, but the Aussie didn't like that idea. It came at him sideways and bumped his leg with its shoulder, turning him toward a long low metal barn, then nipped at his calf to urge him into motion.

"I'm not a goddamn sheep," Peter growled, swaying on his feet. But he wasn't feeling fully human, either.

Maybe the dog had a point. Peter was in no shape to meet Bjarni and the uncles. Despite his intentions, he'd never get a chance to explain things, to warn them of the danger that followed close behind. He'd never find Óskar. Bjarni would knock him down with nothing more than harsh language. The uncles would wrap him in duct tape, then let the river wash him down to the sea. And Peter wouldn't blame them one bit.

No, he thought, the barn wasn't a bad idea. The police had just left. Brunelli's goons would wait until after midnight. Peter could warm up, sleep for a few hours, let the fever run its course. Although he didn't like taking advice from a damn dog.

But he didn't see a door, either. He angled left until the Aussie swung around and bumped him with its shoulder again, herding him to the right, around the corner. And there was the door, large enough for a tractor.

"Nobody likes a smart-ass," he told the dog, leaning against the siding while the snow swirled and the world lost focus. The dog eyeballed him to make sure he didn't make a run for it.

When he finally got the door open, he blocked the gap with his knees to keep the dog out, but the dog didn't try anything. It had done its job, moved a lost sheep back to the barn. Which was more than Peter could say.

Inside, the white static rose and his head throbbed. Only a few dim bulbs shone in the high white ceiling, and the animal smell was strong. The wind moaned as he stumbled down the aisle between rows of waist-high stalls, each big enough for several dozen sheep. They were fluffy and dirty and scared, with horns that curled back over their heads. None of them wanted to be anywhere near Peter.

Large round bales stood at the intersections between stalls, the plastic wrapping cut away. He picked up a sharp-tined hay fork and kept moving away from the door, looking for a place to hide himself. At the rear of the barn, he found a stall with fresh hay and fewer sheep. When he stepped over the barrier, they fled from him, scrambling toward the farthest corner.

Icelandic sheep lived outside for six months or more each year. Farmers on horses brought them down from the mountains in the late fall for shearing, and to spend the winter sheltered from the weather. Unless they were slaughtered for meat.

He forked more hay into the stall as the white static rose higher. He shivered so profoundly that the tool trembled in his hands. The pale ceiling shimmered in his peripheral vision and he considered the lives of sheep. Was it better to be in jail, or dead? Did any of the sheep manage to survive the winter outside the barn? What about the lambs?

Why the hell had Peter come to Iceland, anyway?

Leaning on the fork, he closed his eyes and saw Óskar's face.

At the back of the stall, where the angled ceiling met the wall, he sat and scooped loose hay over his legs. The fever void was held at bay by the internal tension of the white static crackling on his brainstem. Although staying outside in the storm would kill him, the static still didn't want him indoors. Even in this big, open barn, it threw sparks. As if it wanted Peter to die out there.

If he didn't get warm and get some god-damned sleep, he might just die in here. He closed his eyes but his heart hammered. He was afraid of the dreams. Of the dead waking up.

He'd put the bottle of Valium in his coat pocket with his map. Now with shaking hands, he battled the childproof cap. It finally popped off with a jerk and his last four pills flew into the hay. He picked desperately through the brittle stalks, rescuing pills from the manure-stained floor, one by one.

He wiped them off with his dirty fingers and swallowed them dry. His water bottle had frozen.

Despite everything, they tasted fine.

He was glad June couldn't see him now.

As the Valium took hold, he swiped more hay over his coat. His nerves began to unknot and the static hushed. See, this is why drugs are so popular, he thought. Then fell into a bottomless void.

He woke swimming in sweat, the dog's nose cold in his good eye.

57

A broad-shouldered young woman with dark hair falling from an ice-blue stocking cap stood at the edge of the stall.

When she saw Peter push the dog's nose from his face, she turned her head away and called out. She held a square-tipped manure-stained shovel in one hand. She wore a brown jacket and rubber boots.

She carried the shovel like a tool, but it could serve as a weapon, too. Someone turned on more lights and the bulbs wore fuzzy haloes that almost sparkled. The dog whined softly.

Peter tried to bring back his few words of Icelandic. He cleared his throat and his head spiked with pain. His whole body ached. "*Gud dai, ungfru'.* My name is Peter."

She just stared at him. He didn't want to think about what she might see. A battered, one-eyed man covered with hay and sheep shit, passed out in her barn.

A giant in an orange coat stepped into view. He put his hand on the woman's shoulder. Peter was relieved to see that he didn't take the shovel. He just scowled at Peter and spoke into his phone. He had a gold earring. Peter knew his name, but he couldn't remember.

He needed a weapon. Moving slower than he wanted, he scrabbled under the hay but found nothing.

The orange giant shook his head. *"Ku'kalabbi."* Ingo, that was his name.

Peter's hand brushed something hard. The hay fork. He grabbed it and put his elbows back to lever himself up. Ingo called something over his shoulder and put a foot on Peter's chest, pinning him to the floor. The foot might have been an anvil, for all Peter could do to dislodge it. The woman stepped in, knelt on his arm, and pulled off his hat. Peter thrashed and she caught his chin with one hand and stared at his face.

Axel appeared in the aisle and stepped over the stall wall carrying a big sheet of dirty plastic. Bjarni stood behind him with a coil of rope hung over the cast of his broken arm.

"Óskar," Peter said. "They're coming."

Ingo and Axel closed in. Peter fought but

444

they were too many, and too strong.

As the plastic closed over his face, he fell into the void again.

58

He woke on a hard floor in a small, low-ceilinged room with the dirty plastic sheet beneath him. The broad-shouldered young woman knelt on one side, and a slim older woman, with hooded eyes and hair like a gull's wing, knelt on the other. They were cutting the clothes off his body with kitchen knives that slid through the seams like water.

Two lamps stood nearby. Their light hurt his eyes. The walls thrummed and pulsed. His head pounded, an artillery barrage that shook the earth. He turned and saw his winter coat and bibs hanging on the wall. They looked like human skin. Peter was the carcass.

In the shadows stood the enormous uncles, crossed arms like tree trunks. Bjarni still wore his red coat. The floor was hot under Peter's back, but gave no warmth. He tried to speak but the words never got past his clattering teeth.

His fleece sweater and pants were gone. When the young woman reached for the sleeve of his long underwear, Peter jerked his arm back. The older woman spoke and the uncles stepped in and held his arms and legs. Thin fabric parted like gossamer under their blades, releasing the trapped stink of his fermented sweat. His chest and legs were mottled with bruises. The women's faces betrayed nothing.

The older woman looked at Bjarni, who raised his broken arm and muttered angrily. Then Ingo said a few words, and Axel nodded. Bjarni spoke again and gestured at the door. Naked and trembling with fever, Peter didn't need to understand Icelandic to know they wanted to put him out in the snow.

The older woman stood and surveyed Peter on the floor. Her face was creased, her dark eyes set deep. Peter had never felt so exposed, or so lacking. She raked back her hair with a claw-fingered hand, then spoke sharply and turned away.

Ingo moved to Peter's head, and Axel to his feet. They gathered up the plastic sheet and it bunched over his face like a dirty caul. They lifted and carried him, suspended and swinging, to a brighter place, where they laid him down on a hard surface. When the plastic parted, he saw white tiles and felt water falling down all around him. The younger woman pulled on rubber gloves. The dog sat, watching. Peter waited for the knives.

Mercifully, before they could carve him into steaks, he fell into the void.

59

When he woke again, he lay on his stomach on a new sheet of plastic, this time on a low bed. He was naked and dizzy and burning hot. Behind him, the young woman ran an electric clipper across his scalp with crisp indifference. His severed hair fell across his face and onto the sheet.

They were back in the small room with the too-bright lamps on the floor, their bulbs now ringed with pulsing colors. He saw shadowed shapes playing on the walls, dragons or demons. His head thundered and his mouth was dry as the desert.

He tried to turn. "Óskar," he said. "They're coming."

"Shhh." She held his cheek to the pillow with a strong hand on the nape of his neck and kept the clipper moving as if she'd done this every day of her life. He struggled harder. She put a hard knee between his shoulder blades and he was too weak to get free.

When she was done with the clipper, she took her hand off his neck and called out. Bjarni came in with a bowl and a cloth and a cup, and set them on the floor by his head. Then he looked at Peter, took a straight razor from his pocket, and flicked it open with a grim smile. The blade shimmered in the lamplight. Peter tried again to rise but she pushed his face into the bed and held him there.

He felt the odd sensation of a wet paint-brush on his stubbled scalp. Old-fashioned shaving cream. The scrape of the blade against his skin, then a cloth wiping away the remains, and a cold wet painful spike deep into his brain. He tried not to scream, and failed.

The young woman said, "Bjarni?"

Bjarni dropped to his knees and wrapped his good arm around the top of Peter's head, pressing his cheek firmly to the plastic.

"Wait," Peter said, or tried to say. "Wait."

He bucked on the plastic, his skin slick with his own sweat. Bjarni thumped him with his heavy cast. The young woman called out and put her knee on his back again. The older woman came in and sat on his naked thighs, and he was held helpless

450

and frantic.

He felt a stab of pain where Dónaldur had hit him with the bottle, then long moments of agony as she scoured the raw flesh. Then the cold, hard spike again, which he now recognized as alcohol, followed by pressure as she applied a bandage and tape.

"Okay," she said. Bjarni stood away and the women rose to their feet. The older woman sighed, raked her hair back again, then lifted a huge steel Frankenstein syringe and stabbed him in the butt cheek. When she depressed the plunger, it felt like she'd set his ass on fire.

They left him thrashing in a scalding puddle of his own sweat.

"Save Óskar," he said to the empty room. "They're coming."

Then Ingo and Axel came in, picked up the ends of the sheet, and carried him into a bathroom, where they dumped him into a steep-sided white bathtub. The young woman wrapped his shaved head in a trash bag, then patted his cheek roughly and stuck a thermometer in his mouth. Ingo and Axel came in with buckets of snow and dumped them onto his body, again and again, until he lay buried to the neck in Iceland.

They're not cutting me into steaks, he

thought. They're harvesting my organs. But who will save Óskar?

When the void opened up, Peter tried to hold on, but he fell through anyway.

60

He woke with a start in the small room, unexpectedly lucid. The older woman sat in a chair beside the bed. Her gull-wing hair was cut in line with her jaw, framing the kind of face that belonged on a coin. She stared at him with an alarming frankness, as if measuring him for a prosthetic limb, or perhaps a coffin. Behind her, the open door beckoned in a rectangle of light.

He'd been dreaming of Baghdad again, the hot dusty street and the bloody dead rising, reaching for him. He knew this meant that the Valium had finally worn off, the end of his pills. Sparks climbed his spine at the thought. This would be very bad. The static pushed him upright, but he couldn't get free of the sheets.

"Stay," said the older woman. "You are not well." She put a long, bony hand on his chest and pushed him back down. She didn't have to work at it. He was weak enough that she could have suffocated him with a pillow. Watching her face, he knew she was plenty capable of doing just that, and it had crossed her mind more than once. This was Erik's grandmother, Yrsa. The matriarch of the family.

"What's wrong with me?" His tongue was thick.

"Karina believes you have an infection," Yrsa said. "In your blood. There are indications."

Sepsis, he thought. Which would explain some things. "How bad?"

"Perhaps you will die," Yrsa said. "Perhaps not." She held out a large glass of water. "Who else is with you?"

He took the glass and drank. "I'm alone. But the ones who killed Erik, they'll come, too. They want Óskar." He felt the static rise higher. Fight or flight. "Have you seen any strangers? Foreigners?"

"Only you." Yrsa watched him with caliper eyes. "Why did you kill the man from your embassy?" She'd seen his face on the news.

"I didn't," he said. "The ones who killed Erik and Sarah, they killed him."

Clearly, she didn't believe him. "And why are you here?"

"Catherine Price sent me," he said. "Óskar's American grandmother. She's

454

afraid for his life." His tongue felt thick. It was getting hard to organize his thoughts. The fever rose, and he heard his voice as if from a distance. "Why am I still alive?"

"It is poor manners to turn away a traveler in need." She rose to go. "When you are well enough, we will decide." She called, "Karina?"

The young woman appeared with the Frankenstein syringe. The plunger had a thumb ring and a needle like an ice pick. Karina made a circular motion with her hand. "Show me your, ah, backside."

"What is that?"

"Antibiotics," Yrsa said. "For sheep. Karina is the best large animal veterinarian in Nordhurland Vestra."

Caught between the fever and the static, he thrashed in his bed and dreamed of the hot dusty street. Light that fucker up, he said. They did, and the small blue Toyota ground to a halt. He peered through the broken window at the dead, who opened their eyes and climbed into the street, reaching for him like long-lost family.

Now others came, too, from storefronts and side streets. The fat man with the antique rifle who'd refused to surrender. The woman with plastic bags from the market, who'd stepped on an IED. A girl with her clothes on fire from a mistaken drone strike, a young boy playing with a dropped grenade. They stumbled toward him with grasping hands, the countless war dead rising in the wreckage of their bodies.

Peter backed away, hoping for shelter behind the Humvee, but more crowded in. Big Jimmy, who would die years later in Milwaukee. Paul Watson, killed months before in an ambush outside of Tikrit, and Sean Quinn, shot by a sniper in a nameless Afghan valley, and a dozen others Peter knew well or not at all, their familiar uniforms shredded and soaked through with blood and shit and tears.

They surrounded Peter, these men and women, these hungry dead, and reached for him.

He raised his arms to push them away, but they took hold of his fingers and wrists. They clutched at his clothes and pulled themselves close. Hands on his shoulders, hands on his neck, bearing him down, burying him under their weight.

He woke gasping in the small room, arms out to keep them at bay. Heart pounding, head split like a dropped melon. The door stood open a crack, and a sliver of light seeped through. He could hear several conversations at once, along with the cheerful squeal and thump of children.

Óskar. He pushed himself up but felt a sharp tug on his arm. He was connected to a clear IV bag that hung from the back of a chair. The best large animal veterinarian in Nordhurland Vestra. Fluids meant for sheep.

Sparks fired on his brainstem, bright and insistent. Lungs tight, gasping for breath, he pulled the needle from his arm and tried to stand. His feet tangled in the blanket and he fell out of bed, naked and sweating. Driven by static and fleeing the dream, he pulled the sheet around himself and stumbled from the dark toward the light.

At the end of the hall, in a vast room with two dozen people at a long dining table spread with the remains of a feast, he tried to explain something extremely important. "They're coming," he said. "Óskar."

The dog whined under the table. Adults held forgotten forks or coffee cups halfway to their mouths. Children looked up from their books or drawings. He searched their faces but didn't see the boy from the picture. They stared back at him, a wild, one-eyed monster, bruised and swaying in their home.

Then Karina pushed back her chair and spoke softly to them. She wore an elaborately knit sweater over dark pants, her hair in an elaborate plait that made her look like Xena, Warrior Princess. Peter thought of June Cassidy with an ache that went bone-deep.

On the left, past couches and overstuffed chairs, he saw a wide wall of windows and a sliding door with a view of a blizzard. He got the door open and one bare foot in the snow before a hand caught his arm and pulled him back. An ancient man with a hawk nose, his face a map of wrinkles. Thorvaldur, Óskar's great-great-grandfather, who had stabbed his neighbor with a hay fork.

Peter struggled, but Thorvaldur was still tall and sturdy despite his years. With little effort, he moved Peter back to his small room and put him in a wingback chair while Karina made the bed. With the sheets in order, she turned on the small television in the corner. "For company," she said.

The screen showed a crippled tanker, smoke rising from the crumpled hull, then the embassy with blackened holes in its rust-colored walls. Then the famous American newscaster, silver-haired and patrician, asked the American president, "Don't you feel that America must answer this unprovoked act of aggression?" Icelandic subtitles scrolled across the bottom.

Karina made a face and changed the channel, but the interview was on the next channel, and the channel after that. The president looked gravely self-important. "As you know, America does not seek war, but this regime has behaved badly for decades —"

"Ugh." She turned off the television, then put a hand under his overheated arm. "Now. Sleep."

"Wait." The static bloomed electric up his spine. He was afraid of the dead. "No!"

On his feet again, he shook off her hand and pushed Thorvaldur aside. Karina called out and the uncles met him in the hall and picked him up by the armpits and carried him to bed.

They held him there while he shouted. The walls crackled with lightning and the dark ceiling dropped like the lid of a coffin. He roared and thrashed in his fever. Ingo and Axel clutched his arms and Bjarni straddled his legs, but Peter threw them around like children. Faces grim, the Icelanders held tight as if each limb was a lifeline and Peter was the raging sea.

Finally he lay spent and splayed across the bed. Thorvaldur watched thoughtfully from the doorway while Karina poured Bjarni's little plastic packets into a tall glass of water, lifted Peter's head, and poured the bitter brew down his thirsty gullet.

Thorvaldur said something in rasping Icelandic. Karina snorted.

"What." Peter could only whisper.

"He thinks you are like Odin with his one eye. He wonders if you plucked it out for wisdom, as Odin did." Odin was the old Norse god of battle, death, and healing.

"No," Peter said. "Someone kicked me in the face."

Thorvaldur spoke again.

"He says you look like you are still tied to Yggdrasil, the World-Tree. As Odin was when he sacrificed himself."

Peter had nothing to say to that.

When the storm regained strength and the lightning forked once more, Thorvaldur called over his shoulder. The uncles held him down until sleep dragged him under.

The weight of his tactical vest, the grit under his boots. The family from the Toyota, the fat man with the antique rifle, the girl with her clothes on fire, all those dead by his orders, they kept coming. He retreated toward his Marines, but Big Jimmy was dead, too, and Paul Watson and Sean Quinn, the men under his charge were bleeding all around him, reaching out with wet, red hands. They clutched at his arms, his clothes, his neck. It was suffocating, his knees buckling under their weight.

He cried out and jerked awake, unable to catch his breath. He lurched upright in bed and saw Thorvaldur beside him in the wing-back chair. The old man poured water from a pitcher into a tumbler and put it in Peter's hand.

Breathe in, he told himself. Breathe out. Finally he drank and held out the glass for more.

"You were in war." Thorvaldur's accent was very thick. Outside the room, Peter heard children playing some game, and the *clink* of dishes.

"Yes." Peter felt strange, like a window-pane. "Iraq and Afghanistan. How do you know?"

Thorvaldur held up a slim computer tablet. "I read news. You killed American in Reykjavík."

"No," Peter said. "Not me." He remembered that Brunelli's people would come for Óskar, but he also felt Bjarni's drugs working, medical-grade chemicals calming the static. "Do you have any weapons? Any guns?"

"No guns. Just farm tools."

Peter knew the raid would come in the deepest hours of night. "What time is it?"

"Before dinner," Thorvaldur said. "I was in war also. Many years past."

And in halting words, with a voice like an old recording, crackling but strong, Thorvaldur told the history of his war. How, at fifteen, he had crossed the ocean to Edinburgh with his three brothers in an open fishing boat to enlist in the British Army. They had volunteered to parachute into France ahead of the American invasion. Later, he had been at the Ardennes, a brutal winter fight, the last major German offensive.

"We were children," Thorvaldur said. "We thought it would be an adventure, a saga to tell our families. But my brothers, they all died. I tell their story because I dream of them still." Eighty years past, and still the war lived inside him. "You dream also, I think," Thorvaldur said. "Terrible dreams, yes?"

Peter nodded.

"Tell me."

Peter shook his head. He didn't want to talk about the dead who walked through his dreams. He wanted to push away that wildness that grew inside him, push it down before it ate him up. He wanted to walk out into the winter mountains until the wind blew through his bones.

Thorvaldur grabbed Peter's bare shoulder with a gnarled hand, surprising him with its warmth. Something in the old man's face, a kinship. "Come. Tell me."

So Peter did. He told about that dusty Baghdad street and the blue Toyota with bad brakes, the Sunni family just trying to escape their own neighbors, and three hundred rounds fired on his orders. He told about the drone strike on the wrong building, the woman blown from a window with her clothes on fire. He told about collecting the body of Paul Watson, killed by an RPG, his lower half still in the Humvee's gun turret, his upper half blown thirty feet away. Sean Quinn, shot in the groin, his torn femoral artery draining his blood into the dirt. Big Jimmy, wounded in Iraq but killed by it nonetheless, long after he made it home. He told about all of them. He talked about Memphis. He talked until he fell into a fitful sleep.

The dream came again, the Sunni family, the girl with her clothes on fire, his ruined Marines, the bloody grasping dead. The restless souls sought him out and held him tight and his lungs were squeezed empty of air.

He woke, frantic, suffocating. He would not sleep. He lay awake in the dark wash of emotion and Bjarni's drugs, listening to the noise of the house, wondering what time it might be.

The dream returned. He ran but could not hide.

He woke and couldn't catch his breath. He lurched from the bed, or tried to.

Again, he dreamed. And woke. And dreamed again. Bjarni's drugs saturated his blood. The dead chased him. He felt their souls more strongly than ever.

How many times he woke and slept in that fevered night, he didn't know. Ten times or ten thousand. Until finally he stood at the edge of sanity, strength all but gone, and thought to speak to the dead. *You want me?* His voice stronger than expected, a bright clarion, a trumpet call. *Then come get me. I'm a goddamn United States Marine and I'm all yours, motherfuckers.*

This time, instead of sheltering behind the Humvee or running down a side road, he stepped into the open to make room for them. He planted his feet and lifted his arms toward the sky. The Sunni family, the woman with her clothes on fire, Watson and Quinn and Big Jimmy, they crowded in and reached out with desperate hands as if to bear him to the ground with their dead weight.

But they did not.

They wrapped their arms tight around him, they packed themselves closer and closer, the static filled him like a rising flood, but still he did not fight. He breathed in the stink of their ruined flesh, heard the buzz of flies around their wounds. He looked into their desperate lifeless eyes and spoke to them, one by one. He stood in their hungry embrace and took a deep breath, then let it out, again and again and again.

When at last he woke in the small room, he felt lighter. He found a glass by the bed and took a long drink of water. Then he lay back again and closed his eyes.

Okay, he told the dead. Come on back. I'm ready.

When he woke again, the lamps shone plain yellow light. The swelling in his eye had gone down enough that he had binocular vision again. He still felt the static, but in the background, like the idling motor of a high-performance car. He wondered what time it was. The house was silent except for the sound of his own breathing.

What had woken him? Something he'd heard in his sleep, a noise he couldn't identify. His mind had been AWOL, but his ears had been listening regardless. He knew the living sounds of the house, the children playing, the adults talking and cooking and washing up, the dog's nails ticking across the tile.

But he didn't know this soft rasp.

His door was closed for the first time. Maybe Yrsa had made a decision.

His stomach growled. He wondered again what time it was. He pushed himself out of bed, still naked. He wrapped himself in a blanket and went to the door.

The knob wouldn't turn. The Icelanders had locked him in.

He adjusted his hand and tightened his wide, knuckly grip, then gave the hollow knob a short, sharp twist. There was a thin metallic snap, then the knob turned freely.

The hallway was dark. The big room was empty of people. To the left, snow shone through the wall of tall windows. Ahead, past sagging couches and overstuffed chairs, a wall of bookshelves and an opening that would lead to more bedrooms. To the right, an orderly row of coats on hooks, then the long dining table and the kitchen. A clock told him it was three a.m. He saw no source of the unfamiliar noise.

He reversed course. Past his sickroom was the white-tiled bathroom, its high-sided tub still holding the half-melted remains of the snow that had kept the fever from cooking his brain. At the end of the hall was a laundry room, its window showing the empty side yard and sheep barn. The snow had stopped but the clouds were low and dark. Beside the washer and dryer was a long table with neatly folded clothes. On the labels, someone had written *Bjarni* in black pen, as if the big man had gone off to Viking summer camp. Did Bjarni's grandmother still do his laundry?

Peter drew the line at wearing another man's underwear, but he found a pair of soft black gym pants that fit well enough, and a dark-blue long-sleeved T-shirt that felt strange pulled over his shaved scalp. Almost like having his jarhead haircut again.

Then he heard it, more faintly in the laundry room. The softest of rasps. No, not a rasp. A slow, soft crunch. Then another. And another.

Peter needed boots.

He grabbed wool socks and a hooded sweatshirt and floated back to the main room. Under the line of coats stood a row of boots. He didn't see his own, but one of these pairs would do. He tossed the sweatshirt on the dining table and stood on one foot to pull on a sock.

The sound stopped him. Slightly louder

this time, the slow crunch that he now recognized as a cautious footstep in the snow. He turned to the wall of windows as a shadow came into view, silhouetted against the winter landscape. As it advanced toward the glass sliding door, another shadow followed silently, tracing in its footsteps. Behind that shadow, two more.

Shit, shit, shit.

They were here.

61

Tom Wetzel's stomach lurched as the *Valkyrja* heaved over the top of the wind-torn wave, then fell into its trough and buried its nose in the sea. The forward windows showed only ocean for a long moment, until the little tour boat rebounded skyward and water streamed from its high, rounded bow.

The *Valkyrja's* captain, an elderly Icelander named Einar, grumbled to himself as he goosed the throttle and turned the wheel to angle up the side of the next giant swell, which crested well above the boat's pilothouse. Fitzsimmons had to break the man's jaw before he'd agreed to leave the shelter of his home fjord. Fist tight on the grabrail, Wetzel suspected Einar was giving them a deliberately rough ride.

Cassie and Thad, in tactical black, whooped with every wave, while Fitzsimmons stared silently at the darkness. Seamus just grinned at Wetzel, looking entirely at home. "You won't die at sea, lad. I'm almost certain of it."

Wetzel clenched his jaws and swallowed hot acidic bile. Winners did not puke. It wasn't the waves, but the fear, rising. Fear of drowning, yes, but also fear of failure. He needed to finish this thing. If Ash got access to Brunelli's data, Wetzel's life would go to hell in a hurry.

Wetzel wasn't physically afraid of Brunelli. But he was in awe of the man's strategic skills, his ability to game out every contingency, to make all possible threads converge into a single desired outcome. Most of all, Brunelli was utterly ruthless in application of that strategy. He made Machiavelli look like a teenage girl.

Brunelli would have multiple contingencies for Wetzel's failure. Brunelli had more than enough money to retain the best lawyers and buy the congressmen with the most prestigious committee appointments. And if those plans didn't come to fruition, he could flee to his oceanside home in Cabo Verde, whose lack of extradition and excellent exchange rate would allow him to live like a king.

But Wetzel couldn't afford that kind of parachute. His own risk was actually higher than Brunelli's. As the man had reminded him several times already, Wetzel was in this up to his eyeballs, and he'd better get it done.

No, Wetzel did not feel like a winner right now. But he knew who to blame. Peter Ash would die slowly and painfully. Wetzel permitted himself a cold, tight smile.

Time to dish out his revenge and get paid.

Unfortunately, his team had lost several days in the hunt. The accidental dose of date-rape tranquilizer was big enough to relax a rhinoceros, and after Wetzel talked with Brunelli, the side effects got ugly. The Jeep's dark cargo compartment was no place for vivid hallucinations of ravenous monsters chasing him into a bottomless cave. Although Ash had managed to slip the roadblock, Wetzel hadn't been able to keep it together long enough to face the police himself, so Seamus had turned the team back to Akureyri to regroup.

Wetzel was glad he was the unit paymaster. Otherwise they might have dumped him drooling in the snow and gone on without him.

The next morning, with Wetzel fighting a crippling hangover, they'd made a second try at the highway. But the snow was worse and the roadblock hadn't gone away — if anything, there were more cops, and it looked like they were searching every car and checking identification.

Wetzel knew the police were mainly looking for Ash, but apparently the fight at the hotel bar had been caught on camera, and the stepped-up scrutiny was a problem. Wetzel was the only one there on his real name. While the others could make it through passport control just fine, their papers wouldn't withstand the scrutiny of an actual Interpol investigation. None of the team had wanted to see the inside of an Icelandic detention cell, so again they headed back to Akureyri.

It took Wetzel most of the day to locate a charter captain who was available for a quick sightseeing cruise, and Fitzsimmons's fists convinced Einar to take them into the open ocean. A December trip across the north coast of Iceland in the aftermath of a hurricane was a shitty idea in every way, but time was short. None of it would have been necessary if Ash hadn't fucked up their plans at every turn.

But Wetzel was more than motivated to follow through and get it done. Although Brunelli's best-case was for the kid to be dead in that blizzard the year before, Wetzel wanted the kid to be alive and well with his memory intact. Kids were easy to scare. A little pain and blood worked wonders.

Because Wetzel wanted that passcode for himself. He needed access to that server. Brunelli's little motivational speech had made clear that, despite all his bullshit about loyalty, Brunelli wasn't going to take care of Wetzel. So Wetzel needed to take care of himself. The passcode would give him the leverage to extract a financial parachute of his own.

Because that's how Washington worked now, or maybe how it had always worked. People didn't care about ideology, policy, or making things work. They only wanted the power and influence to fill their bank accounts. Nobody cared if they broke the world or ten thousand people died, as long as they got paid.

Wetzel just wanted to get his share, too, before the whole thing collapsed. More than his share, really. If he worked it right, maybe he could get Brunelli's share, too.

If Wetzel had enough money, maybe the fear would finally leave him alone.

Captain Einar turned the tour boat into the waves, using the engine to hold them in place offshore. Seamus dropped the six-man Zodiac down on its davits and pulled the bow close. "Off you go, then."

"I'm staying aboard," Wetzel said. "The rest of you can finally go earn your pay."

"You're trained on this North Sea boat, then?" Seamus asked, pale face pleasant under the dark beard. "You can read the navs, manage the heavy seas, bring her home to Akureyri? Because I came up fishing off Strangford in a boat much like this one. Or are we trusting wee Einar to keep his bloody mouth shut?"

Like every Marine, Wetzel had trained on assault boats. He could manage a Zodiac in the surf just fine, but he was no North Sea pilot and this wild open water scared the shit out of him. "Fuck." He pushed down his fear, shouldered his pack, and jumped down to the little inflatable.

He released the stern davit and got the little outboard started. Cassie jumped next with Thad right behind her, the two ex-CIA killers surefooted as hounds. Timing the wave perfectly, Fitzsimmons dropped in like a ghost.

As Fitz released the bow davit, Wetzel cranked the throttle and angled the Zodiac through the dirty surf toward the narrow sheltered beach across the road from the farm.

Thad gave a woo-hoo. "Time to kill some people and make some money, honey."

62

The four figures stacked up at the glass sliding door, one behind the next. They wore
black tactical gear and face masks against
the cold.

Peter didn't have time to find boots that
fit. He dropped the socks and padded
barefoot around the back of the long dining
table, where a few crumb-specked plates
remained scattered on the surface. He saw
dessert forks and butter knives, not any kind
of useful weapon. After days of fever, Peter
didn't feel very useful, either. His shaved
head was cool, the bandage taped tight at
the back.

At least he'd borrowed dark clothing from
the laundry. In the unlit room, they helped
him melt into the shadows. It was his only
advantage.

The lead man crouched at the latch with
a pick in his hand. The lock wouldn't take
long.

The sliding door was in the middle of the wall of windows, an exposed entry. He hoped that meant they were overconfident. The second figure stepped forward with cupped hands to peer through the glass, and Peter realized his advantage was greater than he'd thought. The dark interior, combined with the bright, snowlit night, had turned the glass into mirrors from the outside. Until they stepped into the darkness, Peter would be invisible.

What was their plan? Come in quiet, he figured. Wound or kill anyone who resisted. Turn the rest into hostages. Leverage the weak to gain access to whatever it was that Brunelli wanted. Whatever Óskar had carried in his head, maybe still carried. And kill Peter, of course.

He would have to work fast, take them one by one as they came through the door. In the hand of the third figure, he saw the glint of a knife. But he didn't see any guns.

If they'd brought firearms from abroad, they'd have had to declare them at customs, leaving a record. They'd have counted on finding guns locally, but guns were hard to come by here. Knives would be easy to find, untraceable, and silent.

Peter had nothing. The orange-handled fishing knife was in his pack, along with the

477

folding shovel and the ice axe, but he had no idea where his pack was. He looked over his shoulder at the open kitchen. It was clean and orderly, the counters empty, dishes and cutlery put away. No knife block with handles sticking out, not even a frying pan. He couldn't afford the time to rifle the drawers, or the resulting rattle.

He considered shouting to wake the family, but quickly decided against it. The noise would remove his only advantage, and even the uncles would take a minute or more to gather themselves. Plus there were too many children who could, in their panic, walk into the fight. So he'd remain silent for the moment.

Bare feet sure on the warm tile, he crept along the line of bookshelves, approaching the sliding door from the shadows.

He didn't consider his own weakened state. There was no calculation. It was not complicated. In fact, it was wonderfully simple. Peter stood between innocents and the darkness. He would hold that line, no matter what. He tasted pennies on his tongue. Adrenaline flooded his tired blood. He bared his teeth at the night. Here we go.

The lock clicked. The lead man stood upright, stowed his picks, took a blade from his belt, then reached for the door handle.

Peter slipped a hardback book from the shelf at his back.

If he wanted a knife, he was going to have to take it.

With the faintest of rumbles, the door slid open and a long-limbed shape stepped through. Peter recognized the swimmer's body. The man in the Ohio State sweatshirt, come to do harm.

Peter held the book with a loose grip, spine out. It was an older copy of that Icelandic classic, *Independent People,* heavy and well bound, designed to last generations. The power of literature at his fingertips.

When Ohio State was fully inside, Peter stepped from the shadows with the book in his hand and punched the spine into the other man's larynx. The cover was thick, the stacked pages were solid, and the strike was hard and true. The crunch of ruined cartilage was barely louder than the sound of the wind pouring cold through the open door.

Ohio State kept coming, but his mouth hung open as realization dawned. Peter kicked him in the side of the knee, he folded to the floor with a *thud,* and the knife flew away. Preoccupied with his asphyxiation,

Ohio State was no longer a threat. He'd be useless in a minute, unconscious in three to five, brain-dead in ten.

The second figure was small but fast with the knife leading the way. Peter recognized the black blade and Spatula Woman's quickness with it. If she took note of her fallen comrade, Peter didn't see it. He was too busy trying to read her eyes and keep his blood inside his body.

After a series of lightning feints and probing slashes, she came for the axillary artery just below his collarbone. It would empty him like a faucet. But Peter was wired tight now, and his arms were longer than hers. This was no time to be a gentleman. She'd made her choice when she came at him with a sharp object. He caught the tip of her knife in the cover of the book, and when she withdrew the blade, his arm was already cocked for the hard jab. He punched a corner of the book into her eye, breaking at least one bone in her face.

She rocked back, half-blinded, knife wandering, but only for a moment. As she found her balance and raised the knife again, Peter brought the heavy book around backhand, slammed the spine into her temple, and knocked her to the floor. Her eyes fluttered, then she vomited and her whole body shuddered spastically, a seizure. She was done.

You can't do that with a paperback, Peter thought.

The next attacker was already stepping through the doorway with a wide sheath knife in his hand. He moved like a discount robot, but by now he'd seen two people go down. His nailhead eyes were bright behind his mask, and he was clearly the most dangerous of the crew. Peter knew this was the silent lurker from the hotel bar.

Peter had lost any advantage of surprise or size. He had a Nobel Laureate's novel against the kind of blade you'd use to gut a moose. Its gleaming tip carved smooth, graceful ellipses in the moonlit air. The man stood in an easy crouch and watched Peter's eyes, waiting to see his fear and desperation. For some, Peter knew, the delight in killing came from drinking your opponent's despair.

But Peter wasn't giving the lurker that pleasure. As the man stepped forward, Peter stepped back. He still held *Independent People* in his left hand. With his right, he reached out to the bookshelves, blindly found another hardback, and flung it sidearm, pages fluttering. It bounced off the other man's chest. A second book, better aimed, hit his knife arm with no apparent effect. Then two more, thrown simultaneously, opened midair like startled pigeons flying into the lurker's face.

For a brief moment, the man's view was blocked. He raised his left hand to brush the books aside. By then Peter was almost on him. He gave a short cry and the man, still mostly blind, instinctively raised the big knife. Peter now held his new favorite novel out and open with each hand gripping a cover and half of the pages, and met the tip of the knife with the inside of the spine. The sharp point punched through the folded paper and glue and cover. Peter slammed the book shut and twisted with both hands, tore the paper-trapped knife from the lurker's hand, and spun the whole thing across the room where it thumped and clattered across the tile.

The dog barked, a muffled sound, as Peter stepped inside the other man's guard. He hit Peter a glancing left in the kidney, but Peter slammed the web of his hand up and under the other man's jaw and popped him back into the wall of windows. Then Peter dipped his other arm down to scoop up Spatula Woman's black blade, and when the lurker lunged forward again, Peter buried the knife in the other man's throat, severing his carotid with a sideways twist.

The lurker was still falling in a red curtain when Peter turned toward the door. A fourth figure stood just outside, eyes wide. He held a knife, but it was down at his side. Then he turned and ran into the snow.

Shoeless, coatless, blood burning like gasoline, Peter ran after him.

63

Tired and hungry and still dehydrated, Peter ran with everything he had, following the dark figure up the long driveway toward the road.

He'd always known the limits of his reserves before, but after this fever, he was unsure of how to pace himself, how much he had left. Regardless, he ran, burning his own flesh as fuel, bare feet already cold in the crusted snow.

The man ahead was too large to be the Irishman. He had to be Wetzel, who'd always taken up the rear anyway. Wetzel, who'd seen Peter as disposable. Wetzel, who'd pulled Peter into this whole goddamn thing.

The subarctic air ached in his chest, but his lungs were open and sucking oxygen. For the first time in a long time, Peter could actually catch his breath. He was warming from the sprint, everything but his feet and hands, but knew that wouldn't last. He had to catch Wetzel before his body seized up, or Wetzel would circle around and attack from behind. That would be exactly his style. And Wetzel still had a knife.

Peter sprinted in the space between the tire tracks, naked toes digging into the granules with each step. Wetzel ran ahead, dressed for the weather in boots and gloves, a coat and thermal pants. He ran for his life. But Peter ran for something else. He ran for the lives of others, and that made all the difference. He drew closer, and closer still.

The driveway came to the road but Wetzel continued straight across it, clearly visible as he leaped the plow berm and ran overland toward the sea. Peter's frozen feet tore on the rocks beneath the snow, but they were too cold to feel pain. He left red tracks behind him. Ahead, the land ended in darkness. The wind threw salt spray into Peter's face, and the waves thumped like falling boulders.

He finally caught Wetzel on the edge of a gray, rocky beach, where an orange Zodiac had been pulled into the shelter of a cluster of boulders. He got a hand on Wetzel's neck and rode him down to the gravel. Wetzel rolled and raised the knife but Peter slammed the hand to the rocky ground and the knife flew away. Peter tore off the mask to see Wetzel's face.

Wetzel shouted, but Peter couldn't hear his words over the wind and the waves. They didn't matter anyway. Wetzel twisted and thrashed and made it to his knees, arms out toward the Zodiac, but Peter threw him into the icy surf, where he knelt on the man's biceps and clamped a hand on Wetzel's face, holding him under.

Wetzel bucked and flailed and tore at Peter's hands. As he ran out of air, he weakened. Then his lungs convulsed and filled with water.

The surf boomed and surged as Peter watched the life drain from Wetzel's eyes. It only took a few minutes, but it felt like forever.

Finally, he rose to his feet and let the waves take the body. Shaking uncontrollably, he looked out across the darkness where a dim light rose and fell, getting smaller in the distance as the waiting boat slipped out to sea.

His legs ached in the icy water. He filled his lungs with the glorious wind. He was alive and glad of it. He had no regrets at killing Brunelli's people, Wetzel least of all. Killing the man with his bare hands freed something vast and glorious inside him, a clean and righteous rage.

He loved it, and it scared the hell out of him.

What had he become?

The incoming waves broke white against his chest, their cold so deep his heart wanted to stop. The waves sucked at his legs, urging him farther out to sea.

"Hey!"

Peter looked over his shoulder. One-armed Bjarni splashed into the surf, eyes wide, mouth open to speak but no words coming out.

Finally he said, "Are you all right?"

Peter didn't have an answer for that. The next wave rolled from the black ocean, the crest turning white and wind-torn as it broke. Its weight crashed against him and rocked him back, then pulled him forward toward the dark.

He felt Bjarni's hand on his arm. The square-shouldered Icelander cleared his throat.

"You killed those people," he said. "But you saved all of us."

Peter still didn't speak. What would he say?

Bjarni shifted his grip and gave a polite tug. "Come," he said. "Please. You need to get inside. Unless you want to freeze to death out here."

Peter had been prepared to die over there, for the men he'd served with. More than prepared, he'd been willing, if that's what it took. But was that the same as wanting it?

No. It wasn't.

In that moment, he saw himself clearly, perhaps for the first time. War had made him. He was a trained hunter and killer of men, and damn good at it. He was still useful. There was work to be done.

He might as well get on with it.

Bjarni shed his red coat and Peter wrapped it around his shoulders. They waded from the water and walked toward the road, where the shit-brown Skoda waited with the doors wide open and the heater going full blast.

64

At the farmhouse, Peter stripped and stood
under the hot shower until he stopped
shivering. Karina dressed his torn feet and
the vodka-bottle wound with fresh gauze
and tape. In the mirror, a hungry stranger
with a bruised face and a bandage on his
shaved head stared back at him. He looked
like a mental patient, he thought. Which
maybe wasn't so far off.

Despite the small bathroom, the static
didn't complain. It just hummed in the
background the way it had when he woke
just a few hours ago, like a high-
performance engine on idle, waiting for
someone to step on the gas.

He found Yrsa in the great room with a
mop and a bucket, scrubbing blood from
the floor. He heard a murmur of conversation through the walls, the children wide
awake but kept in their rooms away from
this scene of carnage. Through the wall of

windows, he saw Ingo and Axel lining up bodies on a dirty sheet of plastic. Maybe the same plastic they'd wrapped him in not long ago.

"I'm sorry about this," Peter said.

Yrsa wore high rubber boots and a striped flannel nightgown, her hair up in short pigtails. She looked at him with those caliper eyes, then held out the mop handle. "Scrub," she said.

Peter rinsed the mop and wrung it. The water ran pink. "This isn't over. He'll just send more men."

"Who?" She put her hands on her hips. "Who threatens my family? Who murdered my grandson and his wife?" She didn't mention Óskar.

"His name is Jerry Brunelli. He's Sarah's stepfather."

Her eyes blazed. "And why did he do this?"

"I'm not sure, exactly," Peter said. "Sarah was an IT security specialist. Brunelli is a power broker in Washington, D.C., with connections to some very bad people. My guess is Sarah found something that threatened him, and he killed her for it. Something that Brunelli hasn't found yet. Because if he'd found it, he wouldn't have sent those people here."

490

"That is all you know?"

"It's not much," Peter admitted. He wasn't going to bring up Óskar, not yet. "Listen, I left my pack out in the snow. Do you have my boots somewhere?"

Her mouth tightened. "That floor is not clean." But she waved her hand toward a closet.

He guessed this meant they would let him live.

It took him a while to find his pack, buried deep under fresh snow. When he returned, the bodies were gone and the floor was clean. Ingo, Axel, Bjarni, and Thorvaldur all sat at one end of the long dining table, drinking coffee.

The other end of the table was packed with children. He counted fifteen of them, aged two to maybe twelve, talking through milk mustaches while eating pancakes with powdered sugar and jam. Like the morning after a sleepover, he thought. Maybe that's what this was, all the kids at Grandma Yrsa's house for the holiday.

Several of the children looked about the right size, including a quiet boy at the far corner of the table, half-hidden behind wavy blond hair that fell across his face. Peter crouched down at the kids' end of the table.

"Who wants to play a game?" he asked.

The kids didn't know quite what to make of the stranger with the shaved head, but they did quiet down a little. They'd started learning English in kindergarten.

"The game is called, What number comes next?" He didn't look at the boy with the hair over his face. "I'll say some numbers. When I stop, you keep going. Got it? Here we go." Slowly and clearly, he said, "Three point one four one five nine."

Every child stared at him like he was crazy, then looked at each other to see if anyone else understood the game. Except for the quiet blond boy, whose lips moved silently with the next numbers in the sequence. He knew four thousand of them.

Yrsa strode from the kitchen, glaring daggers at Peter. "What is the point of this?"

"You know the point," Peter said quietly. "Someone came looking for something hidden. What's the best place to hide something you don't want anyone to find?"

Yrsa's face changed as she figured it out. She clapped her hands. "Children, time to go outside. Who wants to have a snowball war?" She pointed a bony finger at Ingo and Axel, who obediently abandoned their coffee to shepherd the children into their coats and boots.

Yrsa reached out to the quiet blond boy.

"Why don't you stay with me for a minute, *saeti.*" She pulled him gently onto her lap and wrapped her arms around him. He buried his face in her chest. "What else are you carrying in that fine mind of yours, Óskar? Something your mom or dad told you?"

"I'm not Óskar," he said quietly. "I'm Alvar, remember?"

"That's his cousin in Toronto." Yrsa hugged the boy tighter. "We borrowed Alvar's name so we could keep you safe, right? And get you into school? Because you like school."

Óskar nodded.

"Now, *saeti,* I ask again. Did your mom and dad give you something special to remember?"

"It's a secret," Óskar whispered. He was no longer the wild, exuberant boy from Catherine's video. Peter wondered if the damage was permanent.

"You can tell me your secret." Yrsa kissed his forehead. "Grandmothers are very good at keeping secrets."

Óskar gave Peter a skeptical eyeball.

"I'll put my hands over my ears," Peter said.

Yrsa glared at Bjarni and Thorvaldur, who also covered their ears.

Óskar only spoke for a few seconds before Yrsa said, "*Saeti,* wait one minute." Then looked at Peter. "Pen and paper, top drawer by the refrigerator."

When Óskar was done and Yrsa had double-checked her handwriting against Óskar's memory, she gave the boy a hug and a kiss and sent him outside, where miniature Viking raiders were staging a snowball war with Ingo and Axel as their opposing kings. The boy ran up to enormous Axel, jumped onto his back, and pumped his fist in victory. Maybe Óskar would be okay.

Yrsa sighed. "How did I not think to ask?"

"How would you know? Erik has been dead for a year. You had no idea they were still coming for Óskar until four hours ago."

"Well, it's better that we all know the secret," Yrsa said. "That way they're not after Óskar. They're after all of us."

"*Já, já,*" said Bjarni. Thorvaldur nodded, too, a serving fork in his fist.

Peter was really getting to like these Icelanders.

"That reminds me," he said. He went to his pack, opened the top compartment, and pulled out a small Lego bookbag. "I thought Óskar might want this. It washed up in Reykjavík Harbor."

Yrsa unzipped it and examined the contents. Someone, probably Hjálmar, had put the stuffed bear through the wash several times. The book, *Where the Wild Things Are*, was wrinkled and swollen, but dry. The Lego guys were still safe in their plastic peanut butter jar.

"I've been wondering," Peter said. "If Óskar made it here safe, how did his book-bag end up in the ocean?"

"We gave it a Viking funeral," Yrsa said. "Sent it to sea on a toy boat. The end of one life and the beginning of the next."

"The bag made it all the way from here to Reykjavík Harbor?" She shook her head. "From here, the ocean currents would take it to Norway. So we launched from Reykjavík. I wanted it to wash ashore in the city."

It took Peter a moment to understand. "You wanted the backpack found," he said. "You wanted the people who killed Sarah and Erik to come back."

Yrsa pulled the rubber bands from her pigtails and shook out her gull-wing hair. "It was the only way to learn who our enemies were," she said. "The only way to keep Óskar truly safe."

These goddamned Vikings.

65

While Yrsa and Karina got on the computer
to figure out where Óskar's secret led, Peter
went to check the bodies, laid out behind
the barn in the front loader of the big tractor. Bjarni and Thorvaldur stood silently
while Peter searched the pockets.

The two grad students each carried a Ziploc bag with a stack of króna notes and a
cheap Icelandic burner phone, along with a
cargo pocket filled with zip ties. Peter didn't
like the zip ties at all. The lurker carried
twice as much money, two spare knives, and
an expensive, encrypted sat phone.

Peter tried to get them unlocked, but their
facial recognition didn't work, until Thorvaldur reached out his hand and rearranged
the damaged faces. Even the lurker's encrypted sat phone unlocked, a combination
of poor operational security and excessive
confidence.

Only the lurker's phone had anything on

it. Four numbers. Two rang the grad students' phones. The third number rang and rang, but never went to voicemail. The fourth number was answered on the second ring.

"Where are you, laddie?" A certain tension in the voice.

Peter smiled. "Hello, Seamus."

A pause. "I'm sorry, boyo, you've got the wrong number."

"Tell him I'm coming," Peter said. "I'll send you a text so you know what to expect."

The connection died, but Peter knew the Irishman wouldn't dump his phone, not quite yet. Peter took pictures of three dead, ruined faces, then sent them with the words *You're next.*

Bjarni and Thorvaldur looked at the screen over his shoulder, then looked at each other. Thorvaldur said something in Icelandic. Bjarni raised his eyebrows.

"What did he say?" Peter asked.

"He says you must be a berserk, to defeat these three and the other one. A wild man, a fearless bear-warrior."

"Not fearless," Peter said. "Just motivated."

Back in the farmhouse, they found Yrsa and Karina sitting at the table with a laptop, watching grainy video with their hands over their mouths.

Peter said, "What is it?"

As they talked, the news flickered on the corner television, a split screen. One side showed the lacquered newsman talking up the righteousness of the coming conflict, while the other side had footage of a vast carrier group gathering off the coast of Venezuela.

If he was going to stop a war, Peter had to move fast.

But he didn't want to spook Brunelli or the dirtbag TV anchor or the oil executives or any of the others.

The decision wasn't difficult. Everything was easier when you knew good people.

On the lurker's encrypted phone, he typed in the server's address and passcode, triple-checking the long string of numbers, then sent it to June Cassidy's work email. The subject line read *LOOK AT THIS RIGHT NOW.*

More than anyone, he trusted June's ruthless journalistic dedication to the truth, along with her network at the nonprofit group Public Investigations, to get the information into the right hands in a hurry.

Then he realized the unknown sender and

the URL link might get his email dumped into her spam filter. He should just call her. Even if the idea scared the hell out of him.

Her reaction was roughly what he'd expected, although the volume was louder. "What the fuck are you doing in Iceland?"

Of course she'd seen the news about the murder of a U.S. State Department lawyer in Iceland. She was an investigative reporter. Peter's name and photo would have been featured prominently, even with the buildup to war dominating the cycle.

"I'm sorry," he said. "It's a long story."

"Then you goddamn well better start talking, Marine." Her voice crackled, and it wasn't the line. "I was fucking worried about you. Are you safe? Are you in jail?"

He liked that she didn't ask if he'd killed David Staple. "I'm good," he said. "I miss you. Listen, did you get an oddball email?" A pause while she checked. "That's you? What the hell is this?"

"Do you still have contacts in the Pentagon?"

Shouting again, she said, "I thought you were going to the fucking desert to fucking relax."

"June," he said. "When trouble calls my name, you know I have to answer."

"Oh, fuck you." He could hear the tears

in her voice.

"Trouble always knows where to find me?"

"This is not fucking funny."

"Trouble sings a siren song I'm helpless to resist? Bad luck and trouble are my bread and butter? Trouble is my business?"

"Goddamnit, you lied to me. I am really pissed off." She blew her nose loudly. "We need to talk."

"We will," he said. "I promise. And I'm sorry. But right now I have to deal with this. Will you get on the horn to your Pentagon contacts?"

"Yes," she said. And hung up.

Peter sighed. She was right, of course. He was an asshole.

He was grateful that his next call would be easier. He dug his old Icelandic burner out of his backpack, tore off the tinfoil, and found Catherine's number. He got to tell her that Óskar was alive.

A man's voice answered. "Catherine Price's phone."

"Who is this?"

The voice was cold. "No, who the hell is this?" It was Novak, Catherine's bodyguard.

"This is Peter. We met in Portland, after Catherine asked me to find her grandson. Can I talk to her?"

"No," Novak said.

"Why not?"

"She's dead."

Peter closed his eyes. "How did she die?"

"She was mugged. In the District."

"And where the fuck were you?"

"Getting the car." Novak spoke without inflection, but Peter knew the ex-cop was furious. He held himself responsible. Peter knew exactly how he felt.

Brunelli wasn't wasting any time.

Peter glanced at the television in the corner, now showing Icelandic news. The top story was the murder of David Staple. Peter's face filled the screen, followed by shots of a series of police roadblocks on cold, snowy roads.

Getting back to the States was going to be problematic.

Even if Peter could make his way to an airport and charter a plane, he had no passport.

He turned to Ingo and Axel, who had returned to the table with tall stacks of pancakes. "You boys want to go fishing?"

66

POTOMAC, MARYLAND
TWO WEEKS LATER

Jerry Brunelli paced through his house, from his office to the butler's pantry to the kitchen to the dining room, hating how the ankle monitor chafed on his skin. As if he were a common felon, rather than an American patriot.

The confidence of the U.S. Attorney assigned to his case amused Brunelli no end. The very fact that the judge had granted him house arrest was evidence that the machinery of his liberation was already in motion. He'd planned for this contingency as he'd planned for every other, with a complex decision tree accounting for every possibility.

He'd once played this great global game in the White House. Although he now played on his own behalf, with an absurdly higher level of compensation, the larger goal was the same: the greater glory of America through the vanquishing of her enemies.

It wasn't like this war was unwelcome. Brunelli had done his government a favor by finding a way to sell it to the public. America loved a good war. More than that, America needed it. War provided jobs, boosted technological development, opened the way for corporate investment, and helped demonstrate American power to a world that had begun to doubt it. If this war didn't happen, the next one would.

Truth be told, Brunelli was only doing what his own government had done at least twice in the last half century, exaggerating conflict in the Gulf of Tonkin to escalate the war in Vietnam, then inventing nonexistent WMDs as a pretext for the invasion of Iraq.

Brunelli had simply privatized this time-honored process. He was an innovator. He deserved compensation for his genius.

The heels of Brunelli's loafers echoed on the polished floors as he walked from entry hall to living room to grand ballroom. The house had been built by a railroad baron and enlarged several times. In the century before the last one, it was seriously considered for the vice president's residence. Brunelli, to burnish his image and launder his reputation during his K Street years, had thrown lavish parties here, including an annual costume ball whose central conceit allowed anyone to talk to anyone.

To that end, the house was an investment that had paid off many times over. After all, it was at one of those costume balls that Brunelli had met a certain Russian businessman and former GRU general who had given him the speck of polonium that Brunelli had used to eliminate his business partner, Ken Price. Dropped in a cup of herbal tea, the radioactive isotope had lingered in Ken's system just long enough to give him metastatic cancer, leaving the widow Price and her inherited shares vulnerable to a sweetheart takeover and Jerry Brunelli in control of the firm.

Of course, he'd needed to remove Catherine's son from the equation first, but it was a small thing for a man of Brunelli's capacities to arrange for a brake failure on an icy mountain road. He'd also kept young Sarah close first by hiring her fledgling business, then by sending her a steady stream of new clients. By biting the hand that fed her, Sarah Price had practically killed herself.

He'd even maneuvered Catherine into demanding, as a condition of marriage, that he get out of lobbying for "consulting," where the money was better and the oversight was minimal. Brunelli had been her white knight, riding to her rescue in a time of need.

She hadn't even signed a pre-nup. With her unfortunate death in a mugging, actually a carefully planned murder at the hands of Detective Philip Moore of the Metro PD, who had found a small gap in her bodyguard's vigilance, Brunelli now owned it all.

He was pleased to learn that Tom Wetzel and Fitzsimmons were missing and presumed dead, too. The ex-Marine that Wetzel had recommended to Catherine had not performed as promised. Rather than provide the ribbon to wrap up the entire Sarah Price problem, the man had somehow escaped the noose tied around his neck. As a result, Brunelli's leverage had been leaked to the news and his carefully wrought casus belli had been upended.

Of course, Brunelli had immediately set his contingencies in motion. He had a dozen more extralegal operatives coming. He had a telegenic academic expert asserting that the footage had been created from whole cloth with advanced technology. The prominent network personality, who had been so helpful promoting the war against Venezuela, was vigorously denying his sexual proclivities via an energetic social media campaign, claiming that the video was a smear tactic to attack his credibility. Significant technical evidence of Wetzel's involvement, along with his mysterious disappearance, made him a fine candidate for the leader of the plot. Both Brunelli's lawyers and his clients were working hard behind the scenes to make his own role vanish entirely.

They had better, Brunelli thought as he completed the circle to his private office overlooking the pool and the Potomac. His time in the White House had served him well. He knew where too many bodies were buried. They couldn't afford to have him talking to the press, or to Congress.

Time for a drink. As he surveyed the selection of liquors on his bar cart, Brunelli's mind returned to the ex-Marine.

Brunelli's ankle monitor, along with his legal troubles and the small army of federal agents occupying the grounds of his modest estate, were all due to this troublesome person. The fact that he was still at large was only a modest cause of concern, however. Given that the man was wanted for murder, with warrants for his arrest issued in Europe, Canada, and America, rational self-interest dictated that he was almost certainly saving his own neck rather than seeking out Brunelli's own.

Not to mention the fact that Brunelli's extensive network was combing the earth for him at this very moment.

Brunelli lifted the antique crystal decanter and poured himself a substantial measure of the fifty-year-old bottle of Macallan he'd bought at auction the year before. He raised the glass and let the flavor fill his mouth. The scotch truly did taste better because it was so expensive. He'd calculated the cost at ten thousand dollars a sip. And worth every penny.

He put his foot on the windowsill and scratched at the skin under the ankle monitor. Soon enough, this would be over and he'd go back to business as usual. He looked out at the floodlit night, raised his glass, and smiled.

The high chime of breaking glass was the last sound he ever heard.

67

The elderly fishing boat, more rust than paint, rode the East Greenland Current toward Labrador, her high bow and narrow waist slicing elegantly through the waves. She carried extra fuel drums in her fish hold, and her cranes were pulled in and lashed down tight.

Peter and Thorvaldur sat on deck behind the pilothouse, dressed in foul weather gear, heads together in conversation. Together, they remembered their wars, the men they had served with, the friends they had lost.

Inside, the others watched developments on the satellite feed. Things had happened quickly after June Cassidy called her Pentagon contacts. The White House announced renewed talks with Caracas just twelve hours later. June's story went live twelve hours after that. Then the shit truly hit the fan.

So far, all the blame was falling on Tom Wetzel.

Apparently, all the video files had been added to the server using his login and workstation.

Jerry Brunelli was turning out to have a world-class shit-proof umbrella.

In the four days it took Ingo and Axel to drive to Seydisfjordur and return with the *Freyja,* the Icelandic police had come back to the farm twice. Peter had taken a tarp and his new sleeping bag out into the snow to catch up on his sleep.

Once she lost the Labrador Current, the *Freyja* headed south past Newfoundland, Nova Scotia, and New England, always staying far enough offshore to avoid the attention of the Coast Guard.

Ten days after leaving Iceland, Peter ran the orange Zodiac across twelve nautical miles of open water toward a small marina outside of Ocean City, Maryland. The waves were manageable and the sun was warm on Peter's face. The mid-Atlantic coast felt like Bermuda after the icy run across the North Atlantic in a sixty-foot fishing boat.

It was off-season, not to mention almost dark, so nobody saw four men climb out of the small inflatable dinghy at the tender's dock and walk across the boatyard into the parking lot, where Novak sat waiting in a black four-door Silverado pickup.

Even in jeans and a sweatshirt, he still looked like the D.C. Metro cop he'd been for twenty years. The Norwegian had run a background check on him. He was married to Catherine's cousin. His only visible assets were his pension, the truck, and a small condo in Anacostia.

Peter said, "Did you get the stuff I asked for?"

"On the floor." Novak nodded at the paper bag at Peter's feet. Ingo and Axel opened the back doors and climbed inside, pushing Bjarni into the middle seat. The big truck sank on its springs. The uncles put the windows down and sniffed the air.

Novak looked at Peter. "Who the fuck are these guys? What are you looking to do here?"

"They're Vikings," Peter said. "They came to see the Air and Space Museum. For myself, honestly, I'm still figuring it out." He dumped the contents of Novak's bag into his day pack. Zip ties, duct tape, nitrile gloves, a half-decent folding knife you could buy at any hardware store. "Let's just take a look around. What's the security setup?"

Novak put the truck in drive and got out

of there. "The place is huge," he said. "There are two U.S. Marshals at the front, and a pair of cars blocking the driveway. They have four more men watching the doors, and two men patrolling the grounds."

"Only eight guys? For a five-acre property?"

"That's because they're focused on keeping Brunelli inside," Novak said. "Not keeping someone else out." His eyes flicked to the backpack, then at Peter. "Really. What are you thinking here?"

Novak, in his heart, was still very much a cop. Peter reminded himself that Novak had already gone way out on a limb, acting as the driver for a wanted man. That alone was a crime.

"What I'd like," Peter said, "is to find a way to put Brunelli in an orange jumpsuit with a big horny cellmate for the rest of his life. But I'm worried he's going to weasel out of everything. Did you talk to that Metro detective, Phil Moore?"

Peter had suggested Novak reach out to the man who'd run the investigation into Sarah's death, who'd also identified Erik Grímsson as the primary suspect. The Norwegian investigator had recently turned up several overseas bank accounts in the name of Moore's first ex-wife.

"Moore wasn't at work, and he didn't answer his phone, so I went to his apartment. He didn't answer my knock, either." Novak kept his eyes on the road. "But I knew that smell coming under his door. He wasn't going to be talking to me or anyone else."

"How did he die?"

"I got the M.E. report two days ago. Tissue samples put the cause of death as alcohol poisoning."

Peter raised his eyebrows. He hadn't read Moore as an amateur drunk. He'd seemed like a deliberate professional, self-medicating his way toward retirement.

Novak said, "The tox report also showed traces of ketamine in his system. You know what ketamine is?"

"A club drug," Peter said. "Also a date-rape drug." He thought of the syringe in the hotel bar in Akureyri. "Someone's tying up loose ends. Which reminds me. When you were working with Catherine, did you ever run into an Irishman? Smaller guy, very pale, black hair, heavy beard? Maybe went by Seamus?"

"Brunelli's main bodyguard is an Irishman named Fitzsimmons," Novak said. "But he's the opposite of small. He went to Iceland with Wetzel and vanished into thin air. What's the story with your guy?"

The Norwegian had finally tracked down Seamus from the photo Peter had taken in Iceland. His real name was Seamus Conner. A Belfast policeman until he was arrested for murdering four of his fellow officers for the IRA. He disappeared from police custody in 1995, surfacing later in South Africa, Jamaica, and Russia, where he'd worked as an enforcer for various criminal organizations.

"I'd really like to get hold of him," Peter said. "Aside from Brunelli, Seamus is the only guy left standing."

They dropped the Icelanders at the Kimpton in Dupont Circle just after seven. They really did want to see the Air and Space Museum, along with the National Mall at night, and Peter really didn't want them crashing through the woods in his wake.

Peter and Novak arrived in Potomac after nine.

Novak cruised the neighborhood, avoiding Brunelli's street while giving an overview of the wealthy suburb. Most houses stood on large, wooded lots. Many residents had thoughtfully planted evergreen trees for tasteful year-round screening from the neighbors and the road.

Peter had spent part of the drive with a good map. Now he directed Novak down MacArthur Boulevard, with the dark woods of the C&O Canal National Historic Park on the left and a dense veneer of weedy scrub hiding high fences on the right. Past Falls Road and into the park, Novak continued until he came to VFW Post 5633, a low brick building with decommissioned artillery pieces mounted in the yard. He turned into the circular driveway and paused just long enough for Peter to roll out of the truck and disappear into the trees.

The night was moonless and he was effectively invisible in the narrow band of forest between the road and the high iron fences of the houses. Snow stood only in patches where sun would not fall. Peter had the map in his head now, and when the road veered left, he kept his line along the shoulder of an irregular slope, steps muffled in the soft winter loam. He carried his day pack with water and energy bars and the things Novak had bought.

He smiled in the dark, knowing he was home.

He went to the top of the slope with his binoculars and spotted Brunelli's place a half mile away, lit up like a museum on the night of a gala. Every window shone, and the terraces and formal gardens were bright with accent lighting. The house had been built on a level spot where it would look down on the river. Outside the fenced gardens, the terrain rose and fell from angular ridges to steep ravines that drained to the river. Peter marked a modest rise close to the estate, where he could set up for a better view, then set out again.

He hadn't lied to Novak. He had no plan of action other than a night of surveillance. On the other hand, if an opportunity presented itself, he would be ready.

Slow and silent, he worked his way upwind toward the rise. He wondered if there were sensors in the ground or cameras in the trees. He told himself there was too much world out here to monitor all of it, and that any electronic measures would be on the fence itself or inside it. Then the breeze rose, carrying the faint acrid tang of cigarette smoke.

Peter froze in place, ears straining for sound. He heard nothing. The smell of smoke faded. He held that way for several minutes before he moved on, creeping more slowly still, marking each footfall. He didn't want to meet an armed U.S. Marshal in the dark.

The rise turned out to be a cluster of ancient granite boulders too stubborn to wash down to the river. He stood still and silent at its base, eyes searching for a path up, when he heard a soft *phut* overhead, and the distant tinkle of breaking glass.

Peter knew those sounds. He tucked himself into a fold in the granite and waited. The shooter would prize speed over quiet now. A faint mechanical rattle, above and to his left. He circled that way, face down and ears wide open. The brittle crack of a stick. The whisper of fabric against stone. He circled faster, feet soft and sure. The rough rock was cold against his bare hands. Then the scrape of a boot directly above him. He reached up and got a hand around the man's ankle as he sidestepped, pulling him, face-first, six feet down to the ground.

The man hit without crying out, already gathering his feet under him, scooping up a scoped hunting rifle as he came. Tough little fucker, Peter thought, then kicked him in the head and it was over.

His back to a tree, the Irishman's eyes fluttered open as Peter zip-tied his arms around the trunk. He cleared his throat and spat. "I'm a changed man, lad. Handing out justice. On the side of the angels now."

"I can see that." Peter used another zip-tie to cinch the man's neck to the tree. Hard to get out of that one. "You don't like your old boss anymore?"

"I didn't mind him," Seamus said. "He paid well enough. But I've a new employer now, pays much better. Wants to clean up a big mess."

Peter smiled. "Me, too." He pulled the clip knife from his pocket and flicked it open with his thumb.

Seamus dug his boot heels into the dirt to get away, but he was tied up tight. "Surely we can come to an arrangement. There's money enough for everyone."

Peter put the point of the knife to the underside of the Irishman's chin and murmured, "Everyone thinks it's about the money." He pressed the tip gently into the soft skin. Seamus held himself very still. A dark drop of blood welled against the polished steel.

Then Peter took the knife away and, without his hands touching the rifle, smeared the collected blood into the textured plastic of the butt, just where it would meet a sniper's cheek.

Seamus twisted against his bonds and got nowhere. "Ach, lad, you're killing me."

"Actually," Peter said, folding the knife

back in his pocket, "I'm not. No matter how much I'd like to."

He heard the crackle of radios as the Marshals moved across the estate's lower gardens. Soon enough they'd venture past the fence. The Irishman's fingerprints would tie him to his Interpol warrants. If he talked to the feds, he might avoid getting strangled in an Irish prison. Or maybe not.

"Peter," the Irishman called out. "Peter!"

Peter didn't answer. Instead he turned away and angled downslope toward the river. As he walked, the breeze came up again, carrying the smell of wet dirt and rotting leaves and the coming promise of spring.

ACKNOWLEDGMENTS

Some books are easier to write than others.

For various reasons, this book was one of the others.

First and foremost, I owe an enormous debt of gratitude to Margret Anderson Petrie, Duncan Petrie, my parents Pete and Lucia, and my siblings Bob and Maryl Petrie. Your kindness, not to mention your tolerance of my whining, lies beyond even unreasonable expectations. Thank you.

I owe a different but no less enormous debt to every creative professional I know, including (but by no means limited to) Lori Rader-Day, Charles Todd, Mark Greaney, Gregg Hurwitz, Dana Kaye, Michael Koryta, Owen Laukkanen, Erica Ruth Neubauer, Tim Hennessey, Katrina and Chris Holm, Andrew Gross, Bill Schweigart, Don Bentley, John Dixon, Graham Brown, Dan Oko, Jennifer and Andy Rash, Kathleen Kavanaugh and Julio Rivera, Bob Crais, and many, many others. Your words of encouragement were what turned the tide. My community truly is the gift that keeps on giving.

Thanks are due especially to my editors at Putnam, the talented Sara Minnich and Tom Colgan, whose insight and talent are invaluable to this writer, as is their patience. They watched me sail past my deadline with every appearance of Zen calm; if they gnashed their teeth, I never heard it.

I remain, as always, hugely thankful for my agent, Barbara Poelle, whose attitude of semi-benevolent ferocity is alternately a source of inspiration and terror to all who have the privilege to know her.

Next, I must extend my apologies to the people of Iceland. The epic Icelandic landscape is very much as I've described it, but the violent and surly behavior presented in this book comes entirely from my imagination. Over more than three weeks in Iceland, each person I met was unfailingly polite and helpful. Everyone under the age of fifty spoke better English than I did. And more to the point, nobody tried to kill me. *Takk fyrir* for your kindness, your hospitality, your bakeries, and your beer.

As always, this is a work of fiction. I've played with the map and made stuff up to tell a better story.

On the Iceland research front, thanks are due to Alda Sigmundsdóttir, for her smart and thoughtful take on modern Iceland, and to Nanna Gunnarsdóttir and Audur Ösp, whose blogs are both witty and informative. I only wish I could have used more quirky Icelandic sayings, several of which have entered my daily conversation. On with the butter!

Thanks to the Litla Guesthouse, a comfy and friendly place, which is actually in Ísafjordur, not Reykjavík, but was too good not to include in the book.

Many thanks to Duncan Petrie, my Iceland travel companion, who came up with the idea of a backpacking trip across the Hornstrandir National Reserve in 2017. For our 2018 Ring Road trip, Duncan planned our itinerary, took gorgeous photographs, and drove long hours on questionable roads. To see Duncan's astounding Iceland photos, check out his website at DuncanPetrie .com. His ongoing work, along with his terrible horrible no-good very bad puns, can be found on Instagram at @probablydun can.

Duncan also turned me on to the work of Chris Burkard, whose Icelandic surfing documentary *Under an Arctic Sky* provided inspiration for the big winter storm in this book. I cannot recommend this film highly enough. Find it on Netflix or at UnderAn ArcticSky.com. The mini-documentary about the making of the film is equally interesting as a testament to the rewards of persisting in the face of a challenge.

Thanks to the *New York Times* for its excellent ongoing reportage about war and its aftereffects, including several articles about promising experimental uses of MDMA — also known as Ecstasy — for the treatment of post-traumatic stress. If you'd like to learn more, the May 1, 2018, article by Dave Philipps is especially illuminating. Further reading should include Michael Pollan's book about the science of psychedelics, *How to Change Your Mind.*

I'm not suggesting everyone go get high — these are serious drugs administered in a clinical setting by trained professionals — but it's truly wonderful to see such positive results in this still-experimental treatment.

I'm indebted to writers Ken Bruen and Roddy Doyle, whose excellent novels are responsible for all that is lovely about my Irish accent, and none of the shite. I highly recommend their work. Ken Bruen's *The Guards* and Roddy Doyle's *The Commitments* are great places to get started.

Often, something small makes a huge difference. Years ago, I heard Irish poet and Nobel laureate Seamus Heaney give a talk and reading in Seattle, during which someone in the audience asked what he considered to be the most challenging part of writing. He replied, "Getting started, keeping going, and getting started again." How like a poet, to capture in eight words the entire practice of writing: the challenge and failure inherent to the work, along with the necessary effort of always beginning again. Heaney has been gone since 2013, but I hope he wouldn't mind my Irish villain taking on his name. For a taste of his poetry, read his poem "Digging," on the Poetry Foundation's website.

Neil Gaiman's *Norse Mythology* brought brilliant new life to old stories.

Bill Schweigart contributed nautical knowledge and generous wit.

Peter's ice-skating truck was inspired by a man on Washington Island, Wisconsin, who told me about a storm that had blown his parked truck down his icy driveway. This was many years ago, but writers never forget a good story. Be careful what you tell us.

Thanks to Ginger Mulanax, whose generous donation to the St. Louis County Library put her wonderful name in this book, and to Reed Farrel Coleman, mensch among men, for his friendship and an invitation to Suspense Night.

Thanks to Matt George for the right words at the right time. Thanks to Dr. Dean Ziegler for reassembling my shoulder after a gnarly bike accident. Thanks to Dan Oberneder, Physical Therapist Extraordinaire, for his knowledge and humor and gleeful infliction of pain to get my shoulder back to 100 percent.

Thanks to the great crew at Putnam, including Ivan Held, Katie Grinch, Emily Mlynek, Alexis Welby, Ashley McClay, Christine Ball, Tricja Okuniewska, and everyone else on the world-class publicity and marketing and sales teams — your work gets mine into the world, and for that I am grateful. Thanks also to Linda Rosenberg, Meredith Dros, Kylie Byrd, Claire Sullivan, John Sharp, Maija Baldauf, Nancy Resnick, Steven Meditz, and Jeffrey Ward for making this book both beautiful and readable.

Thanks to independent booksellers everywhere, for putting my books in readers' hands, and for introducing me to astonishing books and authors. You are the heart and soul of the book world. An algorithm will never replace a human recommendation. Thanks especially and always to Daniel Goldin of Boswell Books in Milwaukee and Barbara Peters of The Poisoned Pen in Scottsdale for essential and unflagging advice and insight and support.

As you can see, I'm a lucky man surrounded by wonderful people. I owe the world.

But my greatest debt, dear reader, is to you.

Your support and enthusiasm, whether simply reading, at a book event, or online, powers me forward.

Without you, I'd just be howling into the darkness.

ABOUT THE AUTHOR

Nick Petrie is the author of four novels in the Peter Ash series, most recently *Tear It Down.* His debut *The Drifter* won both the ITW Thriller award and the Barry Award for Best First Novel, and was a finalist for the Edgar and the Hammett awards. A husband and father, he lives in Milwaukee.